TO PAY PAUL

[TODAY]

[15,000 YEARS AGO]

[17 TO 14 MILLION YEARS AGO]

MICHAEL SCOTT CURNES

This novel is a work of fiction based on events and people both real and imagined. In instances when real people intersect in a blend of actual and fictionalized events real people's names have been mostly altered. In the interest of preserving historical accuracy, the author has made the decision to include the actual names of elected politicians involved in specific government proceedings or legislation when these associations are already deemed to be part of the public record.

Copyright © 2022 by Michael Scott Curnes

Cover and Interior layout by Masha Shubin, Anno Domini Creative
Edited by Andrew Durkin, Yellow Bike Press
Author Photo by Bernard Sauvé
Cover Photo by Bernard Sauvé
Windmill Photo by John Ferebee
William Witherup Photo from the Estate of William Witherup

The story, while fictional, is based on actual events. In certain cases, incidents, characters, names, and timelines have been changed for dramatic purposes. Certain characters may be composites, or entirely fictitious. This story is created for entertainment purposes. Opinions, acts, and statements attributed to any entity, individual or individuals may have been fabricated or exaggerated for effect. The opinions and fictionalized depictions of individuals, groups and entities, and any statements contained therein, are not to be relied upon in any way.

All rights reserved. No part of this book may be reproduced or transmitted in any form or any means whatsoever, including photocopying, recording or by any information storage and retrieval system, without written permission from the publisher and/or author.

ISBN (paperback) 978-1-7772988-5-2
ISBN (hardback)   978-1-7772988-6-9
ISBN (ebook)   978-1-7772988-7-6

1 2 3 4 5 6 7 8 9 10

Dedicated to the memory and featuring
the "Men at Work" poetry of
William Witherup
(1935 – 2009)

&

to ALL the other outspoken and sadly lost or suffering
Downwinders:
You were robbed and you are remembered.

I cleaned my house and garden
and I was feeling gay;
Then came that nasty wind and blew
my garbage can away.
Blow ye winds of Richland,
Blow ye winds high-o,
Blow ye winds of Richland,
Blow, blow, blow.
That fearful termination wind,
Can't stand it anymore;
Each time I sweep
the dust so deep
blows underneath my door.[*]

---

[*] Lyrics from a song written by Charlie Wende in the late 40s commemorating the dust and winds at Hanford Site—otherwise known as the Manhattan Project's nuclear plutonium production complex on the bank of the Columbia River in south-central Washington State.

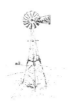

CHAPTER ONE

"YOU KNEW ALL ALONG you were robbing Peter, right?"

"Peter who?"

"Not Peter *who*. Think of Peter as the future, Pops." Gerald Quinlan's over-educated son, Seamus, adjusted the worn bill of his Tri-City Dust Devils baseball cap, squeegeeing the sweat off his forehead and into his hair. "Think of Peter as *now* or even *tomorrow*, if that helps."

"Ah," the father said—thinking, as he always did, that in Central Washington, having a PhD was about as useful as turn signals on a tractor. The skinny octogenarian groaned, realizing his last surviving son was just being clever again. He played along. "And Paul was back then—the *past*, I suppose?" He sucked on his Marlboro, holding the nosepiece and oxygen tubing a cautionary arm's length away from his cigarette. "The same past I suppose you feel I screwed up royally?" he added with a smoky exhale.

"Precisely." Seamus stared his father down for a beat before revealing a trace of that classic Quinlan grin. He shared his father's good Irish looks and the same crooked smile—pleasant features that helped him wriggle out of most entanglements. What he couldn't always sidestep was the quicksand that had oozed between them like a slurry of topsoil after a rigid downpour, ever ready to swallow him whole.

The hunter green painted living room where the two of them sat like a pair of wax figures in an Americana showcase, was all shadows, plaids, and sunlit rays of dust. Seamus, on the made-to-order extra-long sofa from Sears, was bolstered by color-coordinated groupings of his mother's hand-embroidered pillows. He supposed there had never been complete silence—awkward or otherwise—inside that battered, early-twentieth-century farmhouse. Having so far defied every weather-oddity that the past century had hurled at it—from unrelenting dust squalls to extreme temps, droughts and freak out-of-season snowstorms—the dirty white house with the paint-curled green trim, had been the homestead of the Quinlan Family for five generations. With a large covered porch on its leeward side and landscaped by nothing more than Russian thistle (more commonly known as sagebrush) and the occasional tuft of cheatgrass, the two-story, four-bedroom farmhouse was unluckily located halfway between the dusty, nothing towns of Washtucna and Kahlotus, directly east—forty-six miles downwind from Hanford Engineer Works; or *HEW*, as the last two generations of Quinlans rather un-affectionately referred to as their employer and family-killer.

Whether it was the tainted and prevailing wind that scooted down the coulees to sandblast the dickens out of the siding and shingles; the constant rumble of semis hauling grain, sawmill wood chips, or sweet onions on the adjacent State Highway 260; or the summer thunderstorms that rattled the windows but rarely cleaned them or replenished the surrounding gullies—there was never complete silence in this desolate place.

And inside what should have been a very haunted house, but somehow wasn't, there was a constant chorus of noises distinct from the clamor outside. The old copper pipes clanked and groaned in what sounded like a secret language that the Quinlan kids made games out of trying to translate. In later years and stashed behind the ratty blue plaid recliner in the living room, was an oxygen concentrator the size of a bar fridge that vibrated the floorboards and hissed a steady, high-register hum around the clock. An equally audible and wheezing Gerald Quinlan, Seamus's father—or *Pops*, as he'd always called him—was tethered to this machine by a hundred-foot run of tubing that served as his leash, limiting both his mobility and his existence. Pops, the last Quinlan of his generation, was rendered housebound with late-stage prostate cancer paired with a hearty helping of COPD. He stubbornly lived alone on a property that still spanned most of its original 160 acres—minus the state road right-of-way that had expropriated a dozen or so acres from the family holding several decades ago. Nobody who had visited the farm had missed that the closest town was called Harder, Washington—since living anyplace else couldn't have been more difficult.

Gerald's bony hand roughly repositioned the nasal cannula in his hair-choked nostrils, but it was still crooked. "Let me ask you a question," he said. "What choice do you think any of us had back then?"

"How about the choice between wrong and right?" his son said, sending the question back at him like a boomerang he'd barely touched.

"Come on!" Gerald said, coughing. "With all your fancy science degrees, Professor Quinlan—you can't tell me you believe for one minute it was that simple." Rather than make eye contact, the eighty-three-year-old man stared through the dirty glass of the window—his only portal to the outside world. Then, with a flick of his BIC lighter, he lit his second cigarette since the conversation had begun. He uncrossed his legs and leaned forward, lifting a finger with some effort toward his son's face. "How about the choice between abandoning my pregnant girlfriend (your mother, rest her soul)"—he made a lazy sign of the cross with his cigarette hand—"or providing for a family?" He grunted and gasped, brushing ash from his trousers. "Or how 'bout the choice between asking questions and playing dumb? Never mind the choice between staying dumb and getting educated." He took another drag. "The late 50s and early 60s—well, they weren't like today, son. We didn't know what we didn't know, and we couldn't fucking Google it or whatever to find out."

He waved a finger, sending the sunlit house dust into a spiral before continuing. "I was eighteen and a half years old." He started counting, moving to his second finger. "I'd gotten your mother pregnant." The third finger required him to move his cigarette to his other hand. "I went to the only place where there was work and"—he sucked on his cig and extended a fourth digit—"for thirty years, I did what I was told, which was mostly to keep my trap shut because it meant a paycheck, you know? Real security in a goddamn uncertain and scary-as-hell-time." He seemed to feel his rebuttal could use an exclamation point, but he was out of fingers and didn't have the lung capacity to raise his voice. "There weren't any choices back then, son." His hand erased the scoreboard in the stale air. "We were civilians in the throes of a nuclear arms race, and we didn't understand who the real enemy was."

"Your own government, would be my guess," Seamus said, knowing it made him sound like a smart-ass.

These father-son debates always got tripped up on the rhetorical, tumbling fact-over-fiction through the dust that their fantastic theories always kicked up. There was a not-quite-affirming pause between the men as Seamus tried to figure out what Pops was staring at, looking through that dirty eight-paned side window next to his recliner chair like he did all day long. For his part in this brief intermission, Pops issued an impressively long straw of cigarette smoke. Particles of grit levitated between them like miniature helicopters, suspending for seconds before beginning to descend, only to lift again in the afternoon sun that streamed through the chink in the faded orange gingham curtains. Seamus and Gerald knew all about half-lives. Not only was it a term for measuring the interval of time it took for one-half of an atomic nucleus of a radioactive sample to decay and become inert, but it also seemed to describe the fate of each member of the Quinlan Family. Except for these last two, all the others had died from their cancers, with their lives only half-lived.

Father and only surviving son were the latest but not the last of the downwinders to blame HEW for what ailed them. Seamus was 56 years old and outwardly appeared fit and rugged as a 4-H show horse, but he had already overcome his own troublesome interlude of testicular cancer that he'd fortunately caught in his early thirties. He could not name a cancer-free relative on the family tree. For Pops and his "butt cancer," as he jokingly called it, time was sprinting toward the finish line, which is why Seamus could rearrange his work schedule at Hanford. At least three days each week, he would travel to the rural homestead to support his father's dwindling needs and ardent wish to die at home. Seamus brought groceries his father wouldn't eat and medication refills for pills he'd stopped taking. During these visits, Seamus sought advice and sometimes answers. He was always keen to unpack the last of the secrets that no longer served either of them.

Robbing Peter. These days, Seamus overused that cliché—or was it an idiom? (What was the difference?) Maybe it was a metaphor. Or a paraphrase of a parable? The expression struck him as biblical, though Seamus was not scripturally literate, despite his other scholastic achievements. Maybe it referred to a pair of Christ's disciples run afoul. He would have to look that up—Google it. He chuckled at his father's limited grasp of modernity, especially since there wasn't a computer in the house. On second thought, maybe he would just try to stop using the saying so much. More likely, he would do neither. That was okay, too, since everyone but his father seemed to understand what he meant when he said it.

Pops had dozed off again. Seamus extracted the burning cigarette from between his yellowish fingers and snuck a drag even though he had ostensibly quit again. He knew that was just another promise he couldn't keep, like telling Pops that he would never sell the farm after he was gone. Even though he'd mostly grown up in the city, Seamus and his brothers had been shuttled to their grandparent's house for weekend sleep overs where they rode the horses and practiced roping. And during summer chore season, the Quinlan boys came up for extended camp-outs in a musty green, eight-man army tent that their Great Uncle Percy had stolen from the military while stationed at Camp Farragut. Beyond sentimentality, which was neither science nor purposeful, Seamus really had no practical use for the place. He rose from his chair and took the cigarette butt to the sink to douse it. These parts had always been tinder-dry, and the closest fire station had to be over forty minutes away in either direction. In a family of smokers, sink-dousing your butts is just what you did—the second habit you followed religiously.

And why did they all smoke? They'd all worked at HEW, where twenty-five-cent cigarette vending machines outnumbered the employee bathroom stalls. Since becoming operational in the mid-40s, HEW had deviously encouraged its labor force to smoke their lungs out. They built a whole culture around tobacco use. As Seamus understood now, that ploy was so Hanford could avoid liability—any future cancers could be blamed on nicotine instead of radiation. Back then and on his first paying job, even sixteen-year-old Seamus kept his pockets full of quarters—or the similarly sized metal washers that the vending machines also took, since the machines didn't give a shit about his lungs either. He continued to smoke on and off during the decade he was away from Hanford at school, but by the time he returned to Hanford to start his real career, he'd mostly smartened up and was taking his health more seriously.

He turned on the cold-water tap, and air leaked out of the tap with a noise that sounded like the word *no*. He had slightly better luck with the hot water tap where a spurt of rust water sprayed into the stained porcelain basin, but stopped instantly, followed by a clank sound that served as the exclamation mark. The house had no water!

"What the hell?" Seamus whispered as he spit on the end of the cigarette. He parted the orange gingham curtains to let in more light so he could examine the under-sink compartment and have a look at the plumbing. A sizeable house spider seemed surprised to see him and scurried out of the way of the prying hands reaching in to check out the pipes. He righted himself, retrieved his baseball cap and sunglasses off the table and didn't bother tiptoeing across the kitchen, since every floorboard in the place seemed booby-trapped, long betraying any attempt to come or go undetected.

Though his mother was long deceased (thyroid plus metastatic breast cancer), Seamus could still hear her yelling after him to mind her frayed nerves, and so he stopped the screen door from slapping against the doorjamb. Twenty-six years working as a secretary at Hanford, Abigail Quinlan had been absolutely frayed, if the companion definition of frayed also meant cooked. They'd *all* been frayed *and* betrayed by HEW—but somehow, while they were still alive, everyone had derived an almost pleasant, though morbid, solidarity from their various cancers.

Seamus made a beeline for the well at the holding pond, thinking about his dad as he strode past the barn. His baseball cap couldn't shield his eyes from the desert glare that bounced off the beige-almost-albino dirt, and the heat rose in successive waves that forced him to clench his eyes mostly shut and pant through his mouth. He passed under the leafless and fruitless apple tree that his great-great-grandfather Fergus had planted and then grafted, in a failed quest to create a Quinlan variety that was resistant to worms. Though the tree had been dead a hundred years, it still stood, roots cemented in desiccated earth—serving as another parable, idiom, metaphor, and constant reminder that death (and worms) would come for them all. Indeed—on each of the last half-dozen visits to check on Pops, Seamus had sensed that the Reaper had already arrived. He was just patiently biding the time, rocking back and forth in that wicker chair on the front veranda that had always teetered and tottered on the Quinlan porch, in perpetual motion.

Having been a middle child in a brood of his own male siblings, Gerald Quinlan was as clever as he was opportunistic. He had taken advantage of a momentary wealth of related farmhands to make a break with the family farm and strike out on his own. This misunderstood expression of independence resulted in a twenty-five-year stint off the farm while Gerald lived in Richland to be closer to HEW and to start his own family. According to the math, his dad had otherwise spent sixty-three years of his life in that clattering farmhouse. He'd been born in 1935, on the same kitchen table, which was always bigger than their perpetually shrinking family ever warranted. Now that Seamus was thinking about it, that table opposite the kitchen sink had never hosted an impressive gathering of uncles and cousins and grandparents—not at Thanksgiving, and not even on St. Patrick's Day, when you'd expect an Irish family to hoist their shamrocks together. No, sadly, the only significant gathering of the Quinlan clan lay six feet under the hump of a hill that gradually rose in the distance behind the house. The twentieth-century Quinlans had so far been a consistent lot. They worked at Hanford. They propped up the farm. And they died prematurely from their cancers. Pops—Gerald—at age eighty-eight, was an anomaly only because he'd broken the Quinlan survival record and made it to old age.

A younger Gerald had been compelled to take up reoccupation

of the homestead in 1986 when his father passed from liver cancer in his 70s. All his brothers and uncles had already been buried out back. Seamus knew he would be expected to heave the same family mantle onto his own shoulders, because he couldn't sell the family cemetery, and he would soon be the last Quinlan left above ground. Besides, there were no rural house buyers anymore. The pandemic, recession, war in Eastern Europe, and the commodities and stock market crash had all jammed up the prospects of transacting real estate. Plus, any farmland speculators had somersaulted away with the tumbleweeds fifty years ago, chased by the nipping rumors that Hanford had contaminated the soils within a 200-mile radius. Holding onto the farm through this turmoil had worked out okay for Gerald, but it was going to cramp Seamus's future. Either Pops was mostly deaf or he had trained himself to sleep through the noise—but Seamus was a light and fitful sleeper. Already obsessed with impending doom given the state of the environment and other world news, he did not look forward to being harnessed to this acreage for the rest of his life.

Rounding the corner of the faded red-almost-pink barn on its north side, Seamus began ascending the natural and Quinlan-fortified berm that contained the pond that had once been surface-fed by nearby Harder Springs in his great-great-grandfather's time. While the springs still fed the subterranean aquifer via natural plumbing—through fissures and ancient lava tubes—in modern times, the spring water was brought to the surface using a mechanical pump attached to a windmill that never ran out of wind which meant the pond never ran dry. Every few seconds Seamus heard another sixteen-wheeler whiz past on his right, and the hot wind that prevailed from the southwest down the coulee rushed his left ear. What he didn't hear was the windmill's rotors or the squeaks and swooshes of the pump cylinder as it dipped beneath to slurp the dregs of the aquifer as if through a soda straw. When he crested the hill, he could see why. The pond was bone-dry, cracked like a clay bowl left too long in a kiln. Now, how in the hell had that happened? Seamus wondered. Sure, it was coming up on the middle of July, but in his memory not even in the worst drought on record for these parts (it had lasted 116 weeks—from January 2014 to

March 2016) had the pond dried up completely. With his hand extending the bill of his baseball cap to further block the sun from his eyes, he could see across to the windmill on the opposite bank. It wasn't rotating, even though Seamus could feel the wind against his sweaty back. He trudged across the dry pond bed, crouching midway to insert his hand into one of the cracks. He thought his fingertips would touch mud, but they didn't. This desertification was not fresh, he realized, trying to remember the last time he'd checked the water level. The pond was out of sight from the crush gravel driveway where he'd pulled in from the highway. There might have been a sightline through a back bedroom window in the farmhouse, but Seamus hadn't been upstairs for years, and frankly doubted that his father had either, since he'd mostly made himself comfortable on the main floor and slept in his chair.

Seamus reached the base of the windmill and looked up, instantly seeing part of the problem. Something was stuck between the rotors, jamming the blade and chain mechanism. He walked to the ladder side of the derrick, and hand over hand, climbed up to inspect it. The talons at the end of a bracelet of still-connected bones told him it had likely been a barn owl. Whatever the species, it was still clutching a swatch of fur that looked like it might have belonged to a small rabbit, or maybe a very young coyote pup. He imagined the pair struggling in mid-air before accidentally flying into the spinning blades. That miscalculation might have killed them instantly, but something about the way the talon clutched its prey told Seamus there had been protracted suffering. He barely touched the pelt and the last of the tendon-connected bones fell away.

He saw that one of the blades was bent, so he forced the hot and malleable metal back into shape. When he let go of the wheel, it spun freely again. After hearing some clanking from below, Seamus squinted to focus with anticipation on the end of the screened discharge pipe that was supposed to be underwater. He began descending. Cocking his head and straining his ears for the sound of gurgling, he flashed back to earlier summers in his life, which he'd spent splashing, tadpoling, and rafting. He remembered hockey winters, too, when he'd face off against his two older brothers, goalie Sampson (double lung cancer) and forward Sean (hepatocellular carcinoma). The blades of their skates would often catch on the stalks of exposed cattails. Someone would be sent flying into the snowdrifts, while the others fell into unstoppable laughing fits that left the goal undefended.

The right side of Seamus's asymmetrical face had always featured this one permanently arched eyebrow, giving everyone the impression that a smile was always about to follow. Thinking back on his childhood now, the right side of his face did lift into a smile recalling those carefree hockey days with his brothers, while the left side felt so weighted down from the grief of losing nearly every member of his immediate family, that it couldn't really register any emotion at all. Head-on, Seamus thought he must have looked like those Greek tragedy masks of Thalia and Melpomene—two unresolved solitudes but on the same lopsided face. Given the preponderance of that questioning eyebrow, people who didn't know better might have wondered if he'd suffered a stroke. After university, Seamus cultivated a ridiculous horseshoe moustache that he thought would draw the focus away from his hyper-brow. His lip caterpillar went through different iterations of bushiness, but he'd kept it fastidiously trimmed for the past twenty-five or so years. Sure, it made him look like some porn star stuck on the cover of a 70s *Playgirl* magazine, but he never heard anyone mention his eyebrow again. His was just one of those handsomely crooked faces that simply wasn't read easily—something he used to his advantage when delivering good and not-so-good news. Lately, he had to plumb deep for any good news, and since he fretted over everything, he feared the eventual atrophying of his happy face would just get added to the pile of coming disasters he couldn't avoid, stop, fix, or gloss over.

Seamus skipped the last two rungs and hopped flatfooted onto the parched ground, launching a dust cloud. The hot noon wind whisked it instantly away. At ground level, the squeaks and bangs of the windmill getting up to speed sounded like a year-end kindergarten orchestra recital, but the racket wasn't raising water. Not one drop issued from the end of the nearby pipe. At the base of the windmill, Seamus peeled back the cracked rubber well seal and poked his face into the stale void. He didn't smell water, foul or fresh. He shouted a "hey!" into the hole and the echo was dull and delayed. Even as a farm boy, he knew the water table should have sent his voice back to him more quickly. The fact that it didn't wasn't a good omen—not this early in the summer. But then, the world's climate was being upended, and with it, old norms, seasons, cycles, and almanacs. You didn't have to lecture him on climate change. He was usually the one behind the lectern, harping on everyone else to pay more attention to the existential threats faced by all species and ecosystems. With his distinctive and booming baritone voice, he probably gave six, maybe eight talks a year, not just in the Tri-Cities where he lived, but at Central Washington University in Ellensburg where he often guest lectured for their advanced geology department. On the world stage, though he humbly played this down, Seamus was considered a—if not *the*—preeminent authority on prehistoric basalt lava flows; his expertise vaulted by his enthusiastically received and peer-reviewed thesis on the formation of the Columbia Basin. Public speaking was just a hobby for Seamus that played to his middle-child need for attention and his adult passion for geology. After publishing his thesis, he had enjoyed zipping from one international conference to the next, but those opportunities—even the guest-lecturing at CWU—had mostly dried up before the pandemic.

As for his paying gig, Seamus was almost a thirty-year career geophysicist on the US Department of Energy's multidisciplinary field team, part of a tri-lateral partnership responsible for the impossible task of remediating the 586-square-mile, highly radioactive Hanford Nuclear Complex. Thirty-five years after the cleanup had officially started, Hanford still ranked as the most toxic and contaminated place on the planet. While Seamus could recite the numbers manufactured to impress outsiders, he wasn't sure they'd made the place safer. He was more inclined to characterize the whole charade as one of the longest-running make-work projects and public relations stunts in American history. On the one hand, that at least meant Seamus had job security. On the other, he realized he probably should have been more discerning about taking the position when it was offered to him thirty years ago. He had been fresh out of university, armed with a PhD and thinking he wasn't cut out to settle into the boredom of academia. He had already been working at HEW since high school as a soil technician to pay his own way through eight expensive years of schooling. By the time he'd earned his doctorate, Seamus and the family name were known, trusted and bankable entities when the Department of Energy came recruiting in the Hanford lunch rooms. Landing a US Government job had its perks, he'd been counselled and eventually persuaded, but now that this job had swallowed his whole career and eaten up over two thirds of his life, he found himself looking a lot in the rear-view mirror. Wouldn't it have been better to be ending his career at a prestigious university on a high scholastic note, rather than limping out of Hanford with a plutonium-powered wristwatch still sounding the alarms and peddling the apocalypse? Facing imminent catastrophe head-on was damn exhausting work. He had never been a convincing liar, and so he tended to mosey off script, skipping the sugar-coating and window dressing, to tell it as he saw it. This, of course, made the government PR types twitchy. But it also made Seamus almost a cult figure among other downwinders, the enviros, media types, and a handful of podcasting conspiracists.

His expertise was failing him, however, as he baked in the sun, lamenting the disappearance of the farm's pond, which had been around longer than he had. He would have to ask Pops about the pond in case he remembered his father or his grandparents ever talking about a time before this when it might have run dry. But he already knew the response he would get. His old man had made an irritating practice lately of replying to most inquiries with *I can't care*. Despite this honesty, Seamus needed to grasp and understand what he was about to inherit. He wasn't a farmer. His life-weary Pops, asleep in the house, wasn't either. He, too, had been lured to HEW during his working years with the prospect of making more money in raising plutonium hell and mayhem than in farming commodities. Odds were, the water—wherever it had gone—would come back to the pond in time, just not maybe that afternoon. Already, Seamus was making plans for a grocery run to pick up a supply of bottled water to tide the farmhouse over until he could come up with a plumbing workaround.

Seamus walked over to the end of the discharge pipe and knelt to put his ear to the opening. He plugged his other ear with his thumb, listening for drafts of air emanating from the pipe. He had to wait for a semi to pass on the highway and round the ridge of the coulee to the south of the property before he could truly tune into the depths.

And that's when he unmistakably heard what sounded like the planet gasping.

Pre-pare. Pre-pare.

Seamus half-tumbled a step or two backward on the steeply sloped dry pond bank. He recovered his balance and returned to the discharge pipe to listen with his other ear.

Pre-pare. There was a pause, and then the word repeated. *Pre-pare.*

He looked around on a hunch he was being pranked, except there was never anyone else around and his dad couldn't leave the house. Again, he listened, and again, he heard what distinctly sounded like whispered warnings. Trying to think scientifically and keep from overreacting, he began breathing through his mouth, which is what he always did when solving a problem. There was one more *pre-pare*, followed by a *pre* ... and then a mighty whoosh of hot air blasted his ear, followed by water cannonballing out of the pipe, drenching the serious side of his face.

Seamus tumbled out of the way, fussing with his baseball cap and wet hair. He watched as the jet of sulphurous water kicked up dust before disappearing back into the Escher mosaic of interlocking cracks that cross-hatched the bed of the pond. He didn't remember the well water ever smelling like rotten eggs before, but he knew that a buildup of hydrogen sulfide gas was typically caused by the microbial breakdown of organic material. Seamus made the connection that in his commute from town to country, he regularly passed through an unincorporated village named *Sulphur*, with its sky-scraping pair of grain elevators you could spot from miles away. He'd never paused long enough to wonder how it got its name, but it must have been because some of the cold springs in the area had, at one time, been hot. The water hitting his face had been warm enough to suggest subterranean thermal activity, but perhaps that was just from being trapped inside the metal pipe during these triple-digit summer days. Seamus stuck his hand back in the water. To his surprise, it was *still* running bathtub hot. This had him leaning into a geothermal hot springs theory, where he knew that bacteria feeding off sulfides in the water could cause an eggy smell. This was reversing what Seamus normally understood—that no hot springs existed this side of the Cascade Mountain Range.

He modified this hypothesis on the fly, feeding it with facts to help it grow. He had long known that where there was basalt, there had once been lava. Seamus had lectured auditoriums full of people that the expansive landscape that stretched from Ellensburg to the Tri-Cities to Spokane had been the site of one of the world's largest and longest lava eruptions between fifteen and sixteen million years ago. He always pointed out that, unlike a volcanic lava event, a series of fissures in the Earth's crust had opened to discharge rivers of molten lava that filled the basin, eventually covering 45 million acres. Various maps from his meticulously produced PowerPoint presentations strobed through his mind now, as he stared at the bottom of the dry pond, waiting for the water to pool.

When lecturing on his favorite subject that was the Wapshilla Lava Flows, Seamus would project a series of slides and rudimentary animations on the screen to illustrate. His linear, auto-pilot brain went to that spot in his presentation as he absent-mindedly began mouthing the memorized narration from his lecture as he watched the steaming water discharge from the pipe:

Millions of years after these basalt lava flows occurred, an Ice Age—not the last one that ended 25,000 years ago, but the one that happened 2.6 million years ago—plunged these glacial lobes from the Artic into North America. This created several ice dams, behind which giant lakes would form. One of the largest of these was near present-day Missoula, Montana, backing up what today we call the Clark Fork River. And then the ice dam broke.

This is where his presentation could really use fancier CGI work that showed the ice dam breaking, buttressed by dramatic music and stop-motion animation. So far, he hadn't been able to afford or arrange that. Seamus would always delight in revealing to his audiences that not only did this ice dam near Missoula break once, causing this cataclysmic flood that scoured out the basaltic terrain, but that these dams formed, broke, and reformed to break and flood again and again, around one hundred times.

And each time an ice dam broke, its reservoir dispatched colossal volumes of water, sediment, and debris, in tsunamis that traveled overland so fast that they reached the Pacific Ocean in a matter of hours. Each of these events ruthlessly carved out channels and gorges and canyons and coulees that formed most of the topography and visible geology that we can still see today in Eastern Washington and Northern Oregon. Many of you will be familiar with landmarks left over from these abrasive floods in places like the kilometer-deep Columbia River Gorge and the Channeled Scablands between Spokane and Vantage. Even closer to where I grew up in the Tri-Cities, there is an impressive basalt escarpment located just about twenty minutes away from my father's farm, over which the Palouse River plunges an impressive two hundred feet.

Of course, Seamus knew that the lava flows and floods also created the horseshoe-shaped coulee that pocketed the south end of his family's land. You couldn't pick up a rock at the base of those short cliffs just beyond the family cemetery that wasn't pocked with holes from the cataclysmic events he lectured about, but he hadn't included the location of his family's farm in his presentation since he didn't want to attract rockhounds or psychos.

Usually, by this point in his presentation, someone in the classroom or lecture hall would have asked him about Mt. St. Helens trying to draw a comparison, likely for extra credit. He would then have to embarrass that person and explain that the Wapshilla lava eruptions were nothing like what happened at Mt. St. Helens in the 1980s, the latter being a series of stratovolcano eruptions. That explanation, too, was memorized and part of the narration since the question came up every time.

The Wapshilla lava flows had been hydrovolcanic, which meant that red-hot lava rose from deep in the earth until it reached groundwater and freshwater lakes. This pried open an explosive series of vents that stretched for sixty miles and belched out lava that flowed from near Hells Canyon—a spot that straddles the border between Idaho, Oregon, and a bit of Washington—to the Wallowa Mountains in Oregon.

When he'd brought the audience to the edge of their seats—or put them to sleep, as the case might be with students—he'd reveal that these lava flows didn't just last for days or weeks, but for tens of thousands of years, depositing layer upon layer of hardened basalt through the ages.

Seamus shook the lecture notes out of his cranium and returned to pondering the oddity of the thermal water spewing out of the discharge pipe and the ominous warning the plumbing pipe had seemed to whisper. He dismissed outright that the magma might be rising again since the North American continental plate had been drifting in a westwardly direction for millions of years, which meant the former hot spot that had been responsible for the Wapshilla flows was now beneath Yellowstone. He opted instead for a more localized geothermal cause for this hot, but not scalding, water, knowing that east-central Washington State seemed to have a higher-than-expected success rate with heat pump technologies. This, he suspected, was either due to a previously unknown tectonic deformation—possibly new fractures and fault lines that were developing in the mantle that was already under strain thanks to the Cascadian Subduction Zone that has been turning parts of the coast into an accordion—or perhaps this eastern region of the state was just more seismically connected to the active volcanism of the Cascade Mountain Range than most seismologists were prepared to accept.

Seamus was broiling in the sun and knew the temperature must have gone well over one hundred degrees. He lifted his baseball cap and distributed the sweat from his forehead into his hair again. The hot water continued to spurt from the pipe, only to vanish into the baked cracks of the pond bottom as though it were a colander. The shadow of a sizeable bird moving across the terrain caught his eye. When Seamus looked up, there was no bird in the sky that he could see. The unknown flying shadow traced another circle around him on the ground, and stumped by what was casting the shadow, Seamus figured the elongated wingspan suggested a bird of prey. But then it could have been an angel for all he could prove.

Seamus Quinlan was foremost a scientist. He didn't subscribe to spiritualism, beckon ghosts, or keep watch for otherworldly signs. He hadn't been inside a church since his christening. He'd be the last person to embrace mysticism or fall for a hoax. But with no good explanation for what had sounded like a spoken warning coming out of the pipe, for the geothermal water filling up the pond, and now, for the shadow tricks being played by the sun, he freaked out just a little.

With the running water finally puddling and spreading across the bottom of the pond, Seamus seized a shortcut to reach the other side. He hopscotched across the high spots before they became submerged. Just as he turned to head back down to the house, he felt a jolt, like when a ten-speed bicycle chain jumps off its gear. He looked down to see if maybe he'd tripped on a rock or root, but the ground appeared clear. Maybe the nearest neighbor was using dynamite? That seemed unlikely. Perhaps it had been a sonic boom from a plane out of Larson Air Force Base? They regularly made training loops above the hardscrabble landscape. He doubted it was an earthquake. The area wasn't known for seismic activity—not like in the Cascades, on the western edge of the state, where something registered on the Richter nearly every day.

Within seconds, the water from the pipe ceased flowing just as Seamus's cellphone vibrated in his front pocket. It was a text from one of his colleagues over at Hanford, asking if he had felt that. He texted back that he had, knowing he needed to pick up his pace and return to his work site as quickly as possible so he could check the sensor readouts and monitor for further activity. The mystery of the pond would have to wait until the coming weekend, when he'd be back to check on it again. He'd have to talk his stubborn father into coming with him to stay in Seamus's Kennewick townhouse until the water could get sorted at the farmhouse. His cell vibrated once more—this time it was a call coming from Priest Rapids, the dam and reservoir about ten miles upstream from Hanford's boundary.

"Hey there, Seamus. It's Cody up at PR. We're getting confirmation from the Pacific Northwest Seismic Network that we just had a 2.8 blip on the Richter. I imagine you're getting the same information, but I wanted to check in with you."

Seamus did a quick analysis in his head. "Sounds like a pressure release event—perhaps an echo of a tectonic slip closer to the coast," he said, walking over the hump and back toward the house. "I suspect you are still near full reservoir, conserving enough capacity so you can keep feeding the Priest Rapids lateral irrigation channel during these dry months."

There was some crackling on the line that sounded like the dam's structural engineer was struggling to open a vending machine-dispensed bag of Fritos. "Yep. She's full alright." Cody didn't bother disguising his munching. "Remember back in 2015, when we had that explosion in the turbine gallery? We lowered the reservoir table by three feet in a matter of days." He was boasting now. "Half that went over the spillways, a third got flushed down the PR Lateral, and we were damn fortunate that Wanapum Dam was well below max and could shut their outflows off completely. Evaporation took care of the rest."

Seamus stomped the dust off his shoes before stepping onto the back porch. "Let's see over the next twenty-four whether this jolt was an anomaly."

Another call came in—this one from his boss—that he felt he should probably take. He quickly asked about Cody's wife, slowly recovering from a double mastectomy—a procedure Seamus's mother, Abigail, had also undergone. Apparently, it was a Hail Mary pass after all other efforts to conquer Cody's wife's late-stage cancer had failed. "It is what it is," Cody said somberly, and thanked him for asking, before Seamus switched out one call for the other.

"Seamus, here," he announced, as his boss unleashed a string of questions in quick succession. Pausing—suddenly awash with uneasy feelings on the porch—Seamus sucked in a problem-solving gulp of air through his mouth. "Yep, I felt it. I'm on my way back," was all he said before holstering his phone in his front pocket. He had already sensed he needed to beat a path back to Hanford, just in case the seismic activity and the bizarre warning from the well at the pond foretold something much worse to come.

He opened the screen door into the kitchen and simultaneously spotted water cascading over the sink counter onto the yellowed and peeling linoleum, as he heard a rapid beeping sound that sounded like a smoke detector but was more likely emanating from his dad's oxygen concentrator. Seamus turned off the sink tap as he splashed and slipped through the archway to the living room. Suddenly, he felt the blood rushing from his head. Somehow, he already knew he was about to discover that Pops had passed from this realm into the next.

He was right. There he was, slumped in that ratty blue-plaid recliner, the latest downwinder—the very last member of his immediate family—to succumb.

He burns with prostate cancer.
Carried plutonium home in his underwear,
Ashes of Trinity; Ashes of Nagasaki.

"For Christ's sake, dad,
You went to work daily, out of love
And duty, but did the Devil's job.
You guys stoked Hell's ovens,
Brought home shadows in your lunchboxes.

"All the radiation badges can't monitor
How much your children love you
Or measure thirty years of labor
Smoldering in your work pants;
Or count the sperm spitting across
    centuries,
Igniting everywhere karmaic fires."

—William Witherup

CHAPTER TWO

SEAMUS'S BRAIN DIDN'T KNOW what to do next, but his body seemed to be following an itemized checklist he never recalled making. Most likely that was because the list had been made by his Irish ancestors. To the best of his ability, he was re-enacting their traditions, tracing the steps they'd taken and the rituals he'd observed during the staggering score of wakes and funerals that had occurred over the past century in that very farmhouse.

He turned off the oxygen concentrator to stop its alarm so he could think. Outside, the prevailing wind seemed fixated on a piece of loose tin it must have been working to dislodge from the roof for seasons. Over the din of the machine that had helped his father breathe, Seamus hadn't noticed this racket on the roof before now. He leaned over his dad slumped in the plaid chair and tried to wrestle open the closest window, but it had a sticking sash. He threaded his long legs between the chair and the oxygen machine to get greater leverage. Opening a window, he remembered, was done to allow the spirit of the deceased to escape so that it didn't haunt the house. Likely, his father's spirit wouldn't venture far, Seamus figured, since this farmhouse had been his penitentiary for decades, and the Quinlan Family memorial chapel for even longer.

With the curtains and window open, Seamus was seized by a shock as the sunlight revealed how quickly his father's face had turned from orange-yellow to green. His father's mouth was open at a ghastly angle and his pale blue eyes seemed focused on something stationary on the other side of the living room. Seamus followed the line of vision, wondering about the very last thing his father had seen and determined it must have been the dusty low-profile china hutch, with its framed photos of all those who'd preceded him into the afterlife. Their anxious, worn faces seemed ready to receive Gerald on the other side.

Seamus knelt his lanky, six-foot-two frame and while his brain hesitated, his shaking hands were already closing his father's unshaven jaw. Next, with two fingers, he gently and then more firmly worked the eyelids to a mostly closed position. It wasn't like in the movies, where you effortlessly lowered the blinds and they stayed down. The lid on his father's right and most judgmental eye kept creeping open. Seamus held his two fingers there as though he were waiting for glue to dry. It mostly worked, except his own eyes became uncooperative, gushing with gully-washing tears he must have been storing and holding back. He hadn't cried since his younger brother, Sean, had passed from his cancer—one year to the day after their mother had unexpectedly died on the operating table at Trios Women's Hospital in Kennewick, during her double mastectomy. That was in 2014.

His cellphone began vibrating and beeping audibly at the same time. He'd reached the age—his mid-50s—where he now relied on both settings to alert him of incoming calls. He took fists to his eyes and inhaled to pull himself together before extracting the phone from his front pocket.

"Seamus Quinlan, here."

"Shay, it's Dell." The caller did not pause even long enough for a greeting. "We've had another tunnel collapse at the former PUREX site near *200 East*. The take cover alarms are blasting here, and we need a ground stability assessment PDQ before we muster dump trucks to fill it back in."

Seamus inhaled a rivulet of snot just as the house rumbled. He immediately assumed an eighteen-wheeler on the highway, but when Dell exclaimed, "Holy shit! There's another one," he knew it must be the second temblor in a matter of hours. He composed himself, trying to be the take-charge guy everyone relied on, even though he felt like an imposter most days, since geology and physics could be equal parts science and guesswork.

"Dell, I'm on my way, but you've caught me at least thirty-five minutes out, and I'm ... well, I'm in the middle of something." Seamus was grasping but needed to buy some time. "Tell you what—send all non-essential personnel home. Have the trucks load up but stand by. I'll get there as soon as I can." A second call was coming in. Dell acknowledged the instruction, and Seamus took the call after glancing at the screen. It was Cody again, from Priest Rapids Dam.

"Hey, Cody," Seamus said. "I felt this one."

"This a foreshadowing? A precursor to something bigger? Want me to draw down the reservoir now?" Cody was a consummate questions guy. Seamus was supposed to be the answers guy. That had long been their working arrangement, in tandem for different agencies, in offices twenty miles apart. They spoke at least a few times each month, but seldom found themselves in the same room. Today wouldn't change that, but with the odd seismic activity, Seamus had an inkling he'd be spending a lot of time with Cody soon. They'd need to come up with a real strategy for mitigating a water catastrophe that would one day douche Hanford of its nuclear waste—and with its toxic outflow, destroy most living things downstream, and create a dead zone in the Pacific. They, and the generations that had re-imagined and re-engineered nature before them, had been robbing Peter like tomorrow would never come. But it was inevitable, and Seamus knew it. He wasn't the only canary, either. All the insiders he worked with had accepted that aging infrastructure would be the undoing of one future generation or another.

Seamus stood and looked out the open window, wondering if his father's spirit had indeed exited. He leveled with Cody. "Look. I'm not sure what these rumbles mean. We're nowhere near a fault line. We're not sitting on top of tectonic plates, like they are on the coast. I assume someone has already confirmed with Larson AFB that they aren't testing something they might have forgotten to warn us about?"

"Yeah," Cody said. "Barry—you know my counterpart up at Wanapum Dam? He said he just spoke to his cousin who works at Larson, and she told him they felt the first quake, too. It wasn't them."

"I have two irons in the fire," Seamus said, "both burning my hands. Let's keep the communication lines open and our ears to the ground." He was trying to work out the order he'd handle things under this new pressure and realized he could be frank with his colleague, who had virtually the same security clearance. "We had part of another tunnel collapse at HEW this morning, which may or may not be the result of the earlier tremor. We're sending non-essential personnel home until I can assess ground stability and get this latest collapse filled back in. As for your reservoir, I wouldn't start spilling water yet. But like I said earlier, if you could push a little more up the PR Lateral Canal than normal, I'm sure the farmers would be happy in this heat."

He looked back at his dad dead in his chair and gently removed the oxygen tubing from his nose. Another call was coming in. "Gotta go, Cody. I'll connect once I know more." He didn't wait for a goodbye before switching to the other line. "Yeah, Dell?"

The caller cleared his throat and began. "Uh, I'm embarrassed. Turns out our so-called collapse is just a little more than a pothole in size … less than a meter wide. We've cordoned off Area 200. I just didn't want you to break your neck getting here."

Seamus exhaled. "Appreciate knowing, Dell. Look, I'm up at my old man's farmhouse. He just passed away—maybe thirty minutes ago. I need to make arrangements for his body and get the coroner out here before I can be much use on site. Can you let the upper org chart know? I'll be there sometime later this afternoon."

"Oh, geez," Dell exclaimed. "So sorry to hear about your dad, man."

Just the act of sharing the news, though only with one other person, had caused Seamus to experience tremors of his own. He clenched every muscle in his face and upper body so he could keep from losing it on the phone.

"I'll let the higher-ups know," Dell assured him. "You take all the time you need."

"Thanks," Seamus managed before lowering the phone from his

cheek. The Priest Rapids and Wanapum dams together couldn't have held back the tears that gushed down the spillways of his cheeks. He crumpled to his knees near his father's recliner and sobbed violently in the dead man's lap. This was it, he thought: he was now officially an orphan.

Emotions seldom muscled their way into his overly analytical demeanor. It hadn't been a minute before he pulled himself together and got to work on the tasks he'd witnessed his ancestors carry out. Still kneeling, he gently eased his father's body onto a shoulder and, with more ease than he anticipated, rose to his feet. His father couldn't have weighed more than one hundred pounds. He needed to lay him out before he stiffened—to clean him up and get him ready for a coroner and then burial in the family cemetery on the hill behind the house. There was no sense factoring in a wake, since there was nobody left for a proper keening. His father wouldn't have wanted that nonsense, anyway. *Just feed me to the worms and sow bugs*, he'd commanded anytime his mortality came up.

Seamus contemplated laying him out on his bed and pillows upstairs, or down in the root cellar, which had always been the coolest part of the house. The latter had been hollowed out by one of his great-grandfathers beneath an oversized, piano-hinged trapdoor in the mudroom, just off the kitchen and before you reached the back door. Both locations required navigating steep stairs—and to access the cellar where the incline was nearly vertical, it was more ladder than stairs. The kitchen table was the most practical. It was poetic, too—since that was also the spot where his father debuted in this world eighty-eight years earlier. When his father's feet grazed the table, they knocked over the pinecone-shaped salt-and-pepper shakers that one of the great-grandmothers or aunts had acquired while road-tripping through Oklahoma. One of the pair broke on the floor, sending salt in all directions. Seamus was pretty sure that was Irish for good luck.

He gingerly laid his father out on the long wooden table. He stepped back as the early-afternoon sun found its way through the dirty kitchen windows and grease-and-moth-eaten lace of faded curtains to enshrine the room in an amber halo. Seamus thought to open a second window for ventilation but knew he'd have to fight with another stubborn sash. Plus, it was so hot outside. He decided to let it be. He straightened his father's legs with some effort and organized his skinny arms at his sides. He didn't know his father to own a shirt that wasn't plaid, but it didn't seem right not to at least try to gussy the old farmer up some—not that his dad ever gave a lick about his appearance.

The dutiful son left the kitchen and ascended the stairs to the bedrooms for the first time in years. In his parent's room, on top of the fraying quilt of the neatly made bed, Seamus discovered his dad had laid out the clothes for his own burial. Among these articles was a crisp, white shirt with creases from having been folded—almost certain to have come straight from the package. There was also a hand-me-down suit that Seamus thought might have belonged to one of his two brothers, which suggested that one of them had been buried in something else. Tears returned to his eyes as he gathered the clothes from the bed and stopped by the upstairs bathroom to scoop up some toiletries, including a Barbasol shaving cream with a rusted bottom, his dad's mostly toothless comb, and a school-bus-yellow disposable BIC razor. It looked as though his father hadn't understood that the dull and damaged BIC was made to be thrown away.

Downstairs again, Seamus froze in the kitchen archway, shocked a second time by his father's skin tone and not knowing if he was cut out for this. It occurred to him that maybe he should first make sure he could find a coroner who would make a house call. He put the clothes down on the table next to his father's body and reached for the Mid-Columbia Phone Directory on the kitchen counter. He flipped to the blue pages under Franklin County and found the number to the coroner's office. He dialed it using the wall phone that was below the crucifix and next to the curtained pantry. As his improving luck would have it, Seamus learned that the county coroner was already up in Washtucna for the morning—his daughter was showing a goat as part of a 4-H exhibition there. He would swing by the farm on his way back to the office in the Tri-Cities. "Forty-five minutes to an hour, tops," he had added cheerfully, not sounding the least bit creepy. The timing was a relief as it would allow Seamus enough space before the end of the day to dash over to Hanford, make a quick appearance and inspect the latest tunnel collapse for any ground stability issues following the seismic activity.

Seamus moved to the sink, removed the strainer plug to release the water, and dropped a few dishtowels to the floor to mop up the overflow. He refilled the sink with water and tried to make it warm before realizing how ridiculous that was—the temperature wouldn't matter to his father. He added a good dose of Dawn dish soap, thinking that if it was gentle enough for oily sea birds, it would suffice for the delicate task ahead, too. He unbuttoned the long-sleeved plaid shirt and worked the open shirt panels under the shoulder blades before lifting his father's head and neck to extract the shirt from under him. The navy-blue sweatpants he had taken to wearing as daywear and pajamas were easier to remove. He rolled them up with the shirt to create a pillow, supporting the head and neck. Seamus was embarrassed—stunned, really—at how evident his father's skeleton was beneath his almost translucent skin. He could have left his old man's boxers on, but they were wet and soiled. Because Seamus feared this might compromise his dad's reception in the afterlife, he took the boxers down over knobby knees and scabbed and varicose-veined ankles. And there it was, sort of crinkled and hanging off to the side, Gerald's Irish blessing. They'd all had that luck o' the Irish endowment—except Sean, the youngest of Seamus's brothers. "That's because you were supposed to be a lass," his older brother Sampson had relentlessly teased, going as far as nicknaming him *Seana*. To Sean's horror, the nickname stuck with him the whole of his short life.

The thing that bothered Seamus the most was not the fact that his old man had soiled himself—most likely when his heart had stopped, and all his muscles had relaxed. It was the condition of his father's cracked and calloused feet. Yellowed toenails, nearly thick as quarter-inch plywood, looked as though they hadn't been trimmed in a year. *I can't care*, Seamus remembered his father saying, but the reality was that he simply could not reach his feet anymore. Seamus washed them, actively negotiating with his own squeamish resistance. Then he socked them right away. And that's how he started the proper laying out of his father.

Gagging, he used paper towels to remove the excrement, wondering what in the hell his father had been eating. He deposited the towels with the soiled briefs and tied a double knot in a plastic WinCo grocery bag. As the soapy washcloth traveled the older version of his own body, Seamus hummed the tune to "Carrickfergus" because he'd never learned the words—though somebody had sung or played this song at every Quinlan wake and funeral he'd attended.

Shaving his dad's whiskers was, by far, the hardest part of the ritual. He gently pulled the razor over the same prominent, rounded chin they'd all had going back generations, according to the framed photos on the living-room bureau. Seamus knew he didn't have to worry about nicks, but he'd admired and looked up to this face for almost six decades, without ever touching it before now. Only after his late teens, when a growth spurt had him topping at over six feet, did he have to look down to meet his father's narrowly spaced, watercolor-blue eyes. It was that same weathered face that had patiently tutored him on how to shave himself—with the same Barbasol shaving cream, and the same manly scent that had been in his nostrils, he supposed, since birth. Seamus's eyes watered and the folksong he was humming got caught up in a choke at the back of his throat when it suddenly struck him: besides becoming an orphan that afternoon, he was now a farm owner.

Technically, that wasn't news—he'd been added to the title after his brothers and mother had passed away. Likewise, he was co-owner on all his father's bank accounts and vehicles. Aside from a few notifications, there wouldn't be much paperwork. But the farm would be something to contend with soon. What in the hell was he going to do with all that acreage when he already had a townhouse in Kennewick? There wasn't mortgage owed on either property, but there would be taxes. He saw no point—beyond family pride and principle—in holding on to both. He wouldn't relish the hour-plus commute to work each direction if he consolidated households and lived in the farmhouse—but then, he didn't plan to keep working forever, either. Perhaps now, he wouldn't have to at all.

It was the sort of dilemma for which he'd asked his father's advice—though this was usually more to make idle conversation rather than land a decision. Gerald Quinlan would have urged him to keep the farm, no doubt about that. Seamus knew this because his father had been quite dedicated to making these last wishes known every time Seamus stopped by over these last several years. Ever since the doctors had pronounced his cancers incurable, his dad had become this parrot saying the same things over and over; he wished to die at home in the farmhouse, and he wished for Seamus to tend the farm and take care of the family cemetery for the rest of his days. The long medical downhill became much steeper once Gerald had refused any further intervention after the indignity of having his prostate removed. By then he'd been told the cancer had already set up shop in the lymph nodes. That was the moment it was over before it was over, as far as his old man had been concerned.

Seamus began humming again after removing the leftover tracks of shaving cream with a washcloth and while combing his father's white hair. It seemed improper to prep the man's body for burial without giving him underwear. Quinlan men hadn't been able to get away with going commando, though his father had recently mentioned that his Irish blessing wasn't what it used to be since his prostate was gone. Still, his youngest boy Sean probably would have been very happy to have had the ampleness with which their father died. Poor bloke had been shortchanged in that department, Seamus recalled, grinning devilishly, in spite of himself.

Seamus was now mourning the loss of both—of everyone, really. His older brother, Sampson. Their mother, Abigail. Grandparents on both sides, and who he'd barely known, had each made this clapboard farmhouse a death chamber in his lifetime. Seamus wondered whether he was willing to die there, too.

In the meantime, his father's yoke was now around his own neck. Would he be the one Quinlan heartless enough to sell the family cemetery? He pondered this while dashing upstairs to his father's bedroom, hoping to find a clean pair of underwear for the old man. Once there, he found an enveloped letter addressed in block letters to SHAY—his father's (and most everyone else's) abbreviation of the name they couldn't spell and struggled to say. He sat on the edge of the bed, and with trembling hands, he opened the gummed flap and extracted the four pages handwritten on lined paper. He was not ready for deathbed confessions.

Except for a signature, Seamus did not remember ever seeing his father's penmanship before. The writing fascinated him. The letter began …

To my last living son and relative, Seamus:

First things first. You'll find two white pine coffins in the barn where we used to keep the animals and chickens. One for me, and one for you, I guess. I got the second one half-off, so use it or don't. I can't care anymore.

You'll find my grave already dug out next to your mother's. Funny story. Turns out this hippie-looking hitchhiker showed up on the porch about a month back, looking for a drink of water. I asked if he wanted to earn a hundred bucks as a gravedigger. He spent the afternoon on the task and said he got nice and deep but had to go through lots of rocks. I gave him an extra twenty.

Now, I want to get some things off my chest. Things I've never told anybody—not even your mother. It has to do with what went on at Hanford before I got there and what happened after. There were things we heard, things we knew, and things we did—things we were told to do, that were just wrong. You have long suspected we were irresponsible. But honestly, we were just workers following orders. We had no idea what we didn't know. But the government knew, all right.

Here goes.

Back in the 40s, when Hanford started up, less than one percent of folks who worked there even knew they were working on nuclear components for an atomic bomb. I'm not sure it would have mattered if they did. It was a job in a place where jobs off the farm hadn't existed before. Most of my relatives—including my father's brother, who would have been your Great Uncle Percy—were lured to work there back then. I didn't get hired until 1963, your mother in '67. By then, everyone knew

Hanford plutonium had been used in the bomb that destroyed Nagasaki, Japan. Most of us were proud of that. All my relatives except Uncle Percy were gone when I started working there. By then, there were already nine nuclear reactors in full swing and Hanford had made enough plutonium for something like 60,000 bombs, each of the size used on Japan.

My Uncle Percy worked for HEW longer than any of us. He had been trained as a circuit electrician specialist when he was in the Navy, and this earned him an important post at HEW when he left the military. He could have carried his secrets to the grave, but he took me aside before it was too late to tell me about the "Green Run."

Because I was one of the last family members still working for HEW, Uncle Percy felt I should know what he'd done—or rather, what he'd been ordered to do by the higher-ups. Now, I am going to tell you what he told me, because you work there now, you live here, and you are family. You won't want to, but you should know this, too.

In the summer and fall of 1949, the brass at HEW had been approached by the US Air Force, who wanted to develop their technology for detecting radiation using high-altitude reconasance, reconnaisence reconnaissance missions.

Seamus relaxed his forehead, and took a moment, amid all his foreboding, to grin at his father's spelling struggle.

USAF wanted to keep tabs on Russia. They told HEW they wanted to fly behind a high-altitude radioactive plume to see if their instruments could detect the radiation. If this worked, they'd be able to fly over Russia and improve their intelligence gathering. At first HEW had the guts to say no, pretty sure it was going to be far too dangerous for people living here and in the Tri-Cities. Turned out, the mad scientists at HEW had already been keeping around a thousand farm animals in barns and other buildings right there in the middle of Hanford, out near the F Reactor. They'd been giving them feed with iodine-131 in it—the most radioactive of the by-products in plutonium production—to see what happened. My uncle said he knew about the test animals onsite and had heard they were being fed contaminated feed. As a farm boy, he knew those animals weren't right, even though management kept reporting out that they were just fine—fat, happy, and healthy as any farm animal anywhere, they'd said. HEW even gifted butchered quarters of the beef and sheep for employees' Christmas bonuses. Uncle Percy said he would never eat that meat and figured out near the end that they had all been lab rats—the workers included. It hadn't just been the test farm animals that had been exposed to contaminations onsite and daily. He was pretty sure that HEW was lying to everyone back then, that these farm animals were used as a cover-up and a con they were pulling on their employees. But when it came time for this test that the military was demanding, the Air Force insisted it was a matter of national security. That the future of humanity depended on this experiment.

Uncle Percy wanted me to know that he had been part of the delegation that tried to discourage the USAF from going ahead with their test. But in the end, remember, he was also ex-military, having served in the Navy toward the end of WWII. The executives at HEW finally buckled and agreed to do what the Air Force had asked them to do and set the date for the release of radiation for the evening of December 2, 1949. I would have been fourteen years old then. Many years later, before he died from his cancer, he explained something to me. I already knew this, but he said under normal circumstances, irradiated uranium was cooled for just about one hundred days before the worst of the leftover by-products got released into the air and flushed into the Columbia River. But the Air Force was in this great big hurry. They thought the Russians might be short-cooling their nuclear materials and releasing them "green" into the environment without waiting for the chemical elements to dissipate.

The military wanted to stimulate this so they could call-out and punish Russia—slow their race for nuclear supremacy.

Seamus was pretty sure his father had meant to use the word *simulate*, in this context. He gave his head a slow shake from side to side and continued reading.

The US military insisted that this aerial release from HEW consist of similar waste—predominantly iodine-131—that was still green, in other words, that hadn't yet been cooled or cured. That's how the Green Run got its name. They were going to release the worst stuff possible, because they were convinced that was what Russia was doing, but they needed to prove it.

HEW's thinking (and, I take it, their hope) was that by the start of December, all the harvests were finished, the farm animals were in barns for the winter, and colder weather would keep most people indoors during the test. Uncle Percy told me he'd been worried physically sick about the effects this would have on the Quinlan family Farm, his parents, his siblings, and the animals. It fell to him and a handful of other loyal military types to trigger this release from the ground. Uncle Percy says he was ordered by the Air Force to emit one ton of highly radioactive material through the smokestacks, even though it had only been cooled for sixteen days. Uncle Percy told me that he had confided in one of his co-workers that he sincerely hoped—for all of humanity—that the filters and screens on the smokestacks did their job and prevented the largest volumes of the iodine-131 and xenon-133 from leaving the stacks. The co-worker then told this to a superior who told the Air Force. USAF ordered the filters and screens to be switched off for the test and even placed an officer in the control room to make sure it had been done. Uncle Percy was ordered to bypass these safety mechanisms, and an order was an order, he told me—shortly before he died from thyroid cancer.

With knots in his stomach, Uncle Percy overrode the filters on the smokestacks—and because the safety systems were tied together, this also opened the filtering screens on the discharge pipes that normally returned treated and sufficiently cooled wastewater back into the Columbia River—at something like 60,000 gallons a minute.

My uncle said as night fell on December 2, 1949, the weather turned ominous. A thick fog had moved in and once again, he and others at HEW tried to convince the Air Force to call it off or delay for better weather. The Air Force wouldn't have it—they felt the fog would help conceal the venting. At first, the winds seemed to come from the south, which Uncle Percy hoped would push the radiation plume toward Saddle Mountain and away from the Tri-Cities. Almost as soon as the venting had started, though, it began to rain. Then the wind shifted and grew stronger. This time, it was blowing in from the northwest, which Uncle Percy feared would push the toxic plume directly eastward toward the Quinlan family farm and south over the Tri-Cities, potentially poisoning every living relative he had ever known. The rain didn't let up for the first several hours of the test release. This prevented the highly radioactive plume from rising to the elevation the Air Force had planned to be flying—instead, the rain carried the iodine-131 and the xenon-133 with it to the ground, lakes, and rivers.

Uncle Percy later learned that despite the weather, the release had somehow grown to about 40 miles wide and 200 miles long before the venting was stopped. By that time, Uncle Percy figured most of the really bad stuff was already on the ground and in the rivers. The test was deemed a failure by the Air Force.

My uncle remembers that readings later taken on vegetation, from Hanford to Spokane to Walla Walla, and as far south as Pendleton, Oregon, showed off-the-chart radiation readings with microcuries that were ten, even one hundred times the permissible concentrations. Uncle Percy developed ulcers along with his thyroid cancer as he fretted the rest of his shortened life. The immediate and looming consequences of the Green Run seemed to pick off everyone he knew, one by one. Your great uncle was so racked by guilt, that he insisted on single-handedly digging the graves for every member of our family who died before he did. He went to his own grave out back, convinced he was personally responsible for killing his family and for contaminating thousands of people and animals who had unluckily been downwind on December 2, 1949.

As you already know, because we've talked about this, iodine-131 showed up in dairy milk for decades. Hell of a mess as it still shows up in ocean-bound and ocean caught fish to this day. You've seen the Geiger counter tests at Pike Place Fish Market in Seattle on the news. Hanford, Chernobyl, Fukushima—they all fucked us up for good if not forever. Anyway, that's where Uncle Percy's guilt—and his cancer—came from. But I have my own Hanford story to tell. I'm sorry this letter is so long ... I'll try to wrap this up for you and for me. My damn hand is cramping.

    Seamus exhaled long and forcefully into the stale air of that upstairs farmhouse bedroom. He needed a break. Maybe some fresh air. He lowered the pages to his lap. He would have to read the rest later. His heart was beating way more quickly than he thought it should be.
    On the by-now antique walnut dresser across from him, underlined with a rectangular piece of yellowed lace, were framed photographs of his whole dead family, arranged like a skyline. A black-and-white one of his parents was the largest. It must have been taken not long after the two employees had met in a Hanford lunchroom. Arranged on either side were random pictures from different school years of Seamus and his two brothers—always in the same, differently color-striped rugby shirts year after year, since country clothes had to last longer. There were formal couple portraits in wooden frames of the two sets of Irish grandparents. Oddly, there was also a photograph of their celebrated and much-loved 1973 Franklin County Fair-winning heifer, that he and his brothers had named Isa-bells. He was certain that the collection of photos had been curated by his long-departed mother, Abigail. It

probably hadn't been dusted since, he thought, as he drew a finger across one of the frames.

Breathing heavier now and beginning to panic from this newfound abandonment, Seamus took stock. He was having one hell of a morning, and worried that his brain might explode. He flashed back to earlier, when his alarm clock had gone off in his Kennewick townhouse and he had awoken to face a day he had expected would be just like every other. Instead, there had been two earthquakes in a place that wasn't supposed to have any. There had been a jammed windmill and a dried pond—and after the pipes moaned their ominous warning and he coaxed water back to the surface, that water had turned out to be thermal. There had been another tunnel collapse at Hanford, where he really should have been at that moment. And there had been his father's passing—aided by his spreading cancer—which meant Seamus had to wait for the county coroner, set to arrive at any minute.

He snatched the first pair of boxers from the top dresser drawer and braced himself to head back downstairs. Before leaving, he studied the bedroom—its peeling wallpaper with the faded peony pattern, and the July sun spilling through the once-white sheers. Leaning into the doorjamb, he wept for his abandoned self. There was officially nobody else left but him—the last of the Quinlans.

He folded the letter into the envelope and eased both into his back jeans pocket. He was halfway down the stairs when the house shuddered violently and he heard what sounded like a squealing crash outside. At first, he thought it might have been another earthquake, and his heart skipped while his brain scrambled to decode the audible cues. But at the bottom of the stairs, he heard a horn outside. It sounded stuck.

Still holding the boxer briefs, Seamus emerged onto the front porch. He squinted to see a rig tilted in the ditch, and a black Suburban at an odd angle, with its turn signal on, just inside the entrance to the gravel driveway. With a flat hand over his eyebrows to block the intense sun, he ran toward whatever had just happened. A tall man with a beard but no mustache—looking a lot like Abraham Lincoln—emerged from the Suburban. At the same time, a black man, broad as a refrigerator, rounded the back end of the semi. Seamus watched as the men's arms and hands did almost as much talking as their mouths. A metal clipboard in one of the trucker's hands kept catching and reflecting the sun in every direction—but mostly, it seemed, in Seamus's eyes.

When the two strangers looked toward the house, Seamus's first impulse was to wave—but he did so with the hand holding his father's underwear, as though he intended to surrender to invading forces. He walked closer, gravel crunching underfoot, he soon he could see that the back of the driver's side of the suburban had been crumpled—he guessed by the semi, which may have tried swerving, but had still clipped the turning vehicle. When he was close enough to hear the men talking, he held off introducing himself until they had things sorted.

Honest Abe admitted to signaling at the last second, as he hadn't seen the driveway coming up. The truck driver admitted he had likely pushed way over the speed limit, as his AC was broken, and he had been gunning to find anyplace with shade. Neither of them had been hurt, though there was damage to both rigs. The trucker had blown his front right tire when it crushed the culvert sticking out from under the driveway. Seamus smelled onions and said so.

"Early Walla Walla Sweets," the truck driver confirmed with an accent that sounded Southern. "I'm Russ," he said, stretching his gloved hand toward Seamus without needing to move either of his feet.

"I'm Seamus Quinlan." They shook. "This"—he hesitated, arm panning the acreage behind him—"is my farm." It was the first time he had accepted the transfer of ownership. "Welcome, I guess."

"I am at the right place then," said Abraham—but correcting, for the record, that his real name and title was "Mitchell Kennedy, Franklin County Coroner." He shook Seamus's hand and then Russ the truck driver's hand. The latter was checking his phone for a signal.

"Coroner?" Russ squealed the word. "I sure hope you don't have any stiffs in the back of that Suburban. I don't need any zombies in my life right now." The timing of the joke wasn't particularly good, and neither the coroner nor Seamus responded—but they exchanged knowing glances. "What?" Russ asked—but his twisted face suggested he knew he had just stepped in something unpleasant.

"It's okay," Seamus explained. "He's here for my father, who passed away this morning."

"Oh God, I am so sorry." The trucker's demeanor softened, like he'd had all the rigid cartilage suctioned out of him. The sudden pudding of a giant moved in for a bear hug, and Seamus, sensing the first measure of comfort in a normal day turned horrible, hugged back, with every muscle and tendon he could muster.

"Thank you," Seamus mumbled into Russ's neck, which is where his head came to. The much taller man hadn't let go, and Seamus wondered whether he had needed the hug, too, after crashing his rig. "Come," he said, finally pulling away, and addressing both men. "If you move closer to the house, your cellphone signals should improve. Or you're welcome to use the landline." As the words came out of his mouth, he remembered that the phone he'd just offered up was on the wall in the kitchen—next to his naked dead father, still sprawled out on the table.

Russ reached the back of a fist to his eye. "I lost my dad to COVID in '21. I know how hard …" He trailed off. "That was my old man's truck, over there in the ditch. He never had an accident with that rig."

The coroner jumped in with his apology, for the second time. "I didn't see the driveway until the last second and I know I didn't give you enough warning. The fault here is mine, so don't beat yourself up. I just need to phone my office and get the number to the insurance company and start the claim." The coroner looked at his phone again and then showed it to them. "Half a bar. Best to use the phone in the house, and since I am headed there anyway …"

Seamus turned to lead the way. Ascending the porch steps, he realized Russ would probably be the first man of color to step foot inside the Quinlan farmhouse. Holding the front door open, he tried to address and engage the trucker as though this his presence wasn't a novelty.

"Bathroom is the first door down the hall on the right—help yourself," Seamus said to anyone needing it. "My father is in the kitchen," he told the coroner, pointing the way.

The truck driver could see the legs of the dead man on the table through the archway and said he preferred to wait in the living room, where he'd get a start on the accident paperwork that he always carried around in his metal container clipboard, just in case.

The coroner lowered his black backpack off a shoulder and led the way into the kitchen. Seamus pulled the white boxers out of his back jeans pocket and apologized as they entered the kitchen. "I was just about to get him dressed when I heard the crash."

"Ah, don't think twice about it," the coroner reassured him, as he donned latex gloves. "This makes my job easier, and then I can help you get the clothes on him. They never go on as smoothly as you might think."

"I've already cleaned him up—you know, shaved him, and combed his hair. He had cancer, but he was also 88, so—he was getting up there."

"Prostate, removed, I see?" the coroner said, more dictating into his iPhone than asking, as he drew the deceased's privates to one side and lifted the scrotum with a thumb and forefinger pinch. Seamus had not seen that horseshoe-shaped scar before—an indication of how he'd rushed through the sponge bath preparation.

"That was right before the coronavirus pandemic hit—so 2019, I'm thinking. He refused any further treatment after that. Said it was his time, though he stubbornly held on a few more years."

The coroner placed the chest piece of his stethoscope above the sternum and adjusted the ear tips on either side of his Lincoln-esque beard. "Formality," he said. He didn't need to listen long, and then he packed away his gear—except for his phone, which he was recording into. "Date of birth?"

"January 29, 19 ... 38? No ... '35. My mother was born in '38."

"And she's ...?"

"Also deceased—eleven years now. Also cancer."

"Siblings?"

"Of mine?" Kennedy nodded. "Two brothers—one older, one younger. Both deceased. Both from cancer." Internally, Seamus grappled with the totality of his loss, but on the outside, he was trying to be all business.

"Downwinders," the coroner said, without even pretending to whisper. "Let's get your father dressed."

Seamus heard the truck driver talking on his phone in the living room. It sounded as though he was having trouble getting someone to come out to inspect the truck and declare it roadworthy. Meanwhile, the coroner and Seamus got Gerald's suit pants, socks, and shoes on.

"I don't know if my Suburban is even safe to drive now, to tell you the truth," the coroner said as they worked. "He clipped me hard. We might both need a ride into the Tri-Cities if you are headed that way. What would you like done with the body?"

"Sure, uh, I am headed that way, actually. I work for the Department of Energy at Hanford." Seamus wasn't sure whether that was useful information. "And we have a family cemetery on the hill behind the barn. There is apparently a casket in the barn my father intended for me to use."

"Perfect," Kennedy said as he rather roughly raised the body to a sitting position and matter-of-factly threaded the white button-down shirt sleeves over one arm, and then the next. Upon seeing his father suddenly animated, Seamus felt the blood flush from his brain. He took an awkward step back and reached his hand for the wall to steady himself. "I can finish up here if you and the trucker want to retrieve the casket from the barn. No sense struggling with this by yourself when we are standing right here—particularly if you are going to be gracious enough to give us a lift into town. It's the least we can do."

Seamus was surprised and touched and embarrassed. He felt like he was on the verge of becoming quite emotional—at least compared to his regular, scientific state of mind. The unexpected visitors had given him a reprieve from his solitude.

"Sure," he said. "That's great. Thank you." He backed out of the kitchen and into the living room.

There, Russ lowered the phone from his ear. "How's it going in there?" he asked. It was one of those questions where the answer wasn't nearly as important as the gesture in asking it.

Seamus tried to smile, but a tear got away, racing down his

cheek. "We're getting there," he said. "How about you? Are you getting anywhere?"

Russ rose from the sofa. "My mechanic down in Pasco had his driver's license suspended. Says he can't get out here unless I come and get him."

Seamus wanted to be helpful—he just wasn't sure how to go about it. "I don't suppose there is an *AAA* for trucks," he said. The trucker shook his head. "The coroner is almost finished in there," Seamus went on, nodding toward the kitchen. "Then I can drive you both to the Tri-Cities on my way into work, if that helps."

"Wow, okay," said the truck driver. "Thanks. Sorry I wasn't more help in there. I'm not good with bodies."

"I think the coroner is the only one of us who is," Seamus said. "How are you with caskets?" As he spoke, he shut the living-room window next to his father's recliner. Another Irish tradition—so the spirit couldn't slip back into the house.

"Pardon?" A look of panic swept the trucker's face.

"In the barn, my father apparently pre-purchased and stored the box he intended to be buried in. I could use a hand bringing it to the house."

"Let's go," Russ said, tucking his cellphone in the cargo pocket of his side-striped track pants.

By the time the two had returned from the barn, setting the plain pine coffin with the brass rails on the covered back porch outside the kitchen door, the coroner was wrapping up his paperwork. He had placed a white sheet that looked like a shower curtain over the body. Russ waited outside in the narrow patch of afternoon shade cast by the house. Seamus walked through the kitchen and retrieved the plaid cushion from his father's recliner and two of the three seat cushions from the matching and equally ratty-looking sofa that Seamus would be glad to get rid of. "I could use a hand putting him in the coffin, then we can head on down the road if you're ready," Seamus spoke over his shoulder in transit.

"And burial will take place where?" the coroner asked, reaching the last box on his triplicate form.

"In the homesteader cemetery on the hill behind the house, no-frills and no ceremony," Seamus responded. Still carrying the cushions, he passed through the screen door, letting it slap against the doorjamb. He lined the bottom of the wooden box with the cushions and returned to the kitchen.

"I'll take the shoulders. I find the ankles are easier to grab and carry for first timers."

The coroner was already lifting by the time Seamus connected his brain to his willpower and then to his arms and hands. He found his father's ankles beneath the sheet and lifted. The body jack-knifed momentarily until both carriers adjusted their tensions. The coroner walked backward through the screen door, as Seamus tried to direct him. They maneuvered the body into the box on top of the plaid cushions. The coroner retrieved his sheet, made some gentle adjustments with the deceased's head and arms, and then asked, "Are you ready for me to seal the coffin?"

"Wait—I need a rosary!" Seamus exclaimed, dashing back inside the house. All his relatives had been buried with rosaries, and while his father had not been overly religious, Seamus didn't want to screw anything up for him in the afterlife. He dashed up the stairs to his parents' bedroom and looked on top of the dresser and in the nightstands. He finally spotted a string of rosary beads draped and dangling from the crucifix nailed into the peony wallpaper above the bed. He removed the rosary along with the crucifix from the wall. As with the hideous plaid sofa cushions, the circumstances provided an opportunity to dispose of things that Seamus would have no use for now.

When he reappeared on the back porch, he was surprised to find Russ standing solemnly next to the coroner—their heads bowed, and their hands folded with respect for a man they never knew. Seamus tucked the crucifix under his father's crossed wrists and worked the rosary beads between the fingers and thumb of one of the hands. He lowered his head as a few of his tears fell inside the casket to go wherever his father was going. Seamus grinned through tears. Pops was getting a proper wake, and with mourner-witnesses, after all.

Not even a minute had passed, but mindful of the truck driver's squeamishness, Seamus lowered the piano-hinged lid. The three of them exhaled. Out of the corner of one eye, Seamus again spotted a shadow of a large bird that he thought must have been circling overhead. The shadow traced an arch on the ground between the house and the barn. He stepped off the porch and blocked the sun from his eyes, trying to spot the hawk or owl or magpie responsible. He knew they didn't have vultures in this part of the country, though their connection to death was not lost on Seamus. Once again, the sky was empty except for the sun—but the shadow continued its revolutions in the dirt.

Seamus thought about asking the other men if they could see it, too, but elected to leave it be. He'd put them through enough already.

Just before two in the afternoon, Seamus, the county coroner, and the burley teddy-bear of a truck driver squeezed into the only available bench seat in Seamus's 1987 Ford F-150 Custom long bed, along with their backpacks. A metal all-weather box in the bed of the truck was already full of the soil- and water-testing equipment, core samples, picks, shovels, tools, and maps he used every day for work, so Seamus had no extra space to offer. The men turned in unison to examine the disabled semi-truck as they slowly passed it—half in the ditch and marked off by orange cones—before heading south toward the Tri-Cities.

Coroner Kennedy sat in the middle—a tight fit between Seamus and Russ. When nobody said anything or felt an obligation to fill the silence, Seamus was content to be left to his own thoughts, which would have been plentiful even on a less eventful day.

Seamus kept the AC at full blast for the forty-minute commute to the Tri-Cities. The coroner was playing a word game on his smart phone. The truck driver was either asleep or faking it, with his head against the passenger window. Seamus shifted his butt to the left, hoping to give Mitchell's long legs some more room. That's when he heard the crinkle of paper in his back pocket, reminding him of his father's letter about the Green Run—a letter he hadn't finished reading.

Nearing the end
Father was all bones and pain.
The tumor had eaten him
Down to the rind.

Yet little he complained
Or whined. Sulphate of morphine
Eased him somewhat and he kept
His mind and wit—

Though talking was difficult.
A dry wind off the volcanic desert
Went through each of his rooms
Snuffing out cells;

Left an alkaloid crust
On his tongue. We stood by
With Sponge-On-A-Stick
When he was assaulted by thirst

And images. "Give me your hand,"
He said. "And lead me to
The water cooler. I've been
Up in the sky—I'm very tired."

Then, irritated with us,
He would ask to be left alone.
He'd suck a sponge and grab
The lifting bar; be off again.

Brachiating from cloud to cloud.
"Is there a station nearby?
How do we get out of here?
You'll have to help me, son."

He died on graveyard shift.
The train came for him at 3 a.m.,
And when he ran to catch it,
He was out of breath.

—William Witherup

CHAPTER THREE

TRAFFIC WAS LIGHT FOR a summer Wednesday but anyone not needing to drive in this heat had likely elected not to. Seamus and Co. had been stuck behind a double-semi hauling wood chips that he couldn't pass. Chips were flying out the back and hitting his windshield with a sound that reminded Seamus of impatient fingernails drumming a desktop. Russ was snoring and in the middle between them, the coroner was playing a word game on his phone. Seamus was making the best of the drive and some quiet thinking time, like he always did on the road, grateful he didn't have to entertain or hold up his end of a conversation. His one-track mind was stuck between the grooves of an album from his childhood, thinking about his Great Uncle Percy and lamenting the loss of his dad.

He had grown up hearing about the Green Run—like everyone else within a 200-mile radius during the past 74 years, he supposed. There hadn't been a recent member of the Quinlan family who hadn't blamed their cancers on Hanford's slipshod safety records—some downwinders even asserted that the Green Run had been another US-government-sponsored genocide of innocent citizens. At every family gathering, in every phone call or Christmas card, references were made to those who had died, to the contamination that lingered, and to the radioactivity still believed to be leaching into the Columbia River. Seamus had never made the connection before that any of his relatives might have been involved—or even complicit—in some of the more nefarious activities that churned the rumor mill amongst HEW employees. As an insider at Hanford today, Seamus was privy to some classified stuff that had long ago convinced him the rumors weren't that far off the mark. He knew the Green Run was no accident, and he also knew that nobody had ever proved that Hanford had purposely disabled the iodine-131 filters before the Green Run test had begun.

The knowledge that Great Uncle Percy had been the one to flip off all the safety filter switches had been a gut punch. It was part of Seamus's job at Hanford to understand this history. He had of course read the 1992 government report, forced into the open by a media-obtained and court-enforced FOI request. In it, the government reluctantly revealed that roughly 685,000 curies of radioactive iodine-131 had been released into the air and the Columbia River during the four decades HEW produced plutonium. For comparison, the Three Mile Island meltdown in 1979 released less than 25 curies of the same contaminant. On the other hand, the Chernobyl explosion in 1986 released anywhere between 50 million and 200 million curries (depending on which Cold War reporting you believed), and the 2011 meltdown of all three core reactors at Fukushima Daiichi in Japan, 14 million.

Hanford, like most top-secret government-run facilities, had manufactured a slew of misinformation to daze and confuse the enemy and mislead the public. But they had never publicly disclosed how much of its contamination had been intentionally released during the Green Run. Seamus had been told it was upwards of 12,000 curies in an overnight period. But according to the letter from his dad, Uncle Percy had been ordered to vent one ton of the nasty stuff to create the plume. Seamus was no super-mathematician, but he guessed that must have amounted to *more* than 12,000 curies. That reported number was a little over one percent of what the government admitted to releasing during its forty-three years of plutonium production. Of course, the same 1992 report triggered a mass tort lawsuit, which evolved into a class action lawsuit by over 2,000 area residents, who collectively called themselves downwinders. They firmly believed their cancers had been caused by Hanford. Many of Seamus's relatives—including his parents—had been signatories to that lawsuit. Their claim cost the government about $60 million in legal fees, compared to the $7 million it was eventually ordered to pay out in cash settlements to the handful of downwinders with the best cases. "Best cases" meant those with the worst exposures, but who also survived until 2005, when The Green Run case was settled.

Seamus took advantage of a passing lane and overcame the double-trailer of wood chips on a straightaway. At the same time, Mitchell Kennedy was victorious in solving the word game he had been playing on his phone.

While the 1949 Green Run may have garnered the most legal attention, something that happened secretly four years earlier had caused Hanford to produce plutonium in the first place. On August 9, 1945, Nagasaki, Japan was bombed using the first weaponized batch of Hanford's plutonium. The blast from this Fat Boy bomb detonated 1,500 feet above a tennis court in Nagasaki, instantly killed somewhere between 60,000 and 80,000 people. In the year it took Hanford to produce this plutonium, upwards of 350,000 curies of I-131 had been released directly into the air by Hanford. Plutonium for the war effort had gone into breakneck production and smokestack filters had not been thought of or even installed until 1948. Japan needn't have bothered with retaliation for Nagasaki, since Hanford was already in the business of killing its own, Seamus thought, as he fumed behind the wheel.

All of this would have been plenty damning on its own, but he knew that the government report was just a foreword to the real story—the full horrifying legacy of Hanford. Seamus knew this because it was his job to monitor and understand the subterranean geology at Hanford where 53-million gallons of high-level radioactive waste were more-or-less contained inside 177 storage tanks buried in three separate tank farms next to the Columbia River. These had been the top-toxic secrets his father's generation had systematically spent their whole careers trying to cover up (literally and figuratively) and it had been his Pop's responsibility to arrange and plant these tank farms about six feet underground and within a stone's throw from the fourth largest river in the country with the thirty-seventh largest discharge of all the rivers on the planet. *What could possibly go wrong* had been the tongue-in-cheek question of the era. Seamus didn't find that funny or sarcastic now that he had the impossible task of cleaning it up before some globally catastrophic tsunami barreled its way downriver. This feared wall of water could come from any of the ten reservoirs that were being held back by ten aging hydroelectric dams—the oldest of which was turning 88 this year. That was the same age as his dad, who had just given up the ghost.

Since the 40s and up until 1971—when the last of Hanford's nuclear reactors were shut down—the cooling water was only held in open-air detention ponds for, at best, six hours before it was considered treated and flushed back into the river. It's no wonder that radiation kept showing up two hundred miles downstream, like his dad had referenced in the letter tucked into Seamus's back pocket. HEW and the government tried to keep this secret too. They had to, if they wanted to keep operating.

The tell-all 1992 report didn't nearly tell all, and Seamus knew this too. It didn't account for the million gallons of radioactive waste that was still leaking into the Columbia River. During Hanford's heyday, 75,000 gallons of clean river water were sucked from the Columbia every minute, to cool the metal rods containing the enriched plutonium. In the plant, a recipe of powerful chemicals got added to the cooling water, dissolving and separating the metal rods from around the plutonium. When these chemicals met the plutonium, the water became hot, highly radioactive, and nearly as dangerous as the plutonium itself. To maintain the purification standards needed for plutonium, this contaminated water could only be used once. So, the next challenge was to figure out what to do with the contaminated water. The solution came in the development of 200 Area of the sprawling Hanford complex—the site of that morning's tunnel collapse and where Seamus was headed directly after dropping off his passengers. It was there that his father had had some involvement in the placement and burial of the 177 single-lined metal storage tanks that provided Hanford a combined storage capacity of 53 million gallons where it could pump in and store its highly radioactive liquid waste. These tanks were buried near the river and covered up using about six feet of topsoil. This fill, some believed—Seamus among them—was just about as toxic as the materials it concealed. At the time, scientists and engineers expected these tanks to last maybe twenty years. But even with all that subterranean storage, Hanford's plutonium production levels quickly exceeded the tank farm's capacity. Overflows got directed back into open-air trenches and holding ponds for a few hours before getting discharged back into the river. Management claimed, however tongue-in-cheek, that any remaining chemicals and radioactivity would be somehow miraculously diluted or whisked off far away, and so posed no local threat.

In the early 80s, when Seamus started working at Hanford, the Department of Energy excavated additional land for more tank farms in the 200 East Area for the installation of twenty-eight new double-shelled storage tanks encased in concrete. Into these they pumped what was left from 149 of the deteriorating single-shell tanks. In Seamus's air chalkboard calculation, the math didn't work if the remaining volume of radioactive waste from 149 tanks, could fit into twenty-eight new tanks that were roughly the same size, unless there had been a colossal breach in waste containment, but he didn't raise questions and his dad never wanted to talk about it.

Fast forward some thirty years, and it was Seamus who headed up TFIT (Tank Farm Integrity Team), the group that discovered leaks in at least a dozen of the double-shelled tanks they'd planted in the 80s. Seamus knew—despite the publicity smokescreens, and the remedies both heroic and pathetic—that Hanford's radioactive legacy was still leaking into the Columbia River, and still causing cancers and mutations in many species. A large part of his job was to stick to analyzing rocks and soils to find new places to transfer the radioactive waste—to stop the leaks from reaching the river and the water table. But this environmental cleanup—the largest in the world—had no endgame. These days, it included the removal of more than 25 million cubic feet of Technetium-99, also buried near the river, but without containers, as it was already in solid waste form. In 1996, Seamus had discovered the subterranean plume of groundwater that flowed beneath 200 East and connected to the river through a series of interbeds tied into the river's riparian and seasonal flood zone. Contrary to what the public was being told, Seamus knew, there were countless ways radioactive waste was still reaching the Columbia River. This would not be fixed in a dozen lifetimes, never mind Seamus's own.

About five miles from Pasco, Seamus roused the truck driver from his sleep to get directions to the mechanic's shop. He dropped him off on Hillsboro East Street and climbed out of the truck to say goodbye.

"With any luck," Russ said, "my truck will be gone and out of your ditch by the time you make it back home." They shook hands, and the trucker added, "Hey, I really am sorry you lost your dad today."

Seamus thanked him for that. When he turned back around to get into his truck, he saw the coroner standing with his bag over his shoulder.

"My office is just a quarter mile from here, on Fourth Street near Volunteer Park. I can walk it, no issue."

"You sure?" Seamus held a flat hand over his eyes, blocking the sun. "In this heat?" he added.

"Absolutely sure," the coroner said. "Say—should I mail you copies of the death certificate, or did you want to stop by and pick them up? I can have them ready for you by the end of today."

Seamus was momentarily dumbfounded by the bureaucratic finality of it all. "Uh, sure—I can stop by and pick them up from you."

"Great. We're in the county clerk's office. You know the building?"

"Yes, I'm pretty sure I do. And there's no rush." Seamus thought about the unknown scale of the tunnel collapse that might be waiting for him onsite. "I can pick them up tomorrow, or even later this week."

"Sounds good," the coroner replied, already walking away. He suddenly stopped on the sidewalk and turned back. "In this heat, you'll want to get your father in the ground within forty-eight hours."

Seamus nodded. "Right," he said, tensing every muscle in his body to keep his tears inside.

Entering the sprawling Hanford complex via Route 4 South and driving past the weather station and through the gravel pit to reach one of the test wells near where he'd understood the latest earthen collapse had occurred, Seamus spotted the set of double de-contamination tents. This is how he knew where to park his rig and get suited up. He had passed a steady stream of employees in their cars and trucks, heading in the opposite direction. So either the site evacuation was still underway or it had escalated to include the next echelon of workers and contractors.

Most of Seamus's non-field workdays were spent on the third floor of the Pacific Northwest National Laboratory building—not far inside the complex once you'd passed through the security check-in gates. He thought about stopping there first, until Sam at security gave him the update, clearance, and directions needed to proceed directly to the restricted access zone in Area 200. Seamus put his hazard lights on. He couldn't help but feel a bit slighted not to have been issued a suction cup police strobe light, like others got who were on the rapid response team.

Hanford, above ground, was a maze of over 2,800 buildings, trailers, mobile units, towers, tanks, Quonset huts, and missile silos. There had been twice as many buildings during the peak processing years, when his parents, Great Uncle Percy, and other relatives worked there.

Underground was one hot nightmare of buried storage tanks and acres of entombed solid wastes—plus 158 miles of railroad tracks, three-quarters of which ran through excavated underground canyons. The highly radioactive box cars and the locomotives that had pulled them into their crypts were down there, too. The underground canyons had been filled in by thousands of cubic yards of topsoil, trucked in from other locations on the site—so that dirt, just like the fill used to cover the storage tank farms, had to be presumed radioactive, too—hence, all the decontamination tents and protocols. Seamus understood that this partial tunnel collapse was in the same general area as the previous collapse, in May 2017.

He parked his truck next to an incident command crew van and made a mental list of the equipment he would need to grab from the back of his pickup. First things first, though—he needed to suit up. He entered the first tent and was greeted by already-suited personnel who yell-spoke to him through their plexiglass-screened helmets.

"Welcome, Seamus. We're using the Tychem-10,000s today."

Seamus removed his sunglasses and then his wristwatch, placing them along with his truck keys and cellphone in the plastic tray extended to him by a man wearing a pair of astronaut-like gloves. He saw that he'd somehow missed two calls from Cody, ten miles upstream at Priest Rapids Dam. He added a return phone call to his already full to-do list. Working off his hiking boots by stepping on the heels without untying them, he put them on the table where they were fitted into the boot covers that would be taped to his ankles once he'd stepped into the neon, lime-green suit.

The evacuation of personnel and the deployment of heavy suits told Seamus a lot. When the parallel tunnel nearby collapsed six years earlier, it had been the same drill and the same SWIM precautions (*Stop* activities at the scene; *Warn* personnel; *Isolate* the area; and *Minimize* exposure to the hazards). The Geiger team had likely already detected and cordoned off a hot spot. Just what he needed, given the day he was having. Nothing like a little nuclear disaster to squeeze into his packed schedule of earthquakes, Irish wakes, orphanhood, and farm ownership. For some bizarre reason, given his stance as a non-practicing Catholic, he made the sign of the cross as they Velcroed him up and began the taping at the ends of his appendages. He hadn't made the sign of the cross since attending the wake of his sweet mother, Abigail—and then, only because the priest had been watching. Before that, it had to have been during catechism at Christ the King Catholic Church in Richland, where the family attended mass during his teens. None of the Quinlans had been great Catholics, but a few had been good, or at least decent. Seamus did not count himself among the devotees; not then, even less now.

The red-vest-wearing incident commander entered the tent from the de-con side of the command post just as the attendants lifted the helmet to place over and onto Seamus's head. Seamus didn't recognize the incident commander at first, with all the protective gear, but as soon as she spoke, he knew who it was: Jenna Thomason. Jenn was his Department of Energy supervisor on paper, though Seamus's specialty meant he didn't really report to anyone—except during declared site emergencies like this one, when he needed to follow the incident command hierarchy.

"It's not as bad as the last cave-in," she told him. "But you will have to weigh in with your assessment of the ground stability. Part of the buried train is exposed, but I can't tell if it is the engine or a transport car. The Geiger team picked up both gamma and beta hot spots when extending the pole through this new opening, which is why we are suited up today, in case you were wondering."

Seamus's helmet, with its plexiglass face screen, was fitted and then taped around his neck. Talking would steam up the screen, so all he could do was nod or shake his head until the suit was slightly pressurized.

Jenna put a gloved hand on Seamus's shoulder. "I was really sorry to hear that your father passed this morning, Shay." Seamus nodded and sort of sucked in his upper lip, trying to stay composed. She continued: "I am really happy you are here, but we could also have managed this incident without you."

Seamus raised the one permanently raised eyebrow ever higher, emphasizing his doubt.

Jenna grinned. "We would have all probably fallen through the earth's crust because we didn't know what we were doing, but ..." She paused. "Anyway, let me give you a hand with your equipment and I'll take you to the collapse."

Loaded down with his magnetometer, probes, picks, and a shovel, Seamus and Jenna met up with the Geiger team heading back toward the de-con tent. "Sands are shifting," one of them reported. "We're still picking up more gamma than beta, but both are above normal thresholds. I would recommend expanding the isolation zone by another five hundred feet."

Jenna nodded. "So, move the IC tents back ... say, closer to the gravel pit?"

"That would be a good place for it," the other confirmed. "We've cordoned off what we determined to be a safe perimeter around the collapse, but Seamus may read something in the crust that we missed. And like I said—sand is still hourglassing in through the breach. That gap is still growing."

Seamus and Jenna nodded their alien-like heads and continued another hundred yards until they encountered the first in an array of orange landscape flags. Trying to visualize the orientation of the buried tunnels, Seamus scanned the Hanford topography as best as he could through the helmet screen. Using the basalt outcrops of both Gable Butte and Gable Mountain to the north as his reference points, he matched the memorized site map in his head, almost as though he was X-raying the ground. Through the gap between these basalt features, Seamus could just make out the white bluffs on the far bank of the Columbia River that flowed fifty miles to get around the Hanford boundary. The waves and haze of the afternoon heat were visible everywhere he looked but were felt most acutely inside his suit where his perspiration—like the river—was also flowing.

He and Jenna had reached the top of Cold Creek Bar, part of the river's historical floodplain. That meant the undersurface in this area was a mix of sandy loam and loess—wind-blown dust. This made digging easier—one of the reasons the nearby 200 West and 200 East tank farms had been entombed in the stretch of desert just to the south. It also meant the ground here was not very stable.

Most of Hanford's central plateau was between thirty and sixty feet higher than the Columbia River which in this stretch, known as Hanford Reach, was about 340 feet above sea level. Seamus remembered a series of hydrology studies and flood simulations had included a scenario in which the Priest Rapids dam failed, releasing the fury of its pent-up reservoir. In the simulations, since the PR Dam was just ten miles upriver, it had only taken a matter of minutes for large swaths of Hanford to be inundated. In the computer-generated model, the force of the tsunami altered the course of the river just before Coyote Rapids, where it jumped the bank and pushed a wall of water through Gable Gap (between Gable Butte and Gable Mountain) to swamp the spot where Seamus was standing and completely douche (his term, not the computer model's) the excavated tank farms at 200 Area East and West. He had seen for himself that the river, under a dam-failing scenario, could not contain the volume of water within its normal water course.

Still, that wasn't the emergency he was attending to today—at least he hoped it wasn't, thinking back to the two missed phone calls from Priest Rapids Dam. When he and Jenna paused at a test well site, still outside the orange-flagged perimeter, he asked about the two minor temblors that had occurred earlier that day.

"Is it your thinking, Jenna, that this collapse might have been caused by one or both earthquakes we experienced this morning?"

She turned her whole body to address him—the helmet face shields played games with peripheral vision. "That's what you are supposed to tell *me*, isn't it?"

He'd framed the question poorly. He clarified. "No—I'm not saying there is any connection, either. There hadn't been any seismic activity associated with the tunnel collapse in 2017. We'd classed that as a subsidence of soil, so I don't think this collapse and the earthquakes are necessarily related." Seamus paused to give her time to catch up.

"So, we aren't waiting for the Big One like they are on the coast, then?"

"No. This part of the state, this side of the Cascade Mountain Range is not known for big earthquakes." Seamus paused. "I take that back. There was a 5.8 magnitude quake near Milton-Freewater back in 1936—before Hanford was even here—but relatively nothing of note since. That said, earthquakes happen in Washington State every single day. Even I don't feel most of these, but I felt the two this morning."

Jenna frowned. "I suppose it surprises me to hear there was a large earthquake in this area and still decisions were made, not even, what? Eight years later, to site a secret nuclear fuel processing plant here. Never mind the decisions that followed, like building Priest Rapids Dam ten miles upstream from us in 1956?"

Seamus smiled. He liked it when lightbulbs went on with

his audiences—whether an audience of one or a full auditorium. "Hanford is boxed in by a fault line that runs under the Saddle Mountains to the north and the Rattlesnake Mountain Fault Zone, just south of here. Though we get a dozen or so little quakes here every year, they rarely get felt or noticed except by nerds like me. Both of today's events were below 3.0 and quakes this small rarely cause damage. Until we get closer, and I examine the surrounding soils, my hypothesis is that the roof of one of the empty box cars rotted away and the surface dirt and a portion of the tunnel roof fell in."

"Interesting," Jenna said, but not in a way that suggested she had been convinced. "My understanding has always been that none of the transport cars were buried empty; that they were loaded with depleted uranium. To be honest, these buried trains have always spooked me a bit."

Seamus turned to face her, so she could see his smile. "Buried anything that doesn't stay buried, spooks me too."

"I know there was a lot of talk after the 2017 cave-in. If memory serves, there was even a decision made to inject concrete into these train tunnels to grout shut any air pockets. But I also know this didn't happen once the proposed fix was costed out."

"I see," he said. "I thought the tunnels were only meant to store the locomotives and box cars until they'd cooled off, after which they'd get removed and taken some place else to be dismantled and disposed of permanently. Let's have a closer look, shall we?" Seamus gestured with his gloved hand. Jenna, the incident commander, led the way.

Seamus was processing this new information before he spoke again. He had not been told or consulted about any plan to concrete the tunnels and their contents permanently shut. Just because it had been too expensive to carry through with seemed to him to be beside the point. Was he or was he not responsible for decisions involving ground stability? Once again, this job and his role at Hanford struck him as window dressing. He supposed he could be like every other civil servant, bide his time, cash his paycheck, and not give a damn—except he wasn't wired that way. Plus, his life was on the line every day—being suited up drove that point home.

This was not the first time he'd thought seriously about retirement, but it was the first time his personal real estate portfolio included the title, free and clear, to a 145-acre farm.

When he and Jenna crossed inside the orange-flagged perimeter, his radiation badge began clicking and the LED light on both their badges started strobing. This always made his heart race—the investigation felt more real now. It was very different from how he spent most of his professional time—in meetings, running desktop exercises, navigating hypothetical scenarios. Going to work most days at Hanford, you could almost forget your office was sitting atop the most contaminated site in North America—the largest toxic clean-up project on the planet. You could relegate uranium and plutonium and nuclear weapons to a Cold War shelf in an abandoned wing of some history museum. That is, until the nearest radiation detector or alarm went off. That's when everyone was rudely snapped back to reality.

Jenna put her gloved hand on his suited forearm and held him back. Seamus lowered the large pack he carried off one shoulder, and the ground-penetrating radar off the other. He needed to work quickly to minimize the time spent inside the radiation zone. As he got set up, he grew even more suspicious than he already was—first, that he hadn't been told in 2017 that the train cars were fully loaded, and second, that depleted uranium would still give off a level of radiation high enough to set off their badges thirty-four years after plutonium production had ceased in 1989.

Depleted uranium was generally half as radioactive as the pure or enriched kind. And hadn't the Geiger team just told them that gamma levels for this event were off the charts? Uranium normally emitted low beta and gamma particles, instead carrying the signature of heightened alpha particles. Seamus was confident that high gamma readings must be pointing to something else buried underground. Could they be standing on top of a cache of enriched plutonium? He didn't have the right equipment to answer that question—he'd asked for a fission neutron survey meter during each of the past seven budget cycles, but this pricey line item somehow never made the cut as Hanford's annual budget was regularly hacked to pieces. He'd need one of these gadgets to confirm what he strongly suspected now—that a significant amount of plutonium must still be present here, if not above ground, then below the surface. He just didn't think that uranium alone, even if it were depleted, was the reason the badges were going off. Both uranium and plutonium were elements on the periodic table, the main difference being that uranium was mined from ores found in a natural state—which was not to say it wasn't deadly. Plutonium wasn't natural. It was a man-made radioactive product created when uranium-238 was bombarded by neutrons in nuclear reactors, of which Hanford had nine lined up along the Columbia River.

He pulled a binder of detailed site maps from his pack and he and Jenna quickly confirmed the orientation of the underground side-by-side train tunnels. The old PUREX Plant (Plutonium Uranium Extraction) used to be situated on this spot between the two sets of buried tracks, but the four main buildings and the last of the giant venting smokestacks had been demolished and removed by 2020. The test well they had just paused beside was one of more than a thousand such wells situated inside and outside of the Hanford boundary. From these wells, water samples were regularly taken to measure Hanford's latent and not-so-latent contaminants. Seamus had needed to learn their names and elements—uranium, technetium-99, iodine-129, tritium, carbon tetrachloride, chromium, strontium-90, cesium-137, trichloroethylene, cyanide, and lesser but still harmful nitrates. The PUREX Plant had used unknown volumes of these substances while it operated from 1949 to 1989, serving as the final processing step in the production of weapons-grade plutonium. These metal-eating chemicals were used to dissolve the irradiated metal fuel rods that came from each of Hanford's seven reactors so workers could retrieve the plutonium they encased. Then this chemical soup got discarded, sent back to the river to get flushed downstream in the very early days before someone suggested that maybe the soup should be held in retention ponds to cool for six hours before returning it to the river. Even wiser heads came up with the idea of using storage tanks, instead of open-air ponds. His own father had been involved in the assembly of the concrete encased metal storage tanks. As a teenager, Seamus could not get his developing scientific brain around the prospect of using metal storage tanks to hold metal-eating chemicals, but his father was quick to dismiss his inquiries. Gerald Quinlan didn't like to talk about work or what he did there, but even then, Seamus knew that his father's handiwork lay buried beneath them, for as far as his eyes could squint in the blinding desert sun.

He kept these and a barrage of other thoughts to himself. Their visit needed to be brief. He began walking with his radar in wide but diminishing rings, closing in around the staked oval fence of red flagging ribbon that the GT had used to stake off the area around where the ground had given way. With each revolution, he watched the monitor as it mapped the features and irregularities beneath him but also indicated soil makeup and density. All this data was being sent live to the modeling computers in his office at the Pacific Northwest National Laboratory. The monitor also informed Seamus where he could stand and where he probably shouldn't. Jenna's job was to hold the antennae that aided the transmission of data. His badge clicked faster the closer he got to the opening in the ground. It was maybe the size of a grand piano lid. He could not resist his curiosity and wanted to peek inside the breach but the ground beneath him was already granulating.

In two more careful steps, the radar picked up the outline of a rail car directly beneath him, but something about the image on the screen bothered him. In addition to the shaded outline of the buried car, Seamus picked up faint shapes—little circles inside the car. Hundreds, maybe thousands of them—he couldn't be sure.

The rail car was not empty.

The ghost cargo resembled a hidden arsenal of plutonium buttons. These hockey-puck-shaped discs had been the way that the plutonium and plutonium oxide dust had been stabilized for shipping to Los Alamos and Trinity Site in New Mexico. More than two-thirds of the nation's plutonium had been manufactured inside the PUREX Plant that once occupied this quadrant of land. It looked as though this train car may have been packed just before plutonium production wrapped up in 1989. But it never left the station. Seamus wondered if this was why these tunnels were never filled with cement—if the tunnels were a plutonium vault that could be cracked back open for some future application.

If true, that meant DOE had been kept in the dark—unless Jenna Thomason knew about it, given her security level, and had been instructed to keep a lid on it. Seamus considered the possibility of a conspiracy and felt betrayed. He of all people should have the clearance to know where the bodies—or, in this case, the buttons—were buried. The more he thought about it, the angrier he became, watching Jenna standing back a safe distance while he peered into the death hole. He began backing away but continued transmitting his ground penetrating radar data because he wanted to understand how many loaded railcars were beneath him. The sandy loam shifting away under each carefully planted footstep told him that was as close as he would be getting to the cave-in, itself.

The tunnel below was not the same line that had collapsed in 2017. Seamus had understood that a total of twelve rail cars had been buried after operations at Hanford had ended in 1989 The twelve cars—plus, he presumed, at least one, but more likely two, locomotives—had been divided up between the two tunnels. According to all the documentation he'd reviewed, this was only ever meant to be a temporary solution, until technology revealed a better way to relocate and dispose of the contaminated rail equipment. More than three decades on, technology or political will had failed to deliver the desired follow-up. The Department of Defense would know what had been buried inside these railcars, but they wouldn't share that information if he was the one asking for it. He'd start with Jenna and see how far he got.

Seamus had a sudden itch behind his horseshoe moustache that his tongue could not reach. He tried biting the inside of his cheek and then contorting his face—but he could not find relief. Why he'd maintained this ridiculous facial hair all these years— especially now that it was more gray than brown—he didn't know. Maybe he'd figure it out before he turned sixty in a few more years. It wasn't like he'd used it to attract a mate, as he seemed destined to be a bachelor permanently. Maybe the time had come to simplify his haircare. But that was something to worry about later—for now, the itch persisted. If it lasted, he would need to get through de-contamination before he could scratch it.

And to think he had been worried about plutonium. He chuckled to himself inside his helmet.

※

By the time he had reunited with his cellphone, a new team was disassembling the incident command center tents to relocate them a safer distance away, and closer to the gravel pit. He'd decided not to confront his boss about the railcar contents until he could get to his desk and better analyze the 3-D imagery, get the measurements, quantify the contents, make out the textures of the buttons to see if they were intact or breaking down. Then he would make his case. He dialed his voicemail and set the audio to speaker so he could catch up during the fifteen or so minutes it would take him to reach his office building. If he'd had a more modern rig, he could have bluetoothed his cell through the stereo speakers—but like his moustache, his devices were a little outdated.

"Hey Seamus. It's Cody out at PRD. I just heard about your dad and wanted to share my condolences. If there is anything I can do to help you out, I'm here for you, Buddy."

BEEP.

"Say, Shay, it's Cody again. I don't know if your dad had livestock at his place, but if you need to transfer any animals to my farm, we'll make room for them until you sort out what you're going to do."

BEEP.

"Mr. Quinlan, it's Marcia with Pacific Northwest Seismic Network. We understand you have experienced a tunnel collapse at Hanford and wanted you to know we have identified the epicenters for both tremors. We originally thought they were situated around the Toppenish Fault Zone—which would have ruled them out as causes for your collapse. But now we think both events emanated from the Wallula Fault Zone—where seismic activity continues, by the way, just not at a humanly detectable scale. Call me if you have any questions or if this doesn't square with what you're finding."

BEEP.

"Uh, hello—Seamus Quinlan. This is County Coroner Kennedy. I just wanted you to know that I have completed Gerald's certificate of death. I have copies enveloped for you and waiting at the front desk in the Franklin County Courthouse. Thanks for the lift earlier. I am told a tow truck has already retrieved my vehicle from your property. That's it, then."

BEEP.

That was it, Seamus agreed. His father was now officially and certifiably dead. He put the Ford in park inside his assigned parking space at the Pacific Northwest National Laboratory. He kept the truck running—he needed the AC to survive the heat. The rig regularly functioned as his mobile office, particularly when he needed privacy. He reached into his left back jean pocket and extracted his father's handwritten letter. It took him a minute to sort the order of pages so he could pick up where he'd left off.

> I think I had been at HEW for two, maybe two-and-a-half years. I was still in my early twenties, but I rose through the ranks pretty fast because I had relatives who worked there and vouched for my trustworthiness. As you know, I had been trained as an industrial welder. But by the time I am referring to now, I was already supervising the platoon of welders and metal fabricators responsible for constructing the second generation of storage tanks. Nearly a hundred single-shelled tanks had already been filled and buried before my time. These hadn't even been encased in concrete. There hadn't been enough time for this step until later.
>
> The truly reckless speed we were forced to work around the clock left plenty of room for mistakes, and it was my job to catch as many of those as I could. But honestly, because we knew our handiwork was going into the ground, we didn't much care about how things looked—we even joked about our sloppy welds. The way it had been explained to me, the tanks were only meant to slow down the rate of ground and water

contamination—not prevent it. We hadn't expected the tanks to last more than twenty years, given the toxic crap they held. And that was only supposed to be temporary, too—I guess until someone figured out what to do with the whole mess.

But there's more to it than that.

The physicists fully expected the radioactive sludge to eat through the bottoms and sides of our tanks. I found out they'd even secretly nicknamed them "colanders." Truth is, they needed them to leak deep into the earth because there was no place else they could get rid of the 50-some billion gallons of waste. There was no other plan. There never was a "what comes next" because it was wartime and the government had other priorities. When Hanford was running out of storage capacity in the 70s and we couldn't build the double-shell tanks as fast as the singles, I was approached by the site director and offered a hefty bonus to participate in a top-secret mission for our country. That's how they sold it to me, too. I am not proud of this, for the record—especially now that you are partly in charge of cleaning up my mess. I was recruited as one of a three-member tank integrity inspection team, but we weren't inspecting shit. HEW made a big public show for all the earth-loving hippies. That was meant to demonstrate how seriously the government took their concerns about water and soil contamination. We were suited up like astronauts, paraded out in front of the cameras, and expected to pose as heroes—but our secret mission was really to speed up the leakage, to make more room in the storage tanks. Armed with shovels and blow torches, we excavated down a few yards into the earth to punch more holes in the half-empty tanks, about a foot above the waste-level mark on each tank. This way, when the tanks got topped up, their leaking would accelerate. It was crazy, suicidal work, but I had three boys to feed and my parent's farm to maintain, as they were always at financial risk of losing the place. The hazard pay was too attractive to pass up. We were made to believe we were real American heroes, and we were made rich by our silence.

I tell you this now for several reasons, my son. Those storage tanks—all 177 of them, even the double-shelled ones—are still leaking. Our monkey wrenching made damn sure of that! You must be very careful around the tank farms in 200 Area. If I were you, I'd stay clear of both 200 Area East and West. So, there's that.

But you are also about to find out about a bank account I've kept secret from you. You need to visit a manager at the IBEW #112 Credit Union. I think it's called TRI-CU Federal Credit Union, these days. Anyway, it's in Kennewick on West 19th Avenue. They'll probably want a death certificate, but you're the listed beneficiary, as my sole survivor. I don't want to tell you what to do with the money, but I want you to use it to keep the farm in the family. Family ... well, it's just you now.

You will find that you don't have to keep working at Hanford now—not for a paycheck, anyway. It would do my soul good to know that no other Quinlan will be poisoned with cancers because they worked at HEW. Who knows, you may already be growing yours deep inside you—but so far, it seems like you may be the chosen one, spared this fate. What is it you are always telling me? That my generation—the Greatest Generation—robbed Peter, or something or other? I hope you use can this money to start paying back that Paul-fellow you keep talking about. Otherwise, I'm afraid you all will be chasing your tails if you think Hanford can be cleaned up.

We didn't know—or I should say, I didn't know the damage Hanford was doing. Most workers there didn't even know they were making bombs. Look, I never finished high school, so I was never meant to change the world. I just hope I didn't destroy it. And I hope that you can forgive me—for being ignorant, for being a yes-man, for being a shitty father, and whatever else you want to hold me and my generation accountable for. I did it for you, for your mother, and brothers. Don't forget that.

Now that I have ruined your day, I will say goodbye. But before I do, I want to write that I could not be prouder of who you have become. Of any of us Quinlans, you, Seamus, could be the one to change the world. So, get on with it.

Seamus lowered the handful of papers. His eyes were too wet to make out his father's full autograph at the bottom of the seventh page—but what he did see was that he'd dated it the day before yesterday.

My home is Rattlesnake Mountain,
I'm bald as a river goose.
Me and my pal, Coyote
Live on wind and yellow cake snooze.

Oh, we went down to Nuke City
To get drunk and kick some ass,
To grab us a little titty
And piss on the gov'ment grass.

We bust into Uptown Tavern,
We bellied up to the bar.
When the barmaid refused Coyote,
He showed off his keloid scar.

Some Hanford boys was there,
They stood us a chain of beers,
They'd never seen such a wonderful scar
In all their forty years.

Sing ki-yi yippi
And doo-dah, doo-dah,
I'm a Nuke-City Boy!

—William Witherup

CHAPTER FOUR

IT WAS SEAMUS'S SIXTH or seventh attempt to turn over the tractor engine. He'd had lost count along with his patience. He was certain he was the one Quinlan who had never been cut out to be a farmer, and this tractor failure was just more evidence.

It was a shame, because he'd worn Wranglers and a plaid cowboy shirt for the day, hoping to look the part. His only pair of cowboy boots pinched his toes, so he'd tossed on one of his many pairs of Merrell hiking boots instead. His footwear may have been what was jinxing the tractor. He should have worn black. He was there, after all, to bury his father. He'd hated having to wait for the weekend to tackle this task, but the critical incident at Hanford had monopolized his time. He'd packed a mule-load of guilt, knowing his father's body was on the back porch in that heat. But what could he do?

He was doing it now, if only the tractor would start up. He'd checked the fuel tank and oil well. He'd kicked a tire too, in his frustration, wanting to do right by his father. As he sat in the tractor seat at the far end of the barn, counting to one hundred before trying the ignition again, a chicken crossed the hay-strewn floor from one stall to another, like she owned the place. A second chicken followed, trailing behind her a squad of chicks. This meant there was a rooster nearby, too. Seamus was surprised—he didn't think his father had been keeping any animals, especially since he hadn't been able to leave the house to feed them in the past several months. They must have been surviving on bugs, unless somebody else had loaded the auto-feeding hopper. Maybe he got that hitchhiking hippie grave digger to do it.

He hopped off the tractor and cut through the stall to the old coop. The sun had to work through layers of mud and who knows what else had accumulated on the panes of the four coop windows, to push any light into the dank, low-roofed space. Inside was a vomit-inducing mess—the piss- and shit-soaked straw in the laying beds hadn't been changed out for years, it looked like. The foul aroma of ammonia and mold and humidity stuck in his nostrils, and he gagged. In the far corner, he spied the auto-feeder—and sure enough, its hopper was a little less than a quarter full of grain. There was also a shallow water trough, but it had flakes of dried salt residue at the bottom, so the chickens must have been getting their water from the pond, before it too had dried up.

Seamus thought he could have made use of one of those Hanford radiation suits if he was going to clean out that coop. It might just be easier to burn it down. As he backed out of the coop with two fingers pinching his nose, he heard car tires crunching the gravel outside the barn. He emerged into the daylight to find a black Ram truck had arrived. The driver cut the engine, but it took a moment for Seamus to recognize that it was Cody Getz. That was partly because of the sun glaring off the windshield, and partly because he usually spoke to Cody on the phone rather than in person—since Cody worked at Priest Rapids Dam and Seamus worked at HEW.

"Howdy, partner," Cody said, rounding the front of his truck. "You've been on my mind since the loss of your dad. I thought I'd drive out to see if I could give you a hand with anything." Cody moved straight in to give Seamus a hug. "I'm so sorry for your loss," he said before giving a few pats to Seamus's back.

Seamus didn't know what to say, and he said as much. "I'm touched, man. You drove all the way here, from Vantage, just now?" Seamus had to look away when he saw Cody's blue eyes watering up. "Uh, I don't know what to say."

"My place is out between Beverly and Levering, so it's only seventy miles or so to get here. I took Hwy 24." Cody pointed with his blond whiskered chin to the white piping and pearl-snap button shirt that Seamus had on. "Nice shirt."

Seamus was sure he was blushing, so he quickly changed the subject. "Nice rig. Is it a 1500?"

"3500 Hemi," Cody said. "Diesel. I do a lot of hauling."

Seamus was not used to asking for help and he didn't know Cody all that well—but every minute his father's casket baked on the porch in this heat was going to make an already unpleasant task exponentially more so. "You're here," were the two words that came out of his mouth.

Cody waited for more, but Seamus said nothing. "I'm here," Cody said. "What can I give you a hand with? Angie's home, sleeping off her latest round of chemo. I have the day to help."

"She's had a tough go with this," Seamus acknowledged, still processing the timing of the stranger's arrival—because Cody, for the most part, was technically a stranger to him. The two had known *of* each other for the past fifteen years, spoken by phone regularly, and maybe once or twice they'd sat in the same room as members of a joint planning committee. But they didn't really know each other. Yet here they were, standing face to face, at roughly the same height and even dressed just about the same— except Cody was wearing real cowboy boots. Seamus couldn't help feeling astonished. He nodded. "I'm embarrassed to ask, but do you know anything about tractors?"

"A thing or two. Show me what you got." Cody's weathered face softened into a handsome smile. He followed Seamus back inside the barn and climbed onto the machine that had been giving Seamus so much trouble.

The tractor started on Cody's first try. "Where we taking it?"

Seamus inhaled a day's worth of oxygen in one long breath and then gestured. "Follow me."

Cody shouted over the noise of the sputtering engine. "Can you grab my hat from the front seat of my truck?"

Seamus nodded and jogged to the truck, opening the driver's door. Still stung by the scent of the spoiled chicken coop, he was grateful to detect a whiff of cologne that had been heated inside the closed truck cab. It was pleasant, reminding him of sandalwood and freshly cut but slightly still green hay. When he lifted the baseball cap off the center console, he caught a glimpse of the paperclipped sheets of paper beneath—a printout of a rural lands parcel map with the Quinlan acreage outlined with an orange highlighter.

Seamus suddenly wondered about Cody's real intentions with this visit. But he shook the darker suspicions from his head. For once and a change, he wanted to distinguish himself from the Quinlan distrust for outsiders. He pushed the door shut and caught up to Cody, handing the baseball cap up to him. He stepped onto the foot bar of the moving tractor and pointed toward the back porch of the farmhouse. "I don't think you have any idea what you signed up for by offering to give me a hand today," Seamus said, working his right hand behind the operator's seat, trying to find something to hang on to. "I'm afraid I need to bury my father." The words snagged on his vocal cords and he was sure sounded shocking as he said them, but that was his whole agenda for the day. He was ashamed it had been three days that his dad had endured the purgatory of the back porch before getting a proper burial. Seamus didn't know how he could have managed this task by himself, and tears flooded his green eyes. All questioning aside, he was damn grateful that Cody materialized when he did.

From one hundred yards away, Cody spotted the pine coffin on the porch and without saying anything, adjusted the tractor's orientation as he lowered the front bucket. Seamus wiped his eyes with the backs of his hands and hopped off the tractor, creating a puff of dust where he landed. Lined up with the porch, Cody put the tractor in neutral and left it idling. He joined Seamus on the covered porch, removing his baseball cap and tucking its bill into the back of his jeans. After the briefest of pauses, the two men each took an end of the coffin and then lifted it, gently placing it in the receiving arms of the old tractor that at least three generations of Quinlans had operated—and now a Getz.

Cody looked Seamus in the eyes, blue to green and both tear filled, and said, "You driving this hearse, or am I?" Seamus indicated that he needed to do this, and he climbed into the driver's seat. Cody rode on the side of the tractor, and once they were underway, somewhere between the farmhouse and the barn, Cody's hand squeezed the grieving son's right shoulder and didn't let go.

After slowly chugging up the hill on a two-tire track road with cheat grass as the center line, Seamus shifted the tractor into neutral, lowered the bucket a smidgeon and turned the key to silence the monstrously loud engine. The road had ended at the picket fence that corralled the burial grounds in a neat rectangle. Seamus recalled the memory of having to paint that fence—every picket on both sides—with a fresh coat of white before every family burial, and more than once in a bad year. There was little trace of the white paint now, and Seamus thought maybe he should have painted it again before burying his father, but there was nobody yelling at him to do it, so it hadn't gotten done. It was eerily quiet except for the hot winds—they always found something or other to rattle. Today the wind rattled the gate on its rusted hinges and reanimated the stench of death emanating from the payload in front of them. Seamus and Cody dismounted the tractor and lifted the casket from the bucket. Seamus led the way, walking backward past the preceding generations to a row toward the back. There—a hole next to a pile of desiccated earth left by the hitchhiker—was Gerald Quinlan's final resting place. The shovel that had been used for the excavation still stuck out of the mound like a turkey thermometer.

They set the casket down parallel to the dugout, on top of two long hauling straps that Seamus had pre-positioned there. He hadn't quite worked out how he was going to lower the coffin by himself. At first, he thought that Cody's presence had solved that problem—but the task still proved more complicated than either of them could work out in their heads. Cody, a structural engineer, was calibrating how he thought they might manage the task but thinking out loud said it would involve using the tractor as a pulley. When second-proofing his plan, though, he just didn't see how he could get the tractor close enough without desecrating the other graves. As the two stood there in the cruel sun, Cody began reading the names and dates of the gravestones. While Cody probably could have figured the family tree out for himself, Seamus volunteered family introductions.

"This is my mother, Abigail." He pointed. "And my two brothers, one older—that's Sampson. And one younger—that's Sean ... though I suppose I am now older than both, which is strange." He was mumbling now, almost to himself. "I'll be here too, one day. You are looking at the very last of six Quinlan generations to work this stubborn-ass farm." His hand flew to his mouth as the totality of this abandonment returned to him anew.

Cody stood there, listening and watching, and holding his own hands in front of him like a presiding preacher. He admitted this was not what he thought his Saturday drive would entail, but he sure was glad he was there so Seamus wouldn't be facing this alone.

Life events like this hit rural folks differently, was Cody's observation which he shared there on the hillside. He said he knew this having grown up an only child in the sticks, born to parents whose parents had immigrated from Leipzig when Hitler's Nazism showed them the exit out of Germany. His grandparents had worked the orchards around Wenatchee and saved enough to buy an arid tract of land only suited for growing green onions and garlic—so that's what they did. It's also what his parents did, in addition to driving a country school bus (in his father's case), and substitute teaching for three different county school districts (in his mother's). About the time Cody said he inherited the farm, his father had just passed and his mother's Alzheimer's had advanced, making it necessary to move her to a nursing home in Ellensburg. Cody said he and his long-ailing wife didn't really know the first thing about farming either—plus, one of Angie's chemo drugs gave her a violent reaction to onions and garlic. Since they'd known almost since their marriage that they couldn't have kids, they decided to convert the acreage to a hobby-farm with an odd mix of animals. Cody was honest that it had always been more than he could handle with the fifty hours a week he found himself chained to the Priest Rapids Dam and especially after Angie entered Stage IV, well, it had been all he could do to keep from throwing his hands up in surrender. Cody admitted his weekend drives through the country usually calmed him and helped him organize and focus. But not today. Today, he said he was reminded that death would be coming to his farmhouse, too, and soon.

As the two men stood there, in the land of no shade, solace, or shadows, Cody was maybe just being polite by not pointing out the more obvious source of the stench that caught in the backs of both their throats. "I smell onions," he blurted out.

"Really?" Seamus asked him incredulously. "All I smell is the ripeness of my dad in this box that isn't as sealed as I thought. As for the onions, that might have something to do with the semi-truck still stuck in the ditch near the front driveway in front of the farmhouse. It's been there since Wednesday. I think the driver told me he was hauling Walla Walla Sweets."

Seamus could tell that Cody was about to comment that there was nothing sweet about what he was smelling, but instead, he switched back to the task at hand. "What are you thinking as to how we lower your father into the—" Cody stopped abruptly, cutting himself off.

"I was just working that out," Seamus lied, when what he was really doing was delaying that moment when he needed to let his dad go. "But I'm not sure. What do you think? You're the engineer."

Cody inhaled. "If your hauling straps are long enough and you think that fence is strong enough, we could tie one end of each strap to the fence, balance the, uh, your dad on the straps over the opening, and then with each of us on the other strap end, we should be able to lower him down."

"Let's try that!" Seamus's enthusiasm surprised him. He knew it had to be done, and he wasn't about to squander the offer of help. The only hitch, as they shortly found out, was that the straps were not long enough to reach the rickety fence—which, come to think of it, Seamus doubted could support the weight in the first place.

"Plan B," he said. "How about we each tie one end of a strap around our waists so that our bodies act as ballast? Then we can maneuver Pops over the opening and manually lower him into the ground."

Cody pondered the math. The coffin hadn't weighed all that much and they would have a two-to-one counterweight advantage. "Sure," he said reaching for the strap closest him, and tying it off around his waist.

Seamus was a bit surprised his plan had been accepted so readily and hurried to catch up. He reached over the casket to grab the other strap ends on the ground, handing one to Cody. Wrapping the straps twice around their wrists, they pulled them taut and gently edged the box until it was more-or-less over the opening. After a few awkward tilts of the casket at first as they planted their feet, they soon got the level hang of it. Tears filled Seamus's eyes and his vision blurred as he thought about the dozen or so graveside services he'd witnessed on that hill, as cancers had picked off his family one by one over the years. He conjured an ethereal image of his parents reuniting in the hereafter—a notion that didn't come readily to him, but that he hoped would be comforting. Instead, it arrested his soul and manifested in an expulsion of emotion and air that spit from his mouth in a dramatic exhale, just as his knees buckled. This caused the casket to slip from its front harness and drop with a thud that echoed like thunder out of the grave. The two men had zero time to process this before Seamus was yanked off his feet and into the hole by the straps coiled around his wrists. A combination of the torque and momentum jerked Cody, wrists-first, into the grave next—except they weren't in the grave for long. There was this inexplicable sensation of free-falling through space, but that suddenly stopped when the three of them—Gerald, Seamus, and then Cody—crashed into the dirt of a cavern below, each on top of the other, knocking the air out of two pairs of lungs and possibly forcing air back into the third.

Seamus was the first to groan the moment he could coax air back into his lungs. He quickly realized he must have broken a rib at least. He felt sharp pains with each inhalation and sensed that the left side of his body had caved in. Cody was half-straddling Seamus, but Cody's brain couldn't figure out how they'd gotten that way. Both men were in the dark. When they turned to look up at the roughly framed rectangle of sun and sky overhead, just as easily as if they were looking through a skylight or the oculus of the Pantheon, it slowly occurred to them the floor of the grave had given way. They had fallen into a hollow cavity below the cemetery. But how far they'd fallen, they couldn't tell.

"You okay, man?" Cody asked as he tried to find his footing in the dark and lift himself off Seamus, who in turn lay akimbo atop the coffin that held his father. What little light reached them from the hole above suggested the ground beneath them was more-or-less level. Cody stood and fumbled through his front pocket to grab his phone so he could turn on its flashlight. With the other hand, he reached for Seamus's arm and tried to help him off the casket and to his feet.

Seamus kept moaning in pain. "I think I've broken a rib ... or three," he said from his seated position on the only piece of furniture in the place. "Are you all right?" he asked as he untangled the strap tied to his wrist and twisted around his legs.

"You and your dad broke my fall—so yeah, thanks for that, I guess." Cody wanted to make light of their situation, but as far as he could tell, it didn't look good at all. "Where are we?" he asked, plugging his nose with his fingers. The advancing stench of decomposition from inside the casket, had found its way outside of the box. He beamed his phone's flashlight around a space that seemed about the size of an egg-shaped planetarium. It was as though they'd crashed through the top part of an oversized soft-boiled egg and had landed inside the shell where the yolk and membranes were supposed to be.

Seamus had to shake off his shock, trying to think scientifically. "Could be an old lava tube," he said. "And it could be an ancient cistern, where the natural springs were before they migrated just north of the barn, where they are today" was his second thought. He stood and reached into his jeans pocket for his own phone only to find the screen had shattered from the impact, but still working. With two phone flashlights trained on the mostly rectangular opening they had just dropped through, the two separately calculated how far they'd fallen and then compared notes to agree that it had to be twenty feet.

"Do you have a cell signal?" Seamus asked, doubtfully.

"Doesn't appear I do," Cody replied, before trying to put a call through to his wife—the first number on his speed dial. "Nope," he confirmed. "You?"

"No, and I didn't expect to. The damn Wi-Fi doesn't even reach the barn most days." Seamus inspected his shirt for blood. The pain he was experiencing with every breath was intense enough to suggest that something had been punctured. He undid his shirt buttons and tried to shine a light on the spot with his phone.

"Here, let me have a look," Cody said, untying the strap from his wrist and shining his flashlight beam at Seamus's hairy torso. He pulled back the shirt flap, and with his free hand, homed in on a patch of skin that appeared quite red and already bruising beneath the dark hair. "No blood on the surface, anyway, and nothing sticking out. I presume this hurts when I touch it?" Cody applied the slightest pressure and Seamus winced in the phone's spotlight. "Do you hurt anyplace else?" Cody hadn't removed the warm palm of his hand from below his colleague's right nipple.

Seamus couldn't recall the last time he'd been touched. The residual scent of Cody's peppermint gum got him thinking about food and survival. The two of them would need to find some way to get the hell out of this hole.

"Nah, I'm fine," Seamus said. "Just the ribs on that side, I think." He pulled away and with some effort in the diminished light, he snap buttoned his shirt. He turned his phone beam and attention to the dirt and rock walls of their enclosure, wanting to understand the geological makeup and find a way out. "We have much bigger things to be worried about," he announced.

"What do you mean?" Cody asked.

"Well, for starters, even if one of us stands on the other one's shoulders, we won't reach the top. Then there's radon gas."

"Radon? Down here? I don't smell anything—other than your dad," Cody thought to state the obvious.

"You wouldn't smell it. It's odorless. It comes from the breakdown of naturally occurring radioactive elements like thorium or uranium. And now that I'm thinking, it's not so much the naturally occurring stuff I'm concerned about. We're just east of Hanford here." Seamus paused for effect. "We're downwinders in these parts. All kinds of radioactive shit has been falling from the skies for decades here."

"Gas?" Cody seemed stuck on the term. "Like there's a chance of us asphyxiating or something?"

"More like slowly getting lung cancer if we're down here too long." Seamus had meant to put his buddy at ease, but knew it wasn't working.

Cody and Seamus turned away from each other, each now focused on understanding the floor, walls and perimeter of this space. Was there a tunnel that could lead them out or a trap in the floor that would plunge them even deeper into this abyss? Seamus reached the wall on his side of the space after a few exploratory paces and was studying the makeup of its geology. It was layered basalt—no surprise—with a few interbeds of dirt like frosting between cake layers. The wall domed overhead—a concave shape that was clearly unclimbable.

"Over here!" Cody said, with some enthusiasm. "The floor slopes down toward what looks like a passageway."

Seamus had just trained his flashlight on the ceiling, where he saw what looked like tree roots reaching a few feet into the void overhead, like chandeliers or stalactites. That didn't make sense. He didn't remember the family cemetery ever having trees—but that wasn't accurate. What he remembered was there never being any shade. Holding the spot where his ribs still hurt, he quickened his steps past his father's casket to join Cody on the far side of the space. He guessed he was moving in the direction of the farmhouse, away from the cemetery—either east or northeast. But if the cavern was beneath the slope of the hill, did that mean the hill was hollow? And were those overhead tree roots an indication that the cavern had once been filled with soil or water? Could this chamber perhaps have been a part of Harder Springs that got left behind—if indeed the springs themselves had migrated to fill other basalt chambers? He had so many questions—he had no answers, but plenty of theories had started to percolate. He passed through the dim shaft of light that angled down from the opening, toward the other light source—Cody's cellphone.

The engineer was equally stumped by the alien world they'd dropped into, as evidenced by his constant repeating of the phrase, *I can't believe this.* Both men were having to grapple with the denial that they'd found themselves in a space they could not escape, which is why Cody was acting so optimistic about the crevice he hoped was a passageway out of their predicament. In the shadows,

Seamus misjudged how close he was to Cody—not realizing that Cody had extended his cellphone hand in front of him to peer into the passage—and inadvertently rear-ended him.

"Oh—sorry, man."

"No biggie," Cody replied. "We may have to get used to things that go bump in the dark if we can't find a way out of here."

Seamus returned his right hand to the area under his left arm—he felt the need to hold his ribs in place. He supposed his eyes were still adjusting to the subterranean, so he experimented with his phone's flashlight. He wanted his vision to focus on what exactly was being illuminated—more basalt, which was no surprise, though the orientation of the rock seemed to take on a drastic horizontal lean in that narrowing part of the cave. It seemed pretty clear to the geophysicist that ancient lava had flowed out of or into this passage. It also seemed feasible that the lava could have collected here in this spot to expand the chamber that formed the hummock the Quinlans had used to plant their dead. He wet his lips to see whether he could detect any air movement. He couldn't. The air smelled just as musty in that spot as in the main chamber. What he didn't smell, for the first time since falling, was the rancid aroma of his father's decaying body inside the pine casket—though it must have certainly splayed open on impact, as it broke the fall of the two pallbearers. They had bigger things to worry about than the dignity of the deceased, but Seamus paused to consider the kick his father would have gotten from their predicament. Gerald Quinlan was always calling Seamus *Professor Smarty Pants*, and *Too Cool for the Gene Pool*. This comeuppance—or rather, this fall from his high academic pedestal—would have delighted the old man.

"What's your Spidey sense telling you?" Cody asked over his shoulder, with breath that somehow still smelled minty.

"Where to begin the lecture?" Seamus said. "You know, don't you, that this entire region was once one gigantic eruption site, with molten lava spewing out of hundreds of fissures in the ground?"

Cody nodded confidently, inching a few more feet into the grotto. "Angela and I attended one of your lectures at CWU a year or so ago," Cody revealed.

Seamus was pleased, even a bit flattered to hear that. He

continued to add to his theory almost extemporaneously, as though it were excerpted from one of those lectures he'd rehearsed and memorized. "I think this must have been a lava tube," pointing his finger into the light illuminated crevice. "Lava on the move likely bulldozed a sizeable raft of organic material ahead of it creating this bulge over and around which the lava probably continued to flow, then harden. Overtime, the organics under the lava shell would have decayed into dust, and I guess the lava created this dome ceiling and it was sturdy enough to support the accumulation of centuries of blown dirt held together by calcium carbonate to create loess. The natural springs probably had something to do with the breakdown of organic materials, too. Then, human beings, generations of my family, and indigenous peoples before them—went about their lives and the business of hunting and gathering and farming around this hill never knowing what lay beneath."

"Don't forget about the retreat of the glaciers during the last Ice Age and the carving role that raging waters from the Missoula ice dams might have played here." Seamus chuckled, thinking Cody was brownnosing him, demonstrating he had paid attention to that lecture in Ellensburg.

"Gold stars for you." Seamus patted his shoulder. "Ironic, really, when you think about it. We could make use of some of that fire and water if we don't want to end up like my father over there."

"Where is your Boy Scout survival optimism?" Cody turned to face his companion. He knew they were screwed if they didn't come up with something.

"This Eagle Scout wasn't *prepared* for this," Seamus leveled with him, using air quotes to indicate he had flunked the scout motto.

"Me neither," Cody admitted. There was a minute of almost complete silence—the only sound was Seamus whisper-wheezing from labored lungs inside his injured ribcage. "But we have some pretty hefty university degrees that will surely save us."

"Only if you brought them and a match to light them with." Seamus hoped his sarcasm would mask his pessimism. He was reading the rock when he took note of the battery level on his phone. "We should probably conserve our phone batteries, just in case …" He trailed off as he pressed the flashlight icon and pocketed his phone. "I suppose your wife will eventually phone the state police to tell them you're here and that you haven't returned home."

Cody wanted to see the silver lining—but he knew that his wife wouldn't have a clue where to direct the authorities, because he hadn't told her where he was headed when he left her in bed clutching a pillow to quell her nausea. "I didn't tell her where I was heading," he said. This was a departure from all the other Saturdays—he had always been more diligent about sharing the general route and destinations of his weekend drives. When she was feeling better, she sometimes rode along. But 2023 was not turning out to be her year.

Seamus was thinking it, but he didn't say it. The last thing Angela Getz needed was for her husband to go missing. He looked around the dark fringes beyond the shaft of light now coming into the cavern at an angle—it was already afternoon. He took inventory out loud: they had two hauling straps, a pine casket with one of the brass rail handles detached on one end, two baseball caps, two cellphones with no reception. Cody chimed in that he had his truck keys, whatever gum was left in a pack of Chiclets, their two belts holding up the pants around their waists, their boots, and the clothes on their backs. It wasn't worth thinking about what they didn't have, but needed, but Cody did it anyway.

"What we don't have is food, water, blankets, a first-aid kit, a shovel, a pocketknife, matches, a bucket to pee and shit in. Ironically, I have it all in my rig up top," Cody bragged, "including toilet paper."

"Hey, I wonder if you could trigger the alarm on that fancy truck of yours. Wouldn't that get the hazard lights flashing, too?" Seamus was doubtful the remote signal would work that far, but in their situation, you had to try everything.

Cody extracted the bracelet of keys from his front pocket and walked to the center of the cave where he was under the grave's skylight. He reached overhead and pressed the alarm button on the remote several times. "Even if it worked, how would we know down here? We can't hear anything."

"Now who's being Donny Downer?" Seamus said.

Feeling dejected and growing a bit more anxious, Cody returned to the shadows where Seamus was standing—not that he could really see him since they'd both turned off their cellphones. "Say," he said, "I'd like to see if this passage leads somewhere—maybe to water, who knows? What do you say we liberate those hauling straps from under the casket and tie them together, and then tie one of the ends to my belt-loop? I'll go in on my stomach?"

Seamus considered the low clearance and knew his ribcage was not up to it. He licked his lips again to see if he could detect a draft going in or coming out of the small opening. He couldn't—but then again, he was having a tough time concentrating. Every breath felt like he was being stabbed in the side with a hunting knife. Then, a random thought occurred to him—had he known about this cavern as a kid, he would have explored and mapped every crevice, and maybe even connected a secret tunnel from the cellar beneath the farmhouse kitchen. That woulda been so cool.

But since he hadn't done that then, he figured he might as well let Cody see where the passage led now. "Yeah, sure," Seamus said. "We have to try anything and everything."

The pair returned to the casket—which they could have found in complete darkness just by following the unmistakable scent of the decaying corpse. "Here, I'll lift, and you pull," Cody insisted as he raced ahead to lift one end of the box, then the other as Seamus—holding in both his breath and the pain—freed the straps from beneath the coffin. "Each of these is what, maybe a dozen feet long?" Cody asked as he laid the sewn canvas straps out end to end and began walking off the distance, counting his steps.

"Sure, thereabouts." As Cody fiddled with the straps, Seamus felt compelled to apologize for everything—from the odor of his father's body to their subterranean confinement, which would make his visitor late for supper, or worse. "I am so sorry for this—all of this," he said before his eyes unexpectedly watered and his lips quivered. "It's just too much," he said between a series of convulsive sobs that rattled his guts against his riddled ribcage. Cody dashed over to give Seamus a shoulder hug delivering gentle pats on his back—careful to avoid his ribs. Seamus returned the hug though it hurt him to do so.

"Look," Cody said into Seamus's ear, not letting go of the hug just yet. "I came here because I didn't want you to have to face this alone. And you are not alone. I am just keeping my end of the bargain."

Seamus gave Cody's upper butt three pats before pulling slightly away so his vision could adjust. He looked into Cody's blue eyes that looked almost backlit given the shaft of light they were standing under and said, with great sincerity, "Thank you."

Cody couldn't hold the stare without blinking. He smiled in that warmish beam of sunlight and said, "You, my friend, are welcome."

Seamus cleared his throat and pulled himself back together. With a square knot, Cody calculated he'd sacrificed maybe six inches, but he still had a lifeline of more than twenty feet. The darkness was deceptive—he couldn't tell if they were twenty feet below the surface like they'd decided, or half that, or twice that. He lashed one end of the strap through his two back belt loops and turned, asking Seamus to tie him off. In the next minute he was on his knees and beginning to edge into the passage, holding out his cellphone flashlight, which left him only one crawling hand.

There was a reason beyond the ribs that Seamus hadn't argued about which of them should do the spelunking. He just didn't like close quarters. He'd dropped an axe hammer once into a diminishing rock cleft and unwisely went in after it. His boot got wedged in the lower part of the crevice, and after about twenty minutes of struggling in panic, he'd needed to unlace it to free his foot. That outing had cost him a hammer and a boot.

Cody's feet disappeared as Seamus fed the strap into the void, hand over hand. The passageway sloped down at an angle sufficient to have Seamus thinking Cody might encounter water, if they were lucky. But his optimism was countered by the fact that it was still July, and the effects of the drought were visible everywhere aboveground. What Seamus didn't think Cody would find, was an exit. He could envision the surface topography in his head and figured they had fallen below the base of where the hill began. The rest of the property—between the hill and the highway where the house and barn were situated—was flat. There was no natural place—no ravine, no cliff, no rocky outcropping—where Cody could emerge.

The strapping fed through Seamus's hands until there was

about six feet left. Seamus gave it a gentle tug and hollered into the hole.

"You've got about six feet left!"

There was no answer. The strap continued, inch by inch, further swallowed by the passageway. Seamus felt his heart beating rapidly. "Hey, Cody?"

Cody sent a muffled holler back that he'd felt the tug and heard the warning, but he had other issues. His left front jeans pocket—the one that held his truck keys—had snagged on a shard of rock about the same time he began to feel lightheaded. He hadn't reached a vestibule large enough to turn around—that meant the only way out was to reverse inchworm. He was suddenly desperate to hold off panic. He tried not to hyperventilate, or to think that maybe his body was blocking sufficient air from reaching this part of the shaft. He worked his right arm under his chest and around his stomach in an attempt to reach the pocket. His body weight on top of his arm brought on a cramp—and with it, more heavy breathing, just as he felt more forceful pulling on the back of his pants. Using the tips of his cowboy boots for leverage, he tried to pull and wiggle his pocket off the rock that had caught him. Finally, taking advantage of a well-timed tug on the back of his pants, Cody got the pocket free.

He liberated his right arm next, and before continuing to back out, he thought to illuminate and videorecord the abyss in front of him in case Seamus could read something in the rock formations. He pressed his cellphone flashlight on and began recording. He reached around the floor for a loose rock, but everything seemed attached. He usually had a few quarters in his right jeans pocket. While still filming with his left hand, he extracted a coin that felt like a nickel. He wrangled his arm out in front of him and tossed the coin, holding his breath and listening for all he was worth, as the coin fell into the darkness.

He wanted so much to hear a *splash* or a *kerplunk*. Instead, he heard nothing.

He stopped filming. He turned off the flashlight. And in the darkness of that tunnel, Cody Getz came to terms with the circumstances that had conspired against him—against them both.

A jerk on the hauling straps snapped him out of his doom. "I'm backing out!" he yelled over his shoulder. Hooking the toes of each boot and pushing back with his hands, he felt like a slug moving uphill in reverse. His shins ached within minutes, but he had no other way to move.

For his part, Seamus patiently coiled the hauling strap in his hands as the slack became available to him. He'd realized that pulling on the belt loops likely wasn't helping—it might even be pulling Cody's pants down or off. Besides, pulling only intensified the stabbing pain on his right side—pain that had already shortened his breath. He fingered the knot in the two straps, which indicated Cody was just over the halfway point.

Seamus was a little surprised that he'd made it inside as far as he did—he'd expected him to encounter a solid rock backwall. He tried to work it out in his head. If there had been a lava tube branching up and out from a fissure in the mantle, then as the lava flow pressure lessened, the lava would have stopped pushing uphill, and would have pooled and hardened at some lower level in the system, creating a plug. But if, instead of lava, the cavern had been created by ground erosion, the springs and surface water seepage, then the opposite flow scenario would apply, and water would have sought (and might even still be seeking) the level of the water table. Seamus remembered the farm pond that had gone completely dry when the windmill connected to the pump had jammed on whatever creatures had flown into it. Once he'd unstuck the skeletons from the blades, water—albeit hot water but water just the same—was pumped back to the surface again. All the evidence indicated that there was water down there, beneath them in the interbeds, and that some unknown geothermal source was heating it up. If the men spent the night underground—as it appeared they would—maybe it wouldn't be as cold as he had first thought.

The worn soles of Cody's cowboy boots heralded his re-emergence into the larger cavern. Though it hurt his side, Seamus reached out to help the explorer to his feet. Cody brushed the fine dirt from the front of his shirt and pants.

"Well, I am disappointed to report I did not discover a gift shop," Cody said, grinning. "The passageway continues beyond where I stopped, but it doesn't appear to get any larger and it continues to slope down without evening out. Here." He pulled his phone from his pocket. "I shot a video before I backed out."

Seamus noted two things: the battery level on Cody's phone was above seventy-five percent, and his phone's wallpaper was a goofy photo of a black-and-white calf with its tongue sticking out—not a keepsake photo of his wife. Of course, he couldn't judge—his own wallpaper was a photo of his F-150. Not very telling or creative, either.

Cody pressed play on the video. "I flicked a nickel into the abyss, and I didn't hear it connect or splash."

"Wait," Seamus said. "Play that again but turn your phone volume all the way up." Seamus cocked his head, bringing his ear nearer the phone. They both strained to listen, but there was nothing besides Seamus's wheezing.

"Hey Shay, you don't think you punctured a lung in the fall, do you?" Cody said. "Maybe I should take another look at your torso."

"Nah, I'm fine," Seamus said, filled with a need to flex his masculinity and protest the sudden attention. Even if he had suffered internal damage, there wasn't a damn thing either of them could do about it. He wasn't bleeding—at least on the outside.

"Let me take another look at the rock formations in your video," Seamus suggested, trying to change the subject. Cody started to play it again. "Hit pause!" Seamus commanded. "There. See it?"

Cody nodded. "The basalt column-things are on their sides, almost lying down—instead of, you know, vertical, like you normally see them."

Seamus looked at his fellow prisoner and grinned. "You *did* pay attention during my lecture!" He rewarded him with another pat on the shoulder and then continued. "But they are really at an angle, which shows us not only the direction of the lava flow that happened sixteen million years ago, but also gives us a sense of the degree of the plume. In other words, we can speculate that this passageway continues into the earth at this same angle for a ways. Had the basalt columns angled up—toward the surface—we might have had a glimmer of hope that we could have tunneled out of here." Even as he said it, the statement dimmed the hopes for both of them. In the minute that followed without saying anything, Seamus wanted to take a mental eraser to the chalkboard and start all over again. "Our only way out is up," he proclaimed, pointing to where they'd made their dramatic entrance.

The two men stood like statues in the light beam waiting for aliens to beam them up. A gust of surface wind sent dust into the shaft of light and they both shielded their eyes.

"You think that's more than twenty feet up?" Cody asked, already untying the hauling strap from his belt loops. "You think if we borrowed that broken brass railing from your dad's casket and tied one end of the strap to it, we could caber it up, like they do in those Scottish highland games?"

"What do you mean, *caber*?" Seamus said. "I think you just made that up."

"Uh, that's what they call it, when you heave a log by tucking your hands under one end of it. If we could get it to catch on something, like a gravestone, or even get it stuck crosswise over the opening, I could try to shimmy up." His tone suggested the invincibility of a teenager.

"I'm Irish," Seamus stated proudly. "I wouldn't know a caber from a kilt, but, sure. Let's try everything!"

"I'm German," Cody said, moving toward the pine box that had provoked their predicament. "And we don't surrender … not easily, anyway." He paused, lifting his foot over the coffin. "I mean no disrespect to your father," he said, and then stomped on the end of the brass rail. He picked up the railing and instantly realized it was hollow and thus lacked the heft they'd need. Still, it was their only hope for the moment. He brought the pole over to Seamus who held it while he tied off the hauling strap.

"I'm not sure how much I can contribute with my messed-up ribs, but let's give it a heave together," Seamus offered.

The men positioned themselves directly beneath the overhead opening, oriented the brass pipe vertically and placed their four hands, fingers interlocked, to form a launching pocket. They squatted—Seamus in considerable pain.

"On the count of three," Cody said. "One … two … THREE!" They heaved the pole skyward, but Cody's arm got tangled in the hauling strap. The brass javelin jerked back at them, causing both men to duck, with arms flailing over their baseball capped heads. When they realized neither of them had been skewered, they both laughed. They could only get better.

For the second heave, Cody gathered up the full length of the strap in his hands beneath the end of the pole, intending to launch everything at once. Once again, he called the count. "One ... two ... THREE!" The pole sailed upward but at an angle, trailing the strap like a kite tail before arcing and falling back down, landing a short distance from where they stood.

Seamus walked off the pain, pressing an open hand to his side. "We have to keep trying," he insisted—a very different message from the one his face was telegraphing.

Cody picked the railing off the ground and once again organized the strap, this time in alternating ribbons so it would unfurl more easily without creating a drag on his toss. "Let me give it a couple tries by myself. I think I can get more propulsion if I give it a running start and hurl it like a javelin."

Seamus smiled, looking skeptical. But he stood back, saying, "Be my guest."

"Thank you—you've been a great host so far," Cody joked. "I love what you've done with the place, by the way." He hobbled a few steps back, took aim and lunged forward with promising form. The brass pole sailed into the airspace of the domed cavern. The two men squinted, holding their breath, as they watched the hauling strap slip off the end of the pipe, which sailed through the hole overhead and came to a clanging halt against something in the cemetery above their heads.

"NO-O-O-O!" the two screamed in unison, their cries echoing back at them. At that moment Seamus recognized how dry his throat had become. He thought back to the morning's Starbucks latte—sipped during the drive up from Kennewick—still sitting half-full on the cross brace in the open stud wall next to where the tractor had been parked in the barn. This, in turn, got him thinking he also hadn't peed since then. So that was the next challenge on this episode of *Survivor*.

"I need to take a leak," Seamus announced.

"I'd offer you some privacy," Cody replied, "but I am not going back in that passageway."

Funny man, Seamus thought to himself as he cleared his throat. "I was thinking that maybe we designate that passageway as … I don't know … our urinal."

"It does slope down from this main chamber," Cody said. "Go for it. I'm just going to defile your dad's coffin a bit further by prying off that other railing, if that's okay with you."

"Of course," Seamus said, moving toward the ancient lava tube. "We need to work with what we've got, I suppose." He faced the opening and undid the front of his jeans. As dry as his mouth and throat had become, he hesitated to release any of his bodily fluids, not knowing where the replenishment would come from, or when. And then there was the accumulation of ammonia to consider in their confined space—just in case Cody couldn't javelin them out.

Seamus had just begun releasing his stream when Cody stomped on the side of the casket behind him. Seamus jumped, stretching his ribcage, and inadvertently pissing on his hand. Wiping his hand on the butt of his jeans, he knew that things were not going well, but he had a very strong feeling they could turn worse if he and Cody lost focus and gave up. Cody stomped a second time and the deafening clank of metal hitting rock sounded like their best shot at a second chance. Seamus tucked himself and did up his pants, turning around to ask Cody if he had any more gum. He had two motivations: first, he needed to activate his salivary glands, and second, the chewed gum could help them create a gasket on either side of the hauling strap, so it wouldn't slip so easily off the end of the pole when tossed. As the men worked out their escape plan, version 2.0, they avoided elevated panic by working methodically, step-by-step, to improve their survival odds. Neither man said it, but both were grateful for the companionship, and both found purpose in taking responsibility for getting the other out alive.

"Where did you get your javelin-tossing skills?" Seamus asked as he chomped on the two Chiclets he'd been given.

"You'd be forgiven for not recognizing it now, but you're looking at Washington's 1987 Track and Field AAA-Division decathlete of the year."

"No shit, I am?" Seamus was impressed. In his own high school career, he'd preferred books over sports. He hadn't really interacted with any of the jocks—and frankly, with academic scholarships on the line, didn't see the point in athletic distractions. In seventh grade, he had dabbled with becoming a breakaway roping cowboy in the Northwest Junior Rodeo circuit until he had gotten thrown by a mustang and hit his head on a rock. It wasn't just any old rock, but an igneous rhyolite, and that would steer him toward a new career path in geophysics. The same rock—only slightly harder than his own head—sat on the bookshelf in his office at the Northwest National Laboratory building, where he was sure nobody had noticed him missing yet, since it was still the weekend.

The 1987 Decathlete of the Year was readying for his next javelin toss when Seamus suggested they move the casket against the rock wall opposite the new urinal, to give him more wind-up and lunging room. The pine box didn't move as easily without rails, but the pair managed to tuck their cave-mate in the darkness and out of the way. The acrid aroma being emitted from the damaged crate reminded, even incentivized, them to avoid becoming permanent residents in this crypt. Seamus removed the small wad of gum from his freshened mouth and handed it, without thinking about germs, to Cody, who accepted it in his bare hand with a similar lack of concern. As a molding agent the gum wasn't working like putty might, but it seemed to keep the hauling strap knot in the center of the pole.

"I suppose we could lash the belts holding up our pants around the gum on both sides, but that would only add more weight, and we might need those belts for something else," Cody said, "like keeping our pants up, for example." He tested the weight of their new—their *last*—javelin as he spoke. Seamus collected the tail of straps and balled it loosely in his hands—thinking he would lob the straps into the air right after Cody's release so everything became airborne at once as it flew for the bullseye. Cody took three giant steps backward and cocked his body to spring into a running lunge, his eyes on the target. "On three," he said, beginning the abbreviated countdown they both continued silently in their heads. It was tight choreography, and the pair moved as one unit to launch their lifesaving missile.

The pole left Cody's hands, and with an uncomfortable pull on his ribs, Seamus sent the ball of hauling straps chasing it. Sun reflected off the brass the closer it inched toward the opening. But the arc was short, and the pole hit rocks and came cartwheeling down with a two-ended *ker-clunk*—raining straps, dirt clods, and dust on their arm-covered heads.

Cody Getz was no quitter. He tried again and again, for more than ninety minutes, to thread that skylight needle. Just as his shoulder seized in a momentary spasm, and with Seamus sitting on the coffin off to the side, the brass railing slipped the surly bonds of their confinement and thudded on the surface above their heads. Cody tried to whoop with joy, but his throat was so dry he barely squawked.

Seamus didn't want to be a killjoy, but he had to point out that the hauling strap was swaying in the dusty air, well beyond their reach. Not to be defeated, the 1978 Washington State Decathlete of the Year began jumping, then leaping like a lunatic, trying to grab the end of the strap.

"Do you think I could stand and balance on your shoulders?" he asked, out of breath and massaging his shoulder.

Seamus raised one eyebrow and shook his head. "This bruised bag of cracked bones can't support its own weight right now." He watched the enthusiasm drain from Cody's face in the shaft of dust-glittered sunlight that angled into their underworld. "But maybe Pops could help us out again," Seamus suggested, giving the coffin a two-handed drum beat for punctuation. "What if we stood up this box, and you climbed on top?"

"We have to work with what we've got, right?" Cody conceded despite how irreverent it seemed to stand up a corpse.

The men shifted Gerald back to center stage and gently tipped him up on end, gritting their teeth as the coffin's contents slid in the maneuver.

"Sorry, Pops," Seamus whispered, "but you got us into this mess. You're going to have to help get us out, too." He hoped to placate the dead and calm his own nerves. "I will try to brace the box with my back if you want to step into my hands," Seamus offered, already cupping his palms. "And I can try to boost you up, ribs willing."

Cody turned to face his partner as though they were about to begin a waltz and placed his hands on Seamus's shoulders. "Ready?"

"Ready," Seamus confirmed, trying not to sound so tenuous.

Cody placed his booted right foot into the hand stirrups and raised himself up as gently as he could listening to the groaned feedback he was receiving. He placed a knee in the muscled padding of Seamus's right shoulder and collarbone, remembering it was the left side that he'd injured in the freefall. He reached both hands to the angled edge of the wobbling casket—not only did the top flare to accommodate shoulders but the foot tapered in, and maybe they hadn't chosen the most level spot on the dirt and rock floor.

"Steady," Cody commanded.

Seamus held his breath to bear the weight. It felt like one half of his ribcage was about to bust out its side. The pine box creaked, exhaling its odorous gases, giving both men one more reason to keep holding their breath. Seamus felt the weight lift off his shoulder and transfer to the monolith. It might as well have been a unicycle, given how much Cody struggled to maintain his balance. Seamus slowly turned around to embrace the box without ever losing contact with it. He planted his boots and tried to right the tower's lean as Cody rose from his haunches to stand fully upright in one smooth, hydraulic motion. Cody stretched his right index finger within a few inches of the fraying end of the strap dangling in the celestial void. It reminded Seamus a little of the Sistine Chapel.

"If I jump, I think I can grab it," Cody said. "I just don't know if the pole will stay put or if I'll pull the whole works down on top of us again."

Seamus played cheerleader to his new favorite decathlete. "Leap of faith, brother ... go for it!"

Cody sucked in a big gulp of air. "On three!"

Seamus braced. On three, he and the coffin shimmied slightly as Cody sprang straight up; first his left and then his right hands grasped the strap, but it was slipping back down with the weight of his body. He tried aiming his feet to come back down on top of the coffin, but he was a bit off-kilter, or the target had shifted and at least one of his legs was going to miss the mark. The hauling strap was bringing in a downpour of dirt, which made looking up impossible. Cody tightened his grip, willing the pole to snag on anything that would stop him from smacking the ground as he slightly bent his knees at the same time to absorb the impact. Miraculously, the pole caught and snagged on something. The strap jerked. Cody's left tiptoe found the back of Seamus' shoulder. There was a grunt when Cody applied his weight on Seamus's wounded side. A residual sand waterfall continued to spill over the lip in the ceiling. Both men held their breath, waiting for the sky to fall. When it didn't, Cody was the first to let go a chuckle. He swung his other foot onto the top of the casket and pulled his full body up to achieve balance, testing the tautness of the strap with his weight.

Seamus continued bear-hugging the pine box, problem solving as he panted through his open mouth, blowing air through his bushy moustache by jutting out his lower jaw. Unable to see for himself, he asked, "Did it work?"

"I think it did, believe it or not!" Squinting to keep out the shower of debris, Cody examined the hatch above his head. The pole was beautifully braced at an angle across one corner of the roughly rectangular opening. The knot of the strap was not visible on the section he could see, so he couldn't determine if the strap had slipped, or how much of the brass pipe was holding solid ground on either side. He felt the adrenaline threaten to fountain out of his pores.

"I'm going to go for it!" he hollered, already lifting his feet off the coffin top. Seamus released his hold and stepped back into the shadows so he could see. He raised what looked like a sloppy salute to his forehead to block the sudden flurry of sand that assaulted his eyes. He watched his would-be hero and rescuer inch his way up the strap, hand over hand, his legs and booted feet scissored around the tail of strap that trailed and wagged beneath him. Though neither man spoke of it, they were both thinking of the physical education classes of their youth, in which rope-climbing to the gymnasium ceiling was a feat, a rite of passage, and a way to avoid bullying.

Cody kept his eyes on the pipe, which had started to move with the swaying of his body, which he had a tough time controlling. He reached the knot in the two straps and took a moment to pause—encouraged that he had less than half the distance left to climb. Though his biceps and forearms were trembling violently, he pulled himself another armlength higher, and then another. He saw the upper knot now, but not a trace of the two gaskets of chewing gum that were meant to hold the knot in place in the center of the pole. It may have been a trick of the sunlight, but the pipe seemed to move away from the corner, rolling maybe a quarter turn with each pull-up Cody executed. Every time he stopped, the flat strap slipped through his palms—so he kept pulling and lifting himself higher, even though this only made the pole move more.

With maybe six feet left to climb, he paused and watched as the brass tube started to roll inside the knot causing the railing to travel toward the widest part of the opening. Cody had no way of knowing how much of the railing was distributed on either side of the opening, out of his sight—nor did he have any guarantee that the ground surrounding that opening wouldn't cave in with his see-sawing weight. He just had to keep shimmying up and hope he could find handholds or his footing once he reached the top. Suddenly what must have been a dust devil chased a tumbleweed the size of a beach ball down the chute onto Cody's face, along with several shovelfuls of dirt. He coughed and spit, but the dirt had momentarily blinded him at the worst possible time. He continued pulling himself up, no longer able to calculate the distance he had left.

Seamus kept most of the debris out of his own eyes, but he still had trouble gauging how much further up Cody needed to hoist himself. When Cody shouted down that he couldn't see, Seamus knew he needed to step up and coach.

"Another few feet and it looks like you might be inside the grave," he hollered up through the dust. "You've got this," he lamely added, as though it were a cherry on top. He felt instantly dumb for saying that. He didn't want to think about what would become of them if Cody didn't succeed. In the four hours since the accident, this was the closest they'd gotten to the lofty hope of experiencing life above ground again. As much as he loved his father, he was neither ready to spend the hereafter nor willing to endure this botched burial with him for much longer.

"I'm slipping," Cody shouted in panic.

"Oh, man—no!" Seamus wasn't sure what he was seeing, but he blurted it out anyway. "It looks like the pole is bending—"

And that's when Cody, the strap, and the brass pole came crashing down on top of Gerald Quinlan. When the dust cloud cleared, the corpse was no longer standing upright, and no longer in the coffin—his suited father had toppled face-down on the cave floor. Cody—limbs at odd angles—lay moaning nearby. The unmistakable stench of death was released into the cavern, as thought they'd been gassed. Seamus was the first to start coughing involuntarily, but Cody joined in chorus.

Before Seamus could attend to Cody's injuries and ignoring his own, he sprang to his father's stiff corpse. Before really thinking about it, he turned the body right side up, and gasped at the horrific sight of the unrecognizable shrunken head. He pulled the farmer's rigid body across the cave floor, where he pushed it like a plunger completely inside the passageway he'd already used as a urinal. Apologizing to his father's spirit out loud, he next snatched the plaid sofa seat pillows, partly saturated with his father's bodily fluids, and stuffed their stained upholstery sides into the passageway, trying to seal it shut. He dragged the largest pieces of the collapsed coffin to barricade against the cushions, and then, marginally satisfied with the makeshift crypt, he knelt next to Cody, not realizing he was still apologizing.

"I'm so sorry, man," Seamus babbled. "Sorry for the smell, sorry for this whole mess, sorry you fell." His hand went to Cody's cold forehead and stayed there, like a compress. "Can you direct me to what hurts most?"

Cody could only whimper as he struggled to keep from slipping into shock—though he couldn't communicate this, and Seamus, with zero first-aid training, couldn't diagnose it. His breathing was rapid—which was a clue Seamus took as hyperventilation. He placed his other fingers on the side of Cody's throat and found his heartbeat slower than what he thought it should be given the excitement from the fall. Why he thought he needed to elevate Cody's feet and legs, he didn't know—he suspected the idea came from watching too much television. When he moved to straighten his patient's legs, he discovered at least one of Cody's ankles—the left—was obviously broken and at an angle, even inside the cowboy boot, that Seamus could see was not anywhere near normal.

"Listen to me, Cody," Seamus said, in a stern, take-charge voice. "Your ankle is clearly broken inside your boot."

Cody panted, sharp breaths syncopating his speech. "I ... can't ... feel ... my ... legs!"

Seamus reoriented himself to be parallel so that Cody could see his face, though they were both in shadows. He gently but firmly cupped his large hands on both sides of Cody's whiskered chin. "Cody! Breathe with me." Seamus exaggerated his breath, inhaling and exhaling so that Cody could feel it on his face. Cody stared into Seamus's concerned eyes—but the stare seemed vacant, and Cody's pupils weren't tracking as Seamus moved his own head from left to right. Seamus gave Cody's cheek a gentle slap, then followed with one that was firmer when he thought Cody was slow to respond.

"Listen," he said. "I think I need to take your boots off and check your legs. But I'm afraid if I get the one boot off, I won't be able to force it back on around the break." Seamus paused and then spoke louder. "Tell me what you think I should do." He was pleading now.

Cody's lips parted slightly, but no words or sound came out. Seamus realized he was going to have to figure this out for them both. Suddenly, he felt even more responsible than before for Cody's survival. He scooted and knelt to get into a better position to grab Cody under the shoulders and armpits. Without asking, he pulled Cody across the mostly dirt floor under the shape-shifting shaft of late-afternoon light—which wasn't going to last much longer. He didn't have to ask if he was hurting him—Cody's groans made it clear. Seamus reached for the neck brace that had fallen out of the splintered pine box, along with everything else. The device was really a block disguised to look like a satin pillow and had been, until very recently, supporting his father's upper vertebrae and cranium. It had been part of the coffin's accoutrements. Oddly, Seamus raised it first to his nose to see if it smelled badly. He didn't know why he did this, but under the circumstances—for which he was feeling clearly responsible—it was just another ludicrous attempt at being a good host, he supposed. Seamus positioned the block under the calf of Cody's injured ankle. Cody let out a labored yelp that lingered while Seamus tried to work the bottom of his jeans up and over the boot.

Cody finally found the strength to shout, "STOP!"

Seamus did, gently lowering the leg back down to rest on the block. He felt he needed to stabilize the ankle—but again, he could only credit television as his guide. The boot provided some support, but Seamus felt this should be tightened and splinted. He looked on the ground around him for a piece of the casket and found a wooden shard maybe two feet long. It reminded him of the shape of Idaho—skinny at the top and wide at the bottom. He laid this next to the raised boot for sizing even though he knew he just needed to make it work. He thought about using one of the straps to lash it to the leg but decided it would be best to save the joined straps for another escape attempt. That's when he decided to use his belt.

He took it off and lined up the Idaho panhandle with Cody's calf. He encircled the leather belt twice until it was snug around the former athlete's developed leg. Fortunately, with a slight tug, it lined up perfectly allowing him to secure it. As he still needed to lash the lower part of the splint, Seamus eyed Cody's belt next. It had one of those rodeo-style buckles, all hammered and fancy. "Pardon the intrusion, Partner" Seamus said as he fiddled to release the man's buckle. "It's for your own good," he added. "And slow down that breathing. You're in good hands. I sort of know what I'm doing." He was lying, of course. He was relieved Cody couldn't read his face.

With his injured ribs, Seamus had to stand up to get enough leverage to liberate the belt from around Cody's waist. Seamus would have guessed their waists were the same size—both men had stood eye to eye out by Cody's truck when he pulled up, and they carried very similar builds—not skinny, but not stocky either. Positioning and wrapping this second belt, Seamus knew this lower support needed to be cinched much more tightly to gradually bring the broken bones closer to their original alignment. Seamus knew this was not going to be pleasant, even though Cody had said he couldn't feel his legs, but he'd done this once before when he was a kid. He'd caught a baby duckling at the pond after it kept getting left behind by its mother and it couldn't keep up with the other ducklings. Turns out it had hatched with its little foot bent backwards. Seamus had used a spare door key as a splint for this first orthopaedic patient and after a few weeks, it had worked! What was medicine anyway, he wondered, if not one long study of trial and error?

He began to wrap Cody's belt over and around the grossly protruding part of the leather cowboy boot which corresponded with Nixon's chin on the wooden splint. (In Seamus's elementary school, all the students had been taught to draw the states of Washington, Oregon, and Idaho as part of their Pacific Northwest geography lessons. One of Seamus's teachers had instructed the class that the eastern part of Idaho looked like the profile of President Richard Nixon looking in from Montana.) Seamus managed two wraps but to get a third and reach the first eyelet on the belt with the buckle's hook, he realized he was going to have to put some muscle into resetting the broken bone.

"One day, I hope you will forgive me for this," Seamus said. He began tightening the strap and there was an audible crunch. Cody screamed in agony and then used every swear word in his lexicon. "That's what you get for fibbing to me about not being able to feel your legs!" Seamus said. He felt his own cracked (or broken) bones under pressure, but he finally got the belt buckle to hook the eyelet. Gently, he lowered Cody's leg to the block that would keep it elevated. "What about your other leg?" Seamus asked as he palmed the other ankle, calf, and knee.

"Ask me when I'm not hating you," Cody said, suddenly sounding coherent again.

Seamus retrieved the brass pipe that had been rendered into a V-shape, with the gum-stabilized strap still fastened to what was now its trough. "I guess the letter V, in our case, stands for vanquished. Not victory—at least not yet."

Spread-winged in my bag
I take the night sky.
The great star clusters
Are fires on a vast plain.

Families gather at each one
To hear grandfathers
Tell stories of the Old Ways.
Grandmothers gum hides
For winter; elk meat is stripped
And drying; huckleberries
Gathered for pemmican.

I sweep closer, perch
In a gnarled oak; watch
A mouse test a pool
Of moonlight.

Then, softly, drums;
Then, softly, chanting
Spreads from fire to fire
Until the entire, vast deep
Plain resonates with voices,
Ratchets, drums, rattles.

—William Witherup

CHAPTER FIVE

A MONSTROUS CLAP OF thunder sounded above the men, startling them awake, and sending new bolts of pain through their crumpled bodies. Seamus jerked away from Cody, having somehow resorted to spooning him in their sleep, presumably to keep warm. While he could have sworn he hadn't been able to sleep, he'd been having one helluva involved dream about Native Americans who lived, fished, and hunted these lands long before European contact. It left him spooked and wondering if their cave might be haunted by someone other than the recently deceased Gerald Quinlan. Had Native People used this cave before it became sealed off?

Cody began moaning himself awake from a nightmare that wasn't nearly over. They were still stuck underground, and his right leg was throbbing in sync with his anxious heartbeat. "I have to take a piss," he announced before he'd worked out the mechanics of exactly how he was going to go about it. He tried to remember the last time he'd relieved his bladder, but that only made him have to pee more.

"Okay." Seamus cautiously raised himself up from the lumpy rock and dirt floor and onto one knee. It shocked him that he was the one in better shape. Every breath still felt like he was being punched in the left obliques—from the inside. "Let me help you stand," he said, placing a hand and arm within Cody's grasp. "I sort of decommissioned our previous urinal when I stashed my father in it—so you get to choose the next spot to make our marks. I've got to take a leak, too."

Cody rolled away from the wall and onto his back, grabbed Seamus by the wrist, and hinged at his waist to a sitting position. They'd both been sleeping near the short wall opposite the passageway, under a lower rock ceiling—with maybe four-and-a-half feet of clearance. They thought they'd be better able to conserve their body temperatures there, rather than under the opening they'd fallen through. They hadn't spoken much overnight, even when they weren't sleeping. The pain made talking difficult.

They had started out trying to sleep on their backs not more than a foot apart—and Cody with his splinted ankle elevated on the white block. At some point in the night, they'd both rolled onto their good right sides, facing the short wall. When exactly the survival spooning had begun, and for how long it lasted was a mystery that lingered for Seamus as it seemed to him to be so far out of his character. But Cody reported that his shooting pain had kept him twitching and alert most of the night. He also remembered being chilled—maybe even feverish—so the gesture of being held had been welcome, and he hadn't protested.

Seamus stood but stayed hunched over with the lower ceiling clearance. "Watch your head as I pull you up," he instructed, holding out both hands. Cody shifted his butt so that his legs pointed to the center of the cavern. A flash of lightening strobed the tattered opening above them. This was followed very closely by another clap of thunder. "That was a close one," Seamus exclaimed. "I didn't even get in one Mississippi!"

"Maybe it will bring rain," Cody offered with a grunt as he pulled himself up against Seamus's counterweight.

"Here—use my shoulder and we can decide where to piss." Looming above their skylight in the ceiling, was a dark and stormy-looking cloud that only added to the darkness and drama of the cave. It certainly made searching for a toilet a comical affair without the aid of one of their phone flashlights. Seamus was first at the draw and with his beam trained on the floor, the light picked up something shiny. Seamus recognized it instantly as the crucifix he'd lifted from the farmhouse wall to place in his father's cold and very dead hands—proof positive that some of the modern Quinlans made lousy Catholics. It seemed as decent a digging implement as any to hollow out a shit hole. In the time it took for Seamus to bend down to pick it up, Cody was already peeing on one of the plaid cushions, saying he intended to flip it around when he was done.

"We should also prepare for what comes next," Cody said. "It's morning, after all, assuming we are both the regular sort of guys." Cody's staccato speech told Seamus he was working through pain he could only begin to imagine, despite his own injured ribs that seemed really minor, by comparison.

"I am already on the task," Seamus assured him, just as his piss stream began christening the same cushion. "I can try to dig out a little latrine for us against the wall, but I can't do much about privacy," Seamus said, as he turned off the flashlight and holstered his cellphone.

The two men, leaning slightly against each other, had turned a modest few degrees apart as they drained their bladders. Neither had the foggiest notion how they might replenish themselves, but the storm overhead sounded promising. Another lightning bolt whipped through the sky above them—a flash bulb on their tender, private, underground moment. With both their streams diminishing, Cody was the first to shake and tuck. Fastening his pants, he took stock.

"I imagine my Angie is beside herself with worry."

Thunder rumbled in the distance.

"Would she have called the highway patrol by now?" Seamus asked, giving his firehose a tug and shake.

"When I didn't arrive before supper"—Cody paused to swallow hard, with only a trace of saliva to work with—"with the fried chicken dinner I was supposed to be bringing back home so she didn't have to cook, I'm sure she got worried." Cody finished up, and—still using Seamus's back as a brace—he turned away from the wall.

"But then she would have called the police, right?" Seamus hadn't heard what he needed to hear yet—some nugget of assurance that somebody was out there looking for the missing cowboy engineer. Seamus lived alone, and with the death of his father, he *was* alone in the world. Nobody would be expecting him to be anywhere yet—it was only Sunday. On Monday, his co-workers, even *if* they were paying attention, wouldn't notice him missing right away. He spent enough time away from his desk—examining test wells, giving talks, and drilling core samples—that there was a good chance his absence might be brushed off as just another day of field work. Or just another whole week if he was really unlucky.

"I suppose she would," Cody finally said. "I mean, my weekend drives aren't anything out of the ordinary. During hunting season, I am often away for longer than this, and almost always out of cell range. She doesn't pry or prod anymore and seems to have come to terms with my free spirit and her shortened life winding down. The poor woman has cancer pretty bad. It's a relief for her when I keep myself busy tending animals and taking drives. That way, she doesn't have to worry about taking care of me so much."

Seamus helped Cody make it back under the low ceiling—the portion of the cave where they'd been sleeping. When Cody could reach the rock roof with his upstretched hand, he let go of Seamus and used the overhang to ease himself back down to a sitting position. Seamus returned to the other side, retrieving the crucifix sticking out of the dirt to use as his digging implement. He cursed his loaded pickup truck, not more than a hundred yards away, in which he had every tool imaginable. He lifted his Tri-City Dust Devils baseball cap and combed the fingers of one hand through his by-now greasy hair. He turned on his phone flashlight to scan the floor of the cavern like a ship captain reads the surface of the water. In this sweep of the light, he spotted a natural depression to the left of the cushion-blocked passageway. The wall would provide back-support for a rudimentary, makeshift latrine. Seamus gingerly lowered to his knees and began his excavation, hitting more rocks than dirt. Those basalt shards he could dislodge, he did, and those he couldn't, he tried to dig around.

Cody felt the throbbing in his leg must be because the belts were too tight. While Seamus was preoccupied with fashioning their shitter, he worked to loosen the belts a notch. When this brought instantaneous relief, he unfastened and unwound the belts from his leg completely. The pain didn't disappear, but it seemed to zero in on the ankle—around what had to be a break in either the tibia or the fibula—or both. Panting rapidly, Cody was afraid he might black out. He waited for the pain to subside, but when it didn't, he waited instead for the rest of his body to get acclimated. He was overwhelmed with an irrational desire to see his ankle. Keeping the boot on for support and containment probably made the most sense, but the pain was so high that he wanted to confirm that he didn't have an open wound from which he might be slowly bleeding to death. He tried to wedge loose the heel of his cowboy boot with the toe of the other boot but was thwarted by excruciating volts of pain that shocked him into giving up. He lifted his injured leg as high as he could, and when no blood poured out of the top of his boot, he exhaled. At least blood loss wouldn't be what killed him. To give his other foot a similar break from the boot, he worked it off with his hands and wiggled the life back into his pinched toes.

There was another flash of lightning. It must have ripped open a rain cloud, because before the thunder could sound, muddy rainwater began spilling over the lip and through the hole in their roof.

"Water!" Cody exclaimed with renewed enthusiasm.

Seamus whipped around and his ribcage reminded him he shouldn't do that. When he stopped twisting, the pain caught up, and he emitted a leaky-tire sound that was both primal and self-reprimanding. He craned his body and opened his mouth, first to laugh, and then to intercept the flow from the magical tap. He glanced into the shadows and saw that Cody was unstrapped. He immediately cupped his large, dirty hands into a bowl and conveyed the chocolate milk-looking elixir across the cavernous space to his buddy on the floor. Cody lapped from Seamus's hands, not giving his taste buds a chance to analyze the sediment or question the source.

"Your hat," Seamus said, pointing. "Is it waxed or oilskin? You think it will hold water?" He didn't wait for an answer as he snatched the fisherman-style cap off Cody's golden slick back haircut. He held the well-worn chapeau to what little daylight they were getting down in the hole. It was fitted with no adjustable strap and the label indicated it was made from waxed cotton, with no perspiration holes for venting. Seamus extended it under the stream that had already diminished to a trickle. More lightning and thunder danced overhead and loosened the tap, as a fulsome waterfall soon overflowed the cap. Seamus balanced the shifting bounty using both hands and returned the cap to Cody before he returned to drink his fill, straight from the source, knowing it was limited. He noticed the water was excavating a divot between his feet—but it wasn't pooling or running off. It must be percolating down, he figured, through more basalt layers below them.

Chugging from his cap took Cody's mind off his broken leg and gave his brain something else to wonder about—like what might be in that rainwater that had traveled through a graveyard to reach them in their underworld. He splashed some of the brown water on his face and through his hair, which with his cap removed must have looked like wheat straw. The unexpected rush of water was lifting both their spirits. Seamus nearly danced under the stream, sticking his whole head under, and letting the water trickle inside his shirt and down his back into the crack of his ass. The thunderstorm continued and intensified. And then, just as soon as it had arrived, it moved on. Sun once again shone though the skylight at a steep angle, spotlighting the mangled casket stacked in front of the passageway. The scene reminded Seamus of the resurrection story. For a spiritual second, he wished his father would roll away the cushions to emerge, reborn and anew, as their savior. But minutes passed and, of course, there was no miracle. In Seamus's trance, however, he was slow to notice the water, instead of continuing to disappear into the ground, had started pooling, and was now expanding into a puddle that he was standing in. The trickle reduced to steady droplets, then sporadic drips. But the puddle continued to swell and deepen.

"Is it me, or is the water on the floor rising?" Cody asked with his extended legs, one boot on and the other off, pointing toward the pool.

It took Seamus a minute to calculate the possibilities with the water about to overtop his hiking boots. Could the passing rainstorm have caused the water table to rise? Was rainwater seeping in from other spots besides the hole in the cavern's ceiling? He slowly turned around. The cave walls didn't appear to be wet, so he ruled out seepage. Then he remembered what he'd seen at the farm pond a few days back. Once he'd gotten the windmill freed and spinning and the water pump working again, water had disappeared through the cracks until it didn't, and then began slowly filling the pond. This must have meant the ground water table wasn't as deep as he'd always thought it to be.

Then he remembered that he needed to factor in the unknown ghost plumbing of what had once been Harder Springs. One of his great-great-great-grandfathers had chosen this farm site because of the natural springs that watered it year-round. In Seamus's lifetime, the springs needed hydraulic pumps to reach the surface—but in his ancestor's day, freshwater had naturally bubbled to the surface to feed the irrigation ditches that spiderwebbed away from this rare and abundant fount. As the liquid resource became overused in the decades that followed, the water table and the aquifer feeding it must have dropped and nearly dried up.

Suddenly, a wide grin of recognition broadened the horseshoe moustache that straddled the weathered contours of Seamus's lower face. Though late to the punchline, he suddenly understood what must have occurred. It must have become harder to draw water from the springs over time—and that's how the springs must have gotten its name. But it wasn't because the springs had dried up. It was because they had migrated to below where the farm pond was today. Even the slightest precipitation hitting the surface, he postulated, would awaken the former channels and water courses.

Cody removed his cellphone from his jeans pocket just in case the water kept rising. For the hundredth time, he checked for even a single bar of signal, only to verify for the hundredth time that they were still in a dead zone. He punched in 9-1-1 for the hundredth time, and for the hell and habit of it. Nothing.

Seamus followed a narrow rivulet of water as it zigged, zagged, dodged, and flowed toward the downward sloping passageway and under the pine and plaid-pillow barricade. His initial panic that his father's corpse would get wet was followed by a short and explosive burst of laughter—cadaver preservation was now the least of their problems. Accepting now that the water seemed to have an outlet through the passageway, dashed his short-lived hope that if the water kept rising, they might get floated to the surface. With nearly 1,200 dams in Washington State, Seamus knew this was how cargo barges navigated the different elevations of rivers and reservoirs using the hydraulic locks of a dam. The rainstorm appeared to have passed, and Seamus, thinking quickly, realized that the water at his feet was about to disappear back through the layers of dirt and basalt. He heeled off his Merrell boots and used them to scoop up the available water.

Cody watched these antics, trying to imagine what Seamus was thinking. "Are your boots waterproofed?" he finally asked.

"We'll see," Seamus answered, as his last efforts caught mostly thinned mud. He hoped any sediments would settle to the bottom of the boots with time, in the evolving possibility that the men became desperate enough to drink that sludge—assuming the contents didn't leak through the stitched seams of the fifteen-year-old boots in the meantime.

Cody returned his focus to his cellphone. He'd watched enough news and seen the odd movie or television show where missing people's cellphone signals were tracked for pings, which sometimes led rescuers to their hidden locations. He assumed these pings were only transmitted when a phone was within range of a cell tower—and having spent the entirety of his adult life in Central Washington, he knew how far and few between those were. Still, he had to ask, "Any idea how far away the closest cell tower might be?"

Seamus had to think about that. He was used to not getting any coverage until he was close enough to the farmhouse to snag his father's Wi-Fi router, which Seamus himself had installed since Pops had zero use for technology and even less interest in whatever the hell the world wide web was supposed to be about. "I usually have a pretty strong signal around Kahlotus, but it fades to almost zilch by the time I pull into the driveway here."

Cody was thinking that *almost* zilch might be enough of a smidgeon of hope to allow for a miracle, but he hadn't yet formulated what he was going to do with this information. His brain toyed with the idea of creating an antenna using the brass pole he'd mangled and pulled back into the hole with him. Assuming the arrival of another thunderstorm, he guessed that the pipe held more promise as a lightning rod than an antenna. "What's your battery at? I'm down to half charged."

Seamus extracted his phone and realized he had a new text message. "Hey! I've got a text!" he shouted as though he were Guglielmo Marconi receiving the very first trans-Atlantic transmission. His hands shaking, he pressed the green icon on his iPhone. His shoulders slumped, compressing his ribcage. The message was an auto-send regarding his T-Mobile usage plan, sent from his service provider. "SPAM," he reported, holding the pain in his side like a handle.

"Still," Cody said, trying to reassure his colleague, "that message got through to you, and we are underground. Maybe we should keep trying to get a message back out. All my attempts at reaching my wife say *message failed to send*."

"Same," Seamus said. "I have tried two or three SOS texts to my boss at DOE, but they aren't getting delivered."

SOS. They let that sink in. Neither man spoke for at least five minutes, and then the sun broke through the clouds to dispatch a shaft of light onto the muddy floor. The standing water had been sucked back into the earth—and along with it, much of their hopes. But it was a new day. They were still alive.

"How's the leg doing?" Seamus broke the silence with his smooth baritone voice.

Cody straightened his back where he sat in the shadows near the low wall, unintentionally spilling what was left of the water in his baseball cap. He'd forgotten he placed it on the ground at his side. "Better now with the splint and belts off. I was going to take the boot off to have a look, but I almost passed out in the struggle."

Seamus approached and crouched under the lower clearance. "I imagine it's pretty swollen inside your boot," he said. "But maybe it's acting like, you know, a cast or something, to hold the bone in place."

"Yeah, probably." Cody was happy to agree if it meant keeping the boot on his foot. He feared that if he got it off, he wouldn't be able to get it back on again. "I think I'll put the splint back on for support, if you can give me a hand with the belts again."

"Of course," Seamus replied, kneeling closer by in his wet-socked feet.

"How about your ribs? Still hurts to breathe?"

"Yep."

"I was thinking I'd give the brass pipe and straps another throw," Cody said, hopefully.

"You mean the one bent into a boomerang that's probably going to keep coming right back from where it was thrown?"

"I don't know, Shay. I just feel I need to keep trying something to get us out of here, you know?" Seamus flashed a grin, happy to hear that Cody had just familiarly abbreviated his name, like most people did once they'd gotten to know him. The two weren't strangers, or just colleagues any longer. Cody continued. "I don't have a lot of faith in Angela's ability to help us. To be honest with you, I'm not sure she would have called the police by now. Look, I'm scared. I'm hungry. My leg—well, I'm sure it's broken. We're trapped down here with the decomposing body of your dead father. I have lots of motivation to do something right now. I don't know how long this will last, so I want to try everything, so we can know we tried everything before we're faced with only one option—to give up."

Seamus didn't say anything at first. He wasn't about to put his weight on Cody's shoulders too, but he had been pinning his hopes on Cody's wife mounting an all-points bulletin and a statewide missing person's search for her husband. Seamus had no living relatives, nobody who cared about his whereabouts, nobody expecting him to show up or be some place—not on a Sunday, anyway. He had frankly been banking on a midday rescue party to close in on their subterranean prison any minute now, with bloodhounds, search-and-rescue helicopters, and a corps of breaking news crews. He hadn't expected that they would have to face the very real prospect of having to spend another day without food or water, and another night underground.

"You and I are over-educated, high-functioning, and generally bright men," he said. "We don't give up—not ever, okay? I agree with you that we should try everything we can." He moved closer to put a hand on Cody's shoulder for emphasis. "I'm with you in this." He chuckled. "Hell, I got you into this. I will make sure to get you out of this hole, and back home to your wife. That's my promise to you, Cody Getz." He squeezed Cody's shoulder before patting the palm of the same hand on the side of Cody's stubble-shadowed and momentarily downtrodden face.

This pep talk cultivated a smile, and Seamus scoffed at anyone who'd said he wasn't cut out to be a farmer. Optimism in the current situation was the hardest thing to grow.

Emotions stormed Cody all at once—tears came to his eyes, and he blushed in the shadows of their captivity. "I make the same promise to you, Mr. Quinlan. Thank you." He cleared his throat. "Sorry—I have mud breath and cave hair. I must be a sight!"

Seamus motioned with his head toward the blocked passageway behind him. "My ol' man back there, in his fancy new tomb, is the real sight. He makes you and me look positively fantastic!"

"Yeah, right," Cody said. "And speaking of looking all right, we should take another look at your ribcage. How 'bout you move into the sunlight and show me your bruises?"

Seamus rose from his haunches to his knees. He had a devilish grin and that perpetually raised eyebrow lifted even higher. "What? We've just exchanged promise rings and agreed to go steady. But stripping down still seems to be moving things a bit fast, don't you think?"

"Don't be a tease," Cody warned. "Just show me your bruise." Seamus backed up into the sunlight and straightened to his full height. He began coyly unsnapping each pearl button on his cowboy shirt—a shameless and pointless seduction. The joke, as it turned out, was on him—the entire left side of his torso was covered in a crimson patch that started halfway down his long neck and disappeared below his waistline.

"Whoa!" Cody said.

"Holy!" was all Seamus could add as a new wave of worry washed through him. Did this bruise mean he was bleeding internally?

"It's easily a twenty-foot drop. I should know." Cody didn't intend to minimize Seamus's injuries, but neither could he resist bragging that he'd done the bellyflop twice. "I cracked a rib once, and I bruised up nicely too. You hit hard, Seamus, especially with my weight on top of you."

Seamus was already buttoning the shirt back up when he made light of his injuries by commenting, "You ain't heavy, brother."

With that, and the first gut rumblings that signaled his morning call of nature, he commenced, with new purpose, the task of excavating their latrine against the basalt wall to the left of the passageway.

Cody tended to his splint and refastened the belts, just not as tightly. He hoisted himself upright using the low ceiling. While it wasn't a walking cast, the boot and the casket plank gave him enough stability to shuffle around their confines. He first examined the brass pole and untied the strapping. There was no chance that either of them had the strength left to hurl that pipe back to the surface. "What is brass, anyway?"

"It's an alloy, I think," Seamus said. "A hybrid of copper and zinc, would be my guess."

"Can you start a fire with either of those?" Cody had an idea.

"You cold?" Seamus asked over his right shoulder, thinking about his wet socks, and how it would be a luxury to have them dry again.

Cody had gotten cold overnight, but he wasn't cold now. "No, I'm thinking about smoke signals. You know—light a fire when we think we have the best chance of someone checking the property, like when you don't show up for work tomorrow?"

Seamus wanted to be optimistic, but he also needed to set the stark expectation that there was nobody left at Hanford who even knew Gerald Quinlan had lived out there in the middle of nowhere. He couldn't think of a single person he'd worked with who would make any connection between this property and his absence.

Perhaps that was defeatist, though. He decided to keep it to himself. "Whatcha thinking about burning?" he asked instead.

"Well, that tumbleweed, for starters. Then maybe the rest of your dad's broken coffin."

Seamus was suddenly distracted when the end of his digging stick hit something that didn't exactly feel or sound like rock. He tapped again and got a hollow sound in response. He put down the crucifix and began hand-excavating the dirt out from around the immoveable rocks. When he got about four inches deep, he saw something domed and beige—or at least not the black or dark brown of lava rock. The buried object had a jagged seam. And when he realized what it was, it sent him backwards on his heels.

"Um," he said. "In keeping with the Indian theme of your smoke signals, I think we have a human skull at the bottom of our new toilet."

"What?" Cody's voice took on a falsetto quality.

Seamus pressed the flashlight on his shattered and barely readable cell-phone screen, so Cody could better see when he hobbled over for a look.

"That must be a rock. Quartz, maybe?"

"We don't really have quartz in this part of Central Washington. The great Missoula floods really scoured these scablands clean around fourteen thousand years ago." Seamus knew he could easily slip into lecture mode, and he immediately apologized. "Sorry, but I think this is a skull—maybe an infant skull, going by the size of it."

Cody winced from a pain that suddenly bolted up his leg when he shifted his weight. "Sure," he said. "Maybe it's Kennewick Man's daughter."

"Could be," Seamus postulated, ignoring Cody's sarcastic tone. "You probably know, both the Umatilla and Yakima Peoples roamed this area around eight thousand years ago. Their descendants are still scattered around here today—concentrated mostly around Pendleton." He wasn't *completely* sure he was looking at a skull, much more a prehistoric one—but if so, this would indicate that he and Cody weren't the first humans to inhabit this cave. Perhaps this had been a partially open rock shelter at one time. The whole hill south of the farmhouse, next to a water source, would have made a fine spring and summer encampment for the ancient people who moved about the Columbia Plateau.

"Man, would you look at your cellphone?" Cody had just realized the state of his companion's phone.

Returning to his digging, Seamus said, "Yeah, yeah. It's on my list to get fixed"—as though he were being nagged by a spouse.

"Wait. Don't tell me it was that way before the fall?"

Seamus thought briefly about making up a whole different

backstory to pull the engineer's leg, but given how mangled one of his legs already was, Seamus decided to take it easier on him. Instead, he suggested Cody pick another location for their outhouse—and fast. Only slightly dejected, Cody paced a few pitiful steps in each direction. It wasn't like they had lots of choices in a space no larger than a doctor's office waiting room. He didn't know if his dignity could be overcome so that he could use a latrine if they dug one. He walked his hands down the rocks to lower himself to the cavern floor, in a spot his nose told him they'd already marked. He looked at the backs of his broad hands, and at the tufts of blond forearm hair that stuck out of his shirt sleeves. Satisfied the sun wasn't illuminating that part of the cave, he resigned himself to the reality that this location for their loo was about as private as it was going to get. His fingers began hollowing out a depression. "If you aren't using the digging crucifix, mind passing it to me?" he asked, a bit sheepishly.

Realizing he might have been a bit snippy earlier about his damn phone, Seamus extended the crucifix through the shaft of sunlight toward the shadows on the other side. "Of course, my cell screen shattered when we fell on it," he said. "I'm always making to-do lists, even in my sleep. Getting my phone fixed is on the new list I started overnight to give myself hope that we'd get out of here so that I could do chores again."

Cody snickered in the shadows. "What else is on this new list?"

Without hesitating, Seamus said, "Taking you out to dinner in the fanciest restaurant we can find."

"That's a deal," Cody exclaimed, then thought twice. "I hope you aren't referring to Budd's Broiler."

The two men shared a laugh that broke the mid-morning tension into pieces they both knew could be reassembled in seconds. Seamus temporarily abandoned his archaeological dig for more glamorous work helping Cody with the latrine. Before too long they had cratered about twelve inches down into a jagged hole. Seamus took three strides to retrieve the white fabric-covered headrest from the casket that Cody had been using to elevate his leg and positioned it in front of the hole. Next, he grabbed the V-shaped brass pole, cleared his throat, and prepared to demo its new function. Backing up toward the rock wall in shadows, he approximated the length of his legs, thinking his and Cody's were about the same, and dragged out a short line in the dirt using one of the ends of the bent pole. It clanked around the rocks in the parts of the floor that didn't budge. "Here's what you do."

Cody looked up from cleaning the dirt out of his fingernails, hoping his growing smirk was concealed in shadow. He straightened, trying to appear more attentive.

"Stand at this line, your backside to the wall. Next, you take the brass pole to your waist like you were about to Hula-Hoop. Use the ends as a tripod to lower yourself down, keeping the weight off your bad leg and aiming your butt to hang off the back of the stool, like this." Seamus planted the ends of the pole and with some wobbling and a bit of blind luck, lowered backward onto the neck brace—which went shooting off to one side, as it wasn't nearly wide enough to support both cheeks.

Cody was biting his lip now. He raised his hand to signal he had a question, not knowing if he could ask it without bursting into laughter.

"Yes, Mr. Getz?" Seamus said, exasperated.

"At what step do you lower your britches?" Cody got the words out and in the right order but was undone by hysterical laughter he could not control.

"Fine!" Seamus shot back. "Shit in your pants. See if I care."

"No, no—I'm not laughing at you," Cody said. "You've got the right idea with the bar, but you need to hug it, not hula-hoop it." He launched into laughter all over again. "And forget about the neck brace thing," he sputtered. "Just use the bar for leverage to cantilever your butt above the hole." Cody was squealing by this point, like a truck tire rapidly losing air.

Seamus righted the brass V with its point toward the ceiling and pulled his weight off the ground and crossed his rigid arms in an embrace around the pinnacle. He found he could hold himself suspended there quite comfortably—at least long enough to get the job done. But he wasn't about to be the first. "Here then," he said, offering Cody the pole. "As my guest, you should take the maiden shit."

To keep the peace, Cody didn't protest. His laughing fit had rattled his insides loose and after the nearly twenty-four hours since his last movement he really needed to use the facilities, such as they were. He shuffle-dragged himself across the rocky-dirt floor, took the brass pole with both hands and scooted into final position. When he caught Seamus observing his technique, he said, "Can I have some privacy, please?"

Seamus stepped into the shaft of sunshine with his back to Cody and busied himself by removing his wet socks. He stretched them out to dry in the sun patch, though he knew it would move across the floor of the cave during the long summer day. When Cody released a long fart that practically pried the rocks loose from the cave walls, it was Seamus's turn to lose it. The barrel laughing hurt his ribs a lot, but he couldn't stop until tears streamed tracks down his dirty face.

"When you pull yourself together," Cody suggested calmly, "you might think about inventing toilet paper, next."

Seamus wiped both eyes with his shirtsleeves and considered donating his wet socks to the cause. Thinking he'd need to cut them up into smaller sections, he asked Cody if he had a pocket-knife on him, already knowing the answer would be *no*.

"I have a fingernail clipper on my truck key ring," Cody revealed as he fished his truck keys from the front pocket of his jeans that he'd lowered to his knees. The set of keys landed in the dirt close to his partner's feet.

Opening the clippers, Seamus began gnawing a rough square from the first tube sock. It was slow going, but the clippers did the job. When the keys, fobs, and truck remote kept getting in the path of his snipping, he worked to remove the clippers from the key ring. He stopped for a second, eying the truck remote. Even though he knew that Cody had already tried this, he pushed the PANIC button, marked with a red trumpet icon, and cocked his head. He heard nothing beyond Cody's latest grunting push. Seamus stood up and extended his arm another three feet above his six-foot-two-inch frame. He pressed the button again but had to accept they were too far away from Cody's truck in the driveway to activate the alarm and hazard lights.

"What are these other buttons on your truck remote for?"

Seamus absentmindedly turned to ask, since Cody's truck was way fancier than his own.

"Privacy, please ... And a square of toilet paper when you can manage it." There was a demanding tone in Cody's voice.

Seamus mumbled a "sorry," and turned back around to rip the toe part of the sock at the spot he'd gotten started with the clipping. The effort strained his ribcage and he let out a moan—but, with lots of frayed and dangling threads, the toe part separated. He offered it backward into the shadows, where it was received. "The lock and unlock icons, I get," he continued. "Hey, the automatic tailgate is a cool feature. What's the circular arrow for—the one that's marked with an $x2$?"

"That's the auto-start—you know, like when I want to warm or defrost the rig from inside the house during the winter." Cody adjusted his one-armed bear hug on the brass pipe as he went for the wipe. "It has a decent signal distance, but I am pretty sure we are out of range down here." Using the brass triangle as an aid, Cody worked himself to a standing position, balancing on his good leg and pulled up his pants. "I know what you're thinking, though. If only we could somehow get the alarm to trigger, it might get noticed by a passer-by on the highway." Cody zipped up his jeans. "But it would run down my truck battery." As he said the words, he thought how ridiculous they sounded, given that he and Seamus were facing a situation of life and, well—death.

Cody was thinking out loud. "What if we tied the key ring to the double strap and figured out a way to keep the panic button depressed? We could lob it and the keys up through the hole in the ceiling like a fishing lure. Who knows? Maybe above ground, it might be inside signal range? If it doesn't work, we just pull the keys back down, and maybe try again at different hours."

A stomach knot told Seamus it was his turn to use the men's room. He kept the fingernail clippers and the compromised sock but handed Cody's truck keys over to him. "Sounds like something we should try," Seamus agreed as he prepared to squat. "What in Sam Hill did you have for your last meal? My God!"

Cody chuckled. That would be "Huevos Rancheros, yesterday morning. Enjoy."

TO PAY PAUL

The next couple hours progressed but only in the sense of time and their accumulation of it spent underground. For something to do, Seamus had clipped and stacked fourteen more sock wipes after first downsizing the squares and then cutting those diagonally to make twice as many triangles. He'd also gotten the sock off Cody's one good foot, but it had felt like he was asking for a kidney by the fuss Cody kicked up in protest. *My feet get cold*, the other man whined for a good ten minutes before Seamus walked over, pulled the cowboy boot off, and harvested the sock—all for the collective good.

As the July afternoon sun heated things up—tempers included—the trapped smells in the cave began to grate on the men. Cody had worn himself into a foul mood as toss after toss of the keys tied to the strap had not succeeded in clearing the lip of the collapsed grave overhead, and so had not tripped his truck's panic alarm. He'd tightly bound a dime and a penny over the red trumpet button by swiping a triangle of wet sock from Seamus's inventory and using his teeth to knot it around the remote. Utterly defeated, he announced he was taking a nap.

To pass the time while Cody napped, Seamus puttered some with his archaeological dig until he had exposed a few other bones that he also presumed to be human. He didn't wrestle these artifacts free from their earthen grip because he figured the cave was crowded enough with the dead already outnumbering the living—if you considered all the other Quinlans planted around them. Also, he didn't really know what he was doing, and he didn't want to disturb a sacred burial site. This spot might even turn out to be a significant find. But that possibility was of course predicated on them surviving their ordeal so they could tell somebody about it.

On a working theory fueled by the discovery of the skull and other bones, coupled with the nearby natural springs and his overnight dream about Indians, Seamus wanted to find evidence that the closed cave system that they were trapped in might at one time have been a basalt overhang with a natural opening. He recalled having trekked across the Idaho border on a field trip during his early university years, to study the edge of the Camas Prairie at a spot where the high-altitude plateau breaks above the Salmon River near the town of Cottonwood. There was a rock overhang there that had characteristics of a cave but really was just a small niche in the basalt cliffs. For eight thousand years, ancestors of modern-day Nez Perce Indians had inhabited that shelter during a period reaching back until about six hundred years ago. Seamus had read about archaeological excavations conducted by the University of Idaho in the early 60s, and which had unearthed human remains, antler and bone tools, spear points, fishhooks, and basketry. And if he was remembering correctly, a natural spring had also been discovered close by. So, it occurred to him to not be beyond the realm of possibility that the Umatilla, Yakima, or even the far-ranging Nez Perce may have had a camp in this location, too, with open range hunting and not far from the Snake and Columbia rivers.

Why the hell not?

He began a close survey of the cavern's rock walls. He was looking for a cranny or nook that looked like basalt but wasn't—he knew secrets could be found in these interbeds of dirt and sand and other organics. He adjusted his hat by spinning the bill of his Dust Devils baseball cap to the back, turned the flashlight of his cellphone on and looked closely. He was able to loosen the occasional shard of basalt so he could check its viscosity up close. Eruptions involving basalt magma were usually not explosive, since basalt had low silica and gas content, allowing the flows to spread out and layer.

As the state's preeminent expert on basaltic lava flows, he knew what he was looking at. But what he was really looking for was something that would jump out. He wanted to be surprised by something like more human bones or even the sizeable blanched white tree roots dangling from the cave's ceiling like chandeliers. The latter would not have grown into the void he was looking up at now. To Seamus, this meant the cavern was once filled with water or layers of dirt and loess that had eroded and gotten carried away by water—either periodically over time or in one cataclysmic event. And the way the water table had risen to cover his feet during the thunderstorm only confirmed that water had been the sculptor of the space they were trapped inside now—and that hydrology still played a dynamic role in the invisible plumbing all around him.

A waterfall of dirt began spilling through the hole in the ceiling. Seamus cupped his hands to catch the fine grains. The winds that never really stopped in these parts must be kicking up dust devils on the surface—a cyclonic feature so common in these parts they named a minor league baseball team after it. And this constant blowing of dirt was probably how a one-time opening to this undercover space would have gotten sealed up, too—which is what kept him looking for fill material that wasn't basalt. The partially exhumed skeleton at the base of the wall was all the evidence he needed that there had been an ancient way into the cave; there just may not have been a way out. He dumped the fine dirt from his hands over the recent deposits in their latrine.

Cody snored like a hibernating grizzly, in a way that echoed about the chamber. He had been cranky when he went down for his nap, and Seamus wasn't about to poke the bear by making sudden noises. He wanted to come up with a peace offering—or even better, a previously hidden exit. Something, anything to surprise Cody. But he was coming up empty handed. It was hard to hunt and gather and provide for your family when you were stuck at the bottom of a hole.

Seamus was also leaking hope that somebody was actively looking for them—or looking for Cody, anyway. It was mid-July in the desert, so the pair wouldn't freeze to death. They had a few cups of muddy water left in his boots—so dehydration was a way off yet. They were of course hungry, but the rainwater in their stomachs had momentarily calmed the pangs. Complete starvation would come in a matter of weeks and not days. Seamus already knew he wasn't cut out for cannibalism. Spanish-to-English dictionary at his side, he had devoured the thick paperback, *VIVEN!* like a carnivore, for his seventh-grade Spanish class. The book that had nearly rendered him a vegetarian was based on the accounts of survivors from the plane carrying the Uruguayan Rugby Team that had crashed in the Andes in 1971. A new shudder rumbled through his bones at the thought of that level of desperation. Besides, the only available body on their menu was his father's—riddled with cancer and most likely lung disease, and without the deep-freeze atmosphere of the Andes, who knew what other gut-twisting antics were going on inside their resident cadaver. Certainly, other organisms had already beaten them to the buffet behind the plaid cushions.

With the onset of starvation would come hysteria and hallucinations, he imagined, once they'd turned hypoglycemic. And that was if he wasn't already bleeding internally from broken ribs that might have severed arteries. Bleak was a word Seamus hadn't known, since science provided explanations for most of his quandaries. The generations that had preceded him, though, had endured existences that couldn't be described any other way. His privilege and access to education had dispatched him on an entirely different trajectory than his parents and their parents and their parents and their parents and their parents. But in the end—and he had to wonder if this was his end—it didn't matter that he had these advantages. That's just the way it was, he supposed. Maybe now it was his time to face the prospect of the coming requiem that had marked the termination of every Quinlan before him.

Fine dirt continued to trickle down in wispy blonde filaments that caught the sun. It made Seamus think of being inside an hourglass. Seamus examined the pile of dust that was forming at his feet. In time, with these winds, there'd be enough dirt for them to climb out of this hole, but time for geophysicists, moved very slowly.

Seamus hadn't been able to find an irregular break in the basalt from the cave floor to as high as his hands could probe, so he turned his attention to the phantom tree roots in the ceiling. There was a trio of different root systems that his cell flashlight illuminated like a web of almost-connected lightning flashes. Grabbing the length of tied-together hauling straps, Seamus thought he'd try to lasso one of the chandeliers. He began coiling the strap, flipping the direction of each loop so it would release like a spring. He next tied a honda knot from memory at the end of the strap. He opened this adjustable loop and placed his phone, flashlight up, on a basalt ledge. He braced himself and gauged the distance for his first throw. He knew it would pull on his ribcage, but he was also getting used to working around the tenderness. He wasn't about to let some rusty old decathlete overshadow his once and promising prowess at calf and steed roping.

The strap flew up, and the lasso opened beautifully, snagging several of the gnarled roots from one tree and tightening around them—all on his first try. Of course, without a single spectator! But Seamus smiled wide anyway under his horseshoe moustache, nodding in self-congratulation and surprise that he still had it. He tugged, testing how much weight his new skyhook could bear. A small root tentacle broke off and fell, ricocheting off Cody's pineboard splint. Seamus held his breath, which hurt his ribs. The bear didn't stir or growl. While this meant he hadn't hurt him, Seamus could neither showcase nor boast his roping technique.

Seamus considered the situation which involved staring at the roots sticking out of the ceiling. Maybe he'd roped a viable way for one of them to escape and get help. On the other hand, when he squinted to focus his long-distance vision, the space between the tree roots and the roof opening might have been a stretch too far for either of them to reach from the roots. Seamus knew he was in no shape for climbing without passing out from the pressure and pain it would put on his ribs. Cody was down to one good leg and might not be willing to risk messing up the other with another attempted ascent. Seamus wouldn't blame him, but also wouldn't stop him if he wanted to give it another try.

The geophysicist bent to retrieve the section of broken tree root, examining it up close and in the sun. It wasn't petrified, he could see right away—that process could take millions of years—and it didn't seem to be silicified either. But the roots were desiccated and hardened, having been without water, he estimated, for at least a hundred years. He couldn't be certain of that without lab analysis by a geobotanist, but his best guess was that the trio of trees in the ceiling was damn old, and likely predated the earliest Quinlan occupation. So, if the natural spring had migrated toward the farm pond—he was revising an earlier theory on the fly—it had to have happened a very long time ago. He set the tree root down, next to their pet tumbleweed. It suddenly occurred to him that Russian thistle was sometimes edible in the springtime. Now, whether there was any taste or nutrition in the dried-out roly-poly that had dropped in on them—well, that would be for his sleeping inmate to test, when he woke up hungry for lunch.

Time barely passed. Cody snoozed. Bored, but feeling a second wind, Seamus thought he might take a little swing on the hauling strap to test its anchor. He made a loop at the bottom for his bare foot and stepped into it pushing off the ground with his other. He swung into the air, before he stalled like a crop-dusting biplane in a climb after passing under telephone lines. In that moment, he knew he was in trouble. The whole lassoed works—stump, roots, hauling straps, sod, Seamus, and a giant plug of earth—broke loose and plunged to the cave floor, just feet from Cody's feet. The crash was deafening, and it reverberated for seconds. Cody added to the cacophony by yelling his complete repertoire of cuss words. Before the dust could clear, the two men looked up through the gritty air just as another coffin broke through the fractured ceiling, landing with a thud on the dirt and rocky floor of their subterranean lair. Before either of them could cuss or say anything further, the jagged bridge of land between the two gaping holes in their ceiling began crumbling into chunks that dropped one at a time onto the coffin, sounding each time like the whack of a kettle drum. This casket was different from his father's—glossy and metal looking, with competing accents of sleek polished chrome and an unmistakable teal-blue paint. Seamus knew in an instant, whose remains it contained. One final loosened clod of earth became a meteor that comet-dropped with a crash that popped the coffin lid open.

Seamus raised himself off the floor and watching overhead for anymore projectiles, moved to the edge of the casket, folded his hands in front of him and cleared his throat with a quick cough. "Cody Getz—I'd like to introduce you to my great uncle, Percy Quinlan." He bowed his head reverently.

Cody sputtered, clearing the dirt from his mouth. "Holy shit, Shay! And how do you know this is your great uncle, anyway?"

"Well, I'll tell you how I know," Seamus started to explain. "My great uncle Percy drove this outrageous teal-colored 1979 four-door Lincoln Continental in the last decade of his life. Teal was his favorite color, so …"

"I see," Cody said reluctantly, wondering how many more of

Seamus's dead relatives he was going to have to meet before this ordeal was over. "And did Uncle Percy just drop in for a visit, all on his own?"

Seamus gave the most sheepish of grins. "I may have had a hand in arranging this guest appearance." He circled the open coffin as he spoke, daring himself to look inside. It had been more than thirty years since his uncle's burial, so he expected nothing more than a skeleton but the jumbled disarticulation of bones was still a shock. Aside from the skull tilted on its side, what he saw resembled nothing of a human shape. And that's when he spotted two items out of place with the expected contents. He turned on the flashlight and reached his phone inside the casket. He saw the tip of a neon yellow object which struck him as an odd color for a crucifix. Using the phone as an extension of his reach, he scooted away what might have been the phalanges from his uncle's hands. Seamus's heart thumped as he went for the yellow object with his other hand—and that's when he saw the tobacco pipe that his great uncle had never been without. They buried it with him, likely clutched in his tobacco-stained hands! Seamus retrieved it, along with what the yellow object which turned out to be a BIC lighter—full of liquid he really hoped was butane. He held both up for Cody to see and exclaimed in his best prehistoric caveman voice, "I think we might have accidently discovered fire!"

"No shit!" Cody, with much effort and using the wall, righted himself to a standing position and hobbled over to check out the discovery for himself.

Seamus's hazel-green eyes had never been larger. "I never knew Great Uncle Percy to be without his tobacco pipe. Seems to me my family had some twisted sense of the afterlife and thought to bury him with it—and look!" He brought the pipe closer for inspection. "It still has tobacco packed inside."

"Well, I'll be damned." Cody's general outlook improved in an instant.

Seamus was feeling almost cocky thinking he may have just lassoed the biggest prize in his roping life. Just maybe he'd found his redemption for having gotten them into this fix in the first place. But any celebration would be predicated on the BIC lighter working when they flicked the BIC.

Cody was already anticipating disappointment. "What if it doesn't work? You said it's been buried thirty years."

"Only one way to find that out," Seamus said, holding the lighter into the air and readying his thumb.

"Wait!" Cody shouted. "We need to have something to burn! What if we only have one chance at this?"

He was right. Seamus kicked the teal casket. It was metal, just as it appeared it might be. "Well, coincidentally, I was collecting some firewood for us when I pulled part of the ceiling down on top of you," Seamus started to explain. "I lassoed one of those sets of tree roots and I was testing my weight on the strap when the sky started falling." Even as the words were coming out, Seamus knew his story sounded far-fetched. "Just like you were *apparently* your high school's star decathlete, I was somewhat of a junior rodeo roping champion in my day."

"Seriously?" Cody asked. "*You?*"

"Why is that difficult for you to believe?" Seamus took a few strides toward the roped tree roots to retrieve the straps in case a follow-up demonstration was requested. With even better light coming into their confines now that the skylight had been enlarged, Seamus had new confidence he could keep a visual lock on his lasso targets.

"No, it's not that I don't believe you," Cody said. "You certainly have that cowboy swagger to you. It's just not how I'd pegged your upbringing."

"Oh, yeah?" Seamus was flattered to have earned a sideways compliment and pleased to be seen as more complex and interesting than he felt he really was. He gathered the loops in coils between his hands and paused when a new idea popped into his head. Just as he and Cody had been forced to share their cramped, subterranean bachelor pad, Great Uncle Percy could share his metal coffin with his low-country nephew—and that might tidy things up and improve the air quality for the living men. He tested the squeaky hinged lid on the teal coffin, and with Cody's assistance, they righted it, sending the bones sliding back to the bottom of the white-satin-lined box. "Remind me later to tell you something I recently learned about Great Uncle Percy," Seamus said, reflecting on the letter his dad had left behind. "First, though, I think we should put my dad's body in here with him. It should cut down on the stench and then we can burn what's left of the broken pine coffin and add those gross sofa cushions to our fire, too."

Cody steeled himself. Just when he thought things couldn't get creepier, they were about to meddle with a corpse yet again. But Seamus had a point. It was worth trying. "Sounds like a plan," Cody said, trying to raise an enthusiastic note.

They moved the teal casket closer to the cushion-and-coffin-blocked passageway. Seamus suggested they take off their shirts to cover their faces—it was going to be bad on the other side of that barricade. Besides, the July afternoon was setting up to be a scorcher, which gave them another reason to strip down some. Seamus thought a lemonade would have cherry-topped this less-than-ideal summer day, but they worked with what they had. Bare-chested and looking even more like a caveman, he took a swig from his hiking boot before offering the worn leather chalice to his fellow inmate in the underworld.

"Your bruises are looking better," Cody commented, before tipping the boot.

The two of them doubled their shirts in half and tied them around their faces below the eyes. Where Seamus's dark hairy torso made him look like Burt Reynolds about to rob a bank, Cody was more like a rare hairless cat. A clear demarcation at the base of his biceps not only marked the tree line above which blond hair didn't grow—but also where the sun seemed never to have shone. Cody had fairer skin and a farmer's tan, to be precise. Seamus looked positively Mediterranean by comparison, he supposed— even though his Irish skin was probably just as white under the thick mat of dark hair. Cody was lean and fit for his age and obviously took care of himself. He'd benefited handsomely from his Germanic DNA. Seamus was suddenly conscious of his protruding belly and resolved—if they got out of this mess—to trim back down again.

Cody also seemed inspired by their new dress code to share

a memory he thought Seamus might appreciate. He spoke from behind his shirt bandana. "I am just now remembering what Angie said—on the drive home from Ellensburg, after we attended your lecture at CWU last fall—'For a rockhound, that Seamus Quinlan is very easy to look at.'" Cody also remembered the silence that followed her comment—but didn't mention to Seamus that he'd agreed. Seamus claimed he was blushing, knowing there wasn't enough light for Cody to confirm it.

Neither man seemed eager to co-house the corpses—and perhaps to hold off the nasty task that awaited them behind the blue plaid wall—Cody and Seamus felt some obligation to reassemble the bone puzzle that was Percy Quinlan's skeletal remains. They both quickly realized how little they knew about anatomy, but they did their best. Then, taking rib-stretching gulps of air and holding them in, they moved aside the chunks of coffin and the sofa pillows. Cody grabbed Gerald's socked ankles and shuffle-dragged the corpse from the passageway into the open, where Seamus could get his hands under his dad's rigid shoulders. Seamus tried hard to protect his memory of who the man was in life, but the shock of green flesh and the foam issuing from his mouth and nostrils would not be easy to forget. Seamus squeezed his eyes shut the moment his father was re-coffined, and the lid slapped shut. Cody released the air from his lungs, but when Seamus did the same, an urge to vomit made him lunge in the direction of their latrine. There was nothing in his stomach but the off-color water he'd drunk from his boot. It sprayed out in a series of convulsions that felt like dagger points stabbing at his insides.

"Jesus!" he finally spit out once the painful retching had subsided. "Thank you, and I'm sorry." It was maybe his dozenth apology. He turned to lean against the rock wall.

"No sweat," Cody assured him, already thinking that they maybe should have put the soiled and rank sofa cushions in the metal coffin too. Without asking, and to spare Seamus the gruesome chore, he did it on his own—this time turning the fastening clasps to lock the men inside for good. His leg throbbed, but he remained stoic as he lowered himself to rest on their newest piece of chrome-accented and teal-colored furniture.

Just then, a rat the size of a kitten scurried out of the passageway into the enlarged trapezoid patch of sunlight on the floor. The animal skidded in the fine dirt seeming surprised to encounter live humans, before racing for safety back inside the passageway. While Cody thought they might have to start worrying about rabies or worse—maybe a widespread return of the bubonic plague on the heels of the pandemic they'd just come through—Seamus scrambled to understand how a rat had gotten into what he'd thought was a closed cave system. The rat knew how to come and go. Perhaps Cody just hadn't ventured far enough through the passageway. Of course, Cody was no rat, and the alternate entrance was likely no bigger than a gopher hole, or Seamus and his brothers would have discovered it as kids.

"There's some fast food, if we can catch it," Cody commented, pointing to where the rat had disappeared inside the passageway. He untied the shirt from his face and did a sniff test. The air quality had already improved.

"I'd rather eat the Russian thistle," Seamus said, nodding at the tumbleweed.

"I've heard they eat guinea pigs in Peru," Cody offered, though he'd never traveled outside the Pacific Northwest.

Seamus scoffed, returning to the business of fire starting. "Yeah, that really worked out well for the Incas, didn't it?" Seamus untied his shirt from his face and tucked it inside the waistband of his jeans at the back. He began organizing the larger pieces of pine from the broken coffin for his pyre in the center of the space, taking a mock-nibble from the tumbleweed. "Delicious ... tastes nutty," he lied. Seamus decided he didn't have enough wood. If they even got the BIC lighter to ignite, they would need a supply of combustibles to keep the fire going so their smoke had the greatest chance of being noticed. He retrieved the coiled hauling straps as he eyed another set of tree roots overhead.

"Whoa, cowboy. Don't forget that one-ton John Deere tractor sitting up there somewhere. We don't want you bringing that down on top of us, too."

"Come on," Seamus countered. "The more the merrier, right?"

"It's your party," Cody mumbled, before electing to move back to the sleeping area under the lower rock ceiling—as an engineer, he thought it seemed more structurally sound. He elevated his leg, balancing the heel of his cowboy boot on the dirty white neck brace. He leaned back on his elbows and settled in to watch the root roping demonstration about to get underway for his entertainment. "You said you'd recently learned something about your Uncle Percy," Cody prompted.

"*Great* Uncle Percy," Seamus clarified. He lobbed the coiled straps into the air for a couple practice throws, without really aiming but certainly showcasing his wrist-flip technique. "It was in a death-bed confession letter my father left for me. Spilled his secret in the thing, too."

"Are Quinlans known for being great secret keepers?"

"Funny you ask." Seamus coiled the strap with one hand into the other. "My ancestors came from a province called North Connacht on the River Shannon. They fled Ireland in the 1870s when their Catholic secret society was declared illegal and crushed by the Protestant Orangemen. I don't think they ever recovered after the Great Potato Famine a few years earlier, but they must have been good at secrets, because discovery of their sect—I think it was called Ribbonism or something like that—could have got them all sentenced to death."

Practice over, Seamus gave his first serious toss at the root target but missed when the lasso part of the strap failed to open. "Anyway," Seamus continued, "my father wrote me a letter about two incidents that happened at Hanford, both of which carried Quinlan fingerprints."

"Intriguing," Cody said, sitting forward. "Go on."

"Ever hear of the Green Run in 1949?"

"Maybe, vaguely." Cody crinkled up his forehead indicating he might need a clue.

Seamus tossed the strap again. Another miss. "Here's the short version. Right after the start of the Cold War, some years into plutonium production at Hanford, the US Government believed that Russia might be shortcutting the cooling process on its plutonium manufacturing—you know, in the race for nuclear supremacy. The US military wing at the newly opened Pentagon wanted to conduct high-altitude reconnaissance over Russia to see if they could detect these radioisotopes. Before they could be sure their instruments would work and before they took the risk of flying over Russia, they wanted to conduct a test here. My Great Uncle Percy was pretty high up the chain of command at the time. I'm sure he protested the plans for this test, knowing it would expose thousands—including every one of his relatives, friends, and neighbors—to harmful radiation. But he was ex-military, and when given the order from those higher up, he felt he had no option but to comply. He dismantled the filters on the smokestacks so that the test could carry a full release of Idoine-131 and some other nasty stuff." Seamus paused, catching his breath, and setting his eyes on his target anew. He tossed the strap with an extra sharp pull on his ribcage, and this time the lasso opened perfectly, encircling the second root system. He jerked the lasso tight and shouted, "And *that's* how you bring down a heifer!"

Cody's pale blue eyes were large, and he began nodding. "And which of your relatives will I be introduced to next?" he asked, only half joking.

"It's anyone's guess, I suppose." Seamus gave a quick test tug on the line. It felt as though that tree trunk and roots weren't going to budge. "Wanna help me pull the slot machine handle this time?"

"Might as well," Cody said, groaning himself to his feet.

Once four hands were grasped around the strap, Seamus counted.

"On three ... one ... two ..."

The pair pulled, then immediately tugged again. The roots snapped off the trunk like icicles and both men landed on their butts as a half-dozen silver-white daggers came darting down at them. Fortunately, neither man was impaled, but as they sat there, the rat zipped out of the passageway again. This time, the varmint skidded, kicking up a dust cloud in the sunlight as it picked something up in its mouth and reversed direction. The BIC cigarette lighter! Levitated by adrenaline, Seamus ignored his ribcage and launched his body in front of the passageway, momentarily trapping the rat in the space with them. The rat panicked but wouldn't drop the prize. It was a Wild West standoff. Three hearts pumped madly. A winged shadow cast by a raptor flying overhead crossed the cave floor on a diagonal and the rat cocked its head instinctively, distracted. At that moment Cody clubbed the thief out cold—maybe even killing it—with the downswing of a sizeable root. He snatched the lighter back and saw on his hands a mixture of fuel and rodent blood. The plastic lighter had been cracked from the clenched jaws or the impact, or both.

"Shit!" Cody exclaimed. "The lighter is leaking!"

"Quick, see if it works," Seamus commanded, lunging for the tumbleweed. He broke the dried Russian thistle with his hands into kindling and formed a mound in the center of the space, roughly beneath the enlarged opening in the domed ceiling.

Holding his breath and praying, Cody clicked the starter wheel. Nothing. He blew forcefully into the igniting mechanism and clicked again ... and again ... and again. "When was dear Great Uncle Percy buried?" Cody thought to inquire.

Seamus exhaled loudly. "Oh god, thirty years, maybe," he replied. "I could have told you if his tombstone had come down with him. Let me give it a try. Maybe it needs a Quinlan thumb."

Cody passed the lighter, thinking to chew another piece of gum to plug the slow leak of butane. He reached into his jeans and extracted the foil blister pack. There was one Chiclet left. "Here, split this with me," he said, biting the piece in half and putting it into Seamus's mouth. "It's the last piece."

"I hope you are as generous with my share of the rack of rat," Seamus said, chewing the gum.

Cody didn't find the joke the least bit funny if that was what their desperation had come to. How would they have any chance of surviving? He took the small wad of gum from his mouth and held it out to his companion.

"I was just joking," Seamus said quickly. "You keep it."

"Silly! It's for patching the crack in the lighter so we don't lose all the fuel. Dead or not, that fluid still gives me some hope."

Seamus took the wad in his dirty fingers and held the lighter to the sun, trying to find the leak. He was enjoying the peppermint or wintergreen sensation in his mouth, and he admired that Cody had so quickly sacrificed his similar enjoyment to keep them hopeful.

He applied Cody's wad to the diagonal crack in the plastic lighter. He spit his gum into his palm and pressed it next to Cody's gum for extra coverage.

They sat in silence for a while on the rocky dirt floor, as if observing a wake for the rat that didn't rally. They didn't move the rodent's body as the sunlight traveled across the floor over the long, slow afternoon. Without saying it out loud, both men thought maybe the hawk or eagle would spot it laying in the sun and swoop down to grab it. And both men thought that bird would be more palatable than vermin. So, they sat at the ready, stomachs growling, just in case.

Time seemed to be killing itself, so Seamus didn't know why he felt the need to help it along—but he did, by making small talk. He nervously clicked the BIC lighter every so often, like he was punctuating his sentences. He finished telling Cody about his father's death-bed confessions. He talked about what a shitshow the cleanup at Hanford was and how it was only his allegiance to the Quinlans who had worked there over the decades that kept him from taking a fulltime teaching position at CWU in Ellensburg.

Cody was a good listener—like he had any choice. He told Seamus about the dirty rumors he'd heard about Hanford from his colleagues at the Priest River Dam, and Seamus told him about every conspiracy he'd heard whispered about the failing hydro-electric monstrosity choking the Columbia River above Hanford and the Tri-Cities. Why Russia or North Korea hadn't launched a missile at either installation baffled them both—each was a ridiculously crippled and easy-to-reach target. Hitting either would trigger an irreversible Armageddon for countless species, for centuries to come. The nightmarish thought should have kept them awake, but not long after the sun set, they'd talked themselves out and were plunged back into blackness. They curled up close together under the lower ledge of the ceiling and counted hunger pangs instead of sheep. Within minutes, they were snoring in harmony, like they hadn't a care left in the same world that seemed to have forgotten about them.

Sir, if you are, sir—the unnameable flame,
Forgive this lapsed Methodist
His present trade: his gear, tackle
And trim; the company truck—
Twelve foot flatbed International
On which he purveys, delivers
Chemical fertilizers; such pesticides
As *Roundup, Ronstar, Surflan, Baygon*
Metaldehyde, Trimec, Dymec, Gopher Bait
2, 4, D, Mole Blasters—all to blight
And sear the dearest freshness
Deep down things; that a few might golf
On jewelled turf; or Man Suburban
Contemplate a weedless lawn.

Man's smell, man's smudge are everywhere
The soil is bare and we
Have torn a hole in the very sky.
Nestlings are born blind now—
Yet we can't see the evidence;
Getting and spending we lay waste.

Sir, if you are, sir—your supplicant
Wishes he could work for you daily;
Cold walk naked the wild meadows—
Be wafted on flower-light and wind
Up, up, up raptor-like, rapturous.
Yet he is tied down as he ties down
His load, valued for his trucker's hitch—
The craft of ropes; nor for the craft
Of naming and divining the unnameable flame.

—William Witherup

CHAPTER SIX

SEAMUS AWOKE TO THE sound of Cody's voice. The other man was sitting on the casket—their sole piece of furniture—speaking softly into his phone, which he held a few inches from his face as the daylight began to spill into the subterranean space. Seamus wondered if he had a signal, and his heart leapt several beats ahead of reality. He lifted himself to his elbows and cleared his throat, announcing his growing alertness.

"I was trying not to wake you," Cody said, lowering the phone.

"What's for breakfast and who are you talking to?" Seamus asked.

Seamus could see the rosy blush on Cody's cheeks from across the cave and this was followed by the admission that he'd tossed their breakfast up through the hole overhead, as it had started to stink, like—well, like the rest of the space, thanks to Gerald.

"I was recording a message for Angie, you know, in case …" Cody trailed off, raising a fist to his mouth. He recovered after a few seconds. "I also wanted to tell somebody that our latest risk assessment and modeling analysis at Priest Rapids rates the dam at an 83% chance of failing catastrophically within the next five-to-ten years. The public has a right to know this and maybe then they will demand something more out of our fat-cat politicians and government secret-keepers."

"Wow." Seamus had begun to face the music, too—even if it

sounded like a requiem. Maybe the two of them weren't going to survive this accidental plunge into the underworld. If they perished here, they wouldn't have to worry about managing or cleaning up the coming disasters—but of course, if Cody's analysis was accurate, Hanford and the Tri-Cities were not ready. Hanford, especially, was a nuclear sitting duck; sprawled out ten miles below the dam's reservoir. This was the threat facing Hanford while Hanford was already a liability and threat to humanity. Seamus knew that Priest Rapids failing would be a re-enactment of the great floods that had been dispatched by the breaking ice dams. The super cleanup scheme was never expected to do more than appease the skeptics—the residual environmental contamination would still inevitably ride the crest of any coming tsunami, should any of the upriver dams get breached. Seamus had planned to retire and relocate in the next few years anyway—whether this plan was a means to escape culpability or to avoid developing another type of cancer, he vacillated. And maybe it was too late for the latter. He'd stopped seeing a doctor and hadn't had a physical exam in fifteen years—he just didn't want to hear the news that came to every Quinlan. He preferred to live his life oblivious of what his body might or might not be cooking up. It seemed the happier route to take. But then, this calamity had landed him in a cave he might not be able to escape.

"Maybe you should think about recording anything you want to get off your chest, Seamus," Cody suggested, reaching his cellphone to his similarly doomed partner.

Seamus protested. "Let me think about this."

"Let me tell you what I'm thinking," Cody leveled with himself as well as Seamus. "I don't have a signal down here, but maybe if I tossed my phone to the surface with the camera on and the video running, it might get a ping and communicate our location. I want to believe that my wife has half of Washington State out looking for me and the state troopers will be on high alert for ATM and phone activity to triangulate my whereabouts. I figure I have thirty- or forty-five minutes' worth of battery left."

The plan had merit. Seamus nodded in agreement as he

accepted his partner's cellphone. He cleared his throat as he sat up gingerly, trying to protect his ribcage.

"I'll give you some privacy to gather your thoughts," Cody said. "I'll be in the bathroom if you need me." He backed into the shadows. The glint of the bent brass pole catching the morning sunrise.

Seamus pressed the red circle to start recording and reversed the camera lens to frame his face in the screen. He looked a mess with his hair sticking out everywhere and his beard shadow having grown way beyond five-o-clock. He hand-combed his hair. Then he spilled his guts while Cody tried to empty his. The last Quinlan spoke frankly about Uncle Percy, his father, and what lay leaching beneath Hanford. He named every relative he could recall who had succumbed to cancers because of the Green Run or from working at HEW, and he offered a geophysicist's forecast for the future of humanity based on the bygone Missoula ice dams and the abrasive floods that had happened repeatedly toward the end of the last Ice Age. His ominous message boiled down to this: if the Priest Rapids Dam failed, sending Hanford a similar flood, the planet would survive, but countless species would perish. The Pacific Ocean, he prognosticated, would become a radiated dead zone for decades, taking a century or more to recover.

Seamus signed off his video by stating that if he didn't survive, the entirety of his estate—his Kennewick townhouse and the Quinlan Family Farm—should be gifted to his alma mater, and specifically CWU's College of Sciences Geology Department. He'd never made or considered a will, though he'd insisted his father regularly update his, since Seamus had a vested interest as sole survivor. But after Seamus, there was nobody else left to bequeath things to. The university was the only place he could think of that could use whatever his estate amounted to once it was liquidated.

Cody grunted in the shadows, giving Seamus an idea for an addendum. He pressed the record button again.

"I, Seamus Donovan Quinlan, being of sound mind, do hereby bequeath all my possessions to Cody Getz, should he survive me and the ordeal in which we find ourselves stuck on this twenty-fourth day of July, in the year twenty-twenty-three."

"What the hell?" Cody limped out of the shadow and into the shaft of sunlight.

"What do you mean, *What the hell?* I wanted to give you an incentive to live and not give up—not on me, not on your wife, not ..." Seamus wasn't sure what he was building to. "Not on your life," he finally said, stopping the recording. He was happy to have recorded his thoughts and directions for posterity.

Cody didn't know what to make of this gesture or whether he should even take it seriously. "We are both getting out of here alive," he croaked through the phlegm of his emotion. "Any more water left in that boot?"

Seamus lifted the nearby boot above his shoulder to the standing man. "Fair enough, but if you go mad and kill me to get my farm, well then, I vow to haunt your cowboy ass the rest of your miserable days!"

"It's Wilbur, by the way—in case you were wondering," Cody said. "My middle name. Since I already know yours, Seamus Donovan Quinlan." He enunciated the syllables in a terse tone, as though Seamus was in trouble, and being reprimanded. "You should know mine ... you, know ... in case I turn out to be wrong about surviving this, and you need my full name for the tombstone."

Seamus rose to take his turn in their bathroom. "In case you hadn't noticed, this cemetery has a few issues. If I were you, I might want to consider being buried some place else. Somewhere you stand a better chance of *staying* buried."

"True, that." Cody patted Seamus on the shoulder as the other man passed him on his way to the latrine. "I'm just going to record a new greeting on my voicemail before I toss the phone to the surface. I want to be specific about our location in case my wife keeps trying to reach me on my cell."

"Don't you need a signal to get into your voicemail and change the settings?" Seamus knew he was taking a piss in Cody's cornflakes, even though the idea had been a good one.

"Shit! Yeah, I suppose I do." Cody sounded deflated because he was. He had been almost cocky when he woke up with that brilliant idea. He hobbled over to the lower ceiling where he sulked and schemed in the shadows. He checked his battery. Less than half. He'd leave the camera on and recording—that would keep the phone from going to sleep until the battery died completely, giving the stranded pair their best chance for sending out pings with their location.

There was nothing left in Seamus's belly to crap out. He'd been chewing the inside of his cheeks until they were raw, just to give his teeth something to do. His breath was rank, and they'd already split the last piece of gum between them to plug the crack in the BIC lighter. His mouth tasted like his insides had turned against him—and he supposed they had. This was maybe getting dire, he thought.

It was Monday. They'd been in this hole for almost forty-eight hours without food and access to the most basic principles of hygiene, self-care, and dignity. His ribs were cracked or broken, and Cody's leg was likely an orthopedic jigsaw inside his cowboy boot. They needed food and water and medical attention, but neither knew where these things could be found or more accurately, how these things would find their secret hiding place. Not that they could hear it, but cars and trucks of would-be rescuers had been whizzing right past them on Highway 260 not more than a hundred yards away, completely oblivious to the life-or-death plight playing out underground. Seamus's office cubicle desk chair might be observed to be empty this morning, but nobody would think anything of it until he'd missed an important meeting. He couldn't remember what his schedule for the week even looked like. Ironically, his boss, Jenna, had been harping on him to schedule time with Cody Getz at PR Dam to refresh the disaster planning and inundation scenarios, so technically, he was following orders; he was meeting with Cody Getz and they had discussed the dam failing. He supposed he was expected to have written a report or made a recommendation on the latest tunnel cave-in. But beyond that, and maybe a few well inspections, nothing jumped out at him as essential enough that someone would question his absence. How pathetic was that? He was stuck in a hole with the only person left who seemed to give a hoot about him. It was that Cody Wilbur Getz character over there, winding up his arm to toss his phone through the hellmouth overhead, who had been concerned enough to drive across Central Washington to check on him after he'd learned about the passing of his father. Cody even had a highlighted photocopy map of his father's farm in the cab of his truck so his concern was genuine, and the visit had been premediated. The darker, more suspicious side of the geophysicist's brain kicked in, as it often did when he was trying to figure out a person's true character and motivations. Had Cody really come because he cared, Seamus suddenly wondered, or was it because he sensed an opportunity to pick up a farm at below-market value? It didn't matter. He shook his head and dismissed his suspicions. They were two dead men limping, the doomed pair of them. If he weren't so dehydrated, he might have produced a tear of warranted self-pity.

On Cody's first attempt, his phone hit a rock in the ceiling and came ricocheting back to his open hands. Seamus sat off to the side, thumb fiddling with the BIC lighter in his pocket, which had become his new habit on the verge of becoming annoying. "Wanna give it a go?" Cody said.

"With my ribs, I'd likely detach a lung. You're the decathlete. I'll stick to roping." Seamus sounded offended, though he wasn't.

"Suit yourself," Cody replied, dismissing the pouting.

Seamus kept clicking the lighter nervously. Cody tossed the phone again, and this time it went right through the bull's eye. He shot both arms into the air in victory. Seamus tried to imitate a stadium filled with adoring fans—but at the same time, he was trying to work out why his upper thigh felt like it was on fire.

It felt that way because it was! The lighter had produced a spark and the leaking butane in his jeans pocket had ignited.

"Holy shit!" Seamus squealed, jumping to his feet. "My pants are on fire!" He hopped on one leg and tried to get his Wranglers undone. Cody wasn't sure how to help but coached him closer to the tepee of tree roots and tumbleweed kindling that had been assembled in the center of their confinement.

"I'll be damned!" Cody said, almost sounding like he was singing praises from a hymnal. "That BIC lighter still had a flick left in it! Thank you, Uncle Percy!"

By the time Seamus had freed one leg from the flaming pants, the fire had jumped to the other, and was singeing the dark brown hairs on the backs of his hands as they frantically worked to get the pants off. The smell of burning hair was almost a pleasant diversion from the heady stench of decay they had been putting up with since their fall from grace. Seamus's hairy legs were in the path of fire, and the heat fueled his panic. One last shove of the pant leg with his other foot, and Seamus scooted backward on his butt to get away from the engulfed denim.

Their confines were now lit up like a natural history museum panorama depicting a Cro-Magnon cave after the hunt. Cody grabbed the brass V and gingerly transferred the liberated jeans to the stack of woody debris. The Russian thistle was the first to ignite with a *whoosh!* Soon the tree roots crackled to fiery life. While Cody added pieces of Gerald's pine coffin to the fire, Seamus poured muddy water from a cowboy boot onto his legs—though he was sure blisters were already forming there, given the itchy sting of pain. The curls of white smoke found the opening overhead, and with child-like glee, Cody giddily announced, "We have a new pope! Hail to the pontiff!" Wearing his one cowboy boot, he hobble-danced around their growing campfire. Seamus couldn't help but grin at the silliness that something as basic as fire had elicited from the modern man who was still a bit primal on the inside. Then he watched Cody ceremoniously unbelt his splint and start trying to remove his own jeans.

"What the hell are you doing?" Seamus screamed.

"Keeping things even between us, that's what!" But he hadn't quite thought this through since he couldn't get the jeans leg over the cowboy boot containing his mangled ankle. "Can you give me a hand?" he prompted when Seamus just stood there watching. Seamus worked the denim off the snagged boot heel and encouraged him to get his splint belted back in place. Cody donated his pants to the conflagration, then sat back down letting Seamus refasten the State of Idaho to his boot with their belts.

Cody's jeans ablaze eliminated the shadows and increased the luminescence on the inside of their cave. Seamus slowly turned around, marveling at the array of jagged basalt edges. He took a few steps and climbed on top of the teal metal coffin, tracing the parallel basalt columns with his outstretched hand. He had a new theory that he kept to himself as he worked out the variables in his head before presenting his findings to his captive class. What if a geological anomaly—in other words, a big rock or boulder, stood in the way of the basalt lava as it flowed, causing the lava river to back up and expand into a dome that partially collapsed before hardening? This obstruction could have been responsible not only for creating the hill that became the Quinlan homesteader cemetery but also this void beneath it that they were trapped inside. The direction of the basalt columns all around him, seemed configured to prove this new theory.

Dressed in nothing but his unsnapped cowboy shirt and underwear briefs, Seamus stepped off the coffin and hand-over-hand, he surveyed the walls until he'd completed a full revolution. It seemed to Cody as though Seamus had forgotten his excitement at getting the BIC lighter to work and could no longer be bothered by their plan to send up a smoke signal to any would-be passersby. Cody watched his distracted companion as he tended to their fire. He was amused that their bachelor pad had taken on this very casual dress code. A movie reference popped into his head, and not for the first time either, since being trapped underground with Seamus. This time, though, it barrelled out of his mouth before he'd thought to filter it.

"Uh, does it concern you at all that this is starting to feel a little like a scene from *Brokeback Mountain*?" And there it was, out in the open. Cody tried to laugh it off, but his uneasy chuckle was not coming across as confident. Both men wanted to make light of the matter but with Seamus no longer wearing pants and with smoke swirling up and out of their open chimney, the prospect of attracting rescuers seemed possible. Seamus was already anticipating the first question he'd be asked, and that's why did they torch their trousers?

Seamus turned away from the wall. "Are you saying that you might be developing a crush on me?"

"You're the one who's been spooning me from behind at night," Cody redirected the accusation.

"Uh, it's called survival mode, for a reason."

Cody must have felt vulnerable and exposed because he looked like he instantly regretted bringing up that cowboy love story. He added a larger pine plank to the blaze. "So what do you suppose our rescuers will make of our missing pants?"

"Who gives a damn, as long as they find us alive?" Seamus asked, not the least bit ashamed or feeling any need to explain. "Think of this as a shamanic men's retreat. City folks would pay big money for this hippie isolation sweat lodge experience to get in touch with their inner fucked-up selves, you know." When Cody didn't say anything, Seamus wondered if he'd hurt his feelings, or rolled right over the *Brokeback* reference. "As a matter of fact, I still feel over-dressed," he announced, as he unsnapped his stupid-looking cowboy shirt and tossed it on the fire.

"That's the spirit!" Cody rallied. He pulled his shirt over his head and dangled a sleeve in the flames until the polyester threads were shooting off sparks. He stood up to bathe in the smoke, gathering the plume toward his body and under his arms and between his legs. "Do we dare?" he asked, stretching the waistband of his underwear as he pondered removing his soiled briefs.

"Why the hell not," Seamus asked, peeling down his own stained underwear—the lower edge of which was already charred. He held his shorts over the flames until they caught fire, and then he transferred the burning fabric to their make-shift latrine, thinking it would be hygienic to incinerate their wastes. Cody followed the same ritual until he looked like he was about to lose a round of strip poker and was down to the one cowboy boot. The cave was momentarily filled with the scent of burning shit and the men were consumed by uncontrollable laughing and gagging which sent them stumbling to the opposite side of their space where Cody draped an arm around Seamus's shoulders to steady himself.

There, illuminated in all their glory and with all their shadows vanquished, the men appraised each other appreciatingly. Seamus was the first to break the ice and comment that Angela was a very lucky woman to have such a trophy of a husband. Cody returned the compliment, saying "Dude!" in reference to Seamus's endowment. "And I don't mean this in a *Brokeback* way," he added, "but how have you managed to stay unhitched?" As soon as he asked the question, Cody felt himself twitch, and decided to busy himself with tending the fire. He hobbled back to the center of the cave.

Seamus followed him there and proceeded to smoke bathe in a dance of long limbs that was both provocative and irresistible to watch. But when Cody stood to join in, there was more of him showing than Seamus had seen up to that point. "Nice," Seamus said, pointing to Cody's tumescence.

"This is all your fault!" Cody said, for the first time since falling into their current predicament. He was blaming him, of course, for his arousal, but the words were relevant to a wider range of things.

"BOING!" Seamus exclaimed, as he flexed his own erection in the firelight.

Cody got swept up in another, more raucous round of smoke bathing as the two of them played naked in the billowy orange-white puffs, pushing the plume with open hands back and forth between them without touching. This was a spiritual moment. Despite their hard-ons, it wasn't sexual. They didn't have to say anything, but Cody was the first to begin chanting a string of vowels to a melody in his head. Seamus added yips and shouts and clapping until both men had worked themselves into a prehistoric frenzy. Both knew how profound and bonding this moment was—but both also knew it would be fleeting, as their fire would not last long, and soon, they would be plunged again into their shadows, doubts, and despairs.

Cody didn't know why he did what he did next—just that he had to do it. Now that the men were buck naked and in tune with the earth and universe, he bent down to drag his fingers through the residual puddle of mud that Seamus had created while dousing the fire on his legs with what was left in a boot. Then he dragged his muddy fingers across Seamus's face, leaving trails of war-paint that disappeared into his wild mussed-up hair. Seamus repeated the ritual but dragged his muddy fingers down both sides of Cody's long neck to create a delta of parallel trails running down his hairless torso. With some effort, Cody squatted to plant his open palms in what remained of the mud. He held up his open hands and said, "Where do you want 'em?"

Without hesitating, Seamus turned around and bent forward, exposing his elongated, paper-white ass cheeks to his partner, who firmly planted his handprints on each one. "How's that for branding?" Cody asked, appearing quite satisfied with his artistry.

Seamus pressed his right hand in the mud, returned to Cody standing next to the fire, and placed his muddy hand over Cody's heart, saying "Thank you, man. Thank you for driving halfway across the state to check on me. Thank you for being right here so I don't have to go through this alone."

Cody saw Seamus's eyes welling up and before he could check his own emotions, a tear of his own washed a narrow meandering course through the dirt on his face. It seemed the most natural thing for the two men to embrace in that moment, and before either could overthink it, they hugged—body to body, parts to parts—and then pulled away just as quickly. And in that tender moment, the earth shook—literally. It started off with a slow rumble but built until it dislodged rocks from the ceiling. Seamus guided Cody beneath the lower overhang.

"It's another quake," he shouted in their echo chamber. "This one feels stronger and more sustained than the ones last week." He was yelling now over the terrestrial ruckus that seemed poised to deafen them. Cody squeezed his eyes shut, aware that Seamus had not loosened the grip on his bicep. Whatever new hell was coming for them, they were in this together, and that gave him comfort.

And then, as if to bury that comfort, a waterfall of dirt cascaded through the ragged oculus overhead, dousing their burgeoning fire. With one more jolt of the crust beneath them, the shaking suddenly stopped. Both of them scrambled to resuscitate the fire. Excavating dirt and rocks, they blew like human bellows into embers, hoping they hadn't been completely deprived of oxygen from the cave-in. Smoke began to rise again from the mound in the center of the debris, but flames could not be coaxed from the dead pyre. Both men sat back on their haunches and watched as the diminished tendrils wafted through the opening and disappeared from view, like fading hope.

Russ didn't know what the hell had just happened. He was from Florida—a state tied with North Dakota for having the fewest earthquakes. He had just started moseying up the driveway toward the farmhouse when the shaking started. His mechanic had finally agreed to return with him to the scene of last week's accident, to see if they could get his truck started and out of the ditch. While the mechanic tinkered, Russ thought he'd look around. Maybe he'd see if he could find the poor fellow who'd given him a lift into the city last week, so he could thank him. He'd waited out the earthquake crouched between the older Ford and a new Ram—the presence of the trucks made him think *someone* must be here. He ascended the front porch steps and saw the main door open behind the screen door. He hollered inside.

"Hey, man," he shouted, not remembering the guy's name. "Hello? Anyone home?" As a Black man, Russ knew better than to enter any house unannounced or uninvited. This had been even more the case in the Pacific Northwest, where he more than stood out as different. He'd been born in 1967, the third youngest in a family of twelve siblings, in a little town called Defuniac Springs, located in Walton County—about halfway between Pensacola and Tallahassee. He hadn't stood out at all there—and he'd really tried, too, by becoming Florida's first Black high-school drum major—so it wasn't until he joined the air force that he realized how a shift in location could upset the racial applecart. He'd been stationed at Fairchild in Spokane and then McChord in Tacoma and being a person of color in Washington State had taken decades to get used to—indeed, he still wasn't used to it. When his father decided to move west in the 90s to drive trucks and with the rest of his siblings either deceased or scattered, Russ decided it didn't make sense to return home to Florida. He wasn't even sure what "home" was, anyway, so—at his father's urging—he had taken up truck driving.

Wandering between the farmhouse and the barn, he shouted every so often, hoping to get somebody's attention. And that's when he spotted a faint trail of smoke rising from the hill just beyond.

Satan was a mustard eye on a green field.
His hammered scales were rusted
After long duty at the Logos Tree;
His bowels acid with the ration
Of burnished apples; Satan dreamed red meat.

A violet light shone in the rushes.
A smell neither floral nor arboreal
Grabbed Satan's tongue and mustard eye
And just about snapped them out of his skull.
His copper-green tail twitched DANGER.

An animal Satan had not yet seen
Walked out of the reeds. It had
A lion-long mane that flickered
With blue lightnings, like a thunderhead.
Satan radioed, "Logos to Patriarchy!"

Patriarchy sent forth all its power
While centurion Satan laid low,
Jerked with spasms. Adrenaline fanned
Along his scales—He went rigid.
The Logos Tree shuddered; spat fire.

It was a battle of light. The Tree
Crackled, silver, vermillion.
Lt. Satan rose to strike, dripping
Mercury, uranium. The animal came on,
Fearlessly: spread its feet in the mud

Until Satan saw a radiance; his tongue
Sensed a heat that was never before
On earth. He knew it was over; he would
Resign his commission; lay his flat head
In that animal's belly; hole up forever.

—William Witherup

CHAPTER SEVEN

THEY WERE HUDDLED DIRTY together, sitting side by side on the teal casket, naked but for their dry war-paint, when they heard the first shout of another human. Two sets of eyes—one blue, one green—widened in the darkness to take in the full spectrum of light that filtered below the surface of the earth.

"HEL-LOOOO!"

"Down here!" Cody yelled, forcing all his air with reborn enthusiasm through his dried larynx.

"We're down here!" Seamus echoed, nearly pissing himself in excitement as he sprang to his bare feet.

A third set of eyes—these a mustard-brown—doubled in size as the trucker rocked back on his heels from the hole he'd discovered in the middle of an old pioneer cemetery. There was barely a trace of smoke coming out of it by the time he'd climbed the hill to investigate. He'd almost turned back when he couldn't make out the smoke any longer in the midday glare of the summer sun.

"Hey!" he shouted into the hole, his brown hands cupped like a bullhorn around his mouth. "It's Russ the truck driver!"

"Russ!" Seamus called back. "It's Seamus!"

That weird white name. No wonder Russ couldn't remember it. "Whatcha doing down there?"

Seamus and Cody looked at each other—naked, painted, and

dirty—and burst into huge, barrel-rolling convulsions of laughter. The explanation that followed didn't clear up Russ's confusion, but he understood one thing: their rescue was now up to him. He started by calling reinforcements—first, 9-1-1, and then his mechanic buddy's cellphone. Waiting for the police or the nearest fire department, Russ had received requests from the hole for food, water, and clothes. He understood there were two men in the hole, so he went into the farmhouse and through the upstairs bedroom dresser drawers and grabbed a pair of overalls and a pair of black dress pants with the crotch seam ripped out—both having seen better days. He found a Dust Devils baseball jersey with grass stains on it and a sweatshirt hoodie that looked like it had bullet holes. Walking through the kitchen—remembering that a dead white man had been laying on the table the last time he was there—he snatched a box of Hostess Ding Dongs off the counter and found an unopened jug of OJ in the refrigerator. He let the back screen door slap against the weathered jamb. Out of breath after a second time climbing the hill to the cemetery in the July heat, he announced he was tossing the provisions into the hole—the bottom of which he couldn't make out in the shadows.

"I'm gonna wait at the house for the police to arrive, even though I know they are going to want to blame me for all this," Russ shouted over his shoulder, not even knowing if his voice was carrying down into that hole or how far down the two men were stuck.

Seamus divided the clothes, sentimentally choosing the ripped-out dress pants and Dust Devils jersey for himself. He'd taken his father to every home game since the Tri-Cities got their minor league baseball team in 2001. The truck driver hadn't thought to provide them underwear—probably would have never imagined in a million years that those needing rescue were down that hole commando. This didn't bother Cody in the least, as he hitched up the overalls before strapping his leg splint back on with the belts. But Seamus was having trouble staying contained and supported in the ripped-out crotch area, which he boastfully demonstrated to his companion—who had, by this point, seen all there was to see, anyway.

"Show-off," Cody scolded him, waving a finger.

"When you got it, flaunt it," Seamus countered. "And might I add, that ass of yours fills out Gerald's overalls in a way he never could—at least not toward the end." Seamus's thought trailed off when referencing his dead father—the last to wear the clothes they had just put on. And that got him thinking about what to do about Gerald and his Great Uncle Percy. He already supposed he'd leave them down there. Then again, he might need to relocate the whole cemetery one day—both for safety and to keep more relatives from popping through the mantle.

"This has been one campout to remember," Cody said, waxing sentimental now that their rescue seemed imminent. "Thank you, Shay, for helping me get through this."

"Likewise," Seamus said. "I got you into this, and I promised I'd get you out of it."

"Yeah. You also promised me a fancy dinner."

"And the farm, if I recall correctly," Seamus reminded him.

"That's right," Cody said. "And by the way, I was prepared to make you an offer to buy your dad's place and take this acreage off your hands before all this happened."

Seamus realized this was why there had been a map in the front seat of Cody's truck with the Quinlan Farm highlighted. There had been a companion—if not ulterior—motive for the visit Cody had driven halfway across the state to pay him. It hadn't just been compassion and genuine concern as Seamus had credited him during that initial phase of bewilderment when the Ram truck pulled into the driveway. Cody Getz was speculating, and Seamus needed to understand why. "You and Angela outgrowing your hobby farm?" he shorthanded his cross examination.

Cody tightened the belts around his make-shift splint. "I ..." he started to say, before getting choked on his words. "I thought I needed a project—you know—for after Angie passes." Cody stood and shuffled a few steps into the sunlight, inwardly fighting back tears. "Turns out, what I really need is a friend who can help me get through what's coming next."

"Come here," Seamus said, opening his arms for a redo of the hug they hadn't managed well while still naked. This time, the embrace lasted minutes, structurally supporting the exhausted and grateful men, as all their emotions and anxieties and fears were released into the cave they were about to leave behind. Both men were crying, involuntarily quaking with relief. When Cody undocked his head from where it nuzzled Seamus's neck, he kissed him on the mouth. It was not just a peck, but done with full lips that found lips, overcoming beard stubble and a horseshoe moustache.

"Whoa," Seamus exclaimed, as though he were trying to halt a horse.

"I'm sorry," Cody immediately said. "I'm delirious."

The silence that followed was their most awkward. Seamus wanted to say something but didn't have the emotional maturity the moment called for. He was confused and hungry and thirsty. And he was grieving—at not just the passing of his father, but the approaching end of an experience during which he had truly bonded with another human being for maybe the first time in his life.

"That was nice," Seamus said, honestly.

And that was the last thing that was spoken in the almost ninety minutes they waited to be rescued, feasting on a communion of Ding Dongs they washed down with the juice in the jug they silently passed back and forth.

It was a media circus up top, by the time Cody was hoisted up first, strapped inside a rescue stretcher. His sickly wife, Angela, was being supported by two state troopers, but she broke away to throw herself on top of her husband the moment he was set down just outside the white picket fence that encircled the cemetery. Getting Seamus out took longer because of his rib injury and since a rescuer needed to be lowered to get him strapped securely in the stretcher that had just been used to evacuate Cody. Seamus, of course, couldn't see what was happening on top, as he sat on Uncle Percy's casket, having one last moment with his father. He was saddened and feeling abandoned all over again, but this time felt more raw, jagged. Cody had been returned to his wife where he belonged, but where in the hell did Seamus belong, was the question that dogged him to tears during his final moments incarcerated by shadows. There was nobody left up top for him.

His rescuer descended on two lines, and looked like that 1980s actor, Erik Estrada. "Your turn," the toothy smiling man announced. Strangely reluctant to leave a place made even more sacred, Seamus backed into the upright stretcher, squeezing his eyes to keep the rest of his tears to himself.

⬥

Up top, Russ and his mechanic were waiting off to the side in the sun, with a half-dozen reporters with their cameras at the ready. When Seamus emerged from underground, Russ led the applause. As Seamus's eyes adjusted to the daylight, he looked around for Cody, but the other man had already been taken away by ambulance. He thought something was maybe wrong with his heart because a sudden dull pain seemed to be focused there inside his chest. He spent the next thirty minutes getting prodded by paramedics and hounded by reporters all the while wondering how soon he could see Cody again. Theirs was not supposed to have been a *Brokeback* made-in-Hollywood moment, but Seamus could neither explain nor ignore the pangs that lingered after Cody was whisked away from him. He was out of one crisis and falling heart first into another.

Russ waited patiently, even selflessly, for the paramedics to determine none of Seamus's injuries were life threatening before he approached Seamus just inside the cemetery fence. With the media still buzzing around, he knew this moment was not his and so he had been content just to lurk in the background.

"You know, I came back to get my truck fixed and out of the ditch, and to thank you for giving me a ride into town the other day. It looks like now we might be even-steven. You saved me. I saved you." Russ held a broad hand over his brow to shade his eyes from the sun.

"It's hardly the same thing," Seamus said, throwing his arms around the man, who was easily an inch taller than he was. Neither of them knew they were being photographed or that this would be the one image that would land them in the front sections of *The Seattle Times*, *The Tri-City Herald*, and *USA Today*. Unfortunately, the media pool would also caption the photo incorrectly, misidentifying Russ as Cody Getz.

"So, did you get that rotting eyesore of an onion truck out of my ditch?" Seamus teased.

The mechanic, wearing these Tom Cruise Top Gun aviator sunglasses stepped forward to say the rig was idling in the driveway and he was about to take off to head back to the city. Russ indicated he would follow him, then turning back around to Seamus, he smiled and said, "How about we stay in touch this time?"

"I'd like that," Seamus said nodding his head. Russ and his mechanic turned and ambled down the hill, disappearing between the house and barn.

The Hispanic search and rescue tech walked up, unfastening his harness, and said, "As a precaution, I'd suggest you stop by Trios Health Southridge Hospital to get a scan of your torso. I can let them know you are inbound if you'd like. Also, if you don't feel up to driving, we have a second ambulance here and waiting."

"I'm fine," Seamus assured him, but the paramedic raised an eyebrow. "I will stop by the hospital for that X-ray in the next day or so," Seamus added. "Thank you for letting them know I'll be stopping by and thank you for getting us out of this mess."

The Eric Estrada lookalike winked, gave a one chin nod, then waved off the ambulance driver sitting on the hood at the bottom of the hill.

Not even an hour later, the police, fire, ambulance, and media trucks were all gone. Gerald Quinlan's farm next to Highway 260 looked as desolate and abandoned as it ever had. Even Cody's Ram truck was gone—likely removed by Cody's wife as she followed the ambulance back into the city. Seamus wondered if Cody had been taken to Trios Hospital. That would be an added incentive to drive himself there—for his own evaluation and to see the new pal who had planted a goodbye kiss and had then vanished from his life. Seamus was overwhelmed and out of sorts. He didn't know whether to blame the kiss or the ordeal—or both—for his jumbled state of mind.

His cellphone began vibrating in the front pocket of his father's old dress pants without a crotch. Seamus was surprised he still had any battery left but couldn't make out the caller name displayed behind the shattered screen. He answered in the way he always did—"Seamus, here."

"Miss me, yet?" the caller with the voice he more-than-recognized asked, before more seriously adding, "And did you manage to recover my cellphone, by any chance?"

Mister Bullfrog had his breakfast
On his chin, a porridge of algae.
He cocked his head at me
And I cocked my head at him —
It was apparent that he,
Mottled in different greens,
Was sitting for an Expressionist.

No, there was no blazing
Blue dragonfly
Astray from a haiku,

But there is an orange carp,
Also in motley,
The palette of Byron's beret.
He sucks and vacuums
The nether carpets and is, like me
Curator of a sinecure.

At night there is a change
Of tone and wit—
The ghost of Zen Master Suzuki
Strikes the pond's skin
And the moist charcoal sky
Pulses rings and rings,

—William Witherup

CHAPTER EIGHT

SEAMUS DIDN'T GO TO Trios Health right away. In fact, despite what he'd promised the EMTs, he didn't go at all. As much as he could have really used a restful night in his own bed in his Kennewick townhouse, he'd spent the three nights since his rescue tossing and turning in his father's bedroom upstairs in the farmhouse. He'd told himself there was nothing a hospital could do for broken or cracked ribs—so why bother?

Besides, he'd learned that Cody wasn't at Trios. He'd been airlifted from the Tri-Cities to Harborview Medical Center in Seattle, where he underwent surgery to set his tibia and rebuild a shattered fibula. The excruciating pain he must have endured the whole time since his second fall disturbed Seamus profoundly—mostly because Cody had put on a brave face that masked the severity of his injury just to keep their hopes up and their worries down. Panic would have been their undoing, and Cody must have known that somehow from the beginning.

Seamus did miss Cody. There was no denying it, just as whatever had happened between them—he couldn't pinpoint what it was, exactly—had changed him. And it wasn't just that damn kiss! He'd already played that moment—and every other moment they'd experienced together in their captivity—over and over in his head. It left him with a cognitive dissonance he couldn't decipher. Here he was—this healthy middle-aged rockhound, in his fifty-sixth year of solitary life, and supposedly set in his hetero-normative ways. Yet he was pining—that was the word for it—pining for the companionship of a man he'd barely known before the fall, who was married to a dying woman that Cody had said was his best friend and the love of his life. What business was it of his, Seamus wondered, to meddle in that? *Meddle* was not the right word and *compete* was even worse. The beautiful truth was that Cody had been there for him when his dad had passed. He'd stayed brave and optimistic and clear thinking the whole time they had been trapped underground. There wasn't much doubt that Seamus might have ended up entombed like that mostly buried skeleton in the floor of the cave if he and Cody hadn't fallen together through the ceiling of that void. It had taken both their brains to keep each other focused so they could devise a rescue.

Without hesitation in the future, Seamus was already thinking—obsessing, really—that he wanted to be there for Cody in every way possible—without getting in the way—especially if he was about to face losing his wife. Seamus knew he owed Cody that much and likely more, but he didn't see this as a debt. What these new feelings of fondness and absence were beginning to reveal to Seamus was not as startling to him as what was not getting revealed in these intervening days since their rescue and separation. Was Cody feeling these same things for him, too? That's what he really wanted to know.

Seamus had combed every blade of dead grass in the cemetery, looking for Cody's cellphone. Just being there, a safe distance back from the opening they had fallen through together, was a comfort. Jenna Thomason had phoned him shortly after the news of their rescue and ordered him to take a week off work. That was before the latest quake had caused another partial tunnel collapse in the same section as before, and he could tell from her emails that she was already antsy to get him back on site. But at least with his earlier ground assessment and the experience they'd picked up in 2017 when the first tunnel gave in, they knew how to fix things—meaning cover it back up—with or without him. With everything going on, he still hadn't made it back to his office to analyze the data from the ground penetrating radar he had used to scan the buried boxcars after the collapse before last. He did make it a point to impress on Jenna that he was certain there was a cache of plutonium buttons packed onboard. This should trigger a whole different protocol for how the area got remediated—but then again—it was Hanford and common sense or science hadn't—and still didn't—necessarily prevail, once the PR-types got involved.

He'd stayed behind at the farm for numerous reasons. After nearly starving to death, he felt a quirky obligation to eat all the food that had been left in his father's house—plus, there were at least two flats of Budweiser in the pantry to choke down. He'd brought Pops this stockpile of provisions, thinking at the time the supplies had a good chance of outlasting the old man—and they did.

Seamus also worried that, given all the publicity around their rescue, curious or even twisted people might begin showing up to poke around the place. Pops and the family memories were still down that hole, and it was Seamus's duty to keep sentry over them.

Mostly he stayed put at the farm, because that was the one place, other than Hanford, where Cody knew where to find him, in case he had the urge to go looking for something besides his cellphone. Cody must be missing him, too, Seamus kept telling himself. You just didn't share a near-death experience with someone then wash his muddy handprints off your butt, and casually move on, going your separate ways. Or did you?

For his part, Cody, after his operation, was anxious and bored, and itching to get out of his Seattle hospital room. Without his cellphone, he was at a loss for the contact numbers he'd never bothered memorizing. Days before, directory assistance had given him the number for Gerald Quinlan's landline, but Cody was sure Seamus wouldn't have stuck around there for long, given all the sadness and trauma that farm must have held for him. That stupid kiss—Cody had left the recovery room beating himself up over it again—still hung unresolved and unexplained in the growing space between them. It's not that he wanted to apologize for it. He wasn't even sure he'd take it back if he could. But something needed to happen next. He was just at a loss for how, when, and whether it would.

Every time he thought about his cellphone, Cody flushed with new panic. Not only had he and Seamus, when they thought they might not make it out alive, both recorded some heavy and damning information about the places where they worked—there was more. Cody must not have been thinking clearly because he had forgotten to delete a hidden album of rather compromising selfies that were on his phone. He'd taken a half dozen pics of his features and attributes for those occasions when he would take the risk to arrange hooking up with random strangers in the Tri-Cities and occasionally Ellensburg. He and Angie hadn't engaged in sexual activities in years as she lacked the drive thanks to chemo, nausea, and radiation, plus following her double mastectomy, the poor woman no longer felt attractive or worthy—no matter how valiantly Cody had tried to convince her otherwise. He'd been forever meaning to delete this secret album off his phone but hadn't exhausted the purpose why he'd taken the shots in the first place.

With the preoccupation of cancer, Angela hadn't been her insecure, nosy self for several years now. They'd both grown complacent regarding the almost pointless task of living or planning beyond each moment. They both knew how their marriage story would end. Nobody was kidding anybody about that anymore. Cody used to think she'd one day find out about his bisexuality and leave him—which would have been a painful but a welcome release. He also used to think he'd one day come out to her as bi, but lately, he didn't see the point negotiating terms for any future engagement. He'd decided to ride this out without the drama of coming out to her. By this late stage in the progression of her disease, they both knew that her unrelenting cancer was going to beat any other viable endgame to the punch, so what did his sexual orientation matter to her?

Cody's emergency orthopedic surgery in Seattle just happened to coincide with Angela's next appointments in Seattle, anyway. At this moment, while he convalesced in his private hospital room, with four stainless steel rods erupting out of his shin and calf, she was across town at Fred Hutchinson undergoing the latest battery of tests to see if the Hail Mary infusion of an anonymous donor's stem cells, back in February, had tricked her blood into thinking her body was getting the upper hand on her disease. She'd had to spend one hundred days in isolation in a Seattle hospital bed after that procedure, which coincided with Cody's increased needs to tend to his wilder oats; hence the secret photo album on his lost cellphone. Cody was better off surfing the crest of his pain killers, rather than facing up to the likelihood that Angela was already officially in the know when it came to the other clandestine activities he'd been surfing.

It hadn't helped Angela Getz to learn from the state patrol, when they were investigating her husband's disappearance, that his license plate had popped up in their database as belonging to a truck known to frequent an establishment called Elmo's Adult Books & Video off Rainier Avenue in Pasco. They'd also told her that on the day she'd reported him missing, the parking lot security cameras had captured his truck parked at Elmo's for approximately forty-five minutes. After that, his trail had gone cold.

For Angela, this news instantly explained most if not all of Cody's mysterious weekend drives. She took it as evidence of the affairs she was sure he must be having. After she reluctantly reported the disappearance of her husband, the state patrolwoman they had assigned to stay with her so that she didn't harm herself, had been very forthcoming with information about what goes on at that roadside establishment just outside the city limits adjacent to two different truck stops. The patrolwoman also tried to reassure her that his disappearance was not her fault, but then, Angela never really suspected it was to begin with. After Cody had been rescued, she had raised her hand in the air and insisted that she didn't want to speak about where he'd been and what he was doing at that farmer's house; she already had way too much on her mind.

TO PAY PAUL

●

Seamus had spent five minutes staring at the 6x4 floor hatch as he worked up the courage to enter the cellar. By design, the family's refrigeration had always been under the farmhouse. Though still a geophysicist, Seamus had vowed never to go subterranean again—or at least not this soon. He sucked in a gulp of air that tested his still-tender ribcage, and he tugged the ring handle with his middle finger with great force, dislodging the warped sticking points of the linoleum-covered wood hatch. When he opened his eyes after the deafening *smack* of the hatch door hitting the washing machine, he saw muddy water everywhere. The level had reached the second ladder step down. Mason-sealed canned goods and a dead bloated rat with several of her drowned babies bobbed in the muck and the smell of sulphur was so strong it tickled his nose hairs. Out of place in the flotilla of objects was an inflated ziplock bag—the size his mother had used to freeze peaches—except instead of fruit inside, there appeared to be another of his father's handwritten notes and a square of folded linen that Seamus could tell, even through the plastic, was embroidered.

His mother, Abigail, had been quite the rural artisan with a needle and a loom in her day. He was certain this was a sampling of her work. Plugging his nose, Seamus snatched the bag from the swirling filth. He backed his way into the kitchen where he held the inflated pillow of plastic under a stream of fresh tap water for several seconds. Then, he sat at the wooden table atop which his father had been born—the same table where his emaciated corpse had been laid out in preparation for his everlasting rest in peace. Seamus still hadn't decided whether to haul up the casket from the hole for proper reburial. Gerald's was a slumber that seemed stubborn as the family tractor to get started.

Before unsealing the blue-and-yellow ridged plastic flaps, Seamus paused to honor what had to be his father's breath still trapped in the bag. But wait, Seamus reared back in the wooden spindle backed chair that he had sat down in to examine the contents. How in the world did his father know the bag would need to float unless he knew the cellar had flooded before? On a silent count of three, he released the breath of the dead man into the room and extracted the missive and fabric from inside. The note was a single page, written on both sides, ripped from a spiral pocket notebook—like the ones Seamus remembered always sticking out of his father's shirt breast pocket, along with at least two government-issued black pens. Seamus could still remember the smell of those pens. They smelled like the government itself to him. Seamus, like everyone in his family, had followed that scent all the way to the bank, with their secure employment checks. He unfolded the note and began to read.

> Before I forget this detail, Seamus, you should finally know that you had a sister. Well, Sampson had a sister. She was a year older than your older brother and I suppose she was gone before any memory of her could have registered for you. Sally-Sue was her name. A bit of a tomboy, that one. Maybe the only Quinlan in her generation who was cut out to become a farmer—no offense to you and your white-collar brothers. But we lost her.
>
> As we were later able to piece together, it seemed your sister had discovered this new hiding place in the cellar behind the canning shelves lined with your grandmother's apricots, crab-apples, and peaches. Also in that space behind the shelves was a very narrow opening to a tunnel that one of your great-grandfathers or great-uncles must have dug out, prospecting for gold or building a bomb shelter or something. Anyway, that passageway must have run half way to the cemetery out back. It was this search dog they'd brought down from Spokane that must have found her body back in there, because it brought out a ripped piece of the pink-and-green plaid shirt she had been wearing. We had a ceremony and placed a tombstone for her in the cemetery, but we had nothing to bury except for that patch of clothing. We sort of had to accept she was already buried—that she had buried herself maybe having squeezed through a passage that for some reason she couldn't get back through. That woulda been 1968, not even a year

after you came along. I bricked that breach in the cellar shut so her spirit wouldn't re-enter the house to haunt us—but she found other ways to make sure we never forgot her.

So, there you have it.

Dad

Seamus lowered the note to the table and gingerly unfolded the edge-frayed fabric. Encased inside the embroidered swatch was a wallet-size, freckle-faced school photo of his sister in ponytails. The back of the photo had been captioned by their mother's angled penmanship with. *1968*, it said. *Grade 2*. The linen was festooned in wide tatami stitches in four different thread colors creating the block letters that spelled the four names of the last generation of Quinlan children in birth order: Sally-Sue, Sampson, Seamus, and Sean.

Seamus forcibly exhaled. It must have been his own sister's skeleton that he'd uncovered in that pit beneath the cemetery—a sister he never knew he had—and not the artifacts from some ancient Indian tribe. But that didn't explain why the cellar was flooded now. He left the note on the table, scissor-stepped around the open hatch in the pantry floor, and then bolted out the back screen door to head for the farm pond.

He arrived at the pond bank, huffing, clutching his wounded side as a giant cloud passed overhead, blocking the summer sun's relentless assault on the land. There were maybe a couple inches of water where there should have been about eight to a dozen feet. He calculated the water's level when he spotted a bullfrog perched on something that kept his croaking head just above the stagnant waterline. He looked over at the spinning windmill and listened for the clanking of the pump mechanisms below the boards. Everything checked out, but only hot air chugged out of the pipe when he held his hand in front of the dry spigot. Then he remembered how the water table had risen into the bottom of the cave during the thunderstorm—and how it hadn't rained since. The pond was nearly dried up again, but the cellar was flooded. The suddenly spooked bullfrog hopped, trying to find water deep enough to conceal him—but he didn't have many options. As much as Seamus dreaded going back to peer into the underground space beneath the cemetery, he needed to understand this bizarre natural plumbing system. Besides, he felt obligated to pay his respects to his sister—Sally-Sue Quinlan.

Traipsing in long strides between the barn and the farmhouse, Seamus heard a passing truck horn blare twice. He wondered fondly if it might be Russ, back in action at the height of the autumn onion harvest, maybe. He held his right thumb up, high over his head—he doubted that anybody traveling at that speed could have spotted him, but it was a nice thought. As he walked, he watched the shadow of a hawk or an owl move over the ground—but he resisted looking up, not wanting to find a blank sky, as he had before. He wasn't going to fall for that trickery this time. But then, he didn't have to.

A red-tailed hawk dove right in front of him to hook a field mouse in its talons. The mouse had been fixated on judging the pace of the man walking toward it instead of the predator circling overhead. Seamus felt bad for the little guy. At the same time, he was satisfied to witness this moment in the unending predator-prey cycle, which somehow plodded along despite his own round-the-clock fretting for the future of all living things. Seamus, the scientist, lived in a man-contaminated world undeniably undergoing its sixth mass extinction. With more than eight million humans dead from the recent COVID pandemic triggered by a virus that had leapt from the wild to humans, the outlook for homo sapiens was equally grim. And in no place was this more evident to him than on the hillside-clinging Quinlan Family Cemetery, where he was outnumbered forty-seven-to-one by his dead relatives (one more than he had previously known to count).

The Quinlan brothers had an older sister. This was still sinking in. How could he have never known that? Maybe, he thought, that was why poor Sean got teased so much and was given the nickname of a girl. He had been the replacement for the girl the Quinlan Family had lost. Seamus began to climb the hill to reach the white picket fence. His father's ill-fitting denim rubbed the constantly reopening and possibly infected burn blisters on his upper thigh. He would need to head back into the city to reunite with his own wardrobe soon, and maybe get his burns and ribs checked out by someone at Urgent Care. The pain in his ribs would go away, but the burns would scar so at least he'd have something to show for this latest test of his spirit. He opened the rickety cemetery gate to what he supposed would someday become his forever resting place, too. Perhaps later and not sooner, he now thought, having dodged death—last week had been his closest call yet.

His legs trembled as he approached the straw-sodded breach through which he and Cody had been sucked into the underworld. He steadied himself with a hand on the floral-motif-carved headstone belonging to Abigail Marie Quinlan, his mother. Why had she never told him about his sister? Why had Sampson never told him? Kids talked about everything, and he'd been close to both of his brothers. No topic was taboo. It didn't make sense.

"Why?" he yelled at the stone representations of his extended family surrounding him. He knew he was imploring the tombstones arrayed before him like an indecisive jury hearing unconvincing closing arguments from an ineffective rookie prosecutor. "I could have handled knowing I had a sister, just so you know," he told them all with his booming courtroom voice, though he wasn't sure he believed it himself. He was miffed to have been kept in the dark and really wasn't handling the knowing part so well, as it was, after the fact.

Leaning against his mother's grave marker, he calmed down, scanning the ground again for Cody's cellphone. Cody, sort of like Sally-Sue, was another one who had gotten away without a trace. Determined to learn if the water in the cellar was connected to the cave where they had been trapped, Seamus crouched down on all fours and spread his body out flat, distributing his weight as evenly as he could over the unpredictable and torn terrain. He really needed to bring that extension ladder from the barn with him the next time he came up the hill. The last thing he needed was to fall through the looking glass a second time. He put his right ear to the ground and plugged his left with a thumb, listening for plumbing. It seemed faint at first, like something his subconscious might be fabricating, but then it became clearer the more he tuned in and blocked everything else out.

Pre-pare, the ground seemed to say. *Pre-pare*, moaned Mother Earth.

"Holy crap!" shouted Seamus as he scooted his way back from the precipice. Where in the hell was this voice coming from and how could he prepare, he wanted to scream back at the oracle, if he didn't know what was coming? He found a half-buried river rock that one of his relatives must have brought to the homesteader cemetery to place on a tombstone. It fit inside his palm. Listening, he tossed the rock into the hole. It splashed, just as he predicted it might but quicker than he thought, leading him to think that had they still been stuck in that cave, the water now would have been over their heads. In his head, he began to map the hydrological connections he couldn't see. If Sally-Sue and that BIC-stealing rat could reach the cavern beneath him from the cellar under the farmhouse, then a flooded cellar likely backed up through the same passage into the cave. Did that mean that when water wasn't in the pond, it was in the cellar, and vice versa? If so—he scratched the side of his head as he squinted his eyes to focus his long-distance vision in the direction of the pond—then maybe the earthquakes had acted like a geological elevator. Gradually building or lowering underground pressures could raise and lower the ground water to spill into different interbeds or bands of rocks and sediment so that these pressures functioned like valves redirecting and cutting off the flow to and from an aquifer. The remnants of Harder Springs seemed to be playing a shell game on his scientific brain, shifting the localized body of water between the three chambers that he knew about, those being the cave under the cemetery, the cellar, and the pond. There were certainly others—maybe even across the highway—but he was betting that these three on his property were connected and had all once been part of Harder Springs.

He remembered something else he'd heard from a webinar he had attended during those pandemic lockdown months when he was working from his Kennewick townhouse. One of the webinar's speakers had been a National Parks employee from Haida Gwaii off the northern coast of British Columbia. *Gladstone*. Seamus remembered the guy's last name—the perfect nickname for a happy-go-lucky-rockhound like himself. Gladstone spoke about a natural thermal pool tucked in the rock formation just above the Pacific tideline—it had been used for centuries by the Haida People as a gathering and healing center. After a nearby 7.8 magnitude earthquake struck in 2012, the hot springs completely dried up and didn't replenish; its water source believed to have been geologically cut off. The theory, as Seamus recalled, was that the earth shaking must have caused the holes in porous rocks to dilate and take in more water, which in turn dropped the water table. But six or seven years later, the thermal water was suddenly back in the pools. This suggested that the pressure had gradually increased to raise the water level back to its historic levels.

Whether something like that was happening beneath him now, Seamus was not sure. But some kink in the plumbing was introducing ground water through the passage or the floor of the cavernous void below.

Seamus backed out of the cemetery, closing the gate. He pulled himself up and onto the tractor seat where he could see further and think better. He took the underground plumbing theory a fair stretch further. Perhaps the big sister he'd never known hadn't died because she couldn't make her way back to the cellar through the passage, but because she had drowned in the cavern during a sudden and heavy rainstorm. He would never know the truth of course because he had no date or even a time of the year when she'd gone missing. He doubted if local climatology records even went back as far as the 60s, especially for an area as rural and unpopulated as the Quinlan homestead was. It just seemed to Seamus that if Sally-Sue and even the search dog had been able to get through the passage, she should have crawled back home the same way, unless the water table rose so fast it obscured or blocked her way out. Seamus had no recollection of the cellar ever flooding during his childhood. Yet, his father must have known it was possible—otherwise, why would he have blown air into the ziplock bag with the note, before stashing it on a shelf between the peaches under the hatch in the pantry floor? Seamus realized that with climate change and increased seismic activity, the cellar might have only recently started taking on water. If it had been a regular or even a seasonal event, an ancestor would likely have relocated the cellar—if not the whole farmhouse—to some other drier or higher location. Gerald Quinlan, on the other hand, couldn't care and couldn't be bothered. He hadn't even told his son the water taps had gone dry.

As Seamus perched there on the tractor, a dusty wind mussing his hair, his brain—or maybe it was his heart—ushered him back into his sentimental funk. It had been Cody's butt after all, that had been the last to sit where he was sitting. Seamus started the tractor on his first try, and decided to lock up the farmhouse and scoot back to town where he had his own clothes, computers, and a damn better internet connection. He'd even head back into work early the next morning to start reaching out to some of his hydro-geologist colleagues. If he were lucky, he might also get an update on Cody's condition and invent some way for the two of them to connect again.

The mechanic unbuttoned the top half of his greasy coveralls and tied the sleeves at his sweaty waist. The tin-sided truck garage off East Hillsboro Street became a convection oven this time of year. He couldn't drink enough of his home-spiked lemonade or gather enough oscillating fans to make even a quarter-degree difference in the indoor temperature. Opening the three garage doors only made matters hellishly worse—they all faced west, which is where the sun seemed to stall for what he called the "unbearable hours." He'd brainwashed himself into believing it was cooler in the grease pits under the truck bays, and so he'd shift any undercarriage work to mid-afternoon so that it could be completed after his lunch break which he usually wasted up the street feeding tokens into a booth at Elmo's because they had AC and he could sometimes score a ten or twenty off horny truckers. At the very least he could toot some Tina behind the curtain before weaving his way back to the roaster of a truck mechanic shop he owned and operated, called PJ's Lugnutz.

At five-foot-eight and maybe a hundred and forty-five pounds,

Paul Jacobs—or PJ as he was known by—wasn't much to look at. He was just a second-rate truck mechanic with a nasty meth addiction and a cellphone he'd recently pocketed but couldn't manage to unlock, yet.

Morning. Soap-shaving of a moon.
Sky and lagoon nacreous.
Sr. Ortega y Gasset
Stands reed-still
Examining the muck and weeds
For a metaphysical flash—
The meat of things.

Feathered white snake,
The Beautiful incarnate.
Head poised like a javelin.
Or hunched back on his feathers
Like a scholar
Studying an ancient text.

Even when he stalks
He does not move.
He turns the pages of water
Imperceptibly.

While around him,
His noisy students, the gulls,
Who have watched
Too much TV
And gobbled excessive junk food
Can't sit still or concentrate.

They thwack and yawp around his desk,
Complaining about heavy assignments.
They do not understand poetry
Or philosophy. They threaten
To tell their parents
And the School Board
That Professor Egret
Is a martinet.

He closes the lesson
With a firm and irritable croak
And slams the door.
His exit is a marginal note
On Aesthetics and the Real.

Disciplined, economic,
Proving less is more,
He gathers the sky and moon
In his monkish sleeves
And makes his leave-taking
A metaphor.

—William Witherup

CHAPTER NINE

SEAMUS WAS WORN OUT, and it wasn't even noon. He had been graciously accepting nonstop condolences for the passing of his father—which was made a bigger deal than it needed to be since Gerald had also been a HEW employee and longstanding union member.

Seamus was pretty sure that since arriving to work at the Pacific Northwest National Laboratory a little before 8 a.m. that morning, he'd told the story of his subterranean escapade at least once every fifteen minutes. Organically congregating groups of DOE employees and contractors would drift up to his corner cubicle like tides pulled by a full moon. Half of them also knew Cody Getz professionally, given the dam's proximity to Hanford. Toward the end of the recap, Seamus would always hold up his shattered cellphone that the two men had landed on top of, like this was show-and-tell in elementary school all over again and that broken phone was his fossilized fragment of an ancient shark's tooth.

His boss, Jenna, had been the most impersonal encounter of all. After welcoming him back in a tone that made Seamus wonder if he should be submitting a plan to put in overtime to make up for the work hours he'd missed while burying his dad and nearly dying himself, she directed him to drop whatever else he had been working on (which frankly hadn't been much with all the morning's watercooler catch-up). Citing orders from high-up, she directed him to re-prioritize his workload to urgently convene the joint disaster-planning workgroup—the one between Hanford, the Tri-City municipalities, and the Grant County Public Utility District, which owned and operated both the Priest Rapids and the further upstream Wanapum dams. Before the latest tunnel cave-ins and the uptick in measurable seismic activity, she'd maybe mentioned this to him once before, like a spot of housekeeping he might pick up and dust off in his spare time if he felt like it. She tried to blame this new urgency on political pressures, insisting it wasn't coming from her. What with the tunnel collapses and earthquakes and attention on Chernobyl since the Russian invasion of Ukraine, she said, tensions were ratcheting higher. Seamus felt the same way, but he didn't say so. He also felt this may have been a ruse to get him to stop poking around for buried plutonium buttons that shouldn't concern him but did. He didn't mention this either.

As she turned from his cubicle to walk away, he was afraid his response to the re-prioritized disaster-planning assignment may have sounded overenthusiastic. It's just that this would provide an opportunity to professionally collaborate with Mr. Getz from Priest Rapids—and as soon as possible, too, now that Jenna had formally stamped the task as urgent. He decided to follow up with something snider to remind her who she was supposedly managing.

"Say, Jenna, did that second tunnel collapse get filled in, too?"

She looked back over a shoulder. "Yes. That spot was stabilized over the weekend."

Seamus waited a beat. "Doesn't pouring dirt into these tunnels render the tunnels obsolete, you know, as storage that was designed and touted to be temporary only until the train equipment could be removed, scrubbed, and permanently disposed?"

She gave him a curt, pained smile. "You geologists ask too many questions," she said, and continued walking away.

Seamus didn't understand the generalization of those in his profession nor the outright dismissal of his question—but he had expected it. He was certain he was the only geologist she knew—he was the only rock and sediment expert on payroll. He'd made his point, and her response had only confirmed what he'd suspected.

DOE did not plan to remove the hot train locomotives, box cars, and other heavy equipment that had been used to transport irradiated fuel between the B Reactor and the PUREX plant where the critical chemical separation process occurred. Everything they knew they couldn't clean-up or talk some other jurisdiction into taking off their hands had been shoved into the two concrete tunnels and covered over with a few meters of dirt—out of sight, out of mind. Now that the tunnels were beginning to crumble, DOE's infamous on-the-spot decision making had rendered any future removal of the equipment using the buried rail lines, completely obsolete. Dumping fill into the tunnels meant the tracks could never be used again—and now Seamus knew that dirty secret too. The largest superfund clean-up in US History was nothing more— had never been anything more—than a modern-day busy work and public relations mending project.

He still wondered about the even larger quake that had shaken the region on Monday, while he and Cody were still underground. He put on his telephone headset, meant as much to signal to his colleagues that he was busy as it was to cancel out the other noises that came from working in an open office concept. That was another ridiculous ruse—open offices—in a facility rated TOP SECRET. Seamus shook his head as he dialed the Pacific Northwest Seismic Network.

"Hi there, Marcia. It's Seamus out at Hanford."

"Hey, Mr. Celebrity!"

Seamus chuckled. "I escaped the hole but not the publicity, it seems."

"I can't even imagine," she said, "and on top of losing your dad—"

He had started making light of the situation, unsure why he was converting his grief to stand-up. "Technically, I didn't lose my dad. He went down the hole with us. He was there the whole time."

"Oh, you know what I meant!" she scolded.

"Thank you," he answered a bit more genuinely. "Is Jeremy around?"

"He is," she answered, but sounded tentative. "He's in a briefing meeting, but I know he'll want to talk with you. Can you hold on while I slip him a note?"

"I can call back or he can phone me."

"Don't be silly. Hold on." And the phone made a click that placed him on hold, subjected to PNSN's tongue-in-cheek Muzak. Seamus knew the setlist well. It started with Elvis Presley's "All Shook Up," followed by Tori Amos with "Little Earthquakes." Then, depending on how long the wait time was, he might get a few bars of Bill Haley's version of Big Joe Turner's classic, "Shake, Rattle and Roll."

The Muzak stopped and Seamus was suddenly being fêted with hoots and applause by colleagues that must have been sitting around a board table on speaker phone in the UW Earth and Space Sciences building. It took a minute for the noise to settle and for Jeremy to speak for everyone.

"Welcome back, Shay! I think you probably know half the folks around the table here, but everyone sure knows about you, now. Tell us—will your life above ground ever feel normal again?"

"Good question," Seamus said without answering. "Thank you, everybody. I didn't mean to barge into your briefing."

"No, no," Jeremy protested. "It's good timing. We were just reviewing the week's seismicity. You had a notable out by you on Monday that came in at 3.4 mag."

"Okay, so that was the measurement, was it?" Seamus asked, taking note, since that had been the reason for his call in the first place. "We felt it underground, but I didn't have a cell signal to get the alert or see the mag registered on the MyShake app. It felt stronger than the temblors we'd been having at Hanford in the weeks leading up—I guess it's good to know I can still tell the difference between magnitudes. Can you tell me the epi on that one?"

The response came from someone whose voice Seamus didn't recognize. "The epicenter was in the Wallula Fault Zone, Seamus—same as the small clusters you guys would have felt at Hanford a week or two ago."

Seamus considered the proximity to Pasco, and since he was on the phone with the most preeminent panel of seismologists on the planet, he asked if there were any theories around what this activity might be building up to, if anything.

Jeremy fielded the question. "See what I mean about the good timing of your call? We were just discussing the regular flutter along the Cascades—particularly around St. Helens, Rainier, The Sisters, and Hood. You know, our active volcanoes. But I've been noticing—and somebody else can crunch data here—seismic blips have been increasing east of the Cascades in numbers I don't recall seeing before. Anybody else?"

"Seamus, hi there. It's Rhonda Tolstoy. I'm the new dean of the College of the Environment at UW. Full disclosure—I'm a marine biologist." Seamus heard some paper shuffling before she continued. "As I'm certain you already know, climate change and sea level rise will increase the severity of earthquake-triggered tsunamis in the future. Modeling data out of Virginia Tech predicts that in the future 'smaller' tsunamis will carry the same impact of what we consider a large tsunami today—like the ones we saw devastate northern Japan in 2011 and the Sumatra event in 2004. With even a foot of sea-level rise, future tsunamis will send catastrophic floods much further inland than previously thought. Now, you might be thinking that tsunamis don't pose a threat to Hanford but I'm here to tell you that the added weight of the water that tsunamis push onto land could be accelerating the subduction. Particularly so on our side of the Cascadia Subduction Zone, a small or moderate tsunami in the future *could* light up our fault lines like an electrical grid and that's on both sides of the Cascades."

There was a pause. Seamus thought Rhonda might have misspoken when she said *subduction* rather than *subsidence* when referring to the water weight of tsunamis on land. He also might not have been the only one wondering what tsunamis had to do with the question he'd asked about the increasing seismic activity in the Tri-Cities region.

Jeremy tried to bring the discussion back. "Thanks, Rhonda. You know as well as I do, Seamus, that temporary increases and decreases in seismicity is just par for the course when it comes to the fluctuation of earthquake rates. That being said, our records show that in the past forty or fifty years, the Pacific Northwest has exceeded the long-term average number of major earthquakes—not once, but at least a dozen times."

"And that's what makes the Wallula Fault Zone activity so

intriguing for me," Seamus interjected. "Rhonda, your explanation around the weight of water on the land brings up an interesting correlation for me. I don't want to take up your briefing time here, but I'd be interested in popping over to have a longer discussion about this one of these days."

There was some chatter and other noise before Jeremy encouraged Seamus to expand with his correlation.

"Happy to oblige," Seamus said. "Does everybody know the geological significance of the Wallula Gap?"

"I don't," Rhonda admitted.

"Carry on, Professor Quinlan," Jeremy urged.

"The Wallula Gap is the natural pinch point of the entire Columbia River system," Seamus said. "It was formed about 17 million years ago during the Miocene Epoch, when molten lava was rising from the earth's core and came into explosive contact with ground water and freshwater lakes. This caused a series of fissures to open in the earth's crust, emitting these colossal lava flows over the landscape in a region we today know stretched from Hells Canyon all the way to the Oregon Coast. Over millions of years, lava layers built up on top of other lava layers, then warped and folded under powerful stresses happening deep in the crust. This created a narrow water course between two steep basalt lava cliffs—that's what we call the Wallula Gap. It is located about thirty-five miles from my office here at Hanford. Between six and seventeen million years ago, in the final throes of the last Ice Age, giant ice dams built up around Missoula, holding back water." Seamus paused and took a breath. "Someone stop me if you know this."

Jeremy said, "No, go on, Shay."

"These dams would eventually break, releasing an inland sea that scoured these scablands on the mudflow's path to the Pacific Ocean. And geological evidence teaches us that this didn't just happen once. It occurred, like, a hundred times. And during each event, logs, rocks, and other debris would get picked up by the floods, then clog up at Wallula, back-flooding everything to create this massive temporary lake that had a volume of something like 1,600 square kilometers. We geologists today refer to it as Lake Lewis, thinking it maybe lasted a few weeks to a month before draining away. If Lake Lewis existed today, it would submerge the Tri-Cities and Hanford under five hundred feet of water." Seamus knew he tended to get too textbook, so decided to shortcut the lecture. "Just an aside for any history buffs—Lewis and Clark first spotted Wallula Gap in October 1805, wrote about it in their journals, and camped nearby before passing through it the next day. That's how Lake Lewis got its name—even though the lake was long gone by the time Meriwether got there."

"Fascinating." Seamus recognized this as Rhonda's voice, presuming she was likely the only woman around the table. "The Columbia River today has a couple hundred of these Wallulas, doesn't it?"

Seamus always became excited when any of his students indicated they were paying attention. "If you are referring to the more than 250 hydro-electric dams holding back reservoirs in the Columbia River Basin, you're exactly right. Just a few miles downstream from the Wallula Gap and since around 1957, the McNary Dam has been holding back the Columbia River much more effectively than a debris jam ever could. The reservoir behind this dam nearly reaches the Tri-Cities and raises the water level all the way to the Ice Harbor dam on the Snake River. My point—and you may have wondered if I'd ever get here—is that we absolutely need to consider the water-weight impact that all these dams and reservoirs have had on Pacific Northwest geology and seismology. Rhonda is right to consider the weight of added water on the land. Wasn't it NASA that calculated the water held back by the Three Gorges Dam in China had slowed the earth's rotation by something like .06 milliseconds? Multiply this by all the dams we've built in just the last one hundred years that have altered the freshwater hydrology and redistributed the weight of water on our planet, and I think you're looking at the single largest anthropogenic contribution to our own demise. That's all."

The ensuing silence led Seamus to wonder if he'd been disconnected—the equivalent of being given the shepherd's crook. His students, particularly after lunch, had a myriad of ways to communicate when his lectures had gone on too long or wandered too far off the syllabus. Seamus heard a pen tapping on the other end of the line, and then Jeremy piped up.

"Well, that gives us something cheery to chew on. Thank you, Seamus. And speaking for all of us, we are grateful you found your way out of the abyss. If anyone needs Seamus's contact information, I can drop you his digital business card. That's all the time we have. Enjoy your lunches, everyone. Seamus, keep in touch."

Seamus was about to thank everyone for letting him crash their briefing, when the line clicked, and the call was terminated. He removed his headset and stretched his tender ribcage with a long lean backward in his desk chair. *Mag 3.4 on the Wallula Gap Fault Zone,* he jotted down in the margin of his notepad, and then circled it. He was hungry and beginning to get his regular groove and appetite back. There was an L-shaped strip-mall in West Richland, just outside the Hanford gates, with a turquoise-trimmed but otherwise nondescript Mexican restaurant called Rodrigo's, which served this creamy green chili chicken soup that they advertised as "New Mexican Penicillin." Seamus wasn't sick or looking for medicine, but he could use the fresh air and a change of scenery.

He got stopped, congratulated, even spontaneously hugged a few times before reaching his pickup in the parking lot. Once he was underway and heading offsite, other drivers, recognizing his boxy, thirty-six-year-old rig—honked as they passed him going in the opposite direction. Seamus had never felt such comradery at Hanford. It embarrassed him a little to be in the spotlight. He had always been content to be an under-the-radar sort of guy—except when he was lecturing about something he was passionate about, like rocks. At those times, he hogged the attention—in the spirit of advancing science, of course.

His favorite audiences to convert to his way of seeing things, were those who felt they lived in or were passing through a drab, uninteresting part of the world. Seamus loved adding technicolor to these blank, scabland canvases. Which reminded him: didn't he have a public lecture night coming up at CWU? He would need to check the calendar on his phone, but he'd need to get the shattered screen fixed first, since he couldn't make out much of anything behind the broken glass. He waited for an opening in traffic before hanging a left on University Drive. For a split second, his stomach was tempted by the Shogun Teriyaki and Sushi sign, but he forged on a few storefronts further to park in front of Rodrigo's.

He had never noticed before, but one of those storefronts, as blind luck would have it, was a cellphone repair and unlocking outfit called EZ Fix. Risking that Rodrigo's could, as they often did, run out of their green chili chicken soup before he'd placed his order, he couldn't pass up the opportunity to tackle two things at once—and on company time. He opened the glass door to EZ Fix just as a shorter fellow wearing aviator sunglasses was heading out of the store. They locked eyes briefly as Seamus held the door open wide. The face he thought he might have recognized passed under his extended arm, mumbling, "Thanks, man." Seamus thought the guy might have recognized him, too—statistically quite possible, given that something like 9,000 people worked at Hanford. He casually watched from inside the store to see if the guy's vehicle would jog his memory—but the guy was a passenger, and he climbed inside an older model sedan being driven by somebody else.

"What can I do you for?" the dark-skinned clerk asked. Seamus turned and held up the phone. The clerk studied it. "That an iPhone 12?"

Seamus nodded. "I think so."

"Twenty minutes, tops?"

"Wow, that fast? I'll be next door at Rodrigo's. I'll swing back by afterward?"

"I can probably do it in half that time," said the clerk. "I unlocked the previous customer's phone in eight minutes, but just to be safe." Seamus concluded he must be of East Indian descent.

"Do you need a password to get in?"

"I do not need a password. I could get in if I had to, but I am just changing the screen, right?"

"Right," Seamus said. "I'll be back soon."

Walking into Rodrigo's, Seamus had the impression that somebody had cued a waiting mariachi band, but it was just the new recorded entry bell he must have tripped walking through the front door. Rodrigo hollered from the kitchen window, "Hey, *mira*! It's da Cave Man!" Seamus raised his right hand sheepishly. "*Guao, guao, guao*," the owner of the establishment was chanting as he walked up to the counter. "*Dígame*, is dis your first meal after da big rescue? I make someting special for celebrities! Today's lunch is on *la casa*! Rodrigo insist!"

Seamus laughed. "I don't think I am a celebrity—really, I am only here for the creamy green chile chicken soup."

"*Claro, claro*! Take a seat, *señor*. I make it extra special for you today."

Ten minutes later, Seamus's comfort food was delivered piping hot in a crock the size of a small kitchen sink with a heaped basket of chips and guac on the side. The cook—who was also the waiter and proprietor—plopped down in the booth sitting across from him.

"*Dígame*, what was it like being buried alive, hombre?"

Seamus knew he would be relating this tale for several more days, maybe weeks, before the fascination died down. He wondered if Cody was facing a similar grilling by his circle and how their harrowing stories of the same experience matched up. The soup was too hot to eat right away, so Seamus dragged out some of the more interesting details of the ordeal, since Rodrigo's brown eyes had grown to the size of silver dollars.

"*Dios mio*, Hombre!" Rodrigo said when Seamus was done. "Dis story calls for a margarita! Can you?"

"*Por favor*, but better make it a single, Rodrigo. I have celebrated enough co-worker birthdays to know that your margaritas are killers, and I've already escaped death once this month."

"*Ja ja*—funny, man! Be right back."

◆

Seamus still felt the margarita as he slowed his Ford when approaching the checkpoint gate. The DOE decal on the windshield seemed to magically lift the security arm, though he knew he had been recognized by Sammy, a thirty-year security employee who remembered working alongside Seamus's dad, grandfather, and uncles.

His cellphone had a sleek new screen, free of fingerprints. It began vibrating. Seamus looked down as he was pulling into his parking spot. When he saw that the incoming call was from Cody Getz, his heart jumped out of the blocks and began sprinting.

"Seamus here," he answered with a smile that was probably detectable despite his serious government voice. There was a pause of dead air and then the call ended. "NO!" Seamus yelled, hitting the steering wheel with an open hand. He'd waited ten days for an update or a reunion with his new, old, special friend—the one with whom he'd wiggled free from the grip of certain death.

He waited in his truck despite the early August heat to see if there would be a voice message. When there wasn't, he called back. The phone rang three times before someone answered without saying anything.

"Hey there, buddy," Seamus said, rushing right in there like a running back. "You found your cellphone!" There were a few muffled sounds he couldn't place, and then the call went dead again.

Seamus wondered if Cody's wife had answered the phone, after seeing who Cody might have called. He didn't know much about Angela Getz except what Cody had shared. He didn't know if she was the jealous type or if she'd be compelled to verify details of what was already a very public story. She'd been at the cemetery when the two of them were hauled out of the hole. It seemed logical to Seamus that she would have recognized and picked up Cody's cellphone if she saw it laying on the ground. But whatever her reason for not speaking with him now, it looked like he'd have to keep waiting for the reunion he couldn't help thinking about.

Back in his cubicle with a cup of stale cafeteria coffee, Seamus woke up his array of computers screens with a thumb print pressed on the security reader. He checked his calendar and gulped—he had less than two weeks to pull his next CWU lecture together. That was tight. He'd need to check on his collaborators at UC Santa Cruz and the Ice Age Floods Institute to see if they could get him something; he'd be happy with even a draft of the computer simulation that he and their teams had been developing for longer than he could recall. His lecture audiences needed something more than a PowerPoint with graphed timelines and photos of sediment gradients. They needed Hollywood action and sound effects—it was the only way to get their heads out of their phones, and to get them to start paying attention. He pecked out a quick email to the team hoping to dial up the pressure for a quicker delivery.

It wasn't long before his thoughts returned to Cody—his mind wasn't capable of wandering far from the subject of this sudden fixation anymore—and then he couldn't concentrate on work. He preferred to be in the field, rock-hounding, but at least he was good at faking office work. He donned the headset—his most convincing prop—and brought up the direct administration line to Priest Rapids Dam. He waited for the call to connect. He was looking for someone to give him an update on Cody's leg, and maybe an expected return-to-work date. He wasn't about to convene the multi-party emergency planning table without Cody, no matter how much Jenna harped on him. He understood her call for urgency—especially given what Cody had described as the dangerous state of disrepair at Priest Rapids Dam. And after having received what he took as two very ominous warnings from the pipe at the pond and then from the flooded void beneath the cemetery, to prepare for whatever was coming, Seamus was officially on edge.

"Priest Rapids Dam, Oris Barber here."

"Hey, Oris. It's Seamus Quinlan with DOE, over at Hanford." Seamus wasn't sure he'd met an *Oris* before. He wanted to think that was a name he wouldn't forget.

"What can I do for you ... *Seamus*, was it?"

"Yes. Look, I don't suppose you could give me an update on Cody Getz's condition and when you think he might be returning to work, could you?" Seamus had scrunched up his whole face and forehead as he framed his question—afraid the report might be worse than he imagined. But, as if he were a hot potato, Oris put him straight through to HR without explanation.

"PRHR, Julie speaking."

"Say, Julie. It's Seamus Quinlan with DOE over at Hanford. I was looking to see if I could get an update on Cody Getz." Seamus bit his lower lip and held it in his teeth, waiting to be passed off or have his inquiry shut down a second time. Now that he had been transferred to human resources, he fully expected he'd run up against some employee privacy policy.

"Oh—hey, there. You're that fellow that fell into that cave with Cody. I recognize your name." She sounded like she was gushing.

Time for a charm offensive. Seamus straightened his posture and scooted closer to his desk. "Guilty as charged," he said. "Listen—I know this may seem to cross professional boundaries, but Cody and I are supposed to be working together to revamp the joint emergency planning between Hanford and the Priest Rapids and Wanapum dams—"

"Say no more," she interrupted. "Do you need his cellphone number, his email address? How can I help?"

Seamus smiled. "No, I have his cell number and email, but thank you. You might not know this, but he lost his cellphone during the rescue operation, so I haven't been able to reach him to find out how his leg is doing and to see when he thinks he might be cleared to go back to work—you know, so we can get going on that joint emergency planning exercise."

"Right." Seamus couldn't discern in her pause if she was buying his excuse for calling, but he did hear a door close. "This, of course, is confidential, but from what I've heard," she whispered, "he is still at Seattle Harborview. The surgeons there had to, you know, reconstruct his leg, or something major like that. His wife, Angela, is there with him. But as you probably know, she's not in great shape herself."

"Yes, I knew that," Seamus said, in a tone meant to encourage her to continue. She did.

"Cody had already banked a whack of sick time since he never missed work, so he's getting paid whether he's here or not."

"Right—so he hasn't given you a date he plans to return to the office?"

"I don't think he knows, yet. Plus, with his wife's sad situation, and this being summer and all … well, if I were him, I'd take my sweet time rushing back to this concrete bunker." Her laugh seemed a bit carried away, given the delicacy of divulging personal information. She must have figured the two men were bonded for life—like brothers. Of course, he was thinking, she wouldn't be wrong about that.

"Harborview, you said?" he asked, even though he'd jotted it down.

"That's right—but apparently his room doesn't have one."

"Doesn't have one what?"

"A harbor view," she said. Now her laughter was rambunctious, if not obnoxious.

"You've been a great help. Thank you."

"Hey, you two nearly died," she said. "It's the least I ..." She paused and corrected herself, "It's my pleasure. Have a nice afternoon."

Seamus's fifty-six-year-old clumsy rock-hammered fingers were typing too fast—looking up the telephone number for Harborview Hospital before the woman in the HR department at Priest Rapids had even said goodbye. He'd gotten what he was after—a way to talk to Cody directly. Now to make the call, he decided, trying to tame the butterflies in his belly.

The phone rang and rang. Seamus wondered if the hospital had maybe not yet recovered from the pandemic with all its related staffing shortages. Coronavirus had only recently been downgraded from a pandemic to endemic and was really only still raging in certain undeveloped parts of the world. He was about to hang up and dial again when the call was answered.

"Hello," he said. "Can I please be transferred to the room of one of your patients? His name is Cody Getz. Last name spelled G-E-T-Z."

"That's *Getz*, you said?"

"Correct."

"It looks like there is a DND order ... sorry, that's *Do Not Disturb*. Either the family or the doctor has requested that this patient not receive calls or visitors while he recovers."

Seamus exhaled loudly in frustration. He was being blocked, and he suspected Angela was behind this so-called DND. "Could I speak to a nurse on his floor by any chance?"

"Transferring," the attendant said.

Once again, the phone rang and rang and rang. Seamus wondered if Cody could hear a phone ringing from his bed. "Nursing station, fourth floor east—Marcelo, here," answered a man with a high tenor voice and a delightfully lilting accent that Seamus couldn't immediately place.

"Yes, Marcelo, I am phoning to inquire about one of the patients on your floor. Last name, Getz, first name, Cody."

"Yes?" Marcelo seemed to be prompting Seamus for more information.

After a wordless pause, Seamus volunteered that he was a friend; that he was with him when the accident happened. Seamus closed his eyes. He could still see Cody falling, his body—particularly his legs—at the worst possible angle when he collided with the coffin.

"I see," Marcelo said. "The patient's wife has requested that there be no calls or visitors."

"Is Angela there? Could I speak with her, maybe?" Seamus hoped the use of Angela's name would demonstrate he was a family insider—not some random harasser.

"No, she is not," Marcelo said.

Seamus exhaled. Even if she'd been there, he didn't know what he'd have said to the woman whose husband he'd shared, and to whom he hadn't been formally introduced in the first place. By the time Seamus had been lifted out of the cavern, Angela and Cody had already been rushed away by the attending EMTs. That had not even been two weeks ago, though it felt to Seamus like months had passed already. "Marcelo, I know you must be really busy, but could I leave my name and telephone number with you, to give to Cody?"

"Yes, that I can do," the nurse said, sounding happy to have a solution.

Seamus patiently spelled and sounded out the twelve letters of his two names—names that could stump even the best spellers. He thanked the likely overworked, underpaid, and underappreciated nurse by name. And then it was back to waiting and clock-watching. To kill time, Seamus decided he'd drive out to 200 East, to check on the remediation progress being made on the latest tunnel collapse. He turned up the volume on his cellphone to make sure he didn't miss an incoming call, just in case his sweet-talking to Nurse Marcelo had resulted in the immediate delivery of his message.

Opening the door to his pickup that had only been sitting there closed up for less than thirty minutes, Seamus was hit by a wave of heat that smelled like a very hot margarita. He didn't think he was any longer feeling the effects of Rodrigo's mixology, but he must have sweated out a dose of it that lingered during the drive back to the office. He powered the windows down and slid open the rear window, though his phone said it was 111°F outside. He didn't want anyone smelling the cab of the truck and thinking Seamus Quinlan was just another Irish alcoholic. He was all about busting clichés when he could.

Driving past the tank farms for the first time since learning that his father had helped convert the buried, single-lined storage tanks into colanders, Seamus felt real shame. In his decades working at Hanford, he'd cloaked himself in pride for his role in assisting the cleanup. He had felt a similar pride for his family's lineage that had churned out nearly a dozen HEW employees since the 40s. But all of this was being called into question with the bombshell details in his father's letter. Great Uncle Percy and Pops had only been doing what they were told, and for the good of the country, Seamus chose to believe. He supposed he was no different. He was doing what he was told, too, more or less. The difference was that maybe Seamus knew better. That's where the shame snuck in.

What Seamus now knew about the storage tanks and The Green Run bothered him profoundly. It wasn't like he hadn't uncovered or heard about worse atrocities in the mishandling of contaminants at Hanford over the decades, but these two issues had directly involved members of his own family. In his experience, HEW was far better at managing its misinformation campaigns than it was at cleaning up the toxic site, but by the time the communications department had made everybody dizzy with their ready lists of impressive achievements, the damages had been done and there wasn't a damn thing the public could do with the truth or the fabricated version of it.

Seamus had recently re-read the declassified but still heavily redacted 1997 Nuclear Regulatory Commission's report on Hanford, which struck him as the internal rap sheet for all the crimes Hanford had perpetrated against humanity and countless other species during its 44-years of plutonium production. He was recalling that in its first three years of operation alone, Hanford freely spilled nearly seven-hundred-thousand curies of radioactive iodine-131directly into the Columbia River. That had been the standard operating procedure before they came up with the novel idea of burying their dirty secrets in tank farms, which publicists insist to this day, still contain most of the of 53 million gallons of highly radioactive madness; *most*. Seamus found that appalling and certainly false given his father's own involvement in converting containers into colanders. Whenever he thought about Hanford's recklessness, his face turned red with a rage that was now amplified by an embarrassment knowing he had family that had been directly involved. Putting the truck in park and shutting off the engine, he scanned the length and breadth of 200 Area where the worst of the worst contaminants were off cast from the PUREX building currently a hive of heavy machinery as it was finally being dismantled. Beneath the building on both sides were the train tunnels and the tank farms. He knew that of the 177 tanks still buried beneath him, 149 were the original single-shell storage tanks. Many of these, he could now assume, carried the scars of his own father's blowtorch handiwork. As long as he'd been working at HEW, and even before his father's written confession, Seamus had known the tanks were leaking, some up to 300 gallons each year. It's only now that he knew they had been leaking *by design*, and almost from the moment they were filled. During production years when the levels in the tanks dropped, they just got topped back up—storage capacity being so scarce. given that something like 75,000 gallons per minute had been drawn from the Columbia River to cool the reactors. Once used, the water was super heated and had high levels of radiation and couldn't be used again, so much of that wastewater was diverted to storage tanks or open-air retention ponds. This was only done for public relations sake, but the toxic soup was still making its way back into the river a short way downstream, through the ground water plumes and storm water runoff.

Seamus started the truck back up to get some air on his face. As he drove away from the demolition site, he was doing quick math in his head. If even half the tanks leaked 300 gallons a year—and he already knew that estimate was likely another PR distortion of the truth—that meant 27,000 gallons a year had been leaching into the environment annually. That was the equivalent of almost two-and-a-half Olympic-size swimming pools each year, so over the course of seventy-five years, that amounted to more than two million gallons of radioactive waste that had not been contained.

Whereas Pops and Great Uncle Percy had been complicit when following orders, it was Hanford's duplicitous from the start that jeopardized them all. Hell, he thought, slapping both hands on the steering wheel—he was complicit and being used too. His job was to sugar-coat the bitter, ironic truth that Hanford would never be cleaned up completely, no matter how many employee lifetimes or how many trillions of dollars got thrown at it.

He aimed the nose of his truck for the de-con tents still erected on the river side of the road. As he shifted into park, his cellphone began vibrating. He glanced at the screen. Cody Getz. His heart began racing. He answered—not saying his name or even *hello*, but launching right into conversation.

"Hey—I hear you don't have a view of the harbor there at Harborview Hospital. You should demand your money back!"

There was silence on the other end and then the call was disconnected.

"Shit!" Seamus yelled. "Shit, shit, shit!" That had been another call from the wife, or whoever had Cody's cellphone. Then, the phone vibrated again while it was still in his hand—but this time, the call display read *Harborview*.

"Seamus, here," he answered, sounding tucked-up professional.

"Seamus!" Cody said. "It's Cody. Lordy, am I ever glad to hear your voice."

"Cody—my god, man!"

"I know. Seems like forever, huh?"

In the chuckling pause, Seamus decided against telling Cody

about the hang-up calls he'd been receiving from his phone. He didn't want to ruin the moment as both men were content just to be in each other's company again. When they spoke next, it was over each other.

"No, you first," Seamus insisted. When he heard Cody's corny laugh, he grinned widely and his horseshoe moustache did the splits.

"So, I got to ride in a helicopter," Cody said. "That was a first. The pilot came in tight to the peak of Mount Rainier. I tell you, Shay, it was stunning—and good thing too, as I probably could never climb to the top with this bum leg of mine."

When others called him *Shay*, they seemed either lazy or like they were struggling with the pronunciation of his full name. But he liked the sound of it coming from Cody. "How is that leg?"

"Well, there are four steel rods sticking out of it like a giant shish kabob or something."

"Sounds yummy," Seamus said.

"You could have eaten my leg when you had the chance. No seconds for you, now."

They laughed.

"True that, I suppose," Seamus said. "Another twenty-four hours and there would have been no telling what we would have had to resort to, right?"

"I'm telling you—and I've had a lot of time to think about this—but those were the best seventy-two hours of my life. You know why?"

"Tell me," Seamus said, hoping it wouldn't get mushy.

"Because I never felt so alive as when I thought I might die." There was another silent pause on the phone. "You there?"

"Yeah," Seamus said. "Wow. I'm just processing what you said. It's true, right? Same for me, I guess. Not sure how we're going to top that now." He was looking for a way to make light of the heaviness.

"Yeah. Anyway, my tibia is set, but I have a steel rod where my fibula used to be."

"Sounds like Greek food to me," Seamus said. "How many stitches or staples or whatever they use these days?"

"Don't know. I can't really see how they did this, but I've got what is called an Ilizarov apparatus. It's supposed to reshape and lengthen whatever they did on the inside. The rods attach to four wheels that look like giant gears from an Erector Set. If I had my damn cellphone, I'd shoot you a picture."

Seamus felt now was as good a time as any to tell Cody that someone else had his cellphone. "Speaking of your cellphone—" he started.

"Don't tell me you found it!" Cody asked anxiously.

"Well, somebody did—and whoever has it, has phoned me twice now. They don't say anything, and they just hang up after I answer. I tried calling the number back but couldn't get anyone to talk to me. Maybe your wife has it? She would have recognized your phone if she saw it on the ground at the cemetery, right?"

Cody didn't answer at first. He was panicking instead of talking.

"Sure," he said, finally. "She would have recognized it, but she doesn't have it. I asked her if she saw it there, or if she knew if anyone else had picked it up—like a policeman or someone from the media. She was still a bit ragged from the ordeal, but she was crystal clear when she said, and I quote 'I don't know where your damn cellphone is or why you didn't use it to call me to tell me where you were.'"

Seamus let all the air in his lungs exit through the circle he'd made with his lips. He was problem-solving, so he breathed through his open mouth. "Right. So, somebody else has it."

"You need to help me figure out who and how we get my phone back. I'm telling you, Shay—that phone, with the stuff we recorded on there ... we just need to get it back."

"I hear ya. I am on this. I will straighten this out and get that phone back. Maybe one of the ambulance drivers picked it up. I'll make some calls and see if I can track it down. I was only waiting because I thought, you know ... maybe Angela was holding on to it for you. Since she put a block on any telephone calls or visitors coming into your hospital room, I figured maybe she was just protecting you."

"What?" Cody asked, sounding confused. "She put a block on my calls?"

"Well ... yeah. That's what I was told by the switchboard operator when I tried calling."

Cody made an exasperated sound. "All I've wanted since I got here—besides more pain meds—was to hear from you and have, you know, a chance to explain myself and apologize for that kiss and going all *Brokebacky* on you in the cave."

"Ah," Seamus said. "Don't give that kiss a second thought. We were both caught up in that moment, and I can't deny sort of kissing you back. Mind you, I was in shock and traumatized and you know, every other excuse I might come up with. It's not like you spit in your hand and violated me."

"Yeah, like that was going to happen," Cody exclaimed, maybe trying to sound like it was the furthest thought from his mind.

There was more laughter—the kind that happens spontaneously between very old friends. Seamus made Cody promise to phone him anytime he felt like it, and as often as he wanted. "Hey, and if you need anything—besides your cellphone—I am just a couple hours and Snoqualmie Pass away. Just say when, and I'm on my way."

Seamus was sincere about the offer—and then, to his delight, Cody wasted no time taking him up on it.

"Well, Angie and I haven't quite figured out how we are going to get back home in another week when I get sprung from here and she wraps up her treatments at Fred Hutch. Neither one of us will be in any shape to drive—but if that's a big ask to be putting on you, no pressure." Cody paused, and Seamus bet he was biting his bottom lip, like he'd seen Cody do in the cave every time he proposed something or asked a question.

Seamus nearly jumped through the phone in response. "Man, that's the least I could do for you. Just tell me when." Sure, they'd have Angela along as a third wheel. But he felt indebted to Cody for the trouble he'd gone through just to check on him after Pops had passed. Plus, he liked and missed the blond cowboy's company.

"I probably won't get to call shotgun, with this leg needing to be elevated and stabilized. But just being in the same cramped space and breathing the same rank air again would lift my spirits to the clouds," Cody confessed. "You'll probably need to stop near Vantage to switch out your truck for our RAV4," Cody added. "But we can work the details out next week—if you're sure you can get away."

"Absolutely, Cody. Absolutely."

Seamus could hear other voices in the hospital room. "Ah, Doc's here," Cody said. "Gotta scoot and see if I can get this prison sentence commuted on good behavior. I'll call you soon, Shay."

"You do that," Seamus replied, and they hung up. Seamus sat there sweating in the cab of his F-150. This was a big day, he realized. He had reconnected with Cody and now felt truly connected, like they had been in the hole.

Meanwhile, Cody exchanged pleasantries with the surgical team that had stopped by to ratchet his contraption a notch tighter. Despite his discomfort in the torture device on his leg, he felt nothing but joy and relief, and well—confusion and conflict. He recognized he was a jumble of not necessarily compatible emotions. His wife of thirty-four years was across town undergoing a battery of tests and treatments they both knew wouldn't save her life, and yet, he was already pole-vaulting to whatever could potentially come next for him. He hadn't always been the best husband and partner, but he was always a decent and genuinely caring friend since high school who still had her back and would stand by her side until the end. He knew he could be a better man but the man he was pretending to be wasn't working out so well. Looking his own mortality in the face at the bottom of that inescapable hole in the ground had changed him and scared him—well, not so straight.

He didn't fully let on during the call, but that missing cellphone was bugging him something fierce. The moment he had his east-facing room back to himself, he dialed his own cell number. He'd prepared words for whoever answered, but the call just went to voicemail.

Eros and Logos were one to her;
A passion for truth in men.
Her love bites grated on bone.

She left me for love of Nietzsche:
Found men merely mortal;
Went through us all

Like fire in dry chapparal.
An ember smoldered in her womb,
Fed by sexual oils—

Blazed out in the toss
Of her hair. There was
Conflagration everywhere.

Nor am I done with her:
She waits for me
At the top of the stair

Her fevers
Crystallized into the horn
Of 8,000 hungers.

—William Witherup

CHAPTER TEN

ANGELA TWISTED SHORT STRANDS of her black-and-gray hair in her finger as she sat in the front passenger seat of her own car. She was not thrilled by the driving arrangement, but that didn't mean she wasn't also grateful. The Getzes had to get back home from Seattle one way or another, and she couldn't drive in her diminished condition. She was exhausted by her long-running ordeal—the stem-cell transfusion in February had drained her, literally and figuratively, along with every test and alternative therapy she'd undergone since. Grateful for the chauffeur she was just hard-pressed to telegraph gratitude or show she even had a smidgeon of will left to live. She had never been one to fake anything, and it seemed pointless to begin now.

When her husband went missing and she'd learned where his mysterious weekend drives had been taking him, it sort of signaled for her the beginning of the end—not of their marriage which she'd long suspected was one of convenience and companionship, but of the sands left in her hourglass. She'd hoped that her mother would precede her in death, as that seemed the proper order of things—but now that the older woman's Alzheimer's had progressed to an almost enviable stage in which she remembered nothing and no one, Angela knew that she could go without being missed or long mourned. The simple, kind, and secretive man she'd been married to for thirty-four years would be emancipated by her final gesture. While she was a very fair measure angry enough with him for his low-grade betrayal, she lacked the gumption for mounting any equal measure of vengeance.

As for the tall, sage- and musk-scented stranger driving her car, she was sure he must be one of her husband's weekend lovers. Maybe the main one. He was handsome enough—and, like Cody, devilishly subtle in his patience for her to get the hell out of their way. He'd tried to make conversation, smooth-talking like a missionary all the way up Snoqualmie Pass, as if his hot air would get their balloon over the mountain. But she hadn't been very friendly or responsive. His boyfriend, sprawled across the back seat on a raft of pillows, wasn't any better, but high as a satellite on painkillers. Her ears popped with the loss of elevation around Elk Heights—always the halfway point for these Seattle jaunts. She'd be home and done with this charade in an hour, she thought. If she slept, it would go by even faster, and that was something she wouldn't have to fake either.

⬥

Seamus thought that he'd received at least two texts, given the vibrations he'd felt in his front blue jeans pocket. Normally, nobody texted him and vice versa. With his big fingers at the end of meaty hands, he'd spent a lifetime handling picks and chisels that chipped away at rocks and sediment, developing a type of wear-and-tear arthritis that had to be unique to geologists but also an impediment to texters. Curiosity got the best of him, and by the time the giant spinning wind turbines came into view a mile or two before the exit to the Indian John Hill Rest Area, his bladder had given him a second reason to pull off I-90 for a rest stop. Since both his passengers were asleep, he also hoped the opening and shutting of the car door would rouse them so they could help with the final navigation, the closer they got to the Getz farm. Seamus had found it okay on his own, heading from the other direction to switch his rig for theirs, since the latter was better suited for the transport of patients. But going back, he was sure to miss the driveway or the signposts without guidance.

"Pit stop," he announced, putting the RAV4 into park. "I can leave the car and AC running, unless others need the facilities too."

"I'm fine until we're home," Angie said. "It's only another fifteen miles from here."

Cody perked up but didn't sit up. "I'm good until home, too. We'd be here all day if you tried getting me in and out of the car and into the john."

Seamus left the car running and waited until he was inside and peeing before he extracted his phone from his pocket. Two texts, just like he'd thought. The first was only an image, but it surprised and distracted Seamus so much that he momentarily sent his piss stream out of the urinal's stainless-steel bounds. The image was of a naked man with an erection, but his other head—the one that might have identified the proud model—had been cropped off. *Who in the hell?* Then he saw that the texts had both originated from Cody's cellphone. He scrolled down to the second message, which was in ALL CAPS:

> IF YOU DON'T WANT THIS PIC OF YOUR HUNG LITTLE BUDDY AND THE OTHERS THAT I FOUND IN HIS HIDDEN PHOTOS GETTING SENT TO HIS WIFE OR WORSE, EFT ME $500 BY MIDNIGHT TO NUTZO1969@HOTMAIL.COM.

Seamus scrolled back up to the picture. Was that really Cody? He didn't see anything that told him it wasn't. Did this mean he had more photos like this on his cellphone and this is why he had been so upset his phone may have fallen into other hands? Not knowing exactly what to do next and since he had until midnight to respond to the second text, he turned off his phone, stowed it back in his pocket, shook, zipped, and sauntered back to the running car.

As he got closer, Seamus had the impression that Angela and Cody were arguing—but if so, they stopped as soon as he opened the driver's door. The next fifteen miles were like driving a cloistered monastery on wheels—except for the "turn here" that Angela mumbled through the hand she'd held over her mouth for at least half that distance, to prevent herself from saying something she automatically knew she would regret.

But they arrived safely at the farm no worse for the awkward commute. After improvising a pillow-filled wheelbarrow for Cody—Harborview either hadn't thought to send the invalid home with a wheelchair, or the invalid had been too cheap to add one to his hospital bill—Seamus was in his own rig again, tooling down State Highway 243 along the Priest Rapids Lake Reservoir. When he was certain he was well out of sight of the Getz farm, he pulled into the *Volviendo a la Biblia Church* parking lot, empty but for a ratty old school bus, to respond to the texts he'd left unanswered.

> FINE. I WILL PAY YOU $1,000, BUT I WILL WANT THE CELLPHONE BACK FOR THAT PRICE OR NO DEAL!

That, he figured, should resolve the case of the missing cellphone real fast given these hard economic times. He hadn't needed to phone in the Hardy Boys or Nancy Drew, and he pulled back onto the highway feeling pretty good about that.

He'd received another two texts by the time he pulled into the double garage of his townhouse on West Klamath in Kennewick ninety minutes later. The first contained another naked picture, this time of Cody's unmistakeable, smooth white butt. The second read:

> NICE TRY. NO DEAL. NOW THAT I KNOW YOU CAN AFFORD $1,000, THE PRICE HAS GONE UP. YOU WANT THE PHONE BACK? IT WILL COST YOU $10,000. THAT'S FOUR ZEROS AND DON'T TRY TO LOWBALL ME AGAIN. FIRST BATCH OF PICS GET EMAILED TO YOUR BUDDY'S WIFE TOMORROW AT NOON IF $1000 ISN'T TRANSFERRED TO MY EMAIL ADDRESS BY THEN. NUTZO1969@HOTMAIL.COM.

Seamus sat in his truck until the automatic garage door had closed and the overhead light shut off, leaving him in the dark. He scrolled up to study both images. So far, the blackmailer probably hadn't come up with anything Angela Getz hadn't seen before. Still, Seamus felt duty-bound to Cody, but wanted to handle this privately if he could. He felt this was the honorable thing to do after Cody had risked his life for him—even if he hadn't known that was what he was signing up for. He just wanted to spare the two of them this indignity—especially at what was likely the end of Angela's life—so he needed to outsmart the scammer. His earlier attempt to negotiate with the thug had somehow gotten him another twelve hours on the clock. He needed to solve this by noon tomorrow. He'd sleep on it and hope he awoke with a plan.

Inside the three-bedroom, two-level townhome that he had already been thinking he should list with a realtor—since he now owned a farm—Seamus tossed his keys on the kitchen counter. He'd be lucky if he could get a quarter million for it, though he'd only paid one-eighty-five when he upgraded and acquired the place in 1997. He'd bought it because he'd grown tired of renting—or, more specifically, he'd grown tired of being lambasted by his father for throwing his money away, writing rent checks every month. Location had been what attracted him. The building was south of the canal but within a mile of the river and the Columbia Park Trail that ribboned for four miles beside it, and he'd been an avid runner back then. Now that he knew more about the crumbling state of Priest Rapids Dam and the truth leaching out beneath Hanford—and now that he wasn't running anymore—it was high time to sell.

He kicked off his boots and splashed down in his overstuffed chair, reaching in the side pocket for the TV remote. Getting rid of this Tri-City address might be the first step in heeding the warning he'd heard from the pipe at the farm pond, and again when he listened to the ground at the cemetery. *Pre-pare. Pre-pare.*

The incoming call beat Seamus's wakeup alarm by eleven minutes. The display indicated it was Angela—which sent Seamus's morning-fog brain into a panic, thinking there might be an emergency. But it turned out to be Cody. After saying good morning, he explained that his wife had turned her cellphone to him, since she saw no point in carrying one anymore. He was letting Seamus know that his follow-up surgery to remove the Ilizarov apparatus had been scheduled—just in case Seamus was looking for an excuse to travel back to Seattle. "Count on me, Cody," was all Seamus managed to say during the brief pre-coffee call, and after Cody had encouraged him to phone him anytime using this new number.

Seamus cautiously descended the carpeted stairs, pausing at the switchback landing to inhale the new day—he knew it was going to be a busy one. Fearing he might have sounded gruff with Cody, he sent a follow-up text to Angela's phone, confirming he would of course drive him to Seattle for the next surgery. He flicked on the espresso machine and drank OJ from the jug while the machine warmed up. He was relieved that Angie's cellphone was in Cody's hands, in case the blackmail photos began to fly. But he was still anxious about how to defuse the situation. What was at stake was more significant than a few naked selfies. The real trouble would come once the crook discovered the whistleblowing videos the two men had recorded, exposing Hanford and Priest Rapids for their catastrophic shortcomings. Seamus needed to get his hands on the cellphone before that happened—if he still wanted his job and if he wasn't too late already.

Over coffee, Seamus emailed Jenna Thomason to say he would be in the field for the day—not a lie, as he hoped to run up to the farm to snap some shots and video for the PowerPoint he needed to revise for his public presentation at CWU on Wednesday evening—just two days away. Only the day before did he receive via Dropbox a skookum new simulation video from his Santa Cruz collaborators that would amp up his presentation immensely. He next emailed his realtor with the news that he wished to unload the townhouse. Not quite five minutes after he'd sent it, she'd phoned to make an 11 a.m. appointment, to get the photos and other details she needed to build the listing. Lastly, before launching into a dervish of housecleaning, Seamus signed into his online banking and reluctantly made the arrangements to electronically transfer $1,000 to nutzo1969@hotmail.com. He knew that this transaction wouldn't be the end of the mess, but at least it was a starting pistol on what he hoped would be a sprint rather than a marathon. Just to jam up the works for the blackmailer and to prove his theory the thief had been someone on site at his farm the day of the rescue, Seamus had made *July 24, 2023,* the answer to the EFT's security question—what was the date you found the cellphone. This way, the moron would be forced to reveal the date last month when they found and pocketed Cody's cellphone—which would either place them at the scene of the rescue, or sometime later. Seamus had already created a list of suspects in the margin of his notepad—it included police, ambulance personnel, firefighters, and reporters. He still believed he could get the phone back without involving the authorities—but he first needed to know who he was negotiating with and needed to outsmart.

Two textless days had elapsed and the $1,000 was still in his checking account, but Seamus had new preoccupations on top of that and his usual pre-lecture jitters. The drive to the CWU campus in Ellensburg was spent on his earbuds responding to the offers his realtor had received sight unseen after the townhouse listing had gone live earlier that morning. That made things real, he realized, as he tried to hold his second thoughts at bay. There were a thousand reasons he didn't need two homes. And there was one reason he couldn't part with the farm—and it was the same reason that had motivated his father, and maybe his grandfather, too. The family cemetery.

Also, during the two-hour commute from Hanford to CWU, he'd been relayed the nerve-churning last-minute news that his lecture was being moved from room 210 in the student union, his regular venue, to the 750-seat McConnell Hall. Advance ticket sales had been greater than the schedulers had anticipated—something that the caller chalked up to the professor's newfound celebrity. Before Seamus's ego could inflate, the caller reminded him the tickets were selling $5 for adults and the lecture was free for students—but that his regular lecture fee would remain the same.

After a much fancier sound check than he was accustomed to, Seamus walked down East University Way to grab a chicken sandwich at Jack in the Box. He'd thought about substituting the presentation he'd prepared for something more pedantic from what he'd labeled the *re-run folder* on the desktop of his MacBook Pro. He could usually get away with pushing an edgy, non-peer-reviewed theory to students who rarely stayed awake to challenge him. But the lecture he'd cued up for the evening was further out than he usually ventured with a public audience. He was banking on the new ice-flood simulation videos to be all that got remembered or talked about anyway.

Sitting on the edge of the plastic bucket seat in the dining room, he sunk his teeth in the chicken sandwich with gusto. With the day's packed agenda, he'd forgotten to eat. Since going hungry in the cave, Seamus found his appetite more malleable. He liked the sensation of becoming hungry and appreciated that it was something most super-sized Americans never experienced. On his third bite, the chicken breast was too thick for his incisors, setting his jaw on a different angle with the inside of his cheek in the way. In an instant, he tasted the blood. He knew it was bad and sucked on his iced tea to irrigate the wound. He fished out an ice cube placing it on the spot and wrapped his sandwich to finish later.

When he arrived back at the theater stage door twenty minutes before his lecture was supposed to begin, he had to squeeze between two media trucks, one from KOMO in Seattle, and the other from KREW in Spokane. He wondered what other act or sporting event he was up against tonight in the complex of theaters, gymnasiums, and studios located in this part of campus. He couldn't imagine the media being interested in what he had to say. Backstage, his lavaliere mic was getting clipped to the lapel of his sports jacket with the wire threaded over his shoulder and down his back to the battery pack that rode on his belt, just above his butt. "You are free to move around, just no sitting down," the theater tech instructed him before explaining she would help him get the microphone turned on when the time came.

As was his customary practice, Seamus wandered into the audience and out into the lobby, trying to get a sense of the public he hoped to inspire. Normally, he was just another rock guy with a weird moustache, indistinguishable in the crowd. Not tonight. He was recognized first by one of the TV cameramen, and then by a woman reporter Seamus had been long schooled by the communications folks at Hanford to try to avoid—Karen Dorn Steele, a particularly hard-scrapping and really good environmental journalist from the *Spokesman-Review*. Over the past thirty or so years, he'd read with great interest her exposés on Hanford and followed her journalistic crusade to chronicle and humanize the thousands of downwinders who had suffered and died from the thyroid and other cancers they'd developed just by living near Hanford.

It must have been 1986 when Dorn Steele broke the story about Hanford's Green Run. Seamus had been in his late teens. It was in the middle of one of those epic Quinlan family reunions or funerals, when his father and Great Uncle Percy took him aside in the barn where they were supposed to be hand-churning the ice cream to accompany his grandmother's fruit pies. But really, the "Elder Quins"—his grandmother's nickname for the older males in the family who hadn't yet died from their cancers—were there to secretly teach him how to drink Irish whiskey. He remembered the two men arguing points from the article, which had come out in the Sunday paper, and how this lady attack-journalist had only uncovered half the Green Run story. Seamus now knew the other half, thanks to the letter his father had penned—just as he knew the woman making a beeline toward him was Karen Dorn Steele. The tip of his tongue explored the painful divot in his cheek as she introduced herself.

"Seamus, I am Karen Dorn Steele with the *Spokesman-Review*. When I learned you would be speaking tonight, I raced up I-90 to be in your audience." He shook her extended hand.

"I've read your articles for most of my life, Karen. It's my pleasure to meet you." Seamus was a little starstruck.

"Normally, and at my ripe old age, I wouldn't traipse across the state to listen to a rock guy, but with the notoriety of your rescue, I learned that you are also the chief geophysicist working over at Hanford. I suppose I don't need to tell you why that interests me."

"No," Seamus said, smiling. "I expect you and I would have lots to talk about, given the opportunity."

"I don't want to keep you, but I wanted to introduce myself and say that I would surely enjoy that opportunity—on or off the record."

"Thank you," Seamus said, just as he spotted Cody in a chair being wheeled by his sarong-wearing and turbaned wife, Angela. She looked feeble as ever. "Excuse me," he said perhaps a little too abruptly.

"Certainly—" the reporter started to say, but Seamus was already moving away.

When he reached Cody and Angela, he couldn't hide the surprise in his voice. "What are the two of you doing here?"

"You kidding, man?" Cody asked, his face lighting up.

Angela piped in. "Wild horses, his mangled leg, or my losing battle with cancer couldn't keep him away," she explained, though Seamus already sensed the hardships they must have overcome just to be there. He gave Cody's wife an open-armed squeeze at her shoulders as Cody pressed himself out of the chair to a standing position to balance his weight on his good leg so he could receive his hug, too. The fellow with the news camera moved in close to capture the embrace and their reunion, trailing his colleague reporter who had stuck his microphone in their faces asking if the two had time for a few comments.

Seamus looked at his watch. "My lectures always start right on time," he said. "Perhaps afterwards," he teased, doubting the media would bother sticking around until the end of his presentation.

"We should get inside, too," Cody said. "I'd say break a leg, but I don't recommend it."

Seamus winked and laughed at the lame man's even lamer joke. "Thank you both for coming," Seamus said. "I can't tell you how much that means to me." With that, he excused himself, making his way through the crowd to reach a door leading backstage. As he waited in the dark, he reached in his pocket to silence his cellphone—and at that very second, it vibrated in his hands, announcing a new text.

NICE TRY AT TRIPPING ME UP. CAN'T REMEMBER THE DATE YOUR BUDDY'S PHONE TURNED UP IN MY POCKET. NOW THE BANK HAS FROZEN MY ACCOUNT AFTER TOO MANY GUESSES. YOU MADE ME MAD SO I WANT $1000 BEFORE MIDNIGHT. AND MAKE THE

DAMN QUESTION EASY THIS TIME, SOMETHING I'D KNOW, OR ELSE ...

Or else what? Seamus wondered what this idiot was really capable of doing if he couldn't even figure out the date he'd stolen Cody's phone. The houselights dimmed, and the stagehand reached under Seamus's jacket to turn on the wireless microphone. "Show time," she whispered.

After leaving the audience in the darkness for almost a full minute, Seamus clicked the remote. A video began on the giant screen—footage of a lava eruption in Fagradalsfjall, Iceland, in May 2021. This alternated with footage from the Holuhraun lava field, also captured in Iceland, during an eruption in 2014. It was the closest Seamus could come to visually simulating a flood basalt eruption.

As the video continued, he spoke into the mic, his warm baritone voice booming through the theatre sound system. "These lava flows occurred in Iceland within the past decade. I open with this video, so you get an idea of what much of Washington east of the Cascades, along with parts of Idaho, Oregon, and Nevada looked like seventeen to fourteen million years ago. That's when flood basalt eruptions were at their most vigorous, breaking through fissures in the earth's crust—not far from where we are gathered tonight." Seamus walked into the opening spotlight center stage in front of the projection screen. "Good evening. My name is Seamus Quinlan. I am a Central Washington University adjunct professor and a geophysicist."

To his surprise, there was applause—enthusiastic and appreciative, a first in his lecturing career.

"Wow. Thank you," he said, breaking from his script. "I am not used to lecturing crowds this big or this enthusiastic. I mean, I'm just a rockhound. Maybe this is the only venue in town with air conditioning on this hot August night?" The audience laughed. "As I started to say, lava from these flood basalt eruptions reached all the way to the Pacific Ocean near Seaside, Oregon and covered 81,000 square miles—an area the size of Belarus." Seamus advanced through the next series of slides to depict a time-lapse of the iconic eruption of Mount St. Helens. "These images are seared in the memories of those of us who were in the Pacific Northwest on May 18, 1980. This was a stratovolcano eruption. The Icelandic lava flows that I opened with also came from volcanic eruptions. But flood basalt eruptions were different. I stress that they *were* different, because they don't happen anymore. Or rather, they haven't happened since. In fact, the last time one occurred anywhere on Planet Earth was right here.

"The Columbia River Basalt Group is the youngest and smallest example of flood basalt activity on our planet. It's also one of the best-preserved. Like I said, flood basalt eruptions did not spew from stratovolcanoes like Mt. St. Helens, or Kilauea, but from cracks that formed on top of an ancient fault line that ran like a zipper from southeastern Oregon into western British Columbia. The multiple layers of lava that poured from these fissures and accumulated here were more than a mile thick. And this is important for a point I want to make later—the weight from this lava cooled and hardened on the surface, becoming basalt. This caused the ground beneath it to sink into a depressed plain we today refer to as the Columbia River Basin. Or, as I call it—*home*."

He paused to let the point hang in the air. "This advancing lava spreading out from fissures in what is now the southeastern corner of Washington State and reaching the Pacific Ocean near Seaside, Oregon, forced a more ancient version of the Columbia River into its present-day course. As the lava flowed, it filled in stream valleys, sometimes creating dams—behind which, new lakes were impounded." He took a drink of water to irrigate the canker sore in his cheek and continued speaking. "My students ask me, and you might be wondering, too—if lava was everywhere back then, why isn't there lava or hot springs or these types of eruptions here today?" Seamus advanced more slides, explaining that the stationary super magma hotspot beneath Yellowstone National Park used to be under Central Washington, and that the North American continental plate has been migrating westward over it for millions of years.

"Then, around 15,000 years ago, along comes the last Ice Age, when a glacial ice sheet extended from the North Pole into the northern sections of what we now call Washington, Idaho, and Montana."

Seamus began playing his first satellite-view computer simulation video, fresh out of the UC Santa Cruz "nerd tank" (as he called the place where some of his colleagues worked).

"You can see here"—he paused to indicate the spot with his laser pointer—"near the present-day border between Idaho and Montana, that one edge of the ice sheet acted as a dam that was about 750 meters high between steep valley walls. This ice dam backed up what we today call the Clark Fork River creating a lake referred to by geophysicists as Glacial Lake Missoula. Now, Lake Missoula grew to around the size of Lake Huron. It had a water volume of about 850 cubic miles, so when that ice dam gave way, the equivalent of Lake Huron was unleashed over eastern and central Washington. This colossal rush of water—which some estimate had a cubic meter flow rate per second equivalent to 37,000 times that of Niagara Falls, scoured and carved through the basalt layers. But this instant flash-flood erosion didn't just happen once. Oh, no. The ice dam near the Idaho-Montana border kept reforming and Lake Missoula kept re-filling and the ice dams kept breaking, and each time, new cataclysmic floods would be unleashed over the same landscape, deepening the same channels, creating the same transient lakes behind coulees, up to one hundred times before the glacial ice retreated north and back into what we know as Canada, for good. The scars left on the landscape is why our region, east of the Cascades, is sometime referred to as the Scablands, and thus explains the creation of the canyons and coulees and geological wonders that surround us today."

Seamus advanced the slides through what he called his "greatest geological hits," naming the familiar features as they appeared on screen. "Palouse Falls ... the Columbia River Gorge ... Grand Coulee ... Moses Coulee ... the Drumheller Channel and Dry Falls." He returned to the ice dam simulation, allowing it to repeat. He pointed with his laser. "See what is happening right here? Each time the flash flood waters hit this pinch point in the Columbia River. The Wallula Gap, as it's called today, is where debris and mud and the volume of water were too large for the narrow canyon. The floods repeatedly got constipated in this spot with only about a fifth of the water making it through these logjams that were cemented in mud. The rest of the flood waters would back up to temporarily form Lake Lewis, which would swell to the size of Lake Ontario. Lake Lewis was transient—it only existed until the remaining flood waters made it through the Wallula Gap. Then the land turned arid and beige and dusty and boring again—pretty much just like we know it today." Seamus waited for the groans this comment always seemed to elicit so that his next memorized line would work to unify him with his audience.

"Thank you to those of you who just groaned. You are my people if you find this landscape—the Scablands of the Columbia River Basalt Basin—as beautiful and as dynamic as I do." The McConnell Theater audience broke into applause at that point, so Seamus snuck another drink of water.

"So the lava flows laid the groundwork for periodic flooding to carve out the features we still can still see all around us today. For millions of years, water either raced across the Scablands or evaporated in the heat. But then what happened?" Seamus paused for effect. "We did. *We* happened. We showed up on the scene, took one look around, and thought that we could do better. In the last one hundred years, we have built more than 250 dams in the Columbia River Basin, attempting to do what the Wallula Gap couldn't—stop the river almost completely and permanently. Except geology teaches us that nothing lasts forever. Water doesn't race down the Columbia River any more to recharge the oceans and feed the natural water cycle. It sits in reservoirs. In Washington State alone—on the Columbia River, upstream from the Tri-Cities and Hanford (where I work, and daily pray that the dams hold)—that amounts to 40,361,200-acre feet of imprisoned river. That is equivalent to fourteen Lake Hurons—sitting there, right now, flowing nowhere fast."

Seamus paused once more, finger-combing both sides of his horseshoe moustache, and allowing the facts time to sink in. *Sinking*, in fact, was his next theme. He was about to venture further out on a new theoretical limb.

"Imagine—fourteen Lake Hurons crammed into Washington State. Remember what a mile-thick bed of basalt lava did to the region? It caused it to sink, creating a depression in the earth we now refer to as the Columbia Basin. Any idea what a single acre foot of water weighs?" He advanced to the next slide, revealing the answer with a complicated equation that he walked his audience through. "One acre foot of water = 2,718,000 pounds. This times 40,361,200-acre feet which represents just the total reservoir water capacity behind the ten dams on the Columbia River that are upstream from Hanford and the Tri-Cities, equals ... drum roll ..." Seamus advanced to the next slide which revealed the sum of the equation as $1.0970174e+14$. "And in case you are wondering what kind of number is so large it has to be written like this, I'll tell you." Seamus advanced to the next slide which revealed the long version of the truncated number as 109,702,000,000,000.

"That's 109 trillion—almost 110 trillion pounds of water, sitting atop the Columbia River Basin upstream from Richland, Kennewick, and Pasco. When we convert that to tons, we're talking just shy of 55 trillion tons. The Titanic weighed 52,310 tons—so it's as if the Columbia reservoir water weight is equivalent to a little more than a billion Titanics ... on an area of land that was already sinking under the weight of basalt. Think about this a minute—but only a minute, or your brains will explode." Seamus left the podium and walked to center stage. The spotlight tech hadn't anticipated this choreography and jerked to follow.

"Now, let me take you down the rabbit hole a bit deeper. Given recent events in my life, I think it's safe to say I know a thing or two about deep holes." Several in the audience reacted—he guessed that his ordeal was why many of them were in the audience in the first place.

"My use of the Titanic comparison was deliberate. Why? What did the Titanic do?"

"It sank!" the audience responded in unison.

"Precisely. And that is what I believe has long been happening in the Columbia Basin." Seamus returned to the lectern where he'd left his notes and the remote control. "Next, and just for fun, let's factor in a doomsday multiplier. For the past twenty-three years, the western United States has been experiencing a mega-drought—the worst in twelve hundred years. Our human-made climate crisis has altered the jet stream, leading to less rain, spawning more and stronger wildfires, heat domes, and bomb cyclones—oh, my!" There was some audience laughter. Good—they were still paying attention. "And as those of us who live here know, each year we break records with an increasing number of excessively hot days. Higher temps lead to surface evaporation and the depletion of ground water, and less rain means fewer opportunities to recharge." Seamus advanced to the next series of slides, showcasing pictures of sink holes around the world. "In a geologically diverse landscape like ours with a vertical stratification of sediments and interbeds, layer upon layer upon layer, the depletion of underground water combined with the weight of stored surface water—the billion and a half Titanics—can lead to aridification, which is the term many think we should be using instead of mega-drought. The other 'sky is falling' development we should be anticipating soon is what is known as pancaking. This is a particular hazard in a region that experiences regular seismic activity, like we do."

Seamus reached for his water bottle as a new thought popped into his head. "You know what I've left out? The combined weight of the sixty concrete dams in the Columbia River Watershed, I imagine, would add, oh, I don't know, maybe another half billion Titanics to the subsiding Columbia Basin parking lot!"

Seamus advanced to a slide that showed tiled photographs of all sixty dams in the Columbia River Watershed. "How many of these dams, do you think, were designed to withstand the earth sinking beneath all this added weight? Most of our dams are more than half a century old and predate the technology and geological understanding we have today. Let's focus on the one dam on the Columbia River I obsess about the most because it is the closest upstream from where I live—and perhaps more crucially, where I work. It is located at river mile marker 397.1 from the mouth of the Columbia River at Astoria. The Priest Rapids Dam was built eight years before I was born." Seamus cued a series of three images depicting the dam and reservoir from different perspectives. "I grapple every day with the knowledge that my body is falling apart and I'm roughly the same age as the Priest Rapids Dam. At 10,000 feet long and 178 feet tall, this concrete dam holds back 237,100-acre feet of water. I won't subject you to the math again, but that's a lot of Titanics. Priest Rapids Dam is in rough shape—though, full disclosure, this statement is coming from a geophysicist and not a structural engineer." Seamus took that moment to look over in Cody's general direction, since he couldn't see with the spotlight in his face.

He cued the next video, which he'd grabbed from the Internet but had modified to zoom in for a close-up of one of the spillways, spiderwebbed with concrete repairs. "But you don't need to be a scientist or an engineer to see for yourself, this dam has issues and is under immense stress. Just look at the number of cracks that have been repaired in this section of the spillway. An electrical explosion occurred inside this dam in October 2015, tragically injuring six employees. A non-failure emergency was declared. The water level behind the dam was lowered by about three feet as a precaution." Seamus advanced to the next slide. "The year before and a few miles upstream, a crack was discovered in one of the spillways of the Wanapum Dam. The Wanapum Reservoir was lowered almost twenty-four feet and the repair cost more than $86 million. Three years later, back at Priest Rapids Dam, workers discovered leakage in several spots. They believed it was being caused by disbanded lift joints in the structure's spillway monoliths."

Seamus grabbed his water bottle and walked back to center stage. He was veering way off script now, but it had occurred to him that if he took advantage of this large audience, to reveal—with reporters in the auditorium—what he and Cody had confessed on their cellphone videos, Cody's extortionist would have nothing left to hold over them. Seamus knew that Karen Dorn Steele would run with this like Paul Revere. It was a calculated risk—perhaps a stupid one, too, but he was doing it anyway.

"Now, this may get us both in hot water as it casts an unflattering light on both our employers, but I had to ask my buddy, Cody, what a lift joint is and what it does. Cody is one of the structural engineers at Priest Rapids Dam—and, incidentally, the unlucky guy who fell into the partially collapsed cave on my father's property with me a few weeks ago. While we waited to be rescued, the two of us shared a fair bit of down time, if you pardon the pun ..." Seamus paused for those in the audience who got the joke before continuing. "And in that time, Cody explained to me that lift joints are the horizontal joints between the layers of roller-compacted concrete that get between the concrete placing cycles. Think back to those layers of basalt lava that got laid down with each new eruption and think about the layers of dust and dirt that accumulated between these lava eruptions that geologists call the interbeds. Turns out, these lift joints at Priest Rapids Dam are like the interbeds. Concrete needs to dry and cure in layers poured on top of other layers. The lift joints between these layers can be anywhere from six inches to three feet thick—the thicker the better, since this reduces the number of lift joints required in a vertical structure. In a dam, these joints primarily act as shock absorbers that control the shear strength and like caulking that prevents seepage of the dam. When a lift joint becomes disbanded, it can be because of hydrological or seismic movement, but also because of general wear and tear and the age of the joint.

"Some of you might recall the fall of 2002 when a lunatic Greyhound bus driver tried to blow up Dworshak Dam upstream from Lewiston, Idaho. Dworshak—the tallest, straight-axis gravity dam in the world—and for those of you who don't know what straight-axis means, it pertains to a dam structure that is neither concave nor convex. Dworshak already had structural issues before the greyhound bus packed with explosives rolled onto its bridge deck. In the 1980s, not even ten years after construction had been completed, a vertical crack more than two hundred feet long was discovered on the reservoir side of the dam. More than seven thousand gallons of reservoir water a minute were passing through the crack and into the bowels of the dam—so much that holes had to be bored on the downside of the dam so the leaking water could be released.

"The point I want to make—and the alarm I guess I am sounding here—is that even the strongest dams develop age-related problems. Dams fail. A study out of Stanford in 2018, cited that in the US alone, since 1980—the same year the Dworshak crack was discovered and Mount St. Helens blew her top—there have been, on average, twenty-four dam failures per year, with just under four percent of these resulting in fatalities. We should pause to remember the failure of the South Fork Dam near Johnstown,

Pennsylvania, in 1889—it killed 2,209 people. In 1928, the collapse of the St. Francis Dam killed 450 people in California. When this starts happening to the sixty dams in the Columbia River Watershed, it is going to be like the sudden release of Lake Missoula over the Scablands, repeatedly." Seamus held an index finger in the air. "Except now we've built cities and nuclear weapons facilities and other massive dam structures like Wanapum and Priest Rapids dams smack-dab in the downstream paths of certain future catastrophic destruction.

Seamus wandered back to the podium as he began his closing remarks. "Just this morning, I sold my townhouse in Kennewick, in preparation for taking over my father's farm northeast of the Tri-Cities. My realtor said that the townhouse property was FEMA flood rated as a 1 on a scale of 1-10 with 10 being the greatest risk. Today, my townhouse sits about a mile from the Columbia River in a place that I know, as a geophysicist, has historically been five hundred feet underwater about a hundred times—each time the Wallula Gap backed up. What happens to the Tri-Cities when the Priest Rapids Dam begin to fail upstream? What happens to the Columbia River ecosystem—and the Pacific Ocean, for that matter—if Hanford's buried radioactive sludge gets carried out to sea by a catastrophic flood event? Geologists and geophysicists are supposed to be fixated on what happened in the past. But as Shakespeare wrote in *The Tempest*, 'What's past is prologue.'" As he said those words, the quote appeared on the giant screen next to him.

"Thank you," Seamus said to his stunned audience, which took a few seconds to organize its applause.

After the crowd in the lobby had thinned and Seamus had shaken more hands and offered more unsolicited hugs than usual following one of his lectures, he realized he'd missed connecting with Cody and his wife after the talk. Seamus worried that Cody might have gotten upset when Seamus had outed him as a structural engineer at Priest Rapids, but he'd done this deliberately to protect them both from the fallout if their videos got released. The way Seamus saw it, they could either be complicit like his dad and Great Uncle Percy, or they could be whistleblowers—and he'd just chosen the latter—for both of them.

When the telephone
Told us she was dying
We had a Sunday kitchen
Full of guests —
But I hurried out
To clean the fish pond.

I raked from the pool bottom
Leaves as black as the ink
On her note from the hospital.
The orange Koi rose to the roiled
Surface, turned and flashed
Back into the depths.

Monday and an empty Guest House
I sat by the cold fireplace
Watching the feathery branches
Of the huge acacia
Brush her name on the November sky.

—William Witherup

CHAPTER ELEVEN

THE CON MAN MUST have wised up since he or she—Seamus supposed his tormentor could just as easily be con woman—had figured out the answer to the latest security question he'd set to unlock the third EFT of $1,000.

What is the more common term for the crime of extortion? Blackmail.

In his plan to get his hands on the cellphone and be done with this game of cat and mouse, Seamus had needed to shell out three grand in the past few weeks. By making those payments, he had bought enough time to come up with a new plan to blackmail their blackmailer back. Just that morning he had sent a text to Cody's cellphone threatening he'd go to the police and ask them to track the ransom payments already made from his bank account to find out whose bank account the money was being deposited unless the swindler agreed to meet him to turn over the phone in exchange for one final payment of $2,000. Of course, he knew he had no guarantee his blackmailer would agree to this turning of the table and actually meet to make the exchange. Seamus had already decided he would follow through on the threat and take this to the police, if things went sideways. He wasn't sure why he hadn't gone to the police in the first place, but in the end, it was just money, which he had and was about to have a lot more of once the townhouse sale went through.

He'd kept the entire blackmail mess from Cody, who had been carrying a different weight over the past several weeks. The morning after the lecture in Ellensburg that they'd been forced to leave early when Angela turned sick, and then after the really bad night of violent pains and vomiting that followed, Cody had needed to compel her to go to Trios Women's and Children's Hospital in Kennewick. Doctors there agreed that there was really no prognosis left for her but the end. The hastily appointed hospice team thought that outcome would arrive quickly—parts of her cancer-withered body had already begun shutting down. Cody made arrangements with a neighbour to feed and tend his larger animals and his chickens were rounded up and crated for transfer to the Quinlan coop. Seamus took a day off work to move Cody into his Kennewick townhouse and the chickens to the farm. It made practical sense for Cody to stay at his place to be closer to Angela since the closing and occupancy date for the next townhouse owner was still a month away. Collaborating with the Getz's insurance company, Trios had worked with Cody's own medical team to make the unusual arrangements for his Harborview orthopedic surgeon and an assistant to fly into the Tri-Cities to remove the Ilizarov device from his rapidly healing leg, at the Kadlec Regional Medical Center in Richland.

In between shuttling Cody to Trios to spend time with Angela, Seamus had begun shifting his life and belongings to the farmhouse, taking another full pickup load with him each time he swung by the townhouse after work to check on Cody, who still had his second surgery coming up. The pair of them had had several deep conversations and had started to broach the topic of cohabiting the Quinlan farmhouse more seriously. While they were still in the cave, Cody had admitted his interest in possibly buying the farm off Seamus to have more room for his menagerie of animals. The two of them were facing imminent retirement dates—forced if not voluntarily, given the media and public reaction to Seamus's CWU lecture—and they both enjoyed, even missed each other's company. They'd enumerated the many efficiencies that could be gained by combining their two farms into one—once Angela had passed, of course. It seemed the easiest of all the choices facing them both, but Cody had a lot on his mind with the missing cellphone, the tensions at work he was trying to manage remotely, and Angela's final weeks that looked more likely to be days, according to the hospice nurse. On top of all this, while moving in with Seamus had great appeal for him, Cody was still reluctant, having not yet admitted his bisexuality and expressing aloud that he was afraid he might cramp Seamus's independence. Seamus tried to reassure him that after a lifetime of independence and being on his own, it would be easier for him to take on the Quinlan farm if he had a partner, adding that if they moved in together, it wouldn't have to be in a *Brokeback* way, if that was what Cody was worried about. The two of them laughed it off—they had always kidded each other about that damn movie, but Seamus really needed Cody to come around to his way of thinking. Not only did he really like the guy, but he was also having trouble envisioning a future without him by his side. The bond they'd forged while stuck underground was something powerful that neither of them could deny. When it came to the Quinlan family farm, Seamus, like his ancestors before him, had realized he couldn't possibly leave but without any remaining relatives, he just didn't want to be there alone.

The white clapboard farmhouse with the sun-bleached and wind-blasted green trim had also begun its metamorphosis to adapt to the needs and tastes of the new occupants. Seamus wanted to make some modifications before bringing Cody up to take a more serious look at the place as part of his concerted efforts to win him over. Seamus had thrown himself into salvage, demolition, remediation, painting, deep-cleaning, furniture and fixture removal, and any other renovations he could handle on his own. He'd hired a carpenter from Kahlotus and an electrician to do weekend work and a plumber had promised to install new bathroom fixtures just as soon as he could work the job into his schedule. These efforts divided the house so that both men would have equal space. Seamus would get the upstairs for his bedroom and office / man cave. And the three downstairs bedrooms would be converted into one larger bedroom with a den for Cody—just in case his leg made it hard to climb stairs even after it healed.

Seamus increasingly and perhaps unconsciously pulled back

from work during these last summer days. At the office, he arrived later, left earlier, spent longer lunches at Rodrigo's, and calendared more field days than was normal, even for him. The Quinlan farm—and especially Cody's transplanted chickens commandeered much of his time. He didn't mind the new chores and responsibilities, plus the chickens provided endless entertainment and company. Seamus had not been the least bit surprised that his lecture last month at CWU had sent ripples across the executive pool of agencies at Hanford when the media intercepted the football he'd haphazardly lobbed into the air and couldn't resist running with it. Karen Dorn Steele penned a front-page feature that heralded Seamus Quinlan for delivering what she called "the most dire and prescient wake-up call of our time." The higher-ups at an alphabet soup of government agencies were caught off-guard and as Seamus predicted, bungled their defenses. Some notable environmentalists demanded the drawdown of reservoirs and immediate, third-party inspections of all dams built before the 1970s—that is, most of them. Seamus was skeptical, given government hesitation to spend unbudgeted money or accept responsibility. He thought it unlikely that a course change would occur any time soon.

Cody had his heat shields up too. Even though he hadn't yet been medically cleared to return to work and still had a second surgery to go, he was catching flack in absentia for the assumed role he might have played in what were seen as reckless statements made during the CWU presentation about the state of the Priest Rapids Dam. In his written response to the Grant County Public Utility District, he asked for clarification. For one thing, he hadn't made any statements publicly. And for another, it sounded to him as though he was being reprimanded for providing a definition of a lift joint—something anyone could find for themselves on Google and nothing the employee handbook prohibited.

Mayors and public interest groups in the Tri-Cities, along with the elders from the Umatilla Indian Band Office, had been the most vocal following the media storm after the lecture. They collectively raised the alarm—not about Priest Rapids Dam—but about Hanford. But their outrage couldn't be sustained against a platoon of publicists dispatched to all the media outlets to insist that

Hanford's extensive flood modeling had shown that any breach of an upstream dam would be confined and contained within the river's banks. Seamus knew that was patently untrue having participated in these simulations and having seen for himself that for every variable of the simulation that resulted in the flood water being contained, there was a simulation where it wasn't, and catastrophic destruction had been the forecasted outcome. Ironically, Seamus's commentary almost jeopardized his own real estate transaction—but in the end, the buyers went ahead.

Seamus had begun to document the migrating water pattern and the variations in water temperatures he had been observing between the farm pond, the cellar beneath the farmhouse, and the cavern under the cemetery. He'd wondered why the cellar wasn't moldy each time the water retreated, but then he read online that sulphur interferes with the cellular respiration of fungi. He'd smelled sulphur at the pond and maybe inside the cave too, where he'd also been unable to find any mold. The connection between these three spots—the pond, the cellar, and under the cemetery—got him working out a new bathymetric and hydrological theory he had so far termed "earth sloshing." The term was inspired by that funny feeling you get after drinking lots of water and then trying to walk or run. He thought this sloshing might explain the sudden shifting of a subterranean water body either through seismic activity, the seasonal tilt of the earth's axis, or by gravitational pull of the moon during every eight-phase cycle.

On the Friday before Labor Day, passing through Pasco on his way home for the long weekend—his pickup truck empty for the first time in weeks—Seamus stopped at Mac's Garden Center for fence-building supplies. He chatted with Mac, the proprietor, who recognized Seamus from TV and congratulated him for his newfound celebrity. Before he realized it, Seamus had been sweet-talked into buying a large cedar gazebo that was on sale at half price—along with enough cedar decking to build a sizeable walkway and deck on one side of his farm pond. Mac even threw in a promise to deliver and install everything, at no extra charge. Flummoxed by the high-pressure sales tactics and flush with the proceeds from his townhouse sale, Seamus wrote a check like it was play money and signed the landscaping contract. They loaded the back of his pickup with long, cedar rails and what Mac called crucifixion nails—the supplies which Seamus had originally stopped by to grab. He planned to spend his long weekend constructing a simple cowboy fence that would encircle the hole in the cemetery grounds.

Before commencing the fencing project on Saturday morning right after he'd fed and watered the chickens, Seamus wisely thought to retrieve the longest aluminum ladder he could find in the barn. He hauled it up the hill on top of the fencing materials he'd loaded onto a small flatbed trailer he'd hitched to the tractor, that just happened to start up on the very first try. He laid the ladder flat on the ground and carefully lowered it down into the cavernous space that he and Cody had made their first home together. He deployed the ladder for two reasons: first, in case of another cave in while he was encircling the opening with a new fence, and second, in case the spirits of his sister, father, or Great Uncle Percy needed a way out from the underworld. Seamus thought this was somehow complementary to the Irish practice of leaving a window open after a family member dies. He didn't want anyone to be trapped underground if they didn't want to be there. He knew firsthand what that was like.

By late afternoon on Sunday, happy with the corral he'd created around the hole in the cemetery and pleased that his fence looked handsome as the images he'd Googled to learn how to build his own, Seamus shifted focus. He wanted to dedicate what was left of the daylight hours in his long weekend to the site preparation at the pond, where he intended to land the gazebo and new decking that Mac had talked him into. He'd sketched out a rough plan, also based on Internet research, to mimic the look of an overhanging boat dock, complete with swimming ladder bolted over the side. He wanted to level the ground and mark out the dimensions in orange spray paint for the landscaping team he was told to expect the following week. Of course, the pond level had dropped again. It never appeared the same to Seamus, no matter how often he checked it. Seasonal rains, if they were coming at all, would raise the level again shortly after September, he figured. While he raked then shoveled away debris, a bullfrog splashed, just as Seamus spotted the shadow of a predator circling overhead. Shielding his eyes, he scanned the sky—but he already knew he wouldn't spot whatever was casting the shadow. He'd settled on a spiritual or other-worldly explanation for this reoccurring phenomenon and took this as his ancestors' reminder that he wasn't really alone. They hadn't abandoned him and were keeping watch over him and the Quinlan family farm. This was a big leap for a scientist, but it helped him with his grief.

His cellphone vibrated in his front pocket. Cody, on Angela's phone. In the excitement of answering the call, Seamus began bragging about how the other man would be so impressed to see what he'd done with the place.

"Angela passed twenty minutes ago," Cody said.

Seamus let the shovel slip from his blistered hands. "I'm on my way. Where should I meet you?"

"I'm at Trios," Cody answered, clearly sobbing.

When Seamus arrived at the hospital later that evening, Cody was waiting for him, seated in a reception area chair bathed by a shaft of sunlight angling down from a skylight—just as he had appeared to him in the cave, angelic and enlightened but wounded. Cody struggled to stand as Seamus gave him a steadying and hopefully reassuring embrace.

"I am so relieved that her suffering is finally over," Cody said softly into Seamus's right ear.

"I know," Seamus whispered back as he held him there.

"Do you want to see her?" Cody asked before answering his own question. "No, of course you don't. I'm not thinking clearly. Sorry."

"I'd go with you if you needed to see her," Seamus offered.

Cody shook his head, gently pulling out of the hug. "I've said my goodbyes and made my apologies," he said. Tears barrelled out of his eyes, and Seamus drew him into another hug. "The hospital wants to know," Cody started to say but his words got choked off.

"Whether you want them to prepare her for cremation or

burial," Seamus filled in the blanks. Cody nodded; his blond buzz cut grazing the side of Seamus's long neck. "I know a guy," Seamus offered, instantly thinking about the county coroner, with his Abe Lincoln beard. "Have you, did she—?" he started to ask.

"No. We didn't ever take the conversation that far, mostly me pretending she'd get better, and assuming we could hold off the morbid details for later."

"I know a guy," Seamus repeated, "and I happen to own a cemetery. On behalf of the Quinlan family, I would be honored to create a space for Angela Getz." Seamus let go of a few fat tears he'd been trying to hold back.

"That sounds perfect," Cody said, with a growing smile. "Tell me, just how stable is the ground at your cemetery?"

"It's variable," Seamus answered. Still in their embrace, the two tall sunlit men began to shake and sway with familiar laughter.

※

Angela's graveside service was a solemn ceremony, but a highly efficient one, as Seamus had made the necessary arrangements with coroner Kennedy to raise his dad and Great Uncle Percy and to exhume his sister's remains. Sally-Sue's skeletal hands were still clutching a sizeable teddy bear, though it had lost almost all its stuffing too. Seamus had used the backup casket from the barn, to rehouse what was left of his father, giving Great Uncle Percy more room to stretch out in his custom teal chassis. Remarkably, Cody had gotten his own online deal on coffins at Costco, so Seamus had driven into the city and picked up two—one for Angela and one for Sally-Sue. Seamus had opened up the white picket fence to create a new row higher up the hill where the topsoil was thicker for these four burials. With some modifications to the tractor seat, Cody had dug out four perfect side-by-side rectangles using the smaller excavator bucket. Mitchell Kennedy had brought two assistants with him, so the lowering of four caskets was easily completed. Seamus and Cody had organized it so Great Uncle Percy and Sally-Sue were laid to rest to the left of Gerald, who was positioned directly above and adjacent to his wife, Abigail. Angela was on the other side of Gerald, but not at the end of a row that still had space for Cody and Seamus when their planting seasons came. Kennedy and his crew soon after departed, leaving the two farmers on the hill to grieve and fill in the graves. Angela didn't make so didn't have friends to attend her short memorial service. Her surviving mother in the memory care wing of the assisted living complex in Ellensburg hadn't even been told of her daughter's passing since she'd already been robbed of the memory of ever having been a mother.

Giant white clouds with dark grey bottoms floated in an eastwardly procession overhead. Neither man said anything for a long stretch. Then Cody asked, "You sure your ribcage is up to the task of filling in these four graves with me?"

"You sure your leg can support you doing your share of the work?"

"We're partners in this too, I suppose," Cody said, reaching for one of the shovels that had been laid out for the occasion.

The men began scooping the dark brown, almost black earth from the excavated piles until all four caskets were covered. Cody whistled what sounded like "Amazing Grace," but Seamus felt his whistling wasn't all that good, so he began quietly whistling "Carrickfergus" to himself. "You know, speaking of partnership," Seamus said, interrupting their requiems. "I could sure use a hand around this place. Your crazy chickens are already here, and now your wife, too. How about you stop leading me on and we make it official? Will you move in with me, Cody Getz?"

Cody cupped both hands on top of the shovel handle and stared with his washed-out blue eyes across the sprawling, seemingly horizonless landscape. After what Seamus feared was too long of a pause, Cody simply said, "Yes," and went back to filling the grave that held his wife and lifelong friend. He thought of their shattered dreams—like having children and living on a larger farm that was more lifestyle than hobby. This wasn't meant for them, but Cody wasn't out of dreams, yet. He'd always intended to say yes to Seamus when the time was right. From the moment they fell through the earth together, that was the only answer there was.

Cody hadn't found it easy to sell his hobby farm and small acreage. As his realtor suggested, his place was literally in the middle of nowhere—several miles outside the village limits of Beverly, a town of commuters. Though he and Angela had been persuaded (*swindled*, in Angie's view) that the land offered an appealingly simple existence, it was hard to convince anyone else. He had to drop his asking price twice before he got a nibble from the Hispanic pastor of the *Volviendo a la Biblia* church in town—who had to wait until God revealed that it was the right decision. So, Cody waited on God, too. The pastor had been living in a converted school bus, coincidently named *Paciencia y Fe*, that had made it to Beverly before it conked out for good—or God. In the end, the pastor's congregation, lacking the patience or faith that such a sign was on its way, and recognizing that winter was the real thing that was coming, ponied up the money to secure the bank loan in his name.

When the real estate transaction finally concluded on the last day of September, taking much more *paciencia y fe* than Cody had in him, he drove to Hearthstone Eldercare in Ellensburg, where his Alzheimer's-afflicted mother-in-law passed her memory-free days. Meeting with the administrator (his mother-in-law would have never remembered him anyway), Cody presented a certified $25,000 check to be paid toward her account. He updated his contact information with a promise to replenish the funds as needed.

On his way back from Ellensburg, Cody received another text on his dead wife's cellphone, which out of convenience he'd made his own. He pulled into the Indian John Hill rest area, just short of Vantage, and waited for the large attachment to finish downloading. It was the underground video in which Cody had systematically listed everything structurally wrong at Priest Rapids Dam, including his prediction of catastrophic failure within five years' time. Another text immediately followed:

> THIS LITTLE GEM OF YOUR HUSBAND'S GETS SENT TO THE TRI-CITY HERALD AND KFFX IN THE MORNING IF I DON'T GET ANOTHER $1,000 WIRED TO MY ACCOUNT BY MIDNIGHT. YOU KNOW WHERE TO SEND IT: NUTZO1969@HOTMAIL.COM.

Cody had the money, but that was never the point. With his truck and AC still running, he logged into his bank account and set up yet another EFT to the crook that had been blackmailing him thinking he was communicating with Angela. In setting the security question this time, he added a note,

> BTW, MY WIFE IS DEAD. HER FIRST NAME IS THE ANSWER TO THE SECURITY QUESTION. AND I KNOW YOU KNOW HER FIRST NAME SINCE YOU HAD TO USE IT TO UNLOCK MY PHONE. THERE IS NOBODY LEFT TO KEEP MY SECRETS FROM NOW, SO YOU CAN FUCK RIGHT OFF. THIS IS MY LAST PAYMENT TO YOU AND THAT'S TO KEEP YOU FROM SENDING THESE VIDEOS TO THE PRESS.

When Cody in his walking cast limped in the back porch door after having stopped by his place one last time on his way back from Ellensburg, Seamus was in the kitchen texting.

"I didn't know you texted," Cody said, sounding surprised. "You've never texted me."

"That's because you can't manage to hold on to your damn cellphone!"

"Someone is in a mood!" Cody said as he passed through the kitchen on the way to his bedroom and den, to wash up and change clothes for dinner. He'd stopped to clean out the chicken coop at his place near Beverly—a last-minute goodwill gesture to the pastor, who would own the farm as of midnight.

"And someone smells like he was rolling in chicken shit," Seamus hollered after him.

"BINGO!" Cody shouted back, disappearing into his bathroom.

"This is delicious," Cody exclaimed, chewing his first bite of meatloaf. "What's your secret?"

"I add a package of Lipton's onion soup mix to the beef, is all," Seamus answered—happy that on his night to cook, he had produced a hit. "Everything go okay in Ellensburg today?"

"Yep. No drama. No surprises." Cody forked another slice of meatloaf from the casserole dish onto this plate.

"Good." Seamus chewed. "Best to save the drama until you got home, I guess."

"Why?" Cody held his empty fork in the air. "Have you some drama planned for tonight?"

"No, not really." There was something Seamus wanted to discuss, and he looked for a way to broach the subject. "But I have been thinking that you and I ... the two of us ... because we are a team now ..." He let that hang in the air with Cody's fork for a few seconds.

"Yes?" Cody asked, trying to pull it out of him.

"I think we should resign. Retire. And immediately. We've both worked long enough to qualify for our full government pensions."

"Whoa, hold on," Cody said. "I'm only fifty-three."

"You're fifty-four in a few weeks, and I turn fifty-seven in January. But our ages aren't the reason I bring this up." Seamus let a fork full of long green beans dangle off his lower lip as he chewed them shorter. "We have the money and no mortgages. I'm not saying we stop doing everything—just our day jobs."

"I've only ever worked for the government," Cody said, knowing he was mounting perhaps the weakest of arguments.

"And that's my point. Maybe it's time we try something new. Maybe we become serious about farming. And by farming, I mean taming that damn wind that never, ever, *ever* stops blowing. No Quinlan ever made it rich from working this barren acreage, but that's because they were going about it wrong—or their time just hadn't come yet. This is our time, Cody. The world is going green. We have wind—and we have the acreage to turn this farm into a real producer. I'm not suggesting we invest in the technology or start buying up turbine parts in some do-it-yourself scheme. I'm just saying we lease the land to others who are already supplying their megawatts to the grid—people who know what they're doing—while we sit back, growing old, collecting licensing fees, and sipping brewskis and zinfandel out back at the gazebo."

Cody had stopped chewing a few statements back as he took in the pastoral scene that Seamus was painting for him. He'd never been one to hold back a smile, and he didn't then, as he asked, "Fine, but don't turbines cause cancers?"

"Dude. We live downwind from Hanford. Cancer from turbines is the least of our worries."

"Oh, right."

The two finished eating in silence. Later, while tending the dirty dishes, standing side by side—Seamus washing and Cody drying—they brought the topic up again. "Something tells me we should submit our resignations in the morning," Seamus announced.

"This scheme has really been on your mind, hasn't it?" Cody gently ribbed Seamus in the side with his elbow.

"I need to level with you," Seamus said. "I've been keeping something from you." Cody paused his drying of the casserole dish and adjusted his stance, taking more weight off his bashed-up leg. His brain began pinballing off the bumpers and plungers in his cranium. His excited heart pulsed with anticipation and a hunch he knew what was about to be revealed.

Seamus cleared his throat. "I'm being blackmailed," he blurted out. "Whoever has your cellphone has been sending me these images of you from your phone. I have been paying these ransom payments to keep the compromising photos from being emailed to your work and your wife."

That was not what Cody had been expecting to hear, but he knew exactly which images Seamus was referencing. It would have been enough to be seized with embarrassment. But Cody's panic had more to do with the jeopardy this revelation might cause their relationship and the new living arrangement. "Oh, geez," Cody began, not really knowing what to say. "I knew that phone would get me in trouble. Now it is costing both of us."

"What do you mean, both of us?"

"Angela was being blackmailed, too. Except I intercepted

everything because I had been using her cellphone. Whoever this is thinks he has been getting money out of my wife."

"Exactly how much money?" Seamus asked, leaning back against the kitchen counter to steady his growing anger.

"Oh, I'd say about $4,000 so far."

"Plus, my $3,000," Seamus said, scowling. "We aren't very good negotiators, I guess."

Cody placed the casserole dish on the counter and said, "I don't know where this goes."

"This is your kitchen, too," Seamus said. "Put it wherever makes sense to you."

Cody was relieved to hear that, but he knew that Seamus only had half the story about his naked selfies and not why he had them on his phone or for what purpose he used them. "I have to get off this leg," Cody admitted. It had been too much taking on the drive to Ellensburg and cleaning out the chicken coop in one day and so soon after getting his leg encased in a walking cast. "So, what should we do about this phone hostage situation we find ourselves in?" he asked, hobbling to the living room with Seamus in tow. Seamus gathered pillows, and by the time Cody landed his butt on the L-shaped sectional—only recently transplanted from the townhouse—Seamus was right there to get that leg elevated.

"Well, my last payment to the blackmailer was to stop him from sending our workplace confession videos to our employers and the media." Seamus perched on the arm of the matching recliner across from Cody. "Which is why I suggested that we resign. I feel even stronger about this now that I see what a manipulator this person is if he was fleecing both of us at the same time." Just then, Seamus received a text. "Well, someone's ears must have been burning." Seamus read the text aloud:

I'M READY TO DITCH THE CELLPHONE. I WILL MEET YOU AT NOON TOMORROW AT A PLACE IN PASCO CALLED ELMO'S. GOOGLE IT FOR DIRECTIONS. I WILL BE INSIDE BOOTH #8. YOU BRING THE CASH. I BRING THE PHONE. NO CASH, NO DEAL. I'LL BE WATCHING TO BE SURE YOU ENTER ALONE.

OK, Seamus replied.

"I know *Elmo's*," Cody confessed. "I am not proud of this, but I'll go in. It's my cellphone. I've already gotten you more messed up in this than you need to be."

"And I'm the one who got you stuck in that hole—if you hadn't been there, you wouldn't have tossed your cellphone out in the first place. Besides, if this guy sees you, he'll know it's a trap. He has your phone. He's been sending pictures of you to both our phones. He knows what you look like."

"He knows what I look like naked," Cody clarified, through a raging blush.

Seamus sensed Cody holding something back and realized that Cody maybe knew what Elmo's was, but he sure didn't. It sounded like a place that would serve pancakes, to him. "So what's Elmo's?" he asked.

Cody had been holding back. His pause and worried look telegraphed all sorts of alarms.

"Elmo's," Cody said, then clenched his jaw. "Elmo's is an adult bookstore not far from the truck stop just before the interchange as you're heading into Pasco. They sell sex toys and movies and have these porn video booths with different channels so you can, uh," he paused again, "get what you might not be getting at home."

"I see," Seamus said. "It sort of surprises me that I've never heard of the place," he admitted honestly.

"I wish I'd never heard of the place, but I was one of those guys who wasn't getting it at home, so ..." Cody trailed off, leaving it to Seamus to fill in the blank.

Seamus let him stew a moment. "Porn? Is that what this is about? Do you think you are the only one of us to look at a little recreational porn on the side? Isn't that what the Internet is for?"

Cody was biting his lip. "It isn't just the porn at Elmo's, Shay. Plenty of truckers and other married men go there and many are looking for a hand, or more, inside those video booths."

"I see," Seamus said, adding "now, I'm really surprised I've never heard of Elmo's before. I must be living under a rock or too busy, maybe, with my fascination with rocks, is more like it. So you went there. What's the big deal?"

"I didn't just go there, Shay. I was a regular. Part of this secret life I had been driven to lead." Seamus leaned forward, sitting on the edge of the recliner. "When we learned Angela couldn't conceive, she shut down, and we stopped trying. Where she had zero drive, I guess I went into overdrive."

Seamus let loose a chuckle. "You make it sound like you had an addiction of something, you horny little devil!"

Cody was pleased that Seamus was taking this so jovially, but his shame ran deeper than that. "I think it became an addiction. That's the problem. Angie's cancer made things worse and me even bolder. That's where the hidden pics on my phone came into play. I used them to meet people online, people I arranged to meet in person."

Seamus knew how uncomfortable this was making Cody and he really wanted to find a way to interject some levy, make this not such a big heavy deal. "Then how is it, if you can tell me this, Cody, that we didn't meet each other online? You think you're the only one walking around with hidden dick pics on our phone?"

Cody raised his blue and scolded-looking puppy dog eyes in astonishment. "Is that so, Seamus Quinlan?" he asked grinning devilishly. "Text me, then."

Gauntlet on the ground, Seamus had no option but to draw his phone from its pocket holster and choose which pic to fire-off. Cody's cellphone pinged. He looked at Angela's phone screen in his hand and announced in a rather blasé way, "Meh. Trust me. It looks much nicer in person."

And there it was, out in the open. Seamus could almost see the worry drain from Cody's embarrassed face. "What do you say we bang out some resignation letters and make it an early night?" Seamus asked, improvising a path out of these tortured woods. "I plan to head into town early to pay a visit to the Pasco police. See if they have any interest in making an arrest for extortion—not that we'll get our money or jobs back—not that either of us should care about that, anymore."

Cody crinkled his face. "Do we *have to* involve the police?" he asked, in an almost adolescent whine.

Seamus chuckled. "Unless someone's named you sheriff and me deputy of these here parts," he said in his best baritone drawl,

"I don't see any other way we are going to get this creep hauled in and busted. Do you?"

"S'pose not, pardner." Cody hoped his twang masked his panic.

Seamus retrieved Cody's laptop from his room and grabbed his own from the kitchen—where he'd used it to look up that meatloaf recipe, which had been "guaranteed to impress." Cozy and resolute, the two banged out their resignation letters and attached them to emails addressed to their supervisors at Priest Rapids Dam and Hanford.

●

Sitting inside the cab of an overheated Kenworth that didn't belong to him, hours after the service day at PJ Lugnutz had ended, Paul Jacobs checked his bank account on his laptop, having accepted the three EFTs he'd demanded. It took forever to upload the two videos that he'd just sold to an investigative reporter from KOMO News. With time to kill while the uploads completed and feeling proud of himself for executing a daring triple-play that would have made the Tri-City Dust Devils recruit him on the spot, he did what he always did inside the cabs of the big rigs he repaired.

He jerked off.

White crocus and purple hyacinth
In the cracked asphalt street.
Teller-light flickers in the guts
Of wild geese preening on the river bank.
Bleached gravels, dead river, white boxcars.

While my birthday turkey
Sweats in the oven
I polish the house's lens
And pray to a God I do not believe
To spare us the flash, the wind, the ice.

I cupped an exploded milkweed pod —
The air so still
Seeds would not shake out;
The light in the husk
Both blinding and delicate —
Like that moment at Ground Zero
When eye-pods implode
Dark seeds of death-light.

—William Witherup

CHAPTER TWELVE

AFTER HEMMING AND HAWING over coffee, Cody had told him what to expect inside Elmo's when he got there based on his own patronage there. He had asked Seamus to promise him two things: to not judge him and to be careful. The two men had hugged on the front porch, sealing the deal. Joking in the middle of their embrace, Seamus had reminded him that if anything went sideways, somewhere there was a video that promised the farm to Cody. Cody had yelled after him as he walked to his truck something to the effect, he didn't want the damn farm if Seamus wasn't part of it.

It wasn't like the day was going to go off without a hitch. After the officer at the Pasco Police Department politely but firmly passed on Seamus's invitation to raid Elmo's with him, Seamus sat in his Ford pickup and watched the clock.

He'd expected to hear back from Jenna Thomason by now—either begging him to reconsider his resignation or slapping a gag order on him. Cody was back at the farmhouse recuperating—he'd overdone it with his leg the day before. Seamus had left for the Tri-Cities without checking the news. So, he didn't know their leaked videos—with far more damning details than he'd revealed on the lecture stage—had sent shock waves across the Pacific Northwest. To him, it just seemed like the makings of another autumn day.

Then he received the emergency alert on his cellphone. It was a tsunami evacuation notice for low-lying areas of Puget Sound, the Olympic Peninsula, and Western Vancouver Island. Seamus navigated on his phone to the Pacific Northwest Seismic Network, the originator of the emergency alert. A bulletin posted forty-five seconds earlier concerned a rogue wave that offshore buoys had measured to be between four and five stories high. It did not seem to have a corresponding earthquake marker. The tsunami, Seamus calculated by best guess and quickly triangulating the GPS coordinates on the webmap, seemed to be headed for the western entrance of the Strait of Juan de Fuca. Seamus immediately thought about the new dean at the UW College of the Environment, who had been on the conference call several weeks back. What was her name? "Tolstoy!" he said out loud in the cab of his pickup. He went through his contacts, selected her cell number and put the call on speaker phone while it rang.

"Rhonda Tolstoy," she answered.

"Rhonda—it's Seamus Quinlan out at Hanford. I imagine you are swamped with calls, but I just got the tsunami alert and I remembered what you had said about the domino effect a big event like this might trigger."

"Seamus! Are you seeing an associated earthquake event with this?"

"Not yet. I don't see anything on the PNSN website either."

"That's odd. I mean, rogue waves have been known to occur without earthquakes, especially if they are driven by strong surface winds preceding a storm. But it's rare, and I'm not seeing anything on Doppler, either."

Seamus was still Googling and came up with something else. "I'm reading here that La Niña has been building strength again for the past couple weeks."

"Yes, La Niña lowers the surface temperature of the ocean, and in the past few weeks, there have been drastic temperature drops recorded up and down the coast—as much as 4°C below average.

This may or may not be related, but NOAA had predicted that ENSO—the El Niño Southern Oscillation climate pattern—would go haywire as La Niña transitions to El Niño this fall. They said it could wreak havoc with the trade winds."

"Definitely not my specialty," Seamus admitted. "The trajectory for the tsunami—"

But Rhonda knew what he was going to ask, so she volunteered a response. "It's heading straight for the western entrance of the Juan de Fuca within the next hour."

"This is sounding more and more like a Cascadia Subduction event," Seamus postulated.

"I was wondering about that, too."

"Nah." He changed his mind. "It's a too-easy culprit. The Juan de Fuca plate has been acting like a wedge prying its way under the North American plate for centuries. But there would be seismic fingerprints if that were the case, and I'm just not seeing any."

"I'm Googling now and see that there had been a rogue wave with no known associated earthquake, and this had been deemed an orphan wave by a Japanese seismologist, named Kenji Satake—orphan meaning with no parent-source or cause, I imagine," she said.

"Oh yeah? When was that?" Seamus asked, like the answer might have mattered.

There was a pause on the line. "Says here, the year 1700."

The answer did matter. "That was the same year as the Cascadia earthquake—a megathrust event that would have registered, let's say a magnitude of 9.0, possibly higher. Three hundred and twenty-three years ago … that is how long it's been since our last high magnitude quake and tells us just how overdue we are for another major milkshake given that these events had typically and consistently occurred every 200 to 500 years apart."

"Oh—well that makes sense, then. It wasn't really an orphan wave, then. The Japanese wouldn't have felt an associated earthquake, but their tsunami must have originated here and traveled across the Pacific Ocean."

"In probably less than twenty-four hours. But I'm just not seeing any mention of a major quake anywhere else in the world right now—nothing that could have couriered a tsunami our way."

Seamus was puzzled. "Are you and your family heading to higher ground then?"

Rhonda laughed. "I'm a marine biologist and a workaholic. I can't be expected to hold down a relationship long enough to make a family. It's just me to worry about." She sounded resigned. "And I'm safe in my fourth-floor office on campus."

"Safe from high water maybe—but if this turns out to have a seismic signature, I'd be prepared to duck, cover, and hold."

"I'm heading downstairs, and I may lose you in the stairwell," Rhonda said, without responding to his note of caution. "There's a faculty lounge with a television—it might be easier to monitor this situation that way."

Seamus had almost forgotten the reason he had phoned her. "Rhonda, I wanted to ask about something you said on the call the other day."

"Oh, you mean my terrestrial water weight theory I was pleased to see that I'm not the only crackpot losing sleep about the weight of water on land. I saw excerpts online from your lecture at CWU last month. How many Titanics did you say it would take to equal the weight of the dammed reservoirs on the Columbia?"

"About a billion and a half," Seamus answered quickly. "You had hypothesized that a tsunami hitting the Pacific Northwest could push enough water overland to cause a subsidence or a subduction—which was it?"

"I meant subsidence; in other words, a sinking of the earth's crust on a grand scale just like what happened in the Columbia Basin under the weight of the lava, as you've pointed out."

"Right. That makes geological sense, and that's what I thought you meant, since subduction is what is happening off our coast with the tectonics."

"Yes, exactly," she said, sounding out of breath. Seamus assumed she was still running down the stairs.

"Hey! Would you look at that? You're on television, Mr. Quinlan."

"What?" Seamus shrieked into the phone.

"Right now, on the flat screen TV mounted from the ceiling here in the faculty lounge, KOMO 4 NEWS has a tsunami alert ticker running across the bottom of the screen, below a live shot from the Space Needle trained on Elliot Bay. The rest of the screen is you on a cellphone video with the caption: *Seamus Quinlan Warns of Coming Catastrophe for Hanford.*"

Seamus looked at his phone trying to navigate to a KOMO 4 homepage. That's when he saw the call with Rhonda had been dropped. The last bit of the conversation he thought he heard was Rhonda Tolstoy saying that he was on TV. But that couldn't be right. He hadn't given any on-camera interviews lately.

He didn't have long to think about it, though. He spotted a man in dirty coveralls and a pair of aviator sunglasses, trying to look cool. The man sauntered up East Hillsboro Street, toward the chain-link and barbwire-topped perimeter fence that encircled the parking lot where Seamus had stationed himself at Elmo's Adult Books, Videos, and Novelties. The fellow had this lope in his walk that seemed shifty. He was looking all around the place like he knew he was being watched—and then he made eye contact with the mustached driver wearing the Dust Devils baseball cap in the gray Ford F-150 just as he slipped inside the paper-covered glass door below the sign that read *Entrance, Adults 18+ Only.*

In that glance, Seamus realized he had seen that man with the aviator sunglasses twice before—once coming out of the telephone repair shop next door to Rodrigo's, and once standing in the shadow of Russ the truck driver when Seamus emerged from the hole in the cemetery to greet the friend who had thankfully spotted their smoke signal. He'd also had the feeling that he'd been in this industrial park once before, and he now knew it had been when he dropped Russ off at his truck mechanic's shop. So *that* was who had pocketed Cody's cellphone and had been blackmailing them ever since. In their obsession with trying to remember who was on the property that day—the police, EMTs, Russ, the media—neither Seamus nor Cody had remembered the truck driver's sidekick.

Seamus was genuinely torn between desperately wanting to monitor what was happening with the tsunami two hundred miles away and the top-secret mission at hand. He waited until it was almost five minutes after noon before he climbed down from his truck locking the doors with the envelope of real cash inside, tucked under the driver's seat. With a folded manila envelope of fake cash that he and Cody had improvised over breakfast sticking out of his back blue jeans pocket, he strolled across the mostly empty parking lot toward the front door of Elmo's.

Seamus entered. It took his eyes several seconds to adjust to the intentionally low lighting.

"Hey," said a plump and preoccupied female clerk behind the glass counter of sex toys.

"Hey," Seamus responded, looking around. Cody had said the video booths would be lined up along the righthand side of the store, behind ceiling to floor black curtains just past the tall racks of porn movies for sale. He'd also given Seamus an allowance of roll of quarters to feed the video TVs once he went inside one of the cubicles so that he didn't look like he was an undercover cop. The lighting was even poorer the closer he got to the booths with the black shower curtain doors, and so he paused to pretend he was trying to decide on a booth—but really to give his eyes more time to adjust in the darkness. He counted eight booths, three with curtains pulled and each of these had a red light bulb illuminated centered above the curtain—including the eighth one, where he'd been instructed he'd find the bloodsucker. The booth next to it was open and vacant according to the open curtain and no light bulb illuminated, so Seamus walked in and pulled the curtain closed.

In the pitch black, his eyes could barely make out two glass screens set into perpendicular walls that formed one half of the box or closet he was standing inside. He could hear the audio from other booths that showcased the ridiculous over the top screams and moans and grunts of a typical porn movie audio track. He couldn't see or make out any dials or buttons and so he didn't know how to get his television to turn on. Given the activities Cody had said usually happened behind closed curtains inside these cubicles, Seamus was loath to touch anything, but he needed to find the coin slot to get a TV to turn on so he could see how things worked. He heard an impatient clearing of a throat in the booth next to his and knew it belonged to the blackmailer, who was perhaps growing impatient. It was on that common wall between booths numbered seven and eight that the larger of the two glass panels was embedded. Seamus sacrificed his left hand to feel the wall around the smaller screen, sensing that was the one where he would find a place to insert a quarter. His eyes still weren't adjusted. His fingers found the coin slot and his right hand fiddled with the end of the roll of quarters trying to find a place to rip back the paper to free a few coins without dropping any of them—since he was most definitely not touching the floor. With some trial and error, he got a quarter into the slot and the TV screen came alive, as did two control buttons for changing channels. There was, however, no button or dial to turn down the volume and the porn scene that happened to be playing on the screen when the TV came on, featured a raucous group orgy that sounded like it had been recorded in a gymnasium. Seamus quickly pressed the up-channel button to find a less vocal scene. He landed on a scene with two naked women penetrating each other with the very real erect penises each of them had. Seamus was momentarily distracted by the unique set-up. There was a rapping on the glass to his right, which drew his attention to two more illuminated buttons below the larger glass panel, buttons he'd missed in the dark—one red and the other green, like traffic signals.

In the light of the trans sex scene playing on the television, Seamus could better make out the sparce contents of the space and figured it measured maybe four-feet square with a wooden stool, a rubber wastebasket containing used tissues, and a metal Kleenex box with a key lock, fastened next to the TV, which suddenly went dark, turning off the other two illuminated buttons at the same time. Seamus would have thought there was a power outage except he could still porn talk coming from the other booths. Then it dawned, on him. His twenty-five cents hadn't bought him much.

Seamus's heart imitated a drum corps as he lowered his Levi-clad butt to the stool, fishing out another few quarters from the top of the roll to feed the coin slot. The volume and picture came on again at full blast and right back to the orgy scene. Seamus pressed the up-channel button to see what else was on offer and paused at a channel in the gay section of the video library on offer. He noticed the green button was now flashing below the glass in the wall that separated him from his extortionist. There was another rap on the glass from the other side. Seamus didn't know what that meant. Then there was another, and a muffled voice saying, "Turn on your window."

Seamus inhaled deeply and pushed the flashing green button. Suddenly, he saw right through the glass into the booth on the other side. There, perched on his own stool, with his coveralls down around his calves, was the truck mechanic with a hard-on that he seemed very proud to be displaying.

Cody hadn't schooled Seamus on this part and he was confused about what to do next. The truck mechanic motioned for him to lower his jeans, but Seamus shook his head. He was only there for one thing. The mechanic extracted the cellphone from his lowered coveralls pocket to show him. When Seamus showed the dummy envelope from his back pocket that was filled with scrap paper, the screen suddenly went dark, and the green button flashed off and the red button illuminated. Seamus waited to see what would happen. When nothing did, he pushed the green button again and the looking glass was once again transparent. On the other side, the mechanic was now actively jerking off, standing up right next to the glass. Something in Seamus stirred. He knew what it was, but he ignored the mechanic's facial expressions, which seemed to insist he lower his pants to show him what else he'd brought to the party. Seamus refused, and the mechanic pushed one of the buttons on his side, and the glass went opaque again.

Losing patience, Seamus slipped out of his booth and quietly barged into the booth next door. The mechanic got tangled in his coveralls and the stool when he tried to maneuver backwards against the wall, but Seamus had already overpowered the slight-framed guy with a hand over his mouth to hold it shut.

Seamus immobilized him, using his whole body to press the naked grease monkey against the back wall, as he squirmed and groaned. Seamus whispered in his ear. "I am only here for one thing, you little shit," he said as he snatched the cellphone from the top of the bench with his free hand. When Seamus backed off and lowered his hand from the mechanic's mouth, the smaller of the two men didn't yell or spit. Instead, he flashed the biggest shit-eating grin—minus a few missing teeth—that Seamus had ever seen.

"That's *my* cellphone, you idiot! Where's my money?" the blackmailer asked.

Seamus thought about handing over the envelope with the fake stash but knew the con man would want to verify it first. Instead, he asked, "I wonder what your cellphone is worth to you?" Maybe he'd turned the tables.

Again, the other man's grin showed off his neglected dentistry. "It's a burner phone, amateur! You want that cellphone belonging to your buddy with the really nice dick and ass? You'll have to show me yours, first, and pay me the two grand you promised, in cash."

On a hunch that he was lying and sensing that the phone in his hand was Cody's, Seamus stalled. The mechanic went back to jerking off.

"Come on. Don't be a party pooper. It'll be fun. Then we can get down to the other business."

"You don't get it, do you?" Seamus said. "I'm not into this—whatever this is."

The mechanic reached to squeeze the semi-erection he could clearly make out in the tall dude's jeans. "Feels like you're into this, to me. Come on, whip it out!"

Seamus had had enough. He left the booth, powering on the cellphone. In the store's dim lighting, he saw the wallpaper photo on the phone in his hand—the chrome grill of a Peterbilt truck. Cody's phone had featured a photo of Angela.

The mechanic burst out of the video racks, hoisting up his coveralls and shouting, "That dude just stole my cellphone!"

The clerk pushed her panic button, which silently notified the Pasco Police Department. "Take it outside, Boys, or I call the cops," she said, giving the only warning her store policies and procedures manual required of her.

Seamus left the front door of Elmo's and was disoriented in the parking lot for several strides, blinded by the sun. The mechanic came flying out the door like a winged monkey from the Wizard of Oz. "Give me that phone, you asshole!"

Seamus kept moving in the general direction of his truck, willing his eyes to start working properly. The mechanic jumped on his back with a charging leap and a scuffle broke out. The cellphone was knocked out of Seamus's hands, and it went skidding across the hot asphalt. Seamus's knees buckled and the two men went down. Seamus scrambled to subdue the smaller man against the pavement, sitting high on his chest where his knees could pin the madly flailing arms into submission. A distant police siren gave Seamus some hope that this ordeal would be over soon. He just needed to hold this little thief—who was now spitting insults and loogies in his face. The siren seemed closer.

But that's when it started.

The ground beneath them began to tremble, with a low-register rumble at first, followed by a violent lurch that sent the pair one way, and then back the other. It was the sound of a Hollywood blockbuster—like they were stuck in the space between two trains from hell, passing each other at full speed from opposite directions. The shaking intensified. There was another lurch that knocked Seamus on to his overly sensitive ribcage and clean off his prey. The mechanic scurried away from him, got to his feet, snatched his cellphone off the pavement, and tore out of the parking lot gate and around the corner—all before Seamus could right himself to give chase.

That was it. There was silence. The rumbling and shaking stopped. No longer was there any audible police siren. No cops had materialized to shout "Stop, or we'll shoot!" like in the movies. So, the mechanic took advantage of the diversion to flee the parking lot and down the street, hoping to blend back into oblivion. Seamus got to his feet and faced an immediate conundrum; to take chase or enact his professional obligations and expertise to mitigate any further catastrophe. In the minutes that followed though, while the region must have still been stunned by what had just occurred, Seamus's phone wasn't vibrating. He used that reprieve to make his choice. He scuffled into a sprint around the corner just in time to see the mechanic duck out of view at the far end of the long block. As the Tri-Cities began slowly coming back to life, a car alarm sounded in the distance. This was joined by the sounds of his lungs heaving and his boots pummeling the sidewalk to a jingle-bell accompaniment of nine dollars in loose quarters in his front pocket. Running along East Hillsboro toward a very tall, orange-bordered white sign in the shape of a downward-pointing arrow, Seamus read the black block letters: *PJ LUGNUTZ*.

NUTZO1969. Seamus had his man. Right there, on the sign, in the open, he thought, for all to see and none to figure out until now. Seamus had been to this address before. It's where he'd dropped off Russ the truck driver. His cellphone vibrated with multiple calls. First out of the blocks was Jenna Thomason. Against his better judgement, he answered the call. Jenna made a frantic attempt to pull him back to Hanford and his geophysicist senses, but he also saw he had other calls coming in—from Cody and from PNSN. He told Jenna he needed to check with Seattle, and he'd phone her right back.

He let the next calls go to voicemail as he first banged on then kicked in the locked side entrance to the right of the extra tall garage doors. "PJ.!" he shouted, his deep voice ricocheting back to him off a pair of side-by-side truck cabs. "I need a computer and your Wi-Fi password! This is a national emergency!" He looked under and around the two truck cabs up on hydraulics inside the bays. "Listen, I don't give one damn about the cellphone or the extortion. We've had a major earthquake and I need to coordinate with Seattle, Hanford, the upstream dams, and the emergency coordinators for the Tri-Cities." Spotting the office up a wooden staircase, he took the stairs three at a time. In the office, cowering under his desk, was the truck mechanic, hugging his laptop against his chest, with his eyes squeezed shut. "Seriously," Seamus insisted. "I need your help. I need to borrow this office and a landline, and I could really use that laptop. You can sit here and watch every move I make. I promise you. I'm not going to hurt you or even press charges. This quake and the potential for aftershocks and some really catastrophic consequences are far bigger than any of that cellphone nonsense." Seamus paused and then reached an outstretched hand under the desk.

The mechanic reluctantly took Seamus's hand and was pulled out from under his desk. Seamus didn't let go of his hand until he was sure the creep wouldn't bolt on him, and the two stood face to face. "I'm Paul," the mechanic said.

"Paul, I'm Seamus, but you know that. Listen. I am also a

geophysicist and a seismic expert. I need to get on the Internet and make a half-dozen calls. Then I'll be out of your hair forever. Can you help me out?"

"I guess," the shaken mechanic said, opening his laptop on the desk and pulling up the desk chair. "Do you think there are more earthquakes coming?"

"I can let you know in about five minutes. Can you sign in for me and get me to the Internet?" His smile was anxious but grateful.

"It's Nutzo69," Paul said, offering the password so Seamus could sign in himself.

Navigating on the laptop to the Pacific Northwest Seismic Network website, Seamus hit redial on his cellphone, then cradled it to his ear with his right shoulder.

"Cody?" His voice was tender. "I'm safe. I have a dozen calls to make, but you are my first. Are you all right?"

Cody's speech was animated and cutting out a little. "I'm fine," he said, "but the chickens have run out on the highway and there is super-hot water coming up from the cellar in the pantry."

"Listen, don't worry about the pantry right now. Get the chickens off the highway before there is an accident. Then, if you can manage it, jump on the tractor, and check the pond and the cemetery—then call me back and tell me what the water is doing in those two places."

"Chickens, pond, cemetery. Got it. Give me twenty minutes or so."

"Thanks, Code. Be careful!" Seamus had decided to try a new nickname for Cody, since the other man had taken to exclusively calling him Shay.

His cellphone began vibrating before he'd lowered it from his ear. It was Jenna. "Jenna," he said, "you were my next call to return. My phone is blowing up." He scanned the recent earthquakes list with a finger on the laptop screen.

"I need you to retire *next* week," Jenna said. "Not open to discussion. Right now, we need answers and emergency advice. What can you tell me?"

"Okay," Seamus said, tentatively—not sure he was thrilled to be back on the clock but also recognizing his training left him no choice. "Two separate quakes, a 4.9 mag in the Rattlesnake Hills northwest of Hanford and a 6.3 mag with an epi between the Horse Heaven Hills and the Wallula fault zones, roughly just southeast of where I have just set up an emergency post, here in Pasco."

"They've got big problems at Wanapum and Priest Rapids but I'm not getting any clear direction. Can you check in with those sites you know and call me back? We're sending non-essentials home in the meantime."

Paul had turned on the old Zenith portable television set across from his desk in the small office, cranking the volume down and turning the channel know away from the sports stations he usually watched until he found a Seattle news station covering the disaster in real time. He also retrieved a paper notebook loaded with his phone messages and sophomoric doodles and flipped it to a blank page, scooting it with a dull pencil across the desk to Seamus. Seamus motioned his appreciation with an upward tilt of his chin.

"Don't just send them home, Jenna," Seamus said, watching the television. "Tell them to prepare for a full-scale evacuation of the Tri-Cities. And tell them to stay away from the river. Take back roads at higher elevations. I'll call you back in a few just as soon as I can." He hung up and reached across the desk for the filthy motor-oil-splotched desk phone looking like it might have originally been the color of Silly Putty. He scrolled through his cellphone contacts for the number and then dialed Cody's direct line at Priest Rapids Dam, not knowing who might be covering for him.

"Oris speaking."

"Hey Oris. It's Seamus over at Hanford."

"Hey, man. We've got big problems here. Wanapum has apparently pulled away from its anchor points in the earth dike on its west side. The breach is eroding away the buttresses real fast, and the reservoir is shooting a twenty-foot standing wall of water through the gap. We've got full spill underway here which has got to be raising the Columbia for you. We will be at full capacity in eight to ten hours if they can't close the breach at Wanapum. Goose Island in our reservoir is nearly inundated."

"Roger that. You had a 4.9 magnitude earthquake with an epicenter just west of the Beverly Dunes. I assume you've already told

Rock Island Dam to hold its reservoir. Wanapum can't be dealing with anyone's spillway volumes right now. Every dam upstream should be holding, but I know you don't have the jurisdiction to tell them that."

"I hadn't thought of that. I'll call USACE next and see if I can persuade them to turn off the taps. You think we have more tremors coming then?"

"Impossible to predict. There was a stronger quake that happened almost simultaneously south of Pasco. But so far, neither of these appear to have been strong enough to have piggy-backing aftershocks. There are problems in Seattle, too. Hard to say if this is all connected. We're commencing emergency evacuations at Hanford and I'm going to advise the Tri-Cities to evacuate potential low-lying flood zones. I'll try to call you back when I learn more."

"Thanks, Seamus. Be safe and tell Cody we said hello when you see him next."

"You too, Oris and I will pass that along to Cody." Seamus sucked in a gulp of air before dialing his next call to see if he could reach Rhonda Tolstoy. All circuits busy. As he kept hitting redial, he found it curious that Oris seemed to have an inkling that he would be seeing Cody before Oris did, leading him to wonder if the rumor mill might have already cranked out the latest gossip about the two cave dwellers shacking up together. Not that any of this mattered to either he or Cody any longer.

"Do you have a phonebook, Paul?" The mechanic indicated it was in the right-hand drawer of the desk. Seamus had just put his cellphone down on the desk when it began vibrating and crawling across the desktop. It was PNSN this time. He took the call just as there was a loud banging on one of the garage doors downstairs. Paul launched like a rocket off the counter he had been perching on and flew down the stairs to check on it.

"Seamus Quinlan," Seamus said, hoping the call—since it was coming from Seattle—might fill in some unknowns about the tsunami and the spike of seismic activity they were feeling in Central Washington. Were the two associated? Downstairs, he heard agitated voices, and a heated exchange, so he covered his free ear with his hand.

"Oh, hey, Seamus. You're a tricky guy to reach today. Just reaching out as part of our Cascadia protocol to confirm the quakes in your region."

"Yes, I'm on your website and saw the 4.9 and 6.3, both of which rattled the Tri-Cities pretty good about twenty-three minutes ago. They've got real problems at Wanapum Dam on the Columbia which means all of us downstream are paying close attention."

"We've got a world of hurt going on right now in Seattle. Pioneer Square is under about a foot and a half of seawater and mud that pushed onshore. The SR 99 tunnel is filling with water with traffic trapped inside and sections along the Denny Regrade above the tunnel have slumped. Someone said they heard the Yesler Street bridge over I-5 has collapsed, but I haven't seen that confirmed yet. We have no localized or offshore seismic markers to attribute this to, so I wondered if I could get your thoughts. Your two blips are the only things showing on any of our fancy maps. Is there any way your events are associated with our tsunami?"

Seamus attempted to straighten up in the seemingly broken desk chair. PNSN was calling for *his* advice? "Well, you've had that rogue wave originating somewhere outside the western entrance to the Juan de Fuca, and then higher-than-normal Richter activity in the intraplate where I'm located. Something tells me these are bookends to something even more dramatic about to happen in the middle. What is Rainier doing?"

"She's quiet," the caller reported. "Mount St. Helens is seeing its regular low-register seismic swarms."

"Are there patches in the Pacific where you don't have seismic monitoring—you know, like blind spots?"

"Well, there's always Point Nemo. It's known as the oceanic pole of inaccessibility as it is the point in the Pacific that is farthest away from land, but we have a network of satellite sensors tracking seismic waves but there is a lag in data reporting, so we have nothing from space yet to go on."

"Well, my training tells me something must be happening or building up underground, or you wouldn't have the bridge collapse or the slumping you mentioned. It could be a pressure release, or it could be a full-on megathrust event. If you haven't already,

I'd activate the emergency notification system advising folks to take cover. You have enough damage already to warrant it—but if nothing bigger comes, nobody's going to say you cried wolf." He looked up to see Paul arrive on the top stair landing in handcuffs, escorted by a Pasco police officer and two Washington State Patrol officers. "I've got to let you go but will keep my line open if you need to call me back," Seamus said, hanging up. "What's happening here?"

"Why don't you ask them," Paul said, acting cocky and pissed off.

The Pasco police officer, who held the chain connected to Paul's cuffs, spoke first. "Initially, we were responding to an alarm incident at Elmo's up the street, and the staff person there directed us here. In the meantime, our dispatcher pieced together your visit to the station this morning, and the claim you made of being blackmailed and your intention to confront your extortionist at Elmo's."

"Seamus Quinlan?" asked one of the state patrollers, in what Seamus thought was an overly authoritative tone.

"That's me, but wait," Seamus protested. "Why is Paul in cuffs? That whole blackmail thing turned out to be just a big misunderstanding on my part. He and I, we're cool here."

The Pasco policeman nodded. "Well, we had an outstanding failure-to-appear warrant we needed to serve Paul Jacobs, anyway. It just hadn't been prioritized until now."

Paul rolled his eyes and turned away from Seamus. The local policeman continued. "So, if Mr. Jacobs has anything that belongs to you, now would be a great time to square things up."

"It's in the left desk drawer," Paul volunteered.

Seamus pulled open the drawer and saw Cody's cellphone. "Thanks for keeping it safe. It must have slipped out of my pocket when I gave Russ a lift here, after his rig broke down." Seamus was trying to make things right, to pay Paul back for his sudden cooperation during the emergency.

"He'll be released and out by midafternoon," the policeman said. "You can buy him a beer then."

The state patroller took another step forward. "Mr. Quinlan," he said, "we've been tasked with escorting you to the Tri-Cities Airport, where you will be met by the governor at 1400 hours.

The governor's office has specifically requested that you accompany him and his delegation in a helicopter flyover of the region to assess damages. Apparently, this has to do with something you were quoted saying that the governor read in the paper. Some theory or forecast that the Columbia Basin is sinking under the weight of something or other."

Seamus was taken aback. "I didn't even vote for the governor. Are you sure he wants me along as a tour guide?"

"Those are our orders, sir," the officer said. "He wants your read of the landslide and the damage to one of the dams."

"What. What landside? Where did this landslide occur?" Seamus asked, as he closed Paul's laptop and rose from the desk.

"A place called Wallula Gap. You may have heard of it?"

In the time it took for the governor's group to tour the massive landslide blocking a portion of the Columbia River at Wallula Gap, fly over Hanford to Priest Rapids, then Wanapum, and back to the Tri-Cities Airport, evacuation orders had been issued. An exodus was already underway for Hanford and those low-lying areas of the Tri-Cities that computer modeling had flagged as in the potential flood zone. As they descended for landing, Seamus could see that the freeways, highways, dirt roads, and even bike paths were becoming choked with panicked residents fleeing town.

Seamus was busy organizing his notes and calculating what might come next as the helicopter touched down and then taxied to a private and secure hanger. It was his estimation that easily a third of the Horse Heaven Hills basalt anticlines on the western shore of the Columbia had sheared off in the earthquake, blocking a good half of the river. In explaining to the governor and his aides how Wallula would frequently plug up during the Ice Age floods, creating a temporary Lake Lewis behind it, he sensed he had their rapt attention. He took full advantage of the moment. Seamus was not being the least bit cavalier when he suggested that if either or both upstream dams failed catastrophically, the Air Force would be justified in bombing the eastern ridge of the Wallula Gap, triggering a second landslide to block the river completely. This *might* contain the millions of gallons of radioactive sludge that would be hydrologically excavated in the rush of floodwaters over the tank farms at Hanford. And if it didn't, there would be dire, unfathomable consequences for all species, as everything downstream, including the Pacific Ocean, would be rendered a dead zone for centuries to come.

●

It took Seamus a solid three hours of bumper-to-bumper traffic to reach the higher elevation Quinlan-Getz farm—a trip that usually took forty-five minutes. When he got there, the chickens had been corralled, water had been mopped up from the kitchen and pantry floors, and Cody had dinner on the table.

"How was your day?" Cody said, his voice an ironic singsong.

"Oh, you know," Seamus said, playing along. The two had been debriefing on his way home—that's how Cody had known when the tri-tip roast should come out of the oven.

Their long chat had been briefly interrupted by a follow-up call that came in from the Pacific Northwest Seismic Network in Seattle to inform Seamus that the satellite data had come back, and to their surprise, it revealed that at least a 9.2 magnitude earthquake had been detected not far from Point Nemo, north of Australia, West of South America and East of Indonesia—in the dead center of the same blind spot that the two men had talked about earlier in the day. It was now generally accepted that the tsunami that swamped downtown Seattle was caused by this earthquake event. Any linkage to the lesser quakes in Central Washington that afternoon, could be dismissed from having any association with the tsunami.

They'd just sat down to tuck into their meal when they heard the distinctive, two-horn blast of a big rig outside. Seamus got up to part the orange gingham curtains to peer outside into the dark. He saw nothing. A minute later they heard steps on the creaking front porch followed by knocking on the farmhouse door. Seamus rose again, with his mouth full, and crossed the living room in three long strides.

It was Russ. "Hey there, stranger!" Seamus said.

"You're just in time for dinner! Welcome," Cody chimed in, waving from the other room as he propped himself with the table and negotiated the clunky walking cast from under the table.

"You'll have to forgive us the natural disaster in progress," Seamus joked. "We're normally lovely hosts." He led Russ toward the archway leading to the kitchen and dining area, one arm still over the other man's shoulder. "Actually, it's a man-made disaster," he added, in a whisper. "But best to not get me started on that."

Russ turned his broad shoulders sideways to squeeze through the archway with Seamus as they entered the dining room. "Hey, Cody!" Russ said.

"Our hero!" Cody hobbled over to embrace their first official dinner guest since he and Seamus had partnered up. The last time they'd seen each other, Cody had been strapped inside a Gazelle search and rescue stretcher with his hugging arms immobilized, so he made this hug count. "Hope you're not vegetarian," he added, pulling out a chair from the long wooden table that'd had a naked old man lying on it the last time Russ was in that kitchen.

"Pardon my dropping in unannounced," Russ said. "I needed to get my truck out of the Tri-Cities, but this is as far as I got and I saw the lights on, so here I am."

"Oh, you were announced," Seamus interjected from the kitchen. "We heard your truck horn."

"I toot it every time I drive past this place," Russ admitted, though Seamus had already suspected. "Sort of surprised to find you big shots here at home, though. Shouldn't you be managing the emergencies at your jobs?"

"We did the last things we needed to do," Cody said, "and that was to sound the alarms and get out of the way."

"We couldn't in a billion years stop what's coming—whatever that turns out to be," Seamus added. "Except this time, the catastrophe is squarely on us. This is our fault. And I must tell ya, humanity's doing will be humanity's undoing. And you want to know why?" Seamus gave a dramatic pause. "I'll tell you why. It's because our species can't break its addiction to robbing Peter."

Russ took the bait. "Peter, who?"

●

Over dinner, the affable trio exchanged evacuation-from-unfolding-hell stories. They had all but skewered the blackmailing truck mechanic in effigy before dessert. Russ had explained how he knew him and for how long and that the kid had had a drug problem for as long as he could remember. When he inherited his father's mechanic shop, nobody really had much expectation that he could keep it running. Seamus's heart was the first to flip when he suggested they pool some funds so the meth addict could afford a good long stint in rehab. "What's another couple grand between friends?" he asked, polling the table as he served the peach cobbler made with rescued fruit from the cellar.

"To paying Paul!" Cody toasted, raising his wine glass to commemorate consensus reached.

"Yes, to paying Paul," Seamus said, seeming more insistent. "When you think about it, it was because of the mechanic that Russ returned at the moment he did, which enabled him to see our smoke. Without that, nobody would have seen our smoke, and we'd still be in that hole, in far worse shape."

Cody cleared his throat. "That isn't entirely accurate, Shay." He let the challenge hang in the air for a few seconds. Seamus leaned back from the table with his chair teetering on its back two legs. "You had asked me to check the water levels at the pond and the cemetery—you know—on account of the cellar flooding this afternoon." Seamus's hazel-green eyes widened in anticipation and that crazy eyebrow of his disappeared completely behind the bangs of his end-of-the-day mussed up hair. "Pond is at the top of the new decking and easily somewhere around one hundred degrees, and the cemetery—well, it overflowed the cavern and caused a nice little gully from erosion that is probably still running between two pickets of the fence."

"I'll be damned if I wasn't right about these three spots being connected!" Seamus slapped the tabletop, causing the dishware to jump. "And I was right about this seismic activity functioning like turn on and shut-off valves, moving the water around." Seamus beamed, more because he had only been guessing, and was surprised to find out he had been right. He did take a moment to pause, to remember the older sister he'd never known. "To Sally-Sue," he raised the wine glass for another toast.

"I don't know Sally-Sue," Russ admitted, raising his glass anyway.

"Sadly," Cody started to say. "Neither did we."

"And as for Paul," Russ interjected, having more to add to the story. "I had to track that little shit down, too, because he wasn't at the shop when I told him I'd be there to pick him up. I'd almost given up on my plan to get my truck out of your ditch, thinking I'd have to push it until the following weekend. That would have been way too late for you too. It wasn't until I was driving away from JP Lugnutz that I spotted him sauntering down the sidewalk like he didn't have any place he was supposed to be. So, yeah. Without the mechanic, I almost wasn't going to be in the right place at the right time. Wow."

"All the more reason to help the guy out, and besides," Seamus added. "It isn't about the money. It was never about the money, even when he was blackmailing us. It's about the struggle for all of us to get by and stay alive. That isn't unique to your truck mechanic. Each of us fights our own demons every day. Money doesn't fix all problems." Seamus began collecting the dirty dishes from around the table. "As for cash," he continued, "we have plenty. Turns out my dad had a secret war chest—a safe-deposit box at the IBEW Credit Union, crammed with US silver certificates issued in 1896—about the time the first Quinlans immigrated here from Ireland." Seamus's horseshoe moustache grew wider with a smile he directed at the truck driver across from him. "I know you are awfully sentimental about your pop's truck out there, Russ," Seamus said, pointing with his chin toward the front part of the house. "I ..." He paused, reaching to squeeze Cody's forearm. "*We* would like to make a thank-you investment in you, too."

"Maybe get you a new truck," Cody suggested.

"Naw," Russ protested. "I don't need anything. I'm already feeling richer on account of having made two new friends out of this ordeal." It was his turn to raise a glass in a toast. "Besides, you'd think the world was coming to an end, the way you two go on about it."

Seamus and Cody looked at each other, processed the accusation and non-verbally agreed on the spot to stop being so paranoid. The three men had a good communal laugh together.

Looking out the farmhouse living room window, and with SR 420 still looking jam packed heading north, Cody insisted Russ stay the night and use his downstairs bedroom. "Seamus will have to put up with my snoring—something he says he's gotten used to since we were underground anyway," Cody said.

With the dishes done and put away, the three men retired to the gazebo at the pond for a few beers. Seamus set about building a fire in the pit, while Cody detoured through the barn and introduced Russ to the platoon of chickens that had also had a most unusual day.

The first thing Russ said walking across the deck at the pond was, "Hey—that water looks like it's boiling!"

Seamus said, "Yeah, it does that sometimes. Don't ask us why."

And Russ didn't. He figured that just hanging out with two white dudes at a redneck farm in the middle of goddamn nowhere was spooky enough. He didn't need to know about their voodoo plumbing, too.

Drinking brewskis and regaling Russ and Cody with tales of his Quinlan ancestors seemed a mighty perfect way to spend what might be shaping up to be Armageddon Eve, but Seamus had something else in store. He was just waiting for the right moment. To buy more time and work up his nerve, he kept talking about the six generations of Quinlans who had tried farming this arid acreage and that got Russ to open up about his ancestors, too.

"I descend from the Congolese in Sub-Saharan Africa," Russ

explained. "My ancestors came from villages near the Shinkolobwe uranium mine, which, if you didn't know—and this surprised me too when my father told me—is the mine where Hanford got all its uranium to make plutonium for the bombs in the 1940s and 50s."

"Seriously?" Seamus asked. "So, most of my relatives worked at Hanford processing the uranium that your distant relatives may have mined in the Congo. Wow." Seamus reached his arm to tap his beer can to Russ's.

"To ancestors!" Cody exclaimed, joining his nearly empty beer can with theirs. "Don't ask me about mine and I won't tell you that I think they were probably all Nazis."

The men sat in silence, just breathing in the sulphury air coming off the pond and catching up on the latest news coming out of Seattle and the Tri-Cities on their cellphones. Miraculously, no lives had been reported lost in Seattle. Wanapum was a write-off, but the Army Corps of Engineers had plugged the gap with regular helicopter drops of coarse sand mixed with a slurry of semi-hardened cement. According to an email sent by Jenna Thomason to the tri-lateral emergency response team, the Columbia River remained contained within its banks below Priest Rapids Dam as it moved without damaging infrastructure—just at higher-than-optimal levels—for the fifty miles it flowed past Hanford. Benton County emergency work crews were monitoring the landslide at Wallula Gap and reported it was already losing its blockage integrity as the river was carrying away tons of the introduced sediment every hour. Russ let loose a burst of laughter after having sent and just received back a reply text from PJ—or Paul Jacobs, the truck mechanic.

"Let me read you this," he prefaced, causing the other two men to look up from their phones that illuminated each of their faces in the darkness that cloaked the farm pond as they sat in the trio of recycled plastic Adirondack chairs that Seamus had gotten on sale at Costco about a month back.

JUST LANDED ANOTHER FIFTY HOURS OF COMMUNITY SERVICE AND A WARNING TO SEEK COUNSELING AND REHAB (LIKE I CAN AFFORD THAT, RIGHT??). SUCH A JOKE THESE ASSHOLES WHO THINK LIVING MY LIFE IS EASY STREET. GLAD TO HEAR YOU GOT YOUR TRUCK OUT OF DODGE. THEY'VE CANCELLED THE EVACUATION ORDERS FOR NOW, BUT DOESN'T BOTHER ME IF PEOPLE CHOSE TO STAY AWAY— OR EVEN MOVE AWAY FROM THE TRI-CITIES. TOO MANY DAMN REDNECKS HERE ALREADY! LOL. STAY IN TOUCH, MAN AND IF YOU HEAR OF ANY—YOU KNOW—SCHOLARSHIPS THEY'RE HANDING OUT TO ATTEND A FREE RE-HAB, YOU BE SURE TO LET ME KNOW, HUH? LOL.

Seamus didn't miss a beat. "Text him, back, Russ. Tell Paul we've arranged his scholarship."

Russ looked at each of the two smiling and nodding men and texted back the good news.

As the last of the colors drained from the sky and who-knew-what catastrophe was unfolding less than fifty miles away, on the other side of the elevated hump of barren land. A white barn owl, with a massive wingspan, glided down from the barn roof with a whoosh to land on the windmill across from them. It was followed seconds later by the thrum of four, maybe five owlets, noisily taking up positions on the crossbars around their mom.

Seamus pointed. "And there," he said, cooing with family pride, "must be the spritis or reincarnations of my dead Quinlan ancestors now."

"Wow, they are adorable. Look at em!" Cody nearly tumbled out of his chair and into the pond, he'd scooted so far to the edge of his deep bucket chair. "Sort of makes me wish I were a Quinlan," Cody hinted.

"Well, what the hell's stopping ya?" Seamus asked, climbing out of his chair, dropping to one knee and reaching deep into his front jeans pocket to produce his father's narrow, gold wedding band.

"Are you shitting me?" Cody burst out with nervous laughter.

"Oh my god, dudes," Russ said. "This is so *Brokeback*!"

Seamus's eyes grew wider as he looked at Cody trying to hold his laughter in. It was impossible. The two of them cracked up at what had been their inside joke. Russ had just called it as he saw it—as it was.

"Will you?" Seamus asked again. "It was Gerald Quinlan who always said I should be married; thought it was a damn waste of outstanding Irish genes for me to stay single."

Cody didn't know why he suddenly couldn't keep air in his lungs. "I suppose if the world is ending," he said, "then who the hell cares, right?" He was almost panting. He was thinking of Angela and the day he married her. She was his very best friend at the time. A smile wrestled with the scowl his grief had fixed on his face. His new best friend had just asked him a question that needed an answer.

"Hell, yeah, I will!" Cody yelled into the night, scattering the audience of owl witnesses to the dust and wind across the pond.

Just then, the feeder pipe that was connected to the windmill began rattling. Poking just above the surface of the roiling water and acting like the periscope of a submarine in obvious distress, the pipe shook violently for several seconds. The three men braced themselves for another earthquake but what followed was silence—dark and eerie—before the pipe heaved what sounded very much like a resolute and drawn-out sigh.

My problem here is where to end this:
The question of closure in poems written
In free verse and vernacular wit.
If you write in High Court
You come to an end in the rhetoric —
Unless you are one of those scholar-poets
Who never roughened his paws with labor.
Then you might drivel on and on.

—William Witherup

In loving tribute to my father.
Gerald Leroy Curnes
January 29, 1935 — August 12, 2021

ABOUT THE AUTHOR

Michael Scott Curnes is an award-winning American Canadian author. *To Pay Paul* is his fifth novel, and a sequel to his Green Book Award-winning novel, *For the Love of Mother* (2011).

An ode to the countless cancer victims and survivors who worked at, lived near, or got contaminated downwind from the Hanford Nuclear Site in Washington State, *To Pay Paul* marks a return to Curnes's Cascadian roots. He has long considered himself one of those cancer-surviving "Downwinders," having spent his formative years in a small farming town located about a hundred miles east of Hanford. Always remembering the words of an oncologist who once told him he "probably shouldn't count on turning twenty-one," he is thrilled to have recently achieved the age of sixty. Living in Canada since 1995, and cancer-free for thirty-nine years, Curnes lives with his husband in Victoria, British Columbia.

Other novels by this author:
Wicked Ninnish (2020), *Coping with Ash* (2017)
For the Love of Mother (2011), and *VAL* (1996)

ABOUT THE POET

William Witherup Poet, Playwright, and Activist

[Excerpted from an obituary originally published in *The Seattle Times*, June 11, 2009, and written by Armando Montaño]

WILLIAM WITHERUP, A SEATTLE poet, playwright and activist, whose work focused on people who lived downwind of the Hanford nuclear reservation, racism, and technology, has died. He was 74.

In his book of poetry, *Down Wind, Down River*, Mr. Witherup memorialized downwinders and spoke out against the use of nuclear weapons and technology. He was also a member of the Hiroshima Peace Project, an anti-nuclear organization. Altogether, he was the author of eleven books of poetry and two plays.

Mr. Witherup died June 3 from complications of acute myeloid leukemia while in Seattle's veterans' hospital. He believed the illness that ultimately took his life was caused by living downwind of the Hanford Nuclear site, according to Frederick Nelson, his therapist, friend, and fellow artist.

Mr. Witherup was born March 24, 1935, in Kansas City, Missouri, the eldest of four children. The family moved to Richland in 1944 where his father worked as an engineer at the Hanford nuclear facility. In 1957, Mr. Witherup joined the air force as a Russian translator, serving until 1959.

After leaving the air force, Mr. Witherup moved to San Francisco in 1960, and to Seattle in the '80s. Mr. Witherup began writing poetry about downwinders after his father died in 1983 of prostate cancer that had metastasized into a very painful bone cancer, which Mr. Witherup suspected was caused by his father's work in the Hanford site. Mr. Witherup even dedicated his book of poetry *Black Ash, Orange Fire* to his father.

List of William Witherup's Poems used in this novel with the express permission of his family and estate, from his published book of poetry *Men at Work* [originally published by Ahsahta Press/Boise State University and copyrighted by Mr. Witherup in 1989].

Poems of William Witherup

End of Chapter 1: "My Father Dying: 1984"	20
End of Chapter 2: "Mervyn Clyde Witherup"	44
End of Chapter 3: "Nuke City Ballad"	67
End of Chapter 4: "Night Sky: Drake's View Ridge"	99
End of Chapter 5: "Sir, If You Are, Sir"	132
End of Chapter 6: "The Coming of Desire"	146
End of Chapter 7: "Common Bill Visits Laird and Lady Randall at Their Country Estate"	155
End of Chapter 8: "Egret: Bolinas Lagoon, 1986"	170
End of Chapter 9: "Chama"	194
End of Chapter 10: "In Memory of Eve Randall"	215
End of Chapter 11: "Hanford: March 1987; Doing the Storm Windows; and Once By Hanford Reach"	233
End of Chapter 12: "Workman's Comp II"	259

CPSIA information can be obtained
at www.ICGtesting.com
Printed in the USA
BVHW090038010722
641080BV00002BA/5